THUNDER

THUNDER
JAMES GRADY

WARNER BOOKS

A Time Warner Company

Warner Books, Inc., 1271 Avenue of the Americas, New York, NY 10020

 A Time Warner Company

Printed in the United States of America
First Printing: April 1994
10 9 8 7 6 5 4 3 2

Library of Congress Cataloging-in-Publication Data

Grady, James, 1949–
    Thunder / James Grady.
      p.   cm.
    ISBN 0-446-51765-8
    I. Title.
PS3557.R122M37   1994
813' .54—dc20   93-11177
                                      CIP

Book design by L. McRee

for Nathan

GRATEFUL ACKNOWLEDGMENTS TO:
D.C.; L.C.; S.E.; C.G.;
B.G.; H.G.; S.G.; K.H.; R.H.; J.L.;
L.M.; C.N.; N.N.; A.P.; B.P.; J.P.; esp. M.P.;
R.S.; B.W.; D.W.1; D.W.2; C.Y.

Chen/The Arousing (Shock, Thunder)

. . . . This movement is so violent that it arouses
terror. It is symbolized by thunder, which bursts
forth from the earth and by its shock causes fear
and trembling . . . .

THE IMAGE

Thunder repeated; the image of SHOCK.
Thus in fear and trembling
The superior man sets his life in order
And examines himself.

> THE I CHING or Book of Changes
> Richard Wilhelm Translation
> rendered into English by
> CARY F. BAYNES

THUNDER

1

New York City. A January Sunday morning.

Early, when night still clings to that forest of skyscrapers. Empty subway trains clatter beneath streets lined with sleeping cars.

Downtown—way downtown—steam billows from a manhole.

White steam, rising to vanish in the winter air.

A man in a black wool topcoat strides out of that steam. His upturned collar hides the bottom half of a bearded face. Long brown hair swirls in the cold wind. Black-gloved hands swing at his side. Black leather sneakers make no sound on the road.

Behind him, an engine grinds to life as he nears a chrome steel and white marble urban castle.

Corcoran Center: a gleaming tower with a brick plaza and a horseshoe driveway looping in front of its black glass facade.

That ebony mirror reflects the frozen block across the street: a steel-grated Korean greengrocer, an antique store, a barred jewelry emporium. Dark lines of a gigantic "X" of tape are still stuck to the inside of Corcoran Center's tinted glass.

An urban Buddha huddles on the plaza curb, a creature wearing scruffy boots, ragged jeans, torn Army parka. A ski mask cut with eye holes covers his face, he's wrapped in a matted blanket, and he's invisible to city-wise eyes.

The man in the black topcoat walks onto Corcoran Center turf—not toward the tower's locked doors, but diagonally across the plaza's bricks. As if he were taking a shortcut.

Buddha lets his blanket slip, flips his gloved thumb up.

The *whump-whump-whump* of a car with a flat tire fills the Sunday morning silence.

Out of the steam rolls a Datsun, its right front tire flopping with each revolution. The sedan wobbles up the horseshoe driveway, stops in front of Corcoran Center's black glass doors.

The driver staggers out of the car, a cheap coat open to the wind. Her stomach is swollen, clearly heavy with child.

Inside Corcoran Center, two guards at the lobby security desk stare at their TV screens, watch the driver wince at her flat tire, throw her head back in anguish, cradle her heavy belly.

"Oh shit!" says the gray-haired guard who refuses to speak his parents' Greek. "Ain't supposed to start like this!"

The woman beats a hand against the doors. Silent security TVs show her pained face mouthing, *Help me, help me!*

The young security guard from San Juan says: "What should—"

"Come on!" yells the Greek, and they run to the locked entrance. The Greek pulls the door open. The woman staggers inside.

"It's OK!" he yells as the pregnant woman leans against the door. She grips his wrist. His eyes move from her belly to her face: grotesquely thick makeup, pink lipsti—

Like a cobra, her free hand sprays the Puerto Rican with tear gas.

He screams, staggers blind, grabs his face.

The Greek jerks back—is trapped by her steel grip.

Tear gas sears his vision, his lungs.

Black Topcoat races inside the lobby. A stocking cap covers his head and face. He chops the Puerto Rican's neck. The guard drops like a stone.

Outside, a plumber's van parks behind the Datsun.

A fist slams into the Greek's stomach. His lungs overload; he's unconscious before another fist breaks his jaw.

The woman pulls a full-face stocking cap on, deflates her

stomach, props the door open with a rubber wedge and drags the Greek outside.

A masked plumber from the van helps the woman handcuff the Greek's wrists and ankles. They tape his mouth and eyes, throw him on the Datsun's backseat floor. By the time they run inside the lobby, Black Topcoat has cuffed and taped the Puerto Rican guard. The plumber drags the second guard into the Datsun, uses a can of compressed air to inflate the front tire.

Black Topcoat and the woman ferry eight duffel bags from the plumber's van into the Corcoran Center, past the banks of elevators, and stack them in the pay phone alcove.

The plumber drives the Datsun away, abandons it with its immobilized occupants in a bus zone three blocks later.

Inside the Corcoran Center lobby, Black Topcoat connects cables between the duffel bags. Then he and his companion grab the wedge propping open the door, let that portal swing shut and lock behind them as they step outside.

Only Buddha sees.

Black Topcoat drives the van to the street. He pulls off his ski mask. The rearview mirror shows him the van's cargo bay, where his dress-clad companion discards a ski mask, straightens the long wig. In the mirror, Black Topcoat sees stubble beneath those painted cheeks, the gash of electric-pink lipstick.

At the curb, the plumber's van stops. Buddha climbs in. He unpeels his fingers from the silenced pistol, lays it on the van's floor, holds his gloved hands over a heating vent.

Blinker flashing, the van rolls onto the empty street. Drives to the corner and stops for the red light. Turns right.

Gone.

The traffic signal turns green.

Turns red.

The winter sky is clear, like cold tap water.

A yellow taxi rolls out of the steam cloud, rattles onto Corcoran Center's horseshoe driveway, stops at the closed doors.

The cabbie turns to the four people in his backseat: "You guys sure you wanna go here?"

"I've been waiting to come here for twenty-one years!" says the older woman. She'd risen that morning in time to bathe, dress, spray her silver hair, brush the lint off her old wool coat, and have coffee waiting when the others woke up. On the knees of her tailored pants rests a sensible black purse.

"Mother," warns the woman in a blue parka and jeans. The daughter carries no purse. She shares her mother's high cheekbones, blue eyes. The daughter's chemically free, close-cropped burnished brown hair is genetically scheduled to match her mother's gray.

"Wacha you guys doing here?" asks the cabbie. "S'ain't open, got no people, no nothing—am I right or am I right?"

"We'll see," says the older woman.

Her daughter rolls her eyes, twists in the crowded backseat to fumble in her jeans pocket. She bumps her mother's knees. The older woman's purse stays upright, but her legs bump the man sitting beside the far door. He wears a Navy peacoat, brown cords. His thick gloves cradle a plastic-handled rocker seat filled with a snowsuit-bundled sleeping baby.

The grandmother says: "Do you know where we are?"

"I've got cash here somewhere," mumbles the daughter.

"Don't worry," the cabbie tells her, "the meter's off."

To the grandmother, he says: "The Corcoran building."

"Right. The Corcoran building. As in Carole Corc—"

"Mother!"

"Maybe I can reach my wallet," says the husband, but when he shifts, the sleeping baby waves a mittened hand, and the man three months into fatherhood freezes.

"That's her," says Grandmother, pointing to the woman beside her. Her daughter pales—then blushes.

"She's the architect. Had the vision for a nine-sided building, made it happen. Toilets and all. Her first solo project. The tenants don't move in until tomorrow, but she's already been nominated for the Wright Award."

"Which award is that?" asks the cabbie.

The daughter pulls a dollar bill out of her back pocket. The meter reads $4.85.

"Excuse me?" says Grandmother.

"The award she won, the right one. What's it called?"

"The 'Oh God, we're going to be late, too' prize!" The daughter pulls a bill from her shirt pocket—another single.

"A genius-architect award." Grandmother smiles.

"Yeah," says the cabbie, "think I heard of it."

"I'm sure," says Grandmother.

The father/son-in-law laughs—softly, so as not to wake his sleeping son. They named him Peter Ross, first name from the maternal grandfather, last name from the paternal line.

"But why you guys here now?"

"Because we're stuck in your cab!" The daughter straightens her legs, reaches into the last unplumbed pocket of her jeans.

"I want to be in the Sky Suite with my family to see that first sunrise bounce off these nine walls and light up the city!"

"She designed it that way," confides Grandmother. "When she was a little girl—"

"Mother!"

"You can read her name on the plaque in the lobby," says Grandmother. "Carole Corcoran."

"I don't stop the cab much 'less it's a diner."

"Too bad," says Grandmother.

"Oh here, dear," she says, unsnapping the sensible purse she's kept waiting on her knees, "let me pay for it."

"Classic timing," mutters the woman who's added "mother" to her identities of daughter, wife, pianist, and builder.

"What are mothers for?"

The two women climb out of the cab. Grandmother holds out her hands, but the father clings to his strapped-in son as they leave the cab for the cold morning air.

The cab drives away.

Carole Corcoran turns to the doors she sketched four years before, punches the intercom button.

Waits.

The tinted glass filters out 69.3 percent of ambient dangerous ultraviolet solar glare. Carole frowns at the tape's dark "X," presses her forehead against the frozen glass: inside the edifice that bears her name, the security station looks unmanned.

Unattended, she thinks, silently correcting in herself the gender stereotyping she fought all her life.

"You create something beautiful," she tells her family, "then they make you turn it over to careless strangers."

"That's life," says her husband, who can't stop smiling. He uses his Harvard degree to teach at a public high school.

Carole punches the security code into the lock. The door clicks open. She walks inside. The door closes.

The squeak of their shoes echoes off the cool marble walls, the high ceiling, the polished aluminum security desk.

"It's so quiet," says the proud Grandmother.

Carole sniffs: *Not smoke, acrid, but . . .*

That whiff vanishes.

She glares at the deserted security desk, leads her family to the elevator, punches the—

white light

roaring

blasts out Corcoran Center's front wall,

rips a New York January Sunday morning with a billion shards of black glass.

2

A Tuesday morning in March. Rush hour traffic.

"Yesterday's gone," said a bulky gray-haired man piloting a dented white Toyota in that river of cars, "so kiss it good-bye."

His wool topcoat smelled of melted snow. A steel-beaded ID chain snaked over the coat's lapels and disappeared inside its folds. His eyes flicked to the rearview mirror.

Cool spring sunshine lit three packed lanes of vehicles creeping south on a city street. The Toyota passed a road sign:

ENTERING WASHINGTON D.C.

"But we still got jobs," said the driver as he nudged the Toyota into the left lane. "So you can't say we aren't lucky."

The tree-lined suburbs of Maryland slipped away. They drove into a canyon of vertical malls rented to chic stores.

"Luck is what we make it," said the other man in the car.

The passenger had a quiet face. Brown hair cut short and brushed flat, high cheekbones, a half-moon scar near his left temple. His eyes were crystal gray and his name was John Lang.

A red traffic light stopped them. The Toyota's turn signal clicked a steady beat into national public radio's news show: famine in Africa, neo-Nazi violence in Germany, polls on the President's approval rating. Wall Street was anxious.

"No," insisted the driver: "Luck is what we get. All these months, you haven't been paying attention."

"I haven't missed a word you said."

"Yeah, but you haven't *learned* a thing!" The driver trembled slightly, tensed himself into control, sighed: "You kids."

The driver was Frank Mathews, 57 years old to John's 35. John wore a gray and black tweed suit, a black shirt and a gray silk tie from Bangkok. His Burberry trench coat lay tossed on the backseat. He was lean, 6 feet tall. In that dented white Toyota, he sat still: not rigid, *still*. Like a lake.

The left-hand turn arrow changed to green.

They cut through a neighborhood of detached houses with neatly trimmed lawns, followed a blue minivan piloted by a mom who kept turning to talk to a baby lashed into a car seat.

A rasping cough shook the Toyota's driver.

"Are you smoking again?" asked John.

"I try to avoid suicide."

"Then fasten your seat belt."

"The damn strap strangles me." Frank checked the rearview mirror.

They swerved around a rumbling orange street sweeper. A powdery earth smell filtered through the car's closed windows.

Frank licked his lips. "Sorry I was late this morning."

John shrugged. "That's OK. We don't punch a time clock."

"No," said Frank as he drove onto Military Road, "it punches us."

In the mirror on John's door, a motorcycle with a smoked windshield materialized out of the sweeper's dust. The biker's helmet poked above the black windshield.

"I might have to leave the office for a while today," said Frank. "Again."

Protocol kept John from asking why. Again.

Military Road cut across Rock Creek Park. Blocks of homes opened to acres of naked trees and grass fields where netless soccer goals yearned for teams of running children.

"What did you do last night?" mumbled Frank.

"Read."

"Work or pleasure?"

"It wasn't business related."

Frank grunted: "You should get out more."

"Probably." John smiled at himself. "Got any ideas?"

"A guy needs a lot more than ideas."

Just past the turn for the White House, a Japanese sports car crept past John's window. The woman driver had ash-blond tresses. She twisted her rearview mirror and painted her lips the color of blood.

Frank filled the gap she made. A BMW took their space. The man driving it wore a dark suit and picked his nose.

"What did you do last night?" asked John: the senior man had opened that door.

"Didn't sleep."

"Watch any of your movies?"

Frank held the steering wheel with a ringless left hand. He stared through the windshield for a long time before answering, "Wish it were a black-and-white world."

The woman radio announcer said it was 7:38. A Montana writer read from his memoirs, clean prose about pine tree mountains and seas of wheat fields that carried John back to simpler days.

The Toyota left Rock Creek Park's wooded valley for a neighborhood of row houses. They rolled past a tan Ford compact driven by a black woman a few years out of high school, bopping and bouncing with music they couldn't hear.

"The hearing tomorrow," said John, "they're out to nail—"

"Who gives a damn about another Congressional hearing."

John blinked.

"That hearing, all the news that fits in what gets printed or primped on the tube—it's unreal."

"Feels real to me," said John. "Even with who we are."

"Is that right?"

"What—"

"Oh it's real," interrupted Frank, "but all that is like . . . like thunder. Everybody in this town thinks they've grabbed lightning, but all they got is the thunder."

"Except you," said John, but he said it with a smile.

"Just me?" Barbed wire strained in Frank's words.

Easy: "What do you mean?"

"What do you know?"

"I know we don't get paid to riddle each other," said John. "I don't know what's bothering you, but—"

"Yeah, *but.*"

Frank rubbed his eyes, then locked his gaze in the windshield. His tone was softer: "Everything at the shop seem OK?"

"Your desk is ten feet from mine, you tell me."

"So everything's working like it should?"

"This is government, we're lucky it works at all." John said: "Do you know something I should?"

"Lately, I don't know much of anything."

The radio announced 7:41; segued features with jazz piano. Ahead, the traffic light turned green.

Frank sighed, put on the right turn signal.

"Did you see the *Post?*" he said. "Top guns graduating from flight school need to jockey a desk for three years before there's a fighter for them to fly."

John nodded. His job required him to absorb every day's *Washington Post, New York Times, Los Angeles Times* and *Wall Street Journal.* His VCR was programmed to tape news shows.

"The peace dividend," said Frank. "Somebody always pays."

He tapped the Toyota's dashboard: "You should have learned Japanese."

"Now you tell me." John shook his head. "I can't believe they used to pour you into a jet."

"Clearer days, better man," whispered Frank.

Ask: "What's eating you?"

Frank put no smile in his automatic reply: "Anybody who tries to eat me is going to regret it."

"Sure, old man."

"I ain't old—"

"—you're seasoned," finished John.

The Toyota negotiated an S-curve. The ornate dome of Catholic

University gave the day splashes of blue and maroon and gold. A sign pointed the way to the Soldiers Home, where forgotten warriors from forgotten wars waited to die.

John's watch had a luminous analog dial as well as digital display: both systems said it was 7:47 A.M.

Heart of the city. Traffic inched down North Capitol Street, through blocks of flat-faced row houses. Past a storefront church. The three lanes bottlenecked into two at a burned-out car.

Frank bluffed their way into the left lane. They eased around a four-door family Jeep engineered out of a World War II machine. The driver was a woman with curly black hair. She was scowling and pounding the steering wheel. Her frustration infected John as he watched the motorcycle with its helmeted and smoke-visored pilot weave through traffic ahead of them and disappear.

"Tell me again why you want to come to work this way," said John. "We could take Rock Creek Parkway, see the trees . . . "

"Women jogging—"

"Drive along the river. Start our day with a lot less . . . *stark*."

"You drive us your way, I drive us mine."

Frank looked around the aging neighborhood, the vehicles of frantic commuters. He checked his mirrors.

"*Stark* is the real city," he told John.

"Part of it."

"Don't let the white light bouncing off the monuments blind you to the lightning. This town, everything is politics."

"Truth like that takes you nowhere."

"*Nowhere—hell!*" Frank's flip back to anger John. "Don't forget that! And never forget that politics is a cloak wrapped around one rough beast."

"What 'rough beast'?"

"Yeah," said Frank. "Yeah."

A mile away, high above the steel-jammed street, rose the white icing dome of the Capitol.

Back off, thought John. The guy had a bad night. Woke up to no coffee. Back off—at least until the car is safely parked. He said, "Think the cherry blossoms will make it this year?"

"Damn ozone, who knows. There's a hole in the sky, *amigo*. A hole in the damn sky."

John glared at his friend: "What's going on here?"

"Nothing you need to know."

Those familiar words chilled John. "Is that friend-to-friend? Or pro-to-pro?"

Frank swept John with his eyes. "Depends on who you are."

"You know me. But you're making me wonder about you."

"Forget it." Frank looked out the windows. "I'm sorry, I . . . for now, I can't, I don't want to . . . forget it."

Three men shuffled in front of a boarded-up shop. Green paint peeled off the liquor store next door, where a neon store sign flashed "Lottery Tickets!" Torn-coated women pulled shopping carts up the sidewalk. Schoolchildren waited for a Metro bus.

Traffic to their left was light; those lanes were outbound, away from the center of the city. A Federal Express delivery van whizzed by Frank's closed window.

He checked his mirrors.

The digital clock on the dashboard read 7:51.

They drove past a funeral home. Past houses with shattered windows. The billboard on the roof of a convenience store showed a chocolate-skinned beauty laughing as she held a smoldering cigarette between her manicured fingers. A man huddled beneath mud-caked blankets in a warehouse doorway.

The Capitol loomed larger, closer.

"This city does things to you," said Frank. "Big-time."

A Chevy in the right-hand lane ferried four stone-faced Congressional aides to wars over which paper plan would get paper money printed to feed its theories.

"Know what this town reminds me of today?" said Frank.

John recognized one of the Congressional aides.

"Saigon," said Frank.

A horn blared behind them. The traffic light ahead turned from green to yellow. They were four cars back, in the left lane.

The lead car stopped to make an illegal rush hour turn across traffic. Every commuter knew the whole left lane would now suffer through another series of lights before they could progress.

Cars to their right sped forward under the yellow signal, guilty but gleeful as they carved minutes off their trip.

Across the low concrete median, in the outgoing lanes, a garbage truck lumbered toward them, followed by a Mercedes. Another motorcycle messenger whizzed under the changing light, slowed so he wouldn't be a bumper thump on the Mercedes.

Frank braked to a stop in the left lane, three cars from the signal light. This major intersection was open, vacant lots and a gas station, wide avenues stretching through blocks of houses.

For some reason, John thought about lemons.

"Saigon, '63." Frank laughed without joy. "Or maybe better, maybe here in '72. Buddy, what you better remem—"

Glass cracks!

Hot wet splatters John's face, left side—eye stings blind, blink clear as he whirls and . . .

Frank's arms flung wide swinging grabbing toward John and *his head gone red wet* and his bulk lunges at John like a fish—

Frank's leg spins the steering wheel hard left, his foot punches the gas. The Toyota engine roars, the car—

Bump, over the low concrete median *crashing* taillight of the car in front *scraping* bottom John *screaming* as they . . .

Lurch into oncoming traffic.

Horns blare.

Pickup truck slams on its brakes, swerves, misses them.

BAM! a turning station wagon hits their front end.

Tires crying. Glass shattering.

Spinning, whirling around inside the Toyota, Frank flopping on top of seat-belt-pinned John, screaming John, wet *hot&wet* spinning . . .

Shudder. Stop.

Still.

3

John Lang sat in the back of a police car. Alone. Numb. Not there. Coming there, coming back. Slowly. Breathe slowly.

His suit was soaked, caking dry. Marred with huge dark splotches. A policeman had given him a towel, helped him wipe his face, his hair. John stared at his hands: rust stains.

Only it wasn't rust.

He'd stopped shaking.

The police car was running, chugging. Warm. Too warm. John smelled his own sweat, tears. And a sweet meat steam.

Roll the backseat window down.

Cool air.

Red and blue lights spun outside the police car.

A fire truck angled across the intersection. Yellow-slickered firemen milled around. Flares sputtered in the road. Police cars blocked traffic, their uniformed officers waving flashlights, directing motorists through this crossroads.

Where a station wagon with a crumpled grille waited, its driver crying as a policeman wrote her answers on a clipboard.

Where an ambulance was parked, its attendants leaning against the closed doors, plastic gloves sheathing their hands.

Where a police tow truck idled, its driver sipping coffee from a Styrofoam cup.

Where Frank's mangled Toyota sat, hood crumpled, right front tire blown. The windshield was cracked but intact. Smeared.

The driver's window was a spiderweb of cracked glass with a hole at its heart.

An evidence technician flashed pictures of that hole. Walked around the Toyota. Took a half dozen shots of what lay on the front seat. The passenger door gaped open.

Two detectives in tan overcoats huddled with a uniformed police sergeant and the patrolman whose cruiser held John. Their chatter drifted in John's open window.

" . . . couldn't believe that one either," said the sergeant. "A mom driving her three kids home from school . . . "

"New Jeep, right?" asked the patrolman.

"Wasn't new," said the white detective.

"Going home," said the sergeant, "and blammo!"

"Good-bye, Mom," said the black detective.

"Gangbangers pull down on each other six blocks away. They scatter clean, she catches lead in the head."

"Hell," said the sergeant, "what about half mile that way, 'fore Christmas, when a wild slug hit the President's limo?"

"Not the limo," said the white detective, "the Secret Service van. He was parked, the Man was inside some building. The Little Man, too, and their wives."

"The new Man or the old one?" said the patrolman.

"Doesn't matter," said the sergeant. "Didn't happen on our shift."

"Washington, D.C.," said the black detective: *"Death City."*

"Who worked the mom one?" asked his partner.

The cops' radios squawked: *"Scout 57, report to 413 Ivy Street Southeast. Domestic."*

"Anybody see anything on this one?" asked the sergeant.

"No shooters," said the white detective. "Crashing cars. The guy scrambling out the door."

"He was just riding along," said the black detective, "then there it was."

"Lucky his friend had a hard head," said the white detective.

"He see anything?"

"You never see nothing," said the patrolman.

"Just *there it is,*" agreed the white detective.

"How we doing on the drill?" asked the sergeant.

The white detective shrugged. "The two drivers who got crashed are finishing their statements. They know zip."

"ID on the victim?"

"Had a work dogtag around his neck," said the black detective.

"Laminated," added his partner. "Waterproof."

"I found the slug stuck in the back door." The patrolman, trying for points with the sergeant. "Mashed. Looks like a .38."

"Nine mic-mic," said the white detective.

"Scout 21 to Central."

"Figure it came from over there." The white detective pointed to a block of packed earth waiting for a miracle to refinance a bankrupt redevelopment project.

"H Street?" asked the sergeant.

"Maybe, if it ricocheted."

"Central to 21, go."

"Request homicide detectives, Martin Luther King Avenue and Walpole Street."

"Shit," said the black detective.

"Who's up?" asked the sergeant.

"We're it," said the white detective. "Got four guys on that multiple in Northeast, two on that old lady. Guys witness hunting, sick . . . "

"Central to any available homicide unit."

"Figure it's some crack-corner lord," said the patrolman. "Call the Sanitation Department."

"What's left here?"

"Scene sketch is done," said the black detective, "but—"

"Witnesses saw no shooters," said the sergeant. "Shot fired somewhere else. Nothing everywhere but empty sidewalk."

He shook his head: "Random life."

"Central to any homicide unit."

"This is a one-badge job," said the sergeant. "Release the vehicle to Tow, body to the morgue. Door-to-door to pad out the case jacket. Prelim the guy in the car. Clear the streets before the TV crews get here and the Mayor gets a hundred why'd-you-make-me-late calls. Button it up, file it."

"Two hours," said the white detective. "Plus paperwork."

"Any homicide unit, please respond."

The sergeant tossed a coin.

"Heads," called the white detective as the quarter spun.

"Shit," he said a moment later.

"Watch it down there," said his partner.

The white detective raised his radio: "Central, this is Homicide. Detective en route."

He and the sergeant walked to a command car. The sergeant barked orders to the ambulance crew, the tow truck driver.

The black detective climbed in the back of the patrol car. His smile was kind. "How are you doing, Mr. Lang?"

"I don't know."

"My name's Greene. Detective Tyler Greene."

He held out his hand. Didn't flinch when John shook it.

"You're going to be fine," said the detective.

"Is that polite optimism or a professional verdict?"

Greene shrugged.

"What happened?" asked John.

"Your friend—his name was Frank Mathews, right?"

John nodded.

"Mr. Mathews appears to have been shot in the head by a stray bullet."

The ambulance attendants opened the rear doors of their machine. They pulled out a gurney, unfolded a rubber bag, wheeled the stretcher toward the white Toyota. They wore plastic gloves.

John looked away.

"He's dead," said Greene.

"I know."

"Must have been instantaneous. I doubt he suffered."

"You didn't know him very well."

From outside came the whine of the tow truck winch.

"Did you know him very well?"

John stared at this representative of domestic law and order and justice, a creator of official public records.

Detective Tyler Greene had a powerfully built chest and shoulders. His tan overcoat and two-piece suit came from a discount store. Greene had a square ebony face. Black hair and mustache.

"I knew him," said John.

"The two of you worked together. Carpooled."

Nod. The motion cleared fog from John's mind.

"You work for the Senate?"

For a heartbeat, John hesitated.

Then he told the truth. And he lied.

"Yes," said John.

He told Greene the Committee phone number. The detective asked for and was given John's home phone and address.

"Did you see anything or know anything that might help us?" asked the detective.

"I already said I didn't see anything. Why do you think it's a stray bullet?"

"You got any better ideas? Know something I should?"

A car sitting in backed-up traffic honked its horn.

"OK," said Greene. "Here's my card. Tomorrow, call and arrange for a formal statement. In a few minutes, the officer driving this car will run you over to D.C. General."

"It wasn't me who . . . I'm not hurt."

"Shock's a funny thing. Something like this hits everybody hard. Hits everybody different."

"You have a lot of experience with something like this?"

Wheels clattered on the pavement outside the car.

The ambulance attendants rolled the gurney bearing its bulging black rubber bag past John's eyes.

That could have been me.

The ambulance driver peeled off plastic gloves; they were red.

The tow truck winched the Toyota up on its rear wheels.

The ambulance doors slammed shut.

Uniformed policemen flagged traffic through the scene,

picked up flares. Kicked chunks of headlight glass out of the road.

"Will you be OK for about fifteen minutes?" asked Greene.

"Can I . . . I should call . . . call work. Let them know."

"You sure?"

"Supposed to be me. My job."

"You can call from the hospital."

John shook his head.

Greene shrugged.

Slowly, testing each muscle, John opened the cruiser door. Swung his feet outside. His legs worked.

Standing in the fresh air braced him. Winter lingered in the sunlight.

"Hey, Detective!" yelled the ambulance driver. He waved a clipboard. "We need you!"

Greene stood next to the cruiser.

"Don't go away," he told John.

"I'll just . . . walk a little." John nodded toward the bus stop where a dozen people stared at the urban drama. "Phone."

Greene's eyes released him.

The weight of forever pressed on John's shoulders as he walked across the intersection. He felt beyond the dictates of the flares burning in the street. A cop waved at the cars to let John cross. John didn't care, the cars didn't matter.

The bus stop. The plastic-walled windbreak. Strangers staring at the apparition coming closer, closer to them.

To the silver box pay phone.

A bus roared past John, belched diesel smoke. The air cleared. He smelled the road's blacktop warming with the day, the sidewalk, fermenting trash from a blue litter barrel.

One step after another, he could do it.

The curb.

Up. On the sidewalk.

The crowd melted away.

His suit was stiff, heavy. His teeth chattered and he told himself it was because of the cold.

Ten feet from the pay phone, he stopped. Put his hand in his front pants pocket.

Empty. So was his other front pocket.

All his change. Must have tumbled out when . . . When he threw open the Toyota's door, broke free of the seat harness, fell out upside down, screaming, pushing and straining to get out, get free, get out from under . . . He'd flopped to the ground, rolled.

Lost all his change.

"Mithster."

John blinked.

"Mithster."

Her skin was wrinkled, like a prune. She wore a widow's crescent hat and a faded gray coat. She tapped her cane as she came toward him. Cat's-eye bifocals fogged her eyes, and her lips were taut over empty gums as she said again, *"Mithster."*

The hand she didn't need for her cane floated toward him, fingers and thumb pressed together in a dangling hook.

She dropped a quarter in his palm. Tapped away.

Suddenly, he forgot all the right phone numbers. He started to hyperventilate.

Grabbed the metal edge of the pay phone box and squeezed it until the steel gouging his hand overwhelmed everything else. He got his wind back. Sank his breath.

His watch, he looked at his watch: the dial was smeared.

He called directory assistance. Got his work number. The general switchboard. He mumbled the 10 digits to himself, a mantra he dared not forget, a code whose use would bring salvation.

Put the quarter in the pay phone. Hear it clang through. Hear the dial tone. Punch in the digits, one, two, five, all 10.

One ring.

Two rings.

Early, was it too early to—

"Good morning," said a woman's polite professional voice in his ear. "Central Intelligence Agency."

4

The clock in the hospital emergency room read 9:53. John sat by himself on a wooden bench against a white wall, watching the red second hand sweep the circle of black numbers. His hands cradled an untasted Styrofoam cup of tea. He smelled its cranberry tang over the hospital ammonia.

When the patrolman walked John through the sliding glass doors, a resident dropped her clipboard and ran to their horror. She led John to a curtained cubicle, left to whisper with the patrolman. Came back. Shined a penlight in John's eyes. Asked if he was hurt. If he had any open cuts or sores—"shaving cuts, like that." He told her no. She asked if he needed to call anyone. He shook his head. Sirens wailed in the driveway. The doctor excused herself. John sat on the stool. The doctor came back, gave him a bottle of four triangular yellow pills.

"Valium," said the doctor. "Only if you need them, no more than one every eight hours. Could help you sleep deep, but ultimately, it might be better if you dreamed."

John stared at her.

"If you've got a therapist tell him about the Valium. And have your physician contact the authorities about autopsy results of . . . that man."

"Why?"

"Just a precaution."

"Doctor!" yelled a woman's voice outside the curtains.

"Take care," said the doctor, then she hurried away.

An admitting clerk brought a clipboard of forms for him to sign, told him the business office would call.

A nurse asked how he was doing, if he needed a phone, led him to the waiting room bench. She brought him a cup of tea.

"The doctor suggests you stay away from caffeine and other stimulants," she said.

John watched the sweep of the clock's second hand.

A 14-year-old girl waddled in alone to give birth. She was crying. A couple from Guatemala sat beneath the muted TV set. The mother rocked their 8-year-old son in her arms; the boy's face was slick, his eyes glassy. His parents averted their faces when a policeman walked by. An orderly rolled an old man in a wheelchair into an elevator; those steel doors slid shut. Two nurses strolled through the E.R., laughing.

The glass double doors to the street rolled open.

Cold air carried them inside.

The woman wore a camel-colored coat over a plain-skirted suit, low heels. Her brown hair was trimmed, pert.

The man behind her was losing his hair and had eyes like a dragon. He wore a Burberry trench coat identical to the one owned by John and 10,000 other men in Washington, D.C. A second tan coat was draped over his left arm. His shoes squeaked on the hospital floor. He swept the room with his dragon eyes, conferred with the admitting clerk.

The woman came straight to the bench, sat down eye-level with John. Smiled at him.

"Hi, John. My name is Mary. I'm a counselor. Everything's going to be fine. You're OK now. We're here."

Dragon Eyes came over, stood above them.

"We're OK, John," he said. "You're all checked out. Time for us to go."

They waited. Patiently.

John set the tea on the wooden bench.

Dragon Eyes held up the spare coat, opened it wide.

When John stood, Dragon Eyes wrapped him in that featureless garment.

They led him outside through the sliding glass doors.

A man in a green trench coat stood by the emergency room door, watching the street like he was waiting for his football team's bus. His coat was unbuttoned. He glanced at John and his escorts, turned back to scan the sidewalks, rooftops, passing cars.

A Chrysler with antennae on its trunk rolled into the circular driveway and stopped precisely in front of John.

Mary opened the Chrysler's back door.

John got in.

She joined him. Before she could close her door, Dragon Eyes was climbing in the other side so that John sat between them. The ex-football player hustled into the front seat.

A portable tape recorder dangled into the backseat by a strap from the driver's headrest. John saw its wheels turning.

Mary gestured toward the tape recorder.

"You can talk about anything you want," she told him. "Or say nothing at all."

"I want to go home," said John.

"We're on our way there now," she said.

The Chrysler slid into Tuesday morning business traffic, rolled past the Capitol. Past civil service castles built to feed Newark's starving babies and keep Nebraska farmers solvent.

At 14th Street, John realized they were taking the route he'd suggested that morning.

The Washington Monument pointed to the sky as they crossed a street named for a vanished Swedish hero who'd saved hundreds of people from Nazi gas chambers. They passed rows of bare cherry trees. Picked up the Parkway, and cruised alongside the pancake layers of the complex called Watergate.

"Pretty down here," said Dragon Eyes.

"What time is it?" asked John.

"It's 10:32," said Mary.

They knew the way to his house without him telling them.

John's Maryland neighborhood was half a mile from the District border, a hodgepodge of rambling homes encircled by a stone wall and a tissue of incorporating laws.

On his salary, John could never have afforded to own any of these less-than-mansions. He rented one of the last log cabins in the megalopolis, a former slave quarters. John's cabin was behind his landlord's house, through a stand of trees, across a field of grass. No paved path linked the street to the cabin, a major inconvenience for mailmen and his dates when they wore spike heels.

The driver parked on the street, behind John's old Ford.

"We have a meeting to go to," said Mary. "All of us."

"This town," said John, "there'd have to be a *meeting*."

The driver stayed with the car.

What a curious sight we must make, thought John as he led Mary, Dragon Eyes and Mr. Jock through his landlord's backyard. A quartet of bureaucrats, out of the office in the middle of the day, tramping through the winter woods.

Spring, he thought. It's supposed to be spring.

Keys.

Then he felt them, heavy in the side pocket of his suit. The suit jacket had flap pockets; his keys hadn't fallen out.

His front door opened into the living room. To the right was the kitchen, closet and a fireplace. To the left, doors led to the bedroom and bathroom. Walls that weren't covered with crowded bookshelves held Chinese paintings, calligraphy scrolls.

Everything looked as he'd left it. Sunlight streamed through the windows. He smelled the cold coffee on the stove. His brushes and inkstone, ledgers and paper boxes waited on the flat desk. His computer screen was dark. No one had dented the cushions on his couch, or moved his chair from under its reading lamp. The clock on his TV's VCR flashed 10:59, and the dial on his FM receiver showed the same radio station Frank—

No more! thought John.

He struggled out of their coat, dropped it on the floor. Off came his suit jacket, tossed on top of the coat. He jerked free from his tie. His hands shook as he unbuttoned his black shirt, dropped it on the pile of soiled clothing. Kicked his loafers away. Unfastened his watch and threw it on the shirt.

Dragon Eyes shot Mary a look.

So what. John pushed his pants off, thrashed until he was free of them and they were on the pile, the last of what he thought of as his *cool* professional clothing ensemble.

Socks: onto the pile.

Jockey shorts: peeled and dropped.

Naked, he walked to his bedroom, oblivious to their eyes.

Shut the door behind him.

From the bedroom to the bathroom. He turned the shower on as hot as he could stand it. Washed his hair four times. Scrubbed himself over and over again. He opened his mouth to the spray until he choked, then lowered his head and let the water beat down on his back. The hot needles turned to ice.

A knock sounded on the bathroom's door to the living room.

"John," said Mary's muffled voice. "Are you OK?"

He turned off the water.

Steam filled the bathroom. He wiped fog off the mirror.

Saw himself, looking back.

The hell with their meeting. He chose his jeans, an old denim shirt. Comfortable. Comforting. He pulled on a dark navy sweater, laced up his black leather sneakers.

When he walked into the living room, his three escorts pretended they weren't concerned. Mary stood by the bedroom door. Dragon Eyes leaned on the sofa. Mr. Jock rocked in his shoes.

Did they snoop around? Open drawers?

"How are you doing?" asked Mary.

"You look better," said Dragon Eyes. "You look good."

John remembered his trench coat was still in Frank's car. The black mountaineering coat in his closet had molded itself into a comfortable friend. John put it on.

Looked at the strangers in his home.

"OK," he said, "I'm ready."

5

They met in a sixth-floor conference room at Langley head quarters. Beyond the windows, John saw bare March trees.

Eight colleagues sat at a round table. As if they were all equals. As if they were all in this together.

"I can't believe the police are right," said John.

"Can't—or won't?" asked Roger Allen, Deputy Director of Operations. The Operations Directorate controls HUMINT, actual spying. Allen faced the door, the power perch in the room.

"John," said Dick Woodruff, Allen's right-hand man both at this table and on the job, "the facts indicate a stray bullet."

"Unless there's something you forgot to tell us," said George Korn, head of Security, CIA. Tall. Gaunt. Gunfighter eyes honed as a Secret Service agent scanning crowds for assassins.

"Like what?" said John.

"Figure maybe later," said a bulldog in his 50s: Harlan Glass, the CIA executive for the Counter-Terrorism Center.

The CTC was a governmental mist designed to supersede traditional security bureaucracies. Based at the CIA, the CTC had a fluctuating staff of experts from federal agencies. Nominally commanded by a Deputy Director of the FBI, the CTC was controlled by its coordinating committee—which Glass ruled.

CTC executive Glass said: "Figure later, shock wears off, you'll remember—"

"I remember everything now."

Woodruff said: "And you know nothing that contradicts the police stray bullet theory—correct?"

"Factually."

"You saw nothing? No threat? No assailant? Gun smoke?"

"We're riding to work, Frank . . . the world explodes. Car crashes. I scramble free. People help me—they're not ducking bullets, nobody screaming about snipers, nobody knows what happened. Except that Frank is dead."

"Poor guy," said the Agency's Chief Counsel. Harvard, Oxford and the Marines, then Harvard Law and a ticket-punching stint at the Justice Department before joining a law firm that was a respected exile shop during the previous Presidency. The lawyer cradled a leather portfolio in his lap, its covers V'd so that no one could see what he jotted on a yellow legal pad.

"You claim he was paranoid," said Korn.

"I said something was troubling him. A lot. About work, about the world. He didn't tell me what, or why. He should have."

"But it was about work." Allen frowned: "Miguel?"

Miguel Zell was Director of the CIA Offices of Congressional and White House Liaison—Frank and John's boss.

Zell shrugged: "When Frank left Ops three years ago, they assured us he was sanitized."

"And I'm sure our procedures were correct," said Woodruff, defending the troops commanded by his superior Allen. "What did you have Frank doing?"

Blame deflected from his domain, Zell softened his tone: "We put him on Capitol Hill because he could juggle bullshit and keep his hands clean. If he couldn't answer a Congressional query, he bucked it over here. Last few weeks, we've been prepping for tomorrow's hearing. As Frank's partner, John works the same turf."

Zell, who'd learned his politics in boyhood L.A. and during a diplomatic cover stint in the Mexican Embassy, turned his palm up, ferried an invisible weight toward John.

"Not always the same material," said John.

"Was Frank performing as usual?" asked Woodruff.

"He'd spent a lot of time out of the office lately."

"Figure you know why?" said Glass.

"No. And I didn't ask."

Everyone at the table understood the mores of the Agency, why John wouldn't challenge a senior employee about his time.

"I'll check his health insurance records," said Korn. "Dentists, whatever."

"Do what you can, within parameters." Woodruff shrugged: "Ops knows nothing to suggest any Agency concern in this tragedy."

"How about your shop?" head of Ops Allen asked Glass.

The counterterrorism guru shook his head. "DESIST data runs indicate no pertinent hostile operations."

DESIST—the world's most extensive database on terrorists, a revolutionary information system managed by CTC.

Korn grunted: "The CTC is a hostile operation."

"Not to legitimate Agency interests," said Glass.

"Gentlemen," said Allen.

"I knew Frank Mathews," Korn told the room.

"We all did," said Woodruff.

"We weren't tight," said Korn. "A wave in the parking garage. Nod in the hall. But you've been working side by side with him for more than a year."

"Fourteen months," said John.

"You joined Zell's shop after your extended leave."

John said yes.

"After the thing in Hong Kong," said Korn.

John blinked.

Woodruff said: "You mean after John received his medal."

Korn said: "After the money audit."

Financial scandals terrified the CIA after $3.5 million slated for noncommunist Cambodian guerrilla fighters turned up missing in 1988.

"We aren't here to microscope Mr. Lang's fine career," said Glass. He'd met John 20 minutes earlier.

"We aren't here to ignore any patterns of procedure violations." Korn smiled at Glass. "But I should defer to you on stuff like that. You've got more experience."

Allen said: "Refocus, please, Mr. Korn."

"You've run agents in Thailand, Hong Kong," said Korn. "Look at Frank through a handler's prism. Anything unusual about him?"

"Frank Mathews spent more years handling assets than I've been with the Agency," said John. "However you or I looked at him, we'd only see what he wanted us to see."

"A pro," said Glass.

"A good man," said Woodruff.

"I liked him," said John. "I saw him die."

Counselor Mary leaned forward in her chair at John's elbow: "This has been terrible for John. Perhaps another time . . . "

"'Another time' won't change today," said John. His flat gaze took in everyone at the table.

"How well did you know him?" said Korn.

"We worked together, ate some meals, carpooled. Went to a few movies—*JFK*. We knew we'd get questions about it—informally, but on the Hill 'informal' only means a different set of smoke and mirrors."

"Bull's-eye," said Glass.

"We were friends," said John. "Work friends."

"Did Frank have any problems?" asked Korn.

"No more than anyone else," said John. "He was tired."

"Was he drinking?"

"Not that I know of."

"He was a widower. What about women?"

"None that I know of."

"Drugs?"

"Be serious."

"I am. Money troubles?"

"Frank wouldn't compromise his personal security."

"Had he been dealt troubles that could have posed a security risk for the Agency?"

"No."

"You know that for a fact?"

"You knew him longer than me. Do any of you doubt him?"

"No," said Glass.

"How about you?" Korn's question danced in his pale eyes.

"How about me?" said John.

"Do you have any problems?"

"None that are Agency business."

"Really?" said the head of Security.

"It's not my life that's on the table," said John.

Korn shrugged: "But you were in that car."

Ignore him for Allen, the man in charge. Sound sincere. Sane. "What are you going to do?"

"We're going to make certain that this horror has nothing to do with the Agency. That Frank didn't fall in the line of duty."

"You mean you're going to find the truth."

"That's what I said," answered Allen.

Easy, breathe careful, slow. Show calm.

The Agency's counsel said, "You're sure you didn't tell the police that you or Frank worked for the CIA?"

"I told them I was a Senate aide," said John.

"Technically true," said the Agency lawyer. "The Senate gave you and Frank staff IDs and a workplace so you could liaison for them—in essence, be an aide to them."

"That might not satisfy the cops," said Korn.

"No doubt you and the Counsel can flatten the Agency's profile," said Allen. "The Director is adamant about that."

"The Director," said Korn. No one believed his smile.

Allen said: "Is there any link between this incident and the Corcoran bombing?"

"What?" said John.

"Why do you ask?" said Security chief Korn.

"Because" said Allen, "I've gotten a heads-up that at the hearing tomorrow, I'll get questions on the Corcoran attack. This incident—if we can't ride clean with the stray bullet scenario—"

"Only thing that makes sense," interrupted Woodruff.

"I don't want to bluff answers needlessly," said Allen. "And I don't want to generate questions we can't answer. So . . . Harlan?"

Harlan Glass wet his lips, said: "The position of the investigating Task Force and the Counter-Terrorism Center hasn't changed: the Corcoran bombing was a stand-alone incident."

"With obvious caveats," said Woodruff.

"Frank wasn't working on the bombing," added Miguel Zell.

"Fine," said Allen. "Let's be sure there's no linkage."

"For the hearing," muttered Security chief Korn.

"What do we tell the Committee about Frank?" asked Zell.

The Agency's lawyer said: "If there's no connection between his accident and our programs . . . we send the oversight Committees and the White House a confidential report—make it thick. Get the D.C. cops to shoulder the conclusion—in writing. It's a domestic blip anyway, so . . . no problems."

"Except for one dead man," said John.

They all looked at him.

Woodruff rubbed his brow: "John, we lost a friend, too. Our shock can't be as great as yours—hell, he was shot sitting next to you! You feel paranoid. Scared. Maybe even guilty for surviving. Angry. But believe me, we'll nail this down. And we're just all so damn sorry."

"Under fire, you did good," said Glass.

"Hell of a job," added Woodruff.

"All I did was not die."

"No one blames you," said Glass. "For anything."

Don't—don't think, don't be sick, don't—

"People," said Allen, "with our sincere condolences to John—I think we can dispense with any further questions."

"For now," said Korn.

Allen, the senior executive, left.

"Miguel," Woodruff said to the CIA's executive in charge of Congressional relations, "you and I need a moment here."

"And John, please stay, too."

Chairs shuffled as the other CIA executives stood.

Korn glared at Woodruff—then saw Glass watching him. Korn stalked past the counterterrorism guru.

The door closed, left three men seated in a triangle at a round table.

"John," said Zell, his immediate boss, "this is a hell of a thing. Bad as it is, we've got a hell of a thing to ask you."

"Our problem is continuity," said Woodruff.

Zell said: "The accident—"

"The alleged accident," snapped John.

"Frank's death," said Zell. "In this town, perception is reality."

"Reality is Frank's body," said John.

"That's today," said Woodruff. "Tomorrow, reality is a crucial Senate hearing. The substantive setup for the Agency's pending budget appropriation and long-range future."

"*Money.*" John shook his head.

"*Means,*" said Woodruff, "to do our duty. To do what needs to be done."

"Perception," said Zell: "Grant us the probability that Frank's death is a tragic reality, an accident. These days, us, the Pentagon, the Commerce Department: we're all scrambling to remind a bunch of dollar-scared politicians that war and terrorists and economic catastrophes will ambush America if they don't give us the money to gear up for this damn new world."

"What does that have to do with me? With Frank's—"

"Continuity," repeated Zell. "Frank was senior man. With him gone, with the hearings bearing down on us . . . we need you around—not so much to do anything, but—"

"To put up a good front," said John. "One down is a problem, two missing—"

"Raises questions off-point," said Woodruff.

Zell turned a palm up: "If you need to take some time . . . "

"What would I do with it?" whispered John. "I had my long R&R after . . . I'll coordinate the investigation, legwork—"

"That's not where we need you," said Zell.

"That also wouldn't be wise," added Woodruff. "You're part of the tragic package. If you help wrap it, Korn will raise a fuss.

More fuss is the last thing the Agency needs while we and everyone who hates us tries to redefine our existence.

"We'll keep you fully informed," he added.

The two senior men fell silent, their eyes on the man they'd
sat at the point of their triangle.

Company line, thought John. Company logic. Locked in.

Sensible. Admit it. Accept it. Believe it. Try.

"We're professionals," said Woodruff. "We can't lose that
focus."

Tell them what they want to hear: "I can do my job."

John felt tension ease out of the two senior men.

"And I better get cracking on mine," said Zell. He rose,
walked round the table, patted John's shoulder, and left.

Not time to stand yet, thought John.

As soon as the door closed behind Zell, Dick Woodruff moved
to the chair beside John. Woodruff tugged on his earlobe, said:
"It's safe to talk in here. I have Allen's word on that.

"John, are you *really* all right?"

"No, but . . . yeah, I'm OK. I'll have some new nightmares."

"Perhaps a number of bad dreams lessens the intensity of any
one nightmare."

"I'll let you know."

John cupped his forehead and leaned on the table. Dick
Woodruff watched. When John looked up, his eyes were cold,
hard.

"The Agency has already buried Frank," said John, "hasn't it?"

"Burying him isn't my job. Or yours."

"The hell with our jobs! He was my friend—no blood brother,
but we were partnered for more than a year! I owe him!"

"I knew him longer than—"

"Besides," said John, "if someone kills one of us and skates,
then anybody can kill any of us. And will. We'd be fools not to
do something about—"

"We are doing everything *about*," said Woodruff. "*We,* not
you."

"Your word?" John asked the man he'd known for years.

"My *life*," was the answer.

Woodruff said: "I urged you to take the Hill liaison job because you were perfect for it. Congressional Fellow, Asian expertise that didn't scream 'the failure of Vietnam.' You knew covert warfare, HUMINT. Plus I wanted you to work with Frank. Being his shadow could teach you more than most postings."

"It did."

"The perfect man for the job," repeated Woodruff. "So far today, you've proved that. So far. Keep doing me proud.

"Are we clear on that?" he added.

"I am," said John. Licked his lips. His voice softened as he said to the older man: "Tell me why."

Woodruff put a hand on John's shoulder.

"Don't expect reason in every twist of fate. Things happen. As an intelligence officer, you know a chain of events can string together with no meaning other than there it is. Frank's death stays open for us until whoever pulled the trigger is ID'd. But operational reality, experience, all the data—hell, street smarts in this land of the free and home of the heavily armed: he died because he was there."

"So was I. Accident or murder, I could have died, too."

"No one but you can make peace with that. The question is, can you make your peace and still do your job? I will accept either answer. But be sure you give me the truth."

Say it. Believe it: "You can count on me."

"Good. Don't ignore your doubts. The willingness to question is what makes us human. But what keeps us going is the certainty of our beliefs."

John shook his head. "I'm so numb."

"The good news is that'll pass," said Woodruff. "The bad news is, that *will* pass."

Is this room really not bugged? thought John. He said: "I felt like a bone in here. A bone tossed into a pack of dogs."

"Friendly dogs."

"Why was Glass championing me? I don't know him."

"He knows about you." Woodruff sighed. "About Hong Kong."

"What does that have to do with him—"

"Remember Jerry Barber?"

Legends and incomplete news stories, sanitized reports he'd read. John said: "Was he the guy who—"

"Beirut, early '80s. Jerry Barber, Harlan Glass, Roger Allen, me, a dozen others, most of us under diplomatic or friendly-country cover, trying to penetrate warlord armies and terrorist groups, get a line on hostages. Jerry got snatched off the streets on an Op he and Harlan put together—one that should have worked, a simple black bag in a warlord zone. We knew that whoever snatched Jerry would torture him. Harlan didn't wait for Agency sanction. Technically, he jumped the rules. For thirty-two hours, he never left the bricks, followed leads right into rubble hell, no mercenary cutouts or backups. Neutralized the three-man jihad cell who'd grabbed Jerry. Carried Jerry's body out on his back."

"So Harlan, knowing about Hong Kong . . . you'd be his kind of people.

"Besides, he used to be Ops, like you. Probably his heart is still in our black side of the house. And if we have to suffer those damn Centers Casey set up, then at least we're lucky he's in place at Counter-Terrorism, keeping that cancer cell from eating us alive. Plus on this, on Frank, Harlan'll help us keep the lid nailed down."

Easy. Steady. Calm.

"Why was Korn trying to rip my heart out?" asked John.

"Because it's there." Woodruff shook his head. "He's Security. The job makes men lepers and then they think the rest of the world is diseased. Plus he knows you've got Ops blood and no security man will ever rise to head Ops, so he's stuck on a rank level you might pass. Plus, if there had been—is—something hinky about what happened, it would be his trouble."

"I thought finding trouble was what we were all about."

"No," said Dick, "we're about avoiding trouble."

"Can't always do that."

"But we can be smart about it."

The two friends sat quietly for a moment.

"What do you want me to do?" said John.

"Your job. Trust. Believe. And for now, go home."

The same men who'd picked up John at the hospital drove him to his cabin. Mary didn't come with them.

"She had another problem," said Mr. Jock.

She had to report, thought John.

They walked him to his door, came inside and wordlessly assured him it was safe.

"Do you want us to stick around?" asked Dragon Eyes.

"Not around here." John asked him the time.

"It's 4:17."

They left.

John sat on his couch.

When he realized day had turned to night, he got up, switched on all the lights. In his bedroom, he picked up the red wind-up alarm clock: 6:33. He carried the ticking clock back to the living room.

Wind rattled his window. A cold draft.

Just the wind.

Suddenly he was famished. He'd planned on getting a chocolate donut from the Plastic Palace coffee shop in the basement of the Russell Senate Office Building when he and Frank got to . . .

The carcass of a supermarket barbecued chicken waited in the fridge. He pulled it from its plastic sheath, put it on a plate, punched the microwave buttons for 3 minutes, 1 second—he abhorred randomly even numbers.

The microwave hummed.

The alarm clock ticked.

On his desk, the red light on his telephone answering machine flashed a steady, silent beat.

BEEP!

"John! . . . This is Em North."

Throaty voice. A tight smile, red lips.

Don't think about that now. Why think about that now?

Emma North handled foreign relations and intelligence issues for Senator Ken Handelman, a member of the Intelligence Committee. The Chairman and his staff director assigned each Committee member an aide from the Committee staff, but Senator Handelman trusted Emma—who drew her paycheck from his personal staff—more than the Committee-chosen expert, whom the Senator could refuse but not select.

"I heard about Frank and . . . This damn city! America in the '90s. Where the hell are we? If there's anything I can do, I . . . want to be sure you're all right, you're—"

BEEP!

"It's Em again. Hate these machines. If you need something, call me."

More softly, she said: "Take care, John." She gave her phone number and address to the machine.

BEEP!

"Hi, John, Mary from your office. Sorry I couldn't ride home with you. If you need anything, need to talk, call me. Don't worry about the time." She read off her number.

The microwave beeped.

He called his mother. She lived in Black Hawk, South Dakota, alone in the white frame house where John had grown up. The land was a rolling plain that let you see all the way to the Black Hills. The air was clean, 'cept for sage in spring, prairie grasses in the summer and the musk of ripe wheat and red leaves in fall. Winter smelled of ice's fire. You knew everyone in town.

She told him about the freak March snowstorm. And how G&H Furniture was bankrupt. When Jimmy Gustafson—he was a senior on the basketball team when you were a freshman—when he nailed plywood over the store windows he was crying so hard he couldn't see and he broke his thumb with the hammer. *Oh,* said John. She told him about the crazy Adkinses. Do those people back in Washington think we're stupid out here? she said. *What people,* he said. She told him about the pro basketball game on TV. She thought the novel he'd sent her had no point, piss on what the critics said. She said the Golden Years weren't all they were cracked up to be. Asked him how work was, knowing she'd get no details from her son who'd hidden much of his adult life in a cloak she knew but never named. *Work is fine, Mom.* He told her he loved her. She paused. Said she loved him, too. Told him he could always come home. What the hell, teach Chinese on the reservation or go back to work filling potholes for the city, if they got a budget this time. Again he told her what didn't need to be spoken. Again she said she loved him, too.

They hung up.

The chicken was juicy, warm. Cold milk, trace a line in the condensation on the glass.

Maybe the rest of the world was right.

Luck is what we get, Frank'd said.

The phone rang.

John answered it, listened, said OK, hung up.

The room was quiet. The red alarm clock ticked on his desk. Turn on the radio. A talk show on the classical radio station he and . . . Punch the select button: vicious electric guitars screamed on the progressive station. The third palatable choice was a recycled rock station. No more memories now. Turn the radio off, the TV on. Laugh track—turn it off.

The pile of his bloody clothes.

Black plastic trash bag from the kitchen cupboard.

Shoes, watch, shirt, tie, suit, everything: in there. Everything. The coat the CIA sent for him. In the bag.

Tie a knot in its top, so tight nothing will escape.

Trash day was Thursday, two dawns away. If he walked the bag through the dark, put it by the curb in front of his landlord's house, raccoons would have two nights to rip it open.

Can't leave that bag in here. Not inside his home.

The hands on the ticking clock showed 8:07.

All the lights in his house were on; they glowed behind him as he stepped outside. He tossed the black trash bag to the edge of the porch. In misty shimmer of his porch light, John saw the puff of his own breath.

Shoes crunched on frozen earth.

Out there. In the darkness. By the trees.

No.

Closer.

In the night. Shadows move. Become substance.

Become the shape of a man.

Coming closer.

A short man. Topcoat. A hat, a snappy fedora that altered the lines of his profile. Something dangled in his left hand and he stepped closer, closer . . .

Into the mist of the porch light stepped Harlan Glass, the CIA's executive-in-place in the Counter-Terrorism Center, his gloved right forefinger pressed against his lips.

6

Wordlessly, John followed the man wearing the fedora into the cabin.

Heart pounding. *Stay cool.*

Harlan Glass shut the door. He carried a thin attaché case. His gloved thumb flipped a switch on a black plastic box he took from his coat pocket.

Glass swept the box over John's stereo. He unplugged the answering machine. Toured the cabin. Then put the box on the coffee table and sank into the worn easy chair.

Unbidden, John sat on the couch.

The older CIA executive unbuttoned his overcoat. He put his smooth fedora on the coffee table.

"I hate hats," he said. John filled his eyes.

Glass said: "Figure I have to trust you."

"I figure this is my house," said John.

"You think that matters?" Glass kept his gloves on. "Has anyone else been here tonight?"

"No."

"Any phone calls?"

"Is that your business?"

"It's *our* business," said Glass, "or I'm out the door."

He waited, watching the hunger grow in John's eyes.

Finally, John said: "Miguel Zell called. About the hearing tomorrow."

"Yes, I was in on that strategy. Did he talk about anything else?"

"No."

"Have you talked to anyone else since you've been here?"

"Mom and I talked about the weather in South Dakota."

Glass sighed. "Have to trust you. You have to trust me."

"You're an Agency executive: trusting you is my job."

"You better be smarter than that."

Say nothing. Wait.

"Good," said his unexpected visitor. "Patience and discretion are the only necessary virtues for a spy.

"Anytime you want me to stop, say so, because bet your life on this: you can't discuss what I tell you with anyone, not with your supervisor Zell or your mentor Dick Woodruff or DDO Allen or the Director. We're in a minefield."

John shrugged.

"Yes or no?" said Glass.

"So far, yes."

"You'll walk into this like I did," said Glass.

He swung the attaché case to his lap, passed a piece of paper from it to John.

A cardinal rule of the CIA is that work stays at the office. No documents leave the complex.

"Tell me about this," said Glass.

A photocopy of a single-spaced, unsigned, typewritten letter. Words centered beneath the silver-dollar-size eagle and shield symbol for the Central Intelligence Agency.

Dear Senator Firestone:

If you're really interested in bird-dogging the CIA, check out what happened to an American named Cliff Johnson who blew up in Paris this January, and maybe we'll both work our way ahead.

"I've never seen this before," said John.

"Are you sure?"

"Positive—I don't know anything about it."

"I believe you," said Glass. "That makes sense."

"Where did you get it?"

"From Frank Mathews—from your office via Frank."

"A routine buck?"

"At first. An anonymous, vacuous letter to our most vocal critic on the Senate Intelligence Committee. He's stuck with the Intel Committee where he can't pork tax dollars back to St. Louis to buy votes, so headlines are all he can hope for."

"A crank."

"The Senator, the letter or both?" said Glass.

Neither man smiled.

"Senator Firestone's mail room received it," said John. "Saw 'CIA,' gave it to whoever on Firestone's staff handles intelligence issues, and that person bucked this letter over to CIA Congressional Liaison."

"With a 'we're curious' cover letter over the Senator's signature," said Glass. "The CIA 'stationery' saw to that—whether it's a cut-and-paste fake or not. Without it, the letter might have been dismissed as a crank."

"With it," said John, "it might be from a whistle-blower."

"This letter hit my desk eleven days ago. That's when it started. When I first saw it."

"Saw what?"

"What wasn't there: not in DESIST, not in any of our files. Plus none of our old friends in Ops, no one in the Counter-Intelligence Center, no one anywhere had a record of receiving a Liaison buck about an anonymous letter—and no one had any nonpublic data about a Cliff Johnson 'blowing up' in Paris."

"Frank wouldn't have single-shot routed a—"

"He didn't. I went to Frank. He'd already discovered that his routine queries to various Agency offices had vanished."

"Except the query to your Center."

"At CTC, even 'routine' communications from the White House or Congress hit my desk first."

"Makes it easy—"

"Makes it hard for Congressional oversight to hit a stone wall in my shop," said Glass. "And hard for our official chief from the FBI to make a political end run around me or the Agency."

"What did Frank say?"

"That no one else knew."

"What did he do?"

"You tell me."

A wire tightened inside John's spine.

"He and I knew that if someone had intercepted his routine queries, we had a problem."

"To run an intercept like that means—"

"A hell of a lot of work," said Glass. "And risk."

"Why?" asked John. "For what?"

"Figure something that's worth the effort. Perhaps the letter and Frank spotlighted a sensitive operation, one run at the CIA Director's or Joint Chiefs of Staff level. Or from the basement of the White House. Perhaps he'd tumbled into someone's unsanctioned op left over from the old days."

"What did you two do?"

"It was Frank's call. The contact hit his office—your office. He asked me to do no more. To not log or process the query. Certainly not let it percolate up to CTC's illustrious FBI chief or around the office to non-Agency poachers. Frank made me promise to say nothing to anyone. Because he was a pro, a friend . . . "

Glass sighed: "Figure, my personal agendas dictated my professional responses. Not what Agency rules say we should do."

"Why didn't Frank sound the alarms?"

"Frank always had more faith in himself than in the system. Plus on this, we knew the system had already failed."

"Now he's dead."

"Yes. Now he's dead. We're stuck with his legacy. And I'm guilty of having followed his wishes."

The clock ticked in the kitchen.

John said: "I was afraid I was crazy. And alone."

"Maybe we're both crazy," said Glass.

"This is why he was killed," said John.

"*If* he was killed," corrected Glass.

"How can you—"

"Figure, one: all factual evidence indicates a stray bullet. Two: willful murder of a CIA executive takes a lot of balls and not many brains. What could be worth having the entire American intelligence community on your trail?"

"If I knew that . . . What do you want from me?" said John.

"You're a major part of my crisis," said Glass. "So you've got to be a major part of its solution."

"You're after my skin."

Skin. when a CIA agent recruits a spy for intelligence work, the CIA spook nails a "skin" on his trophy wall.

"I've already pledged allegiance," said John.

"To preserve and protect the Constitution. That's what I want you to do."

"The grander the slogan, the greater the lie," said John.

"Find me the truth, we'll both be happy."

"If 'truth' was what you wanted, you would have brought this up at the meeting today."

Glass shook his head: "Truth is a currency. Spend it at the wrong time, it's wasted. In the wrong hands, truth defeats you.

"Frank's first step was into the system," said Glass. "And the system failed. Until I know how and why, no way can I throw the currency of this mess onto the official table."

"Even in that meeting?"

"Frank copied that letter to offices run by people at that meeting," said Glass. "To Ops, run by Allen and Woodruff. To Security, run by Korn. To the lawyer, in case there'd be a red flag from the law. To Miguel Zell, your boss. I waited for one of them to bring it up—Frank had said their copies had been intercepted, too, but I hoped . . . "

"No," said John, "you feared."

"Yes, figure I feared: if one of them ran the intercept of Frank's letter, me bringing it up would give them more incentive and warning to cover their tracks. Rob me of my cloak and the element of surprise."

"But if you told *everybody*—"

"Then we'd lose control. Then we'd generate chaos."

Glass shook his head: "No matter what you hear, I love this Agency—not because it's there, but because it has to be. This is a new era. No more Cold War. No more easy enemies."

"Things weren't so easy or clear then," argued John.

"What was clear then was that we were needed. That need hasn't changed, but the clarity has. Allen was on target today when he talked about the war for the future of this Agency. If we throw this letter like a grenade, the explosion is more likely to rip the Agency apart than clear up . . . whatever needs clearing up."

"Like finding who killed Frank."

"Like finding out *if* he was killed, and *if* it links to this letter, and *if not,* what is this letter worth."

"You're not going to tell the Agency, are you?"

"Not yet," said Glass.

"So this isn't about Frank."

"It's a package," said Glass. "The Agency's future, Frank's past."

Maybe, thought John. Subtle, but maybe.

"You want me to back off," said John.

"You wouldn't do that no matter what you tell me," said Glass. "No, I want you to find the truth. But do it deep cover, leave no tracks, fingerprints. Generate no further turmoil. Or questions. That's what Frank was trying to do."

"Look where he is now. The logical move for me is into as many command offices as I can get: Zell, Woodruff."

"Don't stop there. Go to Allen. And the Director will be back in town tomorrow.

"Of course," added Glass, "Frank's first step was into the system. If there is a problem in the Agency, it would have to be someone capable of pulling Frank's referrals, of thwarting his inquiries. Someone like that will spot us the instant we take a step on any Agency ladder."

"Frank mentioned a rough beast."

"Was he talking about one man or a metaphor?"

"Too late to ask."

"But is it too late to know?" said Glass. "Besides, if you're right, and Frank was assassinated, since you were his partner, whoever killed him has to wonder if you're a threat."

"That's my ambition."

"Fulfill it. But do it smart. Do it with me."

"The Agency—"

"The Agency is satisfied. Oh, they may dance out some sort of study keyed by Frank's death. Spend a lot of time and energy, create a serious document, and thereby 'solve' the problem. You know how that works."

"Working and results are two different things."

"Call it what you want, figure I need to know what Frank was doing, what it means, what it's generated so far—and know it all without generating new crises. Or ignoring my conscience.

"Figure you need to know if someone killed your friend. And if someone thinks you're worth killing.

"Plus," said Glass, "you need to do your duty to the Agency. To what's right and best—for everyone and everything."

Chords of logic. Locked in. True.

"If you're as good as I think you are," said Glass, "my way means I get what I need and you get what you want."

"How could I do all that?" John asked.

"Very carefully. Quietly."

"With only your sanction."

"The problem surfaced in your office. I dominate the CTC, but I can't initiate much without our FBI chief knowing. Besides, we're coordinators. Researchers. In time, the Pentagon and FBI, Customs and CIA may let the Center evolve into an operational force, but tonight I don't command any field people. You're my only chance."

John closed his eyes, rubbed his brow. When he looked again, Glass still sat there.

"This means going covert against the Agency."

"This means giving a dead man his due," said Glass. "This means choosing who you want to be."

"That's not—"

"You were in that car. Be smart. Be a survivor."

"Be a spy."

"That's your calling."

"With you as my case officer. Because—"

"Because if I—if we can't control this operation, no telling what it will ultimately do to the Agency. We've got to do *something,* but we've got to do it smart and do it together. That was Frank's only error that I know of. He insisted on going solo. Consequently, his work died with him."

"What if I say no?"

"Then I'll leave."

"And you'll build a box to drop me in."

Glass said nothing.

"Why should I trust you?" asked John.

"Who else has come to you with their trust? Who else has given your intuition any credit?

"You have to trust someone." Glass shrugged. "First Frank trusted the system, then he trusted just himself."

"I don't want to end up sweating in front of a grand jury," said John.

"Why would that happen? Besides, in all our scandals, from the Bay of Pigs to Phoenix to the assassination programs, Watergate to Iran-contra, name one of us who's been broken."

"I also don't want to end up floating in the Chesapeake, a suicide with a gun that's not around. Or freezing to death outside my cabin. Or having you carry my body through the streets of D.C."

"Then you better be as good as I think you are."

"What about you?"

"No one who harms me walks away."

Believe that.

"Besides, on this, you're the field man, you're the dog." Glass took an envelope from his attaché case. "Limited power of attorney based on documents Frank drew up years ago and filed with the Agency. The law firm belongs to us. You can use these documents to claim his car, be in his house."

Keys dropped on the table from Glass's hand: "Copies from the police that I co-opted from Korn's goons. Frank's car, home."

"How do you know you can trust me? There are things I've done—"

"Don't tell me what I don't need to know." Glass sighed. "Figure I said I had to trust you, not that I wanted to.

"We'll have no insecure contact. Phone procedures, addresses are in that envelope. No reports in writing. You know our objectives. Work this clean but work it hard.

"Work it fast: the letter is already old, and Frank's trail grows colder by the minute. Do your job on the Hill, too. It's excellent cover, and it's crucial on its own."

Glass stood, his motion drawing John to his feet.

"Trust no one," said Glass: "Not Woodruff, not Zell, definitely not Korn: he's paranoid, so his interests parallel our concerns, but he's gunning for you. I wonder why."

"Me, too."

"You'll find $300 in the envelope—my personal money. I can't even get you black funds for this, or guarantee that I can cover any additional expenses."

John stared at the material Glass had put on his table.

"I need an answer," said Glass. "Now."

Going to do it anyway. So do it right. Do it smart.

"OK," said John. "Your Op, my run."

"You and me." Glass shook his head. "You probably grew up believing the Beatles."

"I grew up after they broke up," said John.

Glass sighed, buttoned his overcoat. Carefully, he placed the fedora on his head, shaped its brim into a natty line with steady fingers. He checked his reflection in a night-dark window. With a careful tug, he pulled the hat into proper alignment, gave the night a quick bulldog nod.

At the door, he turned back; said: "You being in that car—figure tough luck."

7

Walk the circle.
Don't think.
Just walk the circle as the night melts away.

John began in darkness, the field outside his cabin lit by the light over his door. He'd been a shadow flitting across dormant grass, practicing *Pa-kua* and *Hsing-i*. He stalked around an invisible opponent, circling one direction, then the other. He walked crouched, his back straight, as if he were sitting in a chair that had been pulled away.

Face the center.

The palm of his inside hand pushed toward the circle's core, his arm bent at the elbow, his eyes focused through the tip of his forefinger. His outside arm hooked down and across his body, palm facing the earth and fingers protecting his ribs. He sank his breath below his navel, to his *t'an tien*. As he walked, he let his mind and spirit open and relax.

Be free of anticipation. Anxiety.

Free of screaming visions.

Forget about who you are. Forget about gotta-do's. Should-do's.
Glass. The air is cold and Frank's hot wet . . .

Walk the circle.

Sweat trickled down John's cheek. His legs ached. The muscles in his arms burned with the posture's dynamic tension.

When he'd started walking the circle, he'd been cold, stiff. Sore from yesterday. Dressed in skier's long underwear. Black lace-up Chinese flat-soled shoes. Gray sweatpants. A white sweatshirt. For the first half hour, he wore a red nylon jacket, black gloves and a navy stocking cap. Now his sides were soaked, his face glistened in the growing gray light, his hair matted to his head. Jacket, gloves and cap lay tossed aside.

After he'd warmed up, John stood in *wu chi,* infinity posture, hands at his sides, heels together, toes fanned out. Long breaths, empty mind. He reverently moved through the formal opening, snapped into the *san-t'i* on-guard position, and sped through the Five Fists' staccato attacks. Worked on *Hsing-i*'s 12 animal styles of fighting. Next came *Pa-kua*'s 64 straight-line counterattacks—grabbing, pulling, striking, kicking, pushing, trying to focus his *ch'i.* Then he'd walked the circle again, alternating the eight whirling changes of direction designed to confound an enemy.

Whoever the enemy was.

As John circled, his eyes swung over the naked trees surrounding his home. His breath made patches of white fog. His cabin came into view over the tip of his forefinger.

Gray dawn melted the night. A bird took wing.

Triggered John.

Sun Lu-t'ang's single palm change: John's right foot swung ahead of his left, then wedged toe-in to the center of the circle. John shifted his weight, whirled to his rear, left palm slamming out at chin level in the blow exported from Shanghai in the 1930s by colonial policeman Captain W. E. Fairbairn, the Machiavelli of British commandos.

John's left palm strike folded thumb-down into a block raising the enemy's punch as he stepped forward, sank his weight and sent his right palm toward an unguarded solar plexus or heart. He flowed left; his hands followed in a scraping block. Looked right and his hands swung that way. He walked the circle, his hands sinking to the ready position as his eyes focused on—

The silhouette of a man in the trees.

Back by the path past the landlord's house, the path from the street to John's house.

Walk the circle.

The silhouette left John's line of sight.

And John whirled through Yellow Dragon Rolls Over, a turn that naturally swung his gaze back along the tree line.

The silhouette in the bare trees shifted from foot to foot to keep warm. Quietly watched as the night died.

The cabin was forty feet from John. The door was closed.

Never beat a bullet there.

Nowhere to run to.

Nowhere to hide.

Walk the circle. Wait. And walk.

John's patience lasted only one revolution. He stopped, stood in *wu chi*, his eyes resting on the figure in the trees.

The silhouette became a recognizable shape. John's gaze pulled him out of the trees, down the path, toward the cabin. The silhouette kept his hands locked at his sides.

When he was a dozen paces from John, the man said: "Where's your pajama suit and black belt?"

"*Pa-kua* and *Hsing-i* are internal arts," answered John. "External things—uniforms, belts, ranks—they don't matter."

"*Ba-gwa* and *Shing-ee*?" mimicked D.C. Homicide Detective Tyler Greene. Stubble on his cheeks showed more gray than his thick mustache. His brown eyes were bloodshot, his tie loose. "Do they teach you that shit in the CIA?"

"I study on my own," said John.

"Where'd you learn to lie to the police?"

"I never lied to you."

"The whole truth, huh?"

"The relevant truth."

"Oh." Greene waved his hand at the vanished martial ballet. "Like your shadow-boxer shit is 'relevant' in a city where every swinging dick with an attitude packs iron and lead?"

The detective squinted at the tops of the skyscrapers visible over the tree line, the open field, the cabin.

"Nice place," he said. "Little small. And close-in."

"Over the Maryland state line."

"Are we talking about *jurisdiction?*"

"You came here. You're the one talking."

"You're Mr. *Relevant Truth.*"

The men blew patches of fog at each other.

"I've been up all night," said Greene. "Hour after I sent you to the hospital, a lawyer pops home to Georgetown during lunch, discovers adultery happening in the guest bedroom. Goes wild with a heavy-duty attaché case. The bitch splatters blood and brains all over the new wallpaper, most of it from her hubby, who expires in the bed, some of it from the other woman, who takes a half dozen hard ones. When her arms get tired, Mrs. Member of the Bar—blood dripping in her $80 haircut—she calls her office, asks if she has any messages. Then she asks for the firm's criminal ace, who tells her to wait in her living room while he phones us.

"Since I'm only door-to-dooring a stray bullet file job, I get red-lighted over to the ghetto of the elite to process truth, justice and the American way.

"The other lady?" said Greene. "The one who made the mistake of falling in love with a married jerk? I spent six hours by her hospital bed, waiting for her not to die. Waste of my time."

"I'm sorry."

"Save your sorry," said Greene. "Give me coffee."

"You get any sleep last night?" he asked as John led him toward the cabin.

John picked up his jacket, gloves and cap. "Sort of."

"You'll have a lot of nights like that." Greene glanced at the black plastic trash bag sitting on the porch.

The aroma of hot coffee greeted them when they entered the cabin. Greene laid his topcoat on the couch, folded his suit jacket and neatly draped it over the coat. A silver badge hung on his belt. On his right hip rode a holstered 9mm Glock.

"You got sugar?" asked Greene when John handed him a steaming mug and a milk carton.

"Anything for you."

"I hope so," said Greene. He sat at the round table in John's kitchen nook, poured sugar from the carton into his cup.

"Breakfast of Champions," said Greene. John sat across from him. The cop kept his right hand flat on the table. A gold band glistened on his left hand as he raised the cup to drink. "This'll carry me home."

"You going off duty?"

"I'm off duty now."

"Are we neighbors?"

"I told you: you live too close-in for me."

John sipped his coffee, showed nothing on his face.

"So I roll from hospital to morgue," said Greene. "Medical examiner gives me tuna fish and a prelim on the lovebirds. Back at the ranch, the U.S. Attorney's Office is hot for that one: a real double murder, not just a teenage crack boy capping a competitor. Fellow barristers chilling in the morgue and waiting to make bail. Everything is hurry up and fly.

"One thing and another, getting pulled off my typewriter to play Bad Cop—you CIA guys use Good Cop, Bad Cop?"

"That's not my department."

"What is your department? The Office of Relevant Truth?"

"Our liaison to your department can answer any questions."

"Liaisons are parrots. They know what they get told."

So, cop, thought John, do you know "liaison" is my job?

"But forget that," said Greene with a wave of his hand.

"What should I remember?"

"That it's just you and me sitting here in your house," said Greene. "And I got problems."

Greene pushed his coffee cup aside, put both hands flat on the table and leaned closer to John.

"Was long dark 'fore I finished up the hot case, got time to start papering your shit."

"It's not my shit," said John.

"Don't *relevant* me," Greene told him.

John raised his coffee cup, drank. Tasted nothing.

"What I found," said Greene, "was a case jacket on the death of Senate aide Mathews, Frank G. Stuffed with reports that should have landed on my desk first. Plus a memo from the Office of the Chief—rubber-stamped, not signed. To wit, all case efforts subsequent to those already performed must be cleared with the Chief's office and 'liaisoned' with 'appropriate officials.' You're an unnamed witness. Cause of death listed as manslaughter, perp unknown. Case open, case filed."

"What's your problem?"

"*Problems.*" Greene stressed the plural. "It's my name typed on all the reports. Some have my captain's signature—in pencil. When I called him, I got told the magic letters *C-I-A.*"

"What else did he tell you?"

"Good job, Detective Greene."

"What did you say?"

"'Thank you, sir. Have a nice night.'" Greene sighed. "Shit like yours, who needs it?"

"Not you."

"That's right. But my name is on the reports. Any trouble, it's me the department will hang."

"Nobody's looking to hang you."

"Better not be," said Greene. "I don't die with bullets still in my gun."

"Why did you come here—off duty?"

"Man to man, working stiff to working stiff, no case jacket notes: is there something out there for me to step in?"

Give him careful honesty: "Not that I know of."

"You sure about that?"

"As sure as I can be."

"That's my other problem," sighed the cop. "I don't know which is worse, if you're lying or if you're telling the truth."

Greene's gun hand stayed flat on the table. His left hand fished a plastic evidence baggie from his shirt pocket.

The baggie held a pencil-nub brass tube.

Don't blink. Show nothing.

"You know what that is?" asked Greene. He laid the baggie

on the table. "Sure you do. It's a spent shell casing. The butt end of a long-gone bullet. Nine-millimeter."

"Why do I care?"

"I found it beside the concrete divider twenty-three feet back up the road from where Mathews, Frank G., got shot through the head by an officially stray nine-millimeter bullet."

The brass glistened in the morning light.

Say: "Bullets aren't my business."

Wait a minute: "You think that somehow I shot Frank in the far side of his head in front of all those commuters?"

"People don't notice what happens outside their car."

"If I shot him inside, how did the casing eject outside to where we'd already driven by?"

" 'Eject'? I thought bullets weren't your business."

"I'm not ignorant."

"You just don't know anything *relevant*." Greene shrugged. "People can work magic you wouldn't believe."

"Not me."

"And you say you saw nobody else?"

"That's right."

"Nothing?"

"Just my friend exploding on top of me."

"The reports in *my* case jacket say his wife is long dead and he lived alone. How good of friends were you two?"

"We worked together. Shared some time. Got along."

"You aren't married, are you?" Insinuation floated in Greene's smile.

"No," said John, "but you are. Plus you're not my type."

"Got something against black people?"

"Some of the best women I know are black," said John.

"Me, too," said Greene. "You and your buddy Frank ever do business together outside your nine-to-five?"

"My business is my business—not his, not yours."

"You and he got money tied up together? Shuffling around and bumping against each other on your work ladder?"

"Questions regarding our work should be officially asked through liaison officers. You plan on doing that?"

"Depends on what worries me most." Greene kept his hand on the baggie while he raised his cup to his lips. "Good coffee. Do you always put cinnamon in it?"

"I like a little spice."

"Really."

The homicide detective walked to the couch. He left the baggie on the table, gave John his back. When Greene turned around, coats in hand, John hadn't moved. Neither had the baggie.

"Lots of spent ammo laying around this town," said Greene. He lifted the evidence baggie off the table, let it sway in the sunlight. The cartridge case shone like gold. "Maybe the lab can tell me where this came from."

"I hope so." John stroked his jaw while Greene watched.

Float it like a favor: "Officially, I'm not supposed to do this, but . . . being in that car blew me past official."

"And *relevant?*"

"If you find any other . . . spent shells you can't explain, come see me. I'll help you all I can—unofficially."

Greene laughed: "What a good citizen."

"The offer is real. Working stiff to working stiff."

"Who's working on what?" The cop walked to the door.

"People get killed on my turf," said Greene. "Pisses me off. I don't care about 'official' or 'relevant' considerations. Murder is murder. And when someone gets murdered and my name gets signed on the line, I take it personally."

"Then you must be a good cop," said John.

"Yeah." At the exit, Greene looked back: "What are you?"

8

At 10 sharp that morning, the Senate Select Committee on Intelligence gaveled into session. For this public hearing, the Chairman's staff snagged a great room: polished front dais, 30 rows of chairs, and a press gallery built high into a sidewall that slid open for TV cameras.

John entered that Hart Building hearing room at 10:29, after the Chairman had read his opening statement, noted undetailed previously agreed-to ground rules, and welcomed CIA Deputy Director for Operations Roger Allen to this continuing series of public hearings on the future of the Central Intelligence Agency.

Allen wore a dark suit, white shirt. His reading glasses were half-moons of curved plastic in steel frames.

" . . . so, Mr. Chairman," Allen read into the microphone at the witness table as John entered, "in many ways, our world today is more dangerous than yesterday, precisely because so many options were freed by the crumbled Berlin Wall."

Big crowd, thought John. Maybe 100 people. Senate staffers monitoring for bosses who couldn't be there but wanted something from the intelligence community. A few tourists, their excitement waning as they sought action in words they heard without context. Staff from think tanks around town. Pentagon execs, out of uniform, hungry for the same pie that fed the CIA. The National Security Agency would be paying attention, but those priests of espionage technology might be staying true to their religion and tracking the proceedings only through C-Span television.

Big mistake, thought John. TV cameras concentrated on who was testifying and who was asking questions. Who was there and who was whispering to who might be more important than the canned statements and staged dialogue.

Which was why John's orders had him arrive too late to create a buzz but in time as a presence to ratify Frank's death as urban tragedy, not Committee business.

The morning *Washington Post* tucked under John's arm had a page C-2, Metro section, six-paragraph story about Frank Mathews, "Senate aide," who'd been killed by a stray bullet while commuting. John was an unnamed and unhurt passenger in the car. The CIA was not mentioned. City police were said to be investigating.

Man bites dog is only a story the first time, thought John as he walked along the wall toward the front of the room.

"The next Pearl Harbor," testified Allen, "may be a covert raid on America's banking system by a hostile nation disguised as a multinational corporation . . . "

Clever: defusing the BCCI criminal and terrorist international bank-kiting scandal the Agency had bungled by turning its ghost into a new threat requiring . . . new dollars for the CIA.

A half dozen reporters sat at the press table, tired eyes floating from the distributed texts of statements to Senators sitting at the dais, to the witness, to attractive members of the opposite sex, to visions of their blue computer screens, silver letters clicking into the lead of their stories.

None of the reporters knew John, but the Senate staff did. As he walked along the wall, John saw them notice him from their chairs behind the thrones of the Senators.

Entrance . . . effect.

John quietly excused himself around the knees of a stranger sitting on the aisle four rows from the witness table, slid toward the empty chair . . .

Saw CIA Director of Security George Korn watching him
from a chair on the far aisle three rows back.

Why is Korn here?

Allen sat alone at the witness table.

In the front row behind Allen, John saw Congressional chief
Miguel Zell, Allen's deputy, Dick Woodruff, Counter-Terrorism
Center bulldog Harlan Glass and one of Allen's personal aides
whose briefcase carried data supporting his boss's testimony and
whose heavy belt required him to badge his way through metal
detectors.

Why wasn't Security czar Korn sitting with them?

Emma North filled John's eyes.

She sat behind her boss, Senator Handelman. Her suit was a
professional brown tweed, with a gold blouse. She wore her
brown hair short and brushed up with a sprayed puff. Ruby lips.

That's just her comforting, supportive smile, thought John as her
eyes flicked away from his.

"So more than ever," said Allen, tapping his glasses on the
table, "the CIA needs to be the crucial first line of America's defense. Thank you for having me here, Mr. Chairman, and, under
conditions previously established, I'd be delighted to answer
questions from the Committee."

Senators, aides and the audience stirred in their chairs.

John looked back:

Korn was gone.

The Chairman leaned into the microphone: "Thank you,
Deputy Director Allen. As always, the Committee is deeply ap-
preciative of your candor. We appreciate the Director agreeing to
let you testify today. The Chair would like to add that should the
day come, as it quite logically could, that you are nominated to
fill the CIA Director's chair, our country would be well served by
having you there."

The TV cameras and tourists didn't register the jolt that shot
through the professionals as the Chairman blessed ambition in
one of the Princes in the CIA's realm, an offhand remark—had to

be offhand—that tipped scales of administration, policy and lust along the shores of the Potomac.

Allen said: "Thank you, Mr. Chairman, it's my pleasure to serve as needed."

No one can knife you for that, thought John. But in the corridors of the CIA, the Pentagon and FBI, the NSA and State Department, other fortresses of foreign policy, John's soul heard a dozen of Allen's equally ambitious peers scream.

John wondered if any of them knew that the Chairman, who had become an increasingly respected guest on news panel TV shows, solicited informal visits and telephone calls from DDO Allen before most of those appearances. Such private "chats" armed the Chairman with rifle-shot facts and clever insider perspectives from his good friend Allen. Miguel Zell had two liaison analysts in the on-call for Allen to use as quick-bite data hunters.

At that morning's formal hearing, four Senators sat at the dais: the Chairman, then to his right, separated by an empty chair, Senators Oliver Obst and Ken Handelman. To the Chairman's left, past another empty chair, sat Senator Ralph Bauman. Empty chairs ran from Bauman to the end of the dais. When the Director of the CIA testified, the Committee chairs were full. When the Deputy Director of Central Intelligence testified, half the Committee showed up. For testimony from third-level Deputy Director for Operations Allen, enough Senators came to justify a hearing.

The Chairman glanced at the empty chair to his right. Usually, the intelligence community's major Congressional critic, Senator Charles Firestone, sat there. As with all absent Senators, the Committee staff made sure Firestone's nameplate was not on the dais in front of an empty chair for any cameras to record.

Firestone, thought John: *That anonymous letter came to you.*

"The Chair has no questions at this time. Senator Obst?"

"Thank you, Mr. Chairman." Obst was the only Senator with a beard. He read from a piece of paper on the dais. "Thank you for your testimony, Mr. Allen. I was wondering if you could identify the most dangerous enemy facing America today."

"Ignorance," said Allen.

"I'll buy that," said Obst, "but selling ignorance as part of the CIA's budget rationale is difficult. You're asking us to spend a planeload of dollars to keep the CIA strong. For what? Against who? In terms of strategic threat, please be specific."

"Without breaching security protocols . . . there are twenty-five countries with programs of varying sophistication designed for nuclear, biological or chemical warfare. Maximum peril could be generated from those political regions."

Emma North scribbled on a yellow pad, passed it to Obst's aide, who quickly laid it next to his boss.

A moment later, Obst said: "I'm assuming that even though it's probably one of the twenty-five political regions you alluded to, we can rule out England as a threat."

He shrugged, smiled with the audience and made his press secretary die (again) when he ad-libbed: "After all, we're two and zero with them in the war score."

"I don't believe we should ever ignore a possible threat to the survival of this country," answered Allen.

"Ah . . . " said Obst.

Caught yourself

"I have no further questions at this time," said Obst as his aide leaned in and then leaned back without having had a chance to speak. The aide whispered to Emma.

The Chairman said: "Senator Handelman."

"Thank you," said Handelman. "Mr. Allen, have any . . . events touching on the national security considerations of the Agency or this body occurred within, say, the last two weeks that the Committee has not been fully briefed on?"

Meaning Frank? thought John. *Where's the trap?*

CIA liaison chief Zell and the Chairman had agreed that the death of a midlevel CIA executive ruled by the police as a stray bullet homicide should not gum up strategic planning discussions about the CIA. Besides, Allen and the Chairman wanted to spare the urban martyr's family the public notoriety.

But Handelman wants something on the record, thought John, just in case.

Not Handelman: Emma.

Allen shrugged, gestured with his glasses. "Outside of what's been reported to this Committee and to the Committee on the House side and to the White House in the daily briefs, at this time I can think of nothing that requires a 'yes' to your question."

That I've now buried in my answer, thought John. He felt Frank's fate drifting away in official winds.

Out of the spotlight now, Senator Obst pushed away from the dais, went into the closed-door room behind where the staffers sat. His aide removed his nameplate from view.

Could be an important phone call to the White House, thought John. Could be calling his office to start damage control before the British Embassy protests. Could be donuts and coffee back there—it was too early for pizza.

"Mr. Allen," said Handelman, "a long-standing concern of mine has been repeated CIA support of dictators and 'leaders' who turn out to be worse than the enemies we feared. The creation by the CIA of Frankenstein monsters."

"Senator, the CIA doesn't act in a vacuum: we carry out policy decided by the White House and overseen by Congress."

"With a lot of latitude," said Handelman. "I'm thinking of the millions of taxpayer dollars we slipped to Panamanian dictator Manuel Noriega. Then we had to send the 82nd Airborne to arrest him as a drug dealer who was poisoning our youth. How can we be sure current CIA programs are not creating monsters like that?"

"Senator, the CIA is not in the business of manufacturing monsters. We carry out policy, sometimes with risks, under your oversight. Perhaps increased vigilance on your part is needed."

"Thank you for that sentiment." Handelman took a breath. "Are you familiar with the terrorist Ahmed Naral?"

Senator Bauman twitched like a puppet brought to life.

"The alleged terrorist," said Allen.

Senator Handelman frowned: "Alleged?"

"Beyond issues of political semantics," said Allen, "we in the CIA, at least, believe in the American principle of giving a man his just due, and the individual you named—"

"Ahmed Naral!"

"—has never been convicted of terrorism in any country."

"He's publicly embraced the concept!"

"I'm not sure I follow your line of questioning."

"Are you aware that Ahmed Naral was found dead in Beirut nine days ago? None of our *routine briefings* from your Agency mentioned that fact."

"Media reports from that area claim that a man who may or may not be Ahmed Naral was found dead in an apartment, yes."

"He was found floating in a bathtub of blood and water. Wrists slit. Supposedly suicide."

"The Agency does not dispute the cause of death reported in the foreign press, but since we have not examined the body, we cannot conclusively state that the deceased is Ahmed Naral."

"But you think it's him?"

"That's our operating relevant assumption."

"What about a report by a Cairo newspaper that Naral had received CIA funds and aid, and that at various times while he was an active terrorist, he was also an asset of the Agency?"

"That unsubstantiated allegation was also in *The New York Times,* I believe. As a matter of course and security, the Agency never confirms or denies the identity of its assets."

"Not even to Congress?"

The Chairman interrupted: "Mr. Handelman, at any public hearing and certainly under today's rules, you're wandering in areas where the witness cannot and should not go."

"I apologize, Mr. Chairman," said Handelman. "I was merely trying to help the witness by linking my earlier questions about recent events and unwise exercises in covert policy with concrete examples."

"Hypothetical examples," interjected the witness.

"Let's stay concrete," said Handelman. "And move on. How can the CIA—which was designed for the Cold War—perform an adequate intelligence role in these days after the Cold War?"

"That's the key question, Senator. Working with your Committee, we surveyed the executive branch—all our consumers— asking them to list what kind of intelligence they were getting, what they thought they didn't need, what they wanted. Not one category of intelligence was dropped. We were asked to provide data in 186 separate categories—six more categories than before."

Smart, thought John: *Define the debate with numbers you control.*

"We are an evolving institution," answered Allen. "We're always looking for a better way to do what we do, but I remind you that given the success of us winning the Cold War, I think you can be confident, even proud, of our institutional dynamics."

Emma leaned forward, pointed to something on one of the briefing papers in front of Senator Handelman.

"By 'us,'" said Handelman, "I assume you mean America and the rest of the West, and by 'winning,' I assume you mean our political and economic system outlurching the Soviets while both sides refrained from destroying the world with nuclear weapons."

"As the Senator knows," rejoined Allen, "assumptions obscure reality, reality creates history, and mankind will argue over history until it stops. What's important is that the CIA has always responded to what the world hands us and what you in Congress and the White House want."

"Nicely put," said Handelman.

"Thank you."

"Tell me, are the various Centers—which extend webs beyond the walls of the CIA—are those Centers going to be a growing— and perhaps eclipsing—institutional force that the CIA will support both administratively and politically?"

"We will support whatever Congress and the White House mandate, but—"

"But," said Handelman.

Laughter echoed in the room.

"While the Centers give us some enhanced flexibility in areas like nuclear proliferation and narcotics and terrorism, they can never replace our Central Intel—"

"Wait a minute!" interrupted Senator Bauman.

Senator Ralph E. Bauman. Small-town lawyer elected to Congress two years before Lee Harvey Oswald died in Dallas. Bauman was a wispy-haired bantam with age spots and temper like a leopard. One year he went through 11 Administrative Assistants, the chiefs of staff for a Senate office. John knew that Bauman's current A.A. had been on the job less than two weeks, and his previous A.A. had lasted only three months. Bauman had turned his service on the Intelligence Committee into a media crusade to keep the children of voters in his home state safe from godless foreign foes.

"Wait just a minute!" said Bauman.

Emma tapped Senator Handelman's watch with her pencil.

The Chairman said: "Excuse me, Senator Bauman, but Senator Handelman has the floor."

Behind the sitting Senators, the door to the staff room opened and Senator Obst walked back onto the dais. He brushed his beard as he took his chair and his staffers returned his nameplate.

Damn, decided John.

"Mr. Chairman," said Handelman, "I'm delighted to yield to my distinguished colleague, providing that the question I was asking and Mr. Allen was answering will be completely addressed in the *Hearing Record,* and that other questions I will submit, with his answers, will be made part of the record."

"Without objection," sighed the Chairman, "so ordered."

"Thank you," said Bauman. "Thank you, Senator Hande'man. I 'pologize for interruptin', but I just heard somethin' that should be the focus of this Committee today and tomorrow and every day until we make damn sure all the folks back home are safe fum't."

Senator Handelman left out the back door.

Emma kept her chair.

TV cameras focused on Bauman. Photographers snapped pictures, bored but just in case.

"Terrorism!" bellowed Bauman. "Mr. Allen, whach you in the C-I-A doin' 'bout terrorism?"

"Everything we can, sir."

"Everything! Well, hell, it's been two damn months since a bomb went off in that skyscraper in New York, and 'Merica and I want to know 'bout it!"

The day that Frank had died, as a courtesy banked against his inevitable future unemployment, Bauman's new A.A. had called the Chief Counsel of the Senate Intelligence Committee, told him his boss would bring up Corcoran Center's bombing. The Chief Counsel passed the heads-up to Miguel Zell at the CIA.

"Senator Bauman," said Allen, "as you know, the FBI—not the CIA—has jurisdiction over terrorist incidents in the U.S. Furthermore, the special joint Task Force of New York and federal authorities—working in conjunction with our Counter-Terrorism Center—is the lead investigative unit for—"

"Two damn months and nobody's in jail yet! What about, I remember, in the news they said you guys got a suspect, a picture of him and everything."

"Senator, without revealing sources and methods which could jeopardize the case—which I'm sure you don't want—the press leak that occurred the day after the bombing has already been confirmed: the New York Police Department has a photo of a *witness* they'd like to interview in—"

"Witness, schmitness, I'm talking about terrorists who killed a bunch of people! I'm gonna stay up here askin' 'bout them until I get some damn answers!"

The Chairman wet his lips. He ruled the glamorous and politically impotent Intelligence Committee. Senator Bauman had more seniority in the Senate and was waiting for the death, defeat or retirement of a colleague to claim either Chairman of the tax-writing Finance Committee or the broad-based Judiciary Committee. Coupled with his seniority, either of those posts would enable Bauman to terrorize any Senator who'd ever crossed him.

John caught the look the Chairman gave Allen.

The Committee's witness sighed, slipped his glasses on.

"Senator, although I'm not on the Task Force, and the CIA is not coordinating the investigation—"

"It's campin' in your Counter-Terrorism Center!"

"You're absolutely correct, Senator." Allen gave Bauman a wan, apologetic smile. Bauman preened.

"Let me tell you this, Senator Bauman," said Allen.

He paused.

Reporters leaned forward.

You'll get your sound bite, Bauman, thought John. *But your getting it was planned by the Chairman. And by us.*

"First, only four people died in that bombing—the architect and her family, who tragically could not have been predicted to be there. The other death, the heart attack of the older guard before he was found in the back of that car, is technically part of the same crime, but also was logically an unplanned event.

"Today, the Task Force will be releasing particulars, but the forensic ordnance experts estimate that 1,000 pounds of C-4 plastic explosives was used. Its placement in the lobby, the choice of explosive, the fact that although the lobby was destroyed and the floors above and below it extensively damaged, all that coupled with the sophistication of the attack indicates that destroying the building was *not* the goal of the terrorists."

Cameras clicked—but it was the CIA witness's crusading image being recorded, not the indignant Senator's.

"Then what was their damn goal?" said Bauman.

"Sending some sort of message," said Allen.

"Well, hell, I got it!: *'Welcome to the new world! You ain't safe and you can't do nothin' 'bout it!'*"

"We would disagree with you, Senator. Respectfully. The CIA's ongoing programs—if adequately funded—create a global intelligence net for all terrorist-related—"

"That's what the newfangled Counter-Terrorist Center is supposed to do!" snapped Bauman. "Sounds like your net's poaching fish in their water and that's tangling everybody up!"

Allen laced his fingers together, pressed that intertwined fist on the table. "As you know, Senator, the CTC is an Agency response, merely a coordinating effort, us reaching out to other national security groups, incorporating—"

"Keeping everything tight and central, right?" interrupted Bauman. "Answer me this: where'd they get all that blowup?"

"Senator, last year over 100,000 pounds of explosives was stolen in this country alone. About the only ordnance that's never been stolen is an atom bomb."

"You sure about that?"

"Yes sir."

"Terrorists did that bomb in New York—right?"

"No group has claimed credit for it, but again, all indications are that you are correct, Senator Bauman."

The flush in Bauman's cheeks subsided. Allen continued:

"Corcoran Center—repaired—houses diplomatic offices from three countries that didn't exist five years ago, a Japanese bank, city and state offices, five multinational corporations, law firms, federal offices. Dentists. Psychiatrists. According to the Task Force, 9,174 man-hours of investigation have failed to turn up any motive for the bombing except terrorism."

Cite a gigantic, quirky number of man-hours expended on a task (fruitlessly or not), thought John, *thereby proving your own competence and justifying your existence. Right out of J. Edgar Hoover's textbook on how to beat Congressional oversight.*

Senator Bauman's beady eyes locked on the dais in front of him: "Do you have a list of possible terrorist group suspects involved in the bombing of Corcoran Center?"

"Excuse me?" said Allen.

John saw Miguel Zell shift in his seat: this tack hadn't been anticipated. John sensed a look from Allen to the Chairman. Seated behind Bauman was his new A.A., who owed some loyalty to the man who controlled his paycheck. That A.A. stared at the ceiling.

Senator Bauman read—obviously read—the question again.

"Ah, we have catalogued many organizations that are terrorist in nature," answered Allen.

Senator Bauman read: "If th' witness says yes, then ask him—"

Bauman's A.A. turned in his chair to stare at the wall.

"I don't need no damn questions!" Bauman yelled, sweeping papers off the dais. The brown patches on his face were islands in a sea of red. "I want a list of terrorist groups and I want you to give it to me and I won't take no for an answer!"

The Chairman cleared his throat.

Bauman thumped the dais: "Not taking no for an answer!"

"And you shouldn't have to, Senator," said Allen.

Bauman blinked.

"Although," said Allen, "I know you don't want to jeopardize American lives or the investigation by getting the list in open committee or releasing it in any fashion. You don't want to be responsible for killing any more Americans."

Bauman wrinkled his brow.

"On your behalf," said Allen, "I will request that the Corcoran Center Task Force release to you the list we helped them compile of terrorist group suspects. The list, of course, will be available on a confidential, by-request basis only to all members of the Committee. Just as you want—correct?"

"Ah . . . Yeah. Yeah. But I want that list! I want to be able to keep my promise to the public that I get that list!"

The Chairman coughed into the microphone: "Gentlemen, we are running over our time. With our thanks to Mr. Allen, I would suggest that all other questions be submitted in writing, and they and Mr. Allen's responses will be part of the permanent record.

"Without objection, so ordered.

"The Chair would entertain a motion for adjournment."

"So moved," said Obst.

The Chairman banged the gavel.

The Senators were out the back door to the staff room behind the dais before most of the audience could stand.

John sat in his chair. The room surged with a sea of exiting bodies, the babble of conversation. He lost sight of Emma.

Frank's dead, and the machine rolls on.

Glass led the CIA delegation up the center aisle. He sent a properly discreet nod to John: an executive acknowledging a subordinate's presence.

Allen and Zell followed a few steps behind Glass. Their nods and smiles were larger.

Emptier, thought John.

Woodruff made his way down the aisle, shook John's hand.

"Who needs baseball when you got this?" said Woodruff, his smile encompassing the emptying room. "You OK?"

"Yesterday was worse."

"Walk with me," said Woodruff.

The Hart Senate Office Building is six stories of offices and hearing rooms built around a sunlit atrium half the size of a football field. A two-section abstract Calder sculpture fills the atrium: *Mountains and Clouds,* black steel ridges pointing up to where a two-ton black aluminum mobile "cloud" sways from the skylight. The building encapsules the atrium in glass; walls of staffers labor in offices transparent to the outer world.

The senior spy led John down a carpeted hall to a long, empty stretch of third-floor balcony overlooking the atrium. The two-ton black *Clouds* hung in front of their eyes; footsteps echoed from the marble floor below. The corridor behind them was empty. Woodruff spoke softly, though no one was there to overhear them.

"We were right," he said. "About Frank. Operations, the Centers, FBI, DEA, the military agencies, D.C. cops—a hell of an indictment of reality, but no doubts: stray bullet."

Show nothing, say: "So that's official."

"Must be a relief to have that behind you."

Smile: "Yes."

Woodruff's eyes narrowed. "Death sometimes fools us into thinking and doing crazy things."

"Like the rules are changed."

"The rules never change."

"No. I don't suppose they do."

"You're not . . . susceptible to crazy things, are you, John?"

"I struggle for sanity every day. So far, I'm winning."

"Good. I thought so. Everybody does."

"There's a crisis-response group forming," said Woodruff. "Drafting recommendations on what to do when tragedies like this happen, interagency procedures. They may want your input."

"Input. To an important study."

"Yes," said Woodruff.

Imperceptibly, the two-ton black metal *Clouds* swayed.

"But if you need some time off, take it."

"We're busy up here," said John.

"Nothing that the boys can't handle. Zell may need your help with this oversight flurry, budget stuff, but basically, we're covered. Just follow his lead."

Woodruff dropped his voice even lower. "Wish I could stay around for you—just in case—but I'm on a noon plane."

John had lived too long in the culture to ask.

"Didn't plan on getting slingshotted, but the world shifts and the Agency countermoves. Gotta put out a fire."

Got to ask. Make it . . . mostly true. "Is something going on . . . somewhere . . . that I should know about—for work up here?"

Woodruff shrugged: "Just business as usual."

Back into it: "Senator Bauman, the terrorism stuff, I'll coordinate with Glass and—"

"Zell will handle Bauman," said Woodruff. "As for Glass . . . Don't expect you'll need to see much of him."

"I thought you liked him."

"I respect him," said Woodruff. "He's a lucky man—like you. Luck is something you're born with or without, but no matter what, we have to respect that."

"Glass is lucky?"

"Well, he married a trust-fund wife, which always makes life easier, though she's . . . troubled. She sprays money around this town like a cat in heat—do-good groups, the soft-money off-shoots of both parties. Just because she can. Social access. Glass has a hell of a time controlling her."

"That's not why you don't like him."

"Harlan . . . Harlan was an Ops man, like I said. It's good that an Ops man runs the Counter-Terrorism Center. And he and Allen and I go back, Beirut and all that."

"But . . ."

"But Glass plays the lines too hard. He's loyal, but . . . He's embracing these ideas of change. Runs his CTC a bit too close to the bone for our Agency's good."

"But his job—"

"'Job,' 'duty,' and 'prudence' are all necessary to maintain the status of an institution like ours, John. Glass sometimes loses sight of that proper mix. Unlike you."

"Change is the rule of life."

"Change is to be managed," said Woodruff. "You don't have a problem with that, do you, John? Because if you do, up here on Capitol Hill is the wrong place for you to be."

Back away: "I know where I belong."

With a smile, a pat on the back, the man in the Agency who John once trusted more than anyone left him standing alone.

9

Careful, thought John as Woodruff walked out of the building on the atrium floor below, *steady and careful.*

John walked down the curved staircase. The red-haired woman who passed him as she walked up was a graduate of OSU employed as a receptionist by a Florida Senator. Her perfume was musk. Out of the corner of her eye, she watched John disappear.

On the second floor, he followed the wide hall toward the glass doors of the Energy and Natural Resources Committee office; through those doors, a receptionist worked at her desk. Ten paces before the Energy Committee door, a narrow hall intersected the main corridor. John turned right, took 20 more paces, turned right again down an even narrower passageway.

A Capitol Hill policeman sat behind a desk; beyond him, a single glass door led to the sequestered offices of the Senate Select Committee on Intelligence.

John showed his ID tag to the policeman, opened his briefcase for cursory inspection and signed the logbook.

"How you doin'?" The young cop held a regular shift on this perpetually guarded door. "Sorry about your buddy. Nice guy."

"Yes," said John. "Thanks."

"Busy day for your people."

Amidst the log entries, three names John didn't believe were scrawled beside the notation "Agency." They logged in at 8:41, out at 10:32.

"Looks like it," said John.

The cop buzzed him into the most expensive Congressional office ever built.

The Senate Intelligence Committee suite is a labyrinth of windowless walls housing 39 Senate staff members. All phones have scramble and antibugging systems. No unescorted visitors are allowed. Plastic burn bags read "Classified Trash."

The labyrinth hums. Word processing keyboards click. In the background drone TV sets tuned to C-Span, the network that broadcasts Congressional hearings and floor action, and Cable News Network. The week before Frank died, the intelligence community bowed to Committee pressure, and wired the office TVs to receive the 12-hour-a-day, five-day-a-week telecasts of the Defense Intelligence Network, a top-secret news and analysis cable-TV network that first went on the air during the Gulf War, and was broadcast only to about 1,000 Pentagon officers and 19 other U.S. military sites. The CIA had requested Congressional funding for a competing classified access civilian intelligence TV network.

As soon as John rounded the partition screening the inside maze from the glass door, a secretary yelled: "John's here!"

Faces he'd come to know over the last 14 months hurried toward him. The assistant staff director touched John's arm. "We're all . . . What a tragedy!"

"It's the damn drugs," said a male staffer assigned to a Senator from Minnesota.

"If families stayed together—" began a woman assigned to a Montana Senator; she'd left Harvard's faculty for *real world* experience.

She was interrupted by a Kremlinologist who relabeled himself a "central European expert" after the Soviet Union dissolved: "They should just shoot all the animals!"

The assistant staff director held up his hand. "We . . . if there's anything any of us can do . . . "

"No, nothing, thanks."

"We passed the hat. Which do you think, a memorial or flowers at the funeral tomorrow?"

"Flowers are more . . . private."

The ranking staffer led John away from the group. "The Chairman is shocked, of course."

"Thank him for his concern."

"You still handling the office?"

"Mr. Zell is running things. I'll be here as needed."

The Senate staffer blinked. "Your people came by today."

"Really."

"Office of Security. They went into the fishbowl. To pick up Frank's personal things. Stuff like that."

"Oh yes."

"They had their own boxes."

John thanked him for his sympathy.

The origins of the idea to station CIA liaison staffers inside the Senate Intelligence Committee are lost in bureaucratic lore. Camps in both the CIA and Senate fought the plan; memos screaming about a fox in the chicken coop and giving slaves to Congress flew back and forth across the Potomac like mortar rounds.

Ultimately, even the CIA hard-liners realized the prize such a "sacrifice" gave them: since the Vietnam War, the CIA had lost budgetary, jurisdictional and political power to techno-spy agencies run by the Pentagon. The presence of two CIA executives in the Senate elevated the Agency's profile. the military branches already had general liaison offices stationed on the Hill.

After the *whats* were agreed upon, months were spent negotiating the *hows*. Security was the watchword—security for the Senate against the CIA.

The solutions were architectural. The Select Committee's suite had been carved out of the Hart Building at great cost because the need for active Congressional oversight of the intelligence community wasn't recognized when Hart was designed. At even greater cost—the budget for which was a two-month dispute settled when the CIA Director agreed to pay the renovation fee out of his $50-million contingency fund—a sealed CIA office was built within the sealed Senate office.

Everyone called it the fishbowl.

The fishbowl fit into a corner of the existing suite, so only two walls had to be built. One was concrete. The other was glass. Which meant the foxes inside could see out, and the watchdogs outside could see in. Which suited no one.

So they built the *fuzzes*.

The fuzzes were vertical blinds, floor-to-ceiling plastic slats mounted on an electric track. A flip of a switch turned them 90 degrees, either sealing the slats in place beyond the fishbowl's glass wall, or "opening" the blinds, allowing visibility both ways.

Since neither side would cede control over visibility, there were two sets of fuzzes, one inside the wall of the fishbowl, controlled by the CIA staffers, and one outside the wall, controlled by the Senate staffers.

The blue translucent slats obscured all images and filtered light into sky tones.

Frank and John had made it a point to leave the fuzzes open as much as possible and always open at the end of the day.

That morning, the fuzzes inside the fishbowl were closed.

John unlocked the fishbowl's door—crafting fuzzes to fit over a working door had been a $3,419.67 expense. He stepped inside. Behind him, the door clicked shut, locked.

Glowing overhead lights mellowed the room's blue tint.

John's desk was bare.

So was Frank's.

So were the walls, where calendars and pictures of the Committee members had hung on Monday.

Their desktop computers were gone.

The file cabinets were unlocked. And empty.

The copy machine's paper tray was empty.

In his desk, John found two paper clips and a broken rubber band.

Frank's desk drawers held only dust.

John flipped off the overhead lights, sat on his desk. The shadowed blue glow made him feel like he was underwater.

The phones were supposedly safe from taps by any enemy.

What about friends? John tapped in a phone number. The line sounded normal, connected in three rings. The secretary who answered told John that "he" had just walked in.

"We were raided this morning," John told his boss Miguel Zell. "Korn's security people—'Smith, Brown and Jones.' They—"

"John—"

"—they gutted the place. Files, computers, Frank's and my personal things. Pens. They even took the coffee can and—"

"You're misinterpreting."

John shut up.

"I'm sorry there wasn't time to tell you," said Zell. "I only learned the details myself this morning on the ride back to headquarters with Director Allen. And Korn.

"You weren't 'raided,'" said Zell's voice in the phone. "Frank's accident requires certain security precautions."

John said nothing.

"Understand, John, we must error on the side of caution."

"I try not to error at all. Are there any other 'cautions' I don't know about?"

"Nothing for you to worry about," said Zell. "In fact, since the hearing is over, why don't you take a little time off? Disappear for a while?"

A chill touched John.

Follow it: "I've got errands. Some things I have to do."

Zell said fine. They said good-bye.

Some things I have to do.

A buzzer sounded in the office.

When he opened the door, he found Emma North.

"Mind some company?" she said.

The door swung shut behind her.

As Emma walked past John, he caught a whiff of coconuts from her shampoo.

"What the hell?" she said, facing the bare walls, the naked desks. She turned to him. "Don't tell me you're leaving."

Her eyes were wide, blue. Smart.

"I don't plan on going anywhere," said John.

"Are you OK? I called last night . . . "

"Thanks."

"I wanted to be sure. Say how terrible . . . "

"How'd you know I was here?"

"When I saw you at the hearing, I wasn't sure where you'd go, but . . . I'd already bribed the cop at the desk to call me if you came in here today."

"Bribed?"

"Deal is, next time I need something brought here, I send it over with Chrissy. She's the lot of blonde in my office."

"Oh."

"Figures, huh?" Clipped laughter. "And I mean *figures*."

Emma was 32. Half a head shorter than John.

"Is this one of those things I shouldn't bother to ask about?" She gave her back to him and scanned the empty walls.

"There's no answer worth having."

"Un-huh."

She was trim. Her hips were round. Belled.

"You still haven't told me." She walked to Frank's desk. Dancer's steps. Trailed her hand over the bare wood, then lifted herself up to sit on it, face him. "Are you OK?"

"Everybody asks. I'm good as . . . What a stupid phrase: good as can be expected. I never expected anything like this."

"Hard rains fall." She shook her head. "But you'll be OK. You're not a folder."

"A folder?"

"Yeah. You won't buckle, fold. You got snapback."

"That's the spy myth."

"I don't buy myths anymore and I know folders. Ask my ex."

"Rather not. I doubt we'd have much in common."

"Tell me about it."

She crossed her ankles. Her legs were smooth. The hem of her skirt reached her knees. Her blue eyes glistened.

"I hate shit like this," she said. "Frank."

"There's no more to say."

"That's a hell of a thing to be true."

Silence.

Then she forced a smile: "Could you believe Bauman? Reading his staff's instructions out loud! Like he's senile!"

"Or something," said John.

"Funny how you guys will get the good press spin on the Corcoran stuff," she said. "Not the Task Force, not the CTC. Not Bauman."

"Just worked out that way." John let himself smile.

Saw her nod, know.

"For what all that's worth," she said. "Only two months gone, and the bombing's already page 4 news."

"Our curse is we live in interesting times."

"With short attention spans," she added. "Only good news is that I persuaded Obst's people to narrow the scope of their questions for the hearing on nonproliferation in central Asia."

"Thanks, that'll be more manageable for my people."

"That's what I thought, too," she said.

"Is your boss hunting for something with those arrows he shot at us?" asked John.

"He hasn't been hot on the CIA since the '60s." She smiled. "That's an attitude open to persuasion."

"We'll have to work extra hard."

They looked at the bare walls.

Silence built. He knew she felt it. He tried to think of what to say—always, he first thought about his words to her. He knew she thought before speaking to him, too. No reason—much of the time. Logically. They spoke the same language. Knew the same songs. Both were small-town escapees, non–Ivy league schools. Their worlds of life and work comfortably overlapped.

Now, thought John, be extra careful with the words.

"Were you . . . Was Frank working anything special for you or your boss?" John asked.

"Not for me. Why?"

"I'm trying to pick up the pieces."

"Anything I can do to help?"

Easy. Go easy with her.

"Are you friends with Senator Firestone's personal staff guy?" he said.

"Steve? His person who handles intel?"

"Yes."

"Not really. They're hotshots. Work with them, there'll be a headline, but your boss won't be in it and he will be pissed.

"Of course," she added, "these days nobody wants to share Firestone's headlines."

The week before, Senator Charles Firestone and a woman 34 years his junior who had a police record for prostitution received minor injuries when they were involved in a traffic accident.

"Steve's OK," said Emma. "But his boss only wants one thing, and it's not oversight or legislation. On Firestone's staff, if you keep the headlines coming, you keep coming to work.

"Why do you want to know about Steve?" she said.

"Nothing special. I just don't know him very well."

"Are you a man who lies to women?" asked Emma.

"I lie to everybody. That's my job."

"How admirable: consistency."

She smiled; her lips were thin. Ruby lipstick.

Dangerous.

Ask her and you rope her in close.

Let her walk away and you might not get another chance.

"There is something you can do for me." He swallowed.

"Just one thing?"

Try not to lie more than necessary.

He said: "A guy just threw a weird question at me."

"A member? A staffer?"

"Hey: I have to have *some* secrets!"

"Really?" she said. "What can I do about that?"

"He asked if I knew about an American in Paris named Cliff Johnson."

Emma stared into John's eyes: "Never heard of him."

"Me either. My guy isn't certain, but he thinks Johnson died this year."

"Been a rough year."

"Yeah, rough. My guess is this is macho staff bullshit. Make the Agency jump through hoops. I should have called his bluff on the spot. But I didn't, and if I ask him for more details now, I'll look like a fool and this office will look incompetent."

"You're no fool," she said.

"Let's keep it that way. Your desk computer is hooked up to the Library of Congress newspaper data search banks, right?"

"Aren't you?" She looked around the stripped office. "At least, weren't you?"

"This is just our chaos after . . . you know."

"Yeah. I know. Damn world." Emma sighed: "You want a public search on Biff Johnson?"

"*Cliff* Johnson—and no big deal. *The International Herald Tribune, New York Times,* Paris papers if you can do it."

Emma frowned. "This is a nothing little favor. Kind of thing a high school kid could do. Doesn't fit with . . . Why ask me?"

"I don't know a high school kid I can trust."

Her smile was slow, sharp. "And you trust me."

"If this is too much to ask . . . "

"Save it. I'll do it today."

"Thanks. I'll call you."

"Or come by." She smiled, as if she knew a secret. "My boss wants to send a condolence. Who should he address it to?"

"Thank Senator Handelman. I'll let you know."

"Please."

Sitting on the desk, she swung her feet. Her suit jacket hung open. A thin yellow chain looped around her neck, disappeared beneath her gold blouse.

Don't think about that. Why think about that now?

"You want to get some lunch?" she asked.

They'd had lunch in the cafeteria more than a few times. With other staffers, Frank. Shared communal pizza in the staff office behind the hearing room when the Committee was in session.

"What time is it?" he asked.

"Eleven thirty-five," she told him.

"I've got some things to do," he said.

"Oh," she said.

"All this." He waved his hand around the office. "And because of yesterday."

"Oh," she said. "OK."

When she slid off the desk, he heard her panty hose hiss.

Her eyes were blue and bright.

See you, she said.

10

The city impound shop smelled of gasoline, grease, tools and cold coffee. From behind the counter, the ebony-skinned man in overalls told John: "You sure you got enough paperwork?"

An air-pressure wrench whined in the garage bay.

"Not enough to take it," said John, "but I'm supposed to inventory it."

"Crime scene boys already checked it."

"They found nothing, right?"

"Yeah, said the car was clean as—" The foreman of the impound lot frowned. "You has to ask them 'bout that. Or the detective in charge."

In the garage bay, a hammer banged on car metal.

"The detective ain't in charge anymore." John shrugged. "If we want to bother somebody, gotta bother the Chief's office."

"Say what?"

"My office called downtown, and that's what they told me. And I ain't going to piss off a bunch of brass about bullshit."

"Who'd you say you was with?"

"The permission letter says it all." John nodded to a copy of the vague power of attorney document. "I work with that law firm. Guy's dead, I gotta inventory his estate for the court."

"He's dead, all right."

The foreman glanced at the letter on the counter.

John yawned, leaned on the scarred wood counter and craned his neck to peer at an open box of sugar donuts.

His motion drew the foreman's eyes: "You want one?"

"No thanks," said John. "I got a late lunch with a lady, and she's sweet enough."

The foreman let John cheerlead him into polite laughter.

"Just tell me where to sign, and I'll get out of your hair and into hers."

"You watch that stuff," said the foreman. "It ain't like when we were kids."

"Never is," said John.

The foreman grunted. Stared at the letter on the counter.

The door to the yard flew open and a tow truck driver popped inside: "Yo, Burt! Where you want me 'put that torch job?"

"What you talking about?" said the foreman.

"The one what's been sitting on North Capitol. I got it hooked up out here."

"Just a minute."

"I be a busy man," said the tow truck driver.

With his back to the tow truck driver, John arched a sympathetic eyebrow to the foreman.

Who shook his head in silent reply, told the tow truck driver: "Ain't we all?

"Here." The foreman passed a clipboard to John. "Find a line, sign."

Skim notes on the clipboard from the crime scene search team: nothing significant.

John scrawled a signature for Harold Brown.

"Can I keep this?" The foreman tapped the Xeroxed letter.

"You're supposed to," said John. "That covers us."

"Come on, Burt!" yelled the tow truck driver.

Burt tossed John a set of keys: "Far end of the lot, by the fence. Bring the keys back when you're done."

"No problem." John's pocket was heavy with his own set.

Outside, he walked past a charred car hoisted on the rear end of a tow truck. Burt would be busy with the tow truck driver for five minutes, maybe 10.

The city impound lot filled a ragged block across the Anacostia River in a neighborhood where dreams were paved with broken glass. John hurried through rows of cars, some abandoned, most towed for unpaid parking tickets.

Frank's Toyota sat in a corner by the chain-link fence. Yellow crime scene tape on nearby cars fluttered in the cool wind.

A black-hearted spiderweb filled the driver's window.

You can do it.

A hunk of scarred metal, brownish stains inside the windshield, on the dashboard and upholstery. *Doesn't matter—now.*

Truck horn's blare—*up front, by the distant gate.*

Nobody looking.

Heart pounding. Breathe deep.

Unlock the passenger's door . . .

How may miles did I ride sitting . . .

The car smelled of cold steel. Upholstery and rubber.

Only dirt under the floor mat. Inside the jockey box: registration, car insurance card, a credit card slip for gas, owner's manual, a pen and a broken pencil.

John's stained trench coat lay on the backseat. He left it there, looked on the floor, felt beneath the backseats. Got filth under his fingernails.

The search form on the clipboard had been perfunctorily completed. Everybody knew what had happened; no one believed there would be anything in that disgustingly soiled car worth finding.

He unlocked the trunk. A blanket, an old parka, a pair of rubber boots, a couple wrenches. Crowbar.

Laughter from an unseen child floated through the impound lot. Handclaps.

The driver's door was dusted with pink fingerprint powder.

No need to justify my prints. Don't shake the metal, shatter the cobwebbed glass.

Open the door Frank hadn't unlocked alive.

The driver's seat was remarkably clean.

John looked beneath the overturned floor mat, felt under the driver's seat where the search team had looked.

Nothing.

Squatting in the dirt outside the open car door, John remembered a Triad gangster he'd known in Hong Kong.

The steering column was smooth plastic. John ran his hand down it, under the dash, up under the dashboard where there were wires and fuses and . . .

Something . . . taped.

Metal, secure but . . .

With a quick jerk, John pulled the metal-something loose.

A .45 automatic, the pistol issued U.S. Armed Forces from the dawn of the 20th century until after Vietnam.

Cold steel in John's sweaty grip.

Black electrician's tape on the handle and barrel had kept it under the dash. Snug, but easy enough to rip free with a one-handed grab, even without leaving the driver's seat.

A strip of Scotch tape covered the muzzle's black-eyed bore. Scotch tape kept the dust out, blew off with the first shot.

John glanced over his shoulder. Saw no one watching him.

He peeled the black tape off the gun, pulled out the .45's ammunition clip: packed with six rounds. John worked the slide, and ejected a squat bullet from the firing chamber: the safety was on, but the gun had been ready to fire.

Neither Frank nor John had CIA authorization to carry weapons, nor had they been issued any.

The pistol barrel was smudged, as though it had been taped and retaped under the dash. Frank couldn't have carried the gun into work at the Senate, but everywhere else . . .

John made sure the safety lever was on, slapped the clip into the handle, chambered a round into the barrel, dropped the clip out and loaded the bullet he'd ejected into it, slapped the clip back in the gun. He safely half cocked the spur wing hammer.

Rock 'n' roll. Seven kisses.

For who? Frank never raved about guns. Never ranted about crime. Never took a step he didn't need.

The cold breeze whipped John's jacket. When he stood, he held the gun close to his side.

Spotted no eyes in the projects beyond the chain-link fence. Inside the lot, the unblinking headlights of impounded cars stared at him.

John stuck the .45 down the back of his belt, buttoned his suit coat.

Walked away from the gun-shot car.

11

The dashboard clock read 2:10 when John parked in front of Frank Mathews' two-story town house that was sandwiched amidst identical homes a mile farther into Maryland than John's cabin.

Drapes covered Frank's front windows.

The .45 weighed down John's briefcase.

At the house's front door, he fumbled with Frank's keys.

Wood creaked, clicked—to his right.

An eye stared at him through the slit of the chained front door of Frank's neighbor.

"Hi," said John.

Old Woman's Voice said: "Are you one of them?"

A tingle ran up John's spine.

"One of who?"

"Mr. Mathews' houseguests. They were here last night. This morning. They're gone now."

"I'm a friend of Frank's," said John.

She opened the door another half inch, showed her white hair, quilted robe.

"Who were they?" asked John.

"I don't know. Not my business. Didn't see anything."

"You saw them."

"Just when they came last night."

"This morning . . . ?"

"Only heard them. Took in the paper."

"When you got your newspaper."

"I don't read newspapers. What good does it do?"

They tell you your neighbor is dead. John said: "Have you seen Frank today?"

"Seen nobody. Heard them come home. Leave."

"Maybe they were some friends we've been expecting," said John. "Were there three of them? Was one tall? Or fat, was—"

"I don't remember."

She shut the door. John heard her dead bolt ram shut.

"I'll talk to you later," he said loudly.

The keys let him in Frank's home.

Frank's furniture was comfortable, worn, a modest dining room set, couches, chairs. The kitchen was open, yellow. John smelled old coffee, saw the plastic coffeemaker on the counter, a quarter inch of black sludge in its glass pot.

The living room/dining area was a giant box. Curtains hung across the front picture window and over the sliding glass door leading to a fenced-in backyard. One wall was floor-to-ceiling bookshelves, another held an electronic tech lover's dream: an FM receiver, tape deck, two VCRs and a color TV facing the couch. The electronic equipment was housed in open wooden cabinets with shelves of videocassette tapes. Remote control wands waited on the glass coffee table next to a small stack of magazines.

The air was still, flat.

Silent.

Who'd already been here? Korn's people—or . . . ?

A quick run-through. To be sure he was alone.

Up the stairs.

A guest bedroom decorated in soft pink tones, a painting of boats on the Seine. A closet with a mixed selection of women's clothes, old coats, out-of-fashion men's suits, dusty shoes.

Bathroom: men's toiletries, shower tub. Spotless toilet.

Master bedroom: Frank's bed. A book about the mystical shimmers of physics and a history of Japan on the nightstand.

Like he would have left it. Whoever had been here in the night, that morning, had been careful to preserve Frank's order.

Back downstairs. A desk stood beside the wall of books.

John put his briefcase with the .45 on the couch.

The checkbook in Frank's desk told John nothing. The drawers held innocent bills, notices from the Administration Directorate about pension rights, bank statements showing a modest savings. The desk calendar showed no appointments. No address book. Nothing was taped to the bottoms of the desk drawers.

Crowded bookshelves. Histories. Volumes on movies, a dozen novels. A red paperback of William Butler Yeats's poems. No time to flip through all the pages—had that been done?

The cabinets and drawers in the kitchen held utensils, pots and pans, silverware and dishes.

In the freezer, carelessly wrapped packets of frozen meat.

Rewrapped, he thought.

The ice maker clunked, slowly filled its tray.

Refilled.

The clock on the kitchen wall read 3:17.

He circled to the high-tech entertainment wall.

The drawer in the cabinet held cables, connectors, odds and ends of video and stereo equipment, pliers.

The floor-to-ceiling shelves of videocassettes reflected Frank's best-known passion: movies.

"Not this new crap," Frank once told John: "Classics."

Alan Ladd and Veronica Lake in *The Glass Key* and *The Blue Dahlia*. Bogart in *To Have and Have Not, The Big Sleep, The Maltese Falcon, Casablanca*. A boxed set of *The Best Years of Our Lives*. Six Hitchcock titles. *High Noon* and *The Magnificent Seven*. *Butch Cassidy and the Sundance Kid. The Manchurian Candidate*. A row of foreign films: *Jules et Jim, The 400 Blows, The Bicycle Thief, Rashomon, The Seven Samurai, A Man and a Woman*. The middle shelf surprised John with Vietnam-based stories: *Who'll Stop the Rain, The Deer Hunter, Apocalypse Now*. John's fingers lingered on *Chinatown*, where it stood next to the first two *Godfathers*, and, incongruously, *An American in Paris* and *Seven Brides for Seven*

Brothers. On the top shelf, John saw *Breakfast at Tiffany's, Nashville*. Beside them, he spotted *McCabe and Mrs. Miller*, wondered if the carton showed a picture of the movie's heartbreaking blonde actress. John reached up and pulled it down.

Through that gap, in the shadows behind the top row of videocassettes, he spotted a dark shape.

A kitchen chair put him eye-level with the shelf. He moved a half dozen classic movies out of the way.

A stack of videocassettes lay behind those with the title spines out to the world. John lifted them down—the rest of the space behind the outward row of cassettes was empty. Six boxes of hidden cassettes filled his hands.

The two titles he recognized were movies he'd never seen, *Behind the Green Door* and *Deep Throat*. He'd never seen the other films either: *Backstreet to Paradise*, whose box photo showed the naked back-to-shoulders of a kneeling, curly-haired brunette, her eyes closed, head arched and slick-lipped mouth open in ecstasy. The thick-lipped, sultry blonde on the box of *Exxiles* pouted at the camera; she sat in a reversed wooden chair, wore nothing but a black garter belt, fishnet stockings and strapped high heels; her breasts were heavy. The logo beneath the title read: "Wilder than your darkest fire's dreams!" *Love Never Rusts* showed a redheaded woman wearing a wispy crimson gown leering out from a dry-ice fog. *Health Spa's* box had an active group shot in a hot tub.

John trembled as he stared at the cassettes in his hands. He stood on a kitchen chair in a dead man's living room. The mushrooming heat of embarrassment engulfed him; embarrassment, astonishment, and shame—a sliver of shame for the surge of curiosity these cassettes stirred, but mostly shame for the weight of this secret he'd stolen from a dead 57-year-old widower. A man who'd been his friend, a man whom John thought he'd known. Secrets are power, perspective.

Never imagined, never wanted to know this.

Quickly, look around: no one watching this sin.

Had *they* found this secret, too?

Had there been anything else back there for *them* to find?

John put the X-rated cassettes back where he'd found them, replaced the row of classic movies.

The hall coat closet held nothing of interest.

Upstairs.

He spent 20 minutes in the guest bedroom, rummaged through mothballed drawers of women's clothes, looked under the mattresses on the bed.

In the master bedroom, framed photographs of a middle-aged woman hung on a wall. Two other photographs showed Frank and the woman side by side, smiling for the camera.

A picture standing on the bureau showed a 20-something Frank and that woman posing for their white wedding portrait.

His wife had a handsome face. Bold. Intelligent.

John stared at the pictures, tried to reconcile that face with the pouted leers hidden behind the classic movies.

Didn't hear a key slide into the lock on the front door.

Upstairs, John didn't hear the front door swing open.

Gently close.

He shook himself, moved to the night table and bureau drawers. The sounds of his rummaging rolled over light footsteps on the downstairs carpet.

His mind flashed on his briefcase on the couch in the living room, his briefcase zipped shut around a loaded .45.

The louvre doors of the master bedroom's closet were stuck shut. John had to shake them, rattle them loudly, then snap them open with a loud *whirr*.

Frank's stairs were carpeted.

The pair of black shoes walking up them made no sound.

John pushed a space between the suits on hangers and the shirts still in their dry-cleaning plastic sheaths; hanger hooks screeched on the closet pole. Ran his hands over the suits, squeezed pockets. His back was to the door, he didn't see the shadow ride afternoon sunlight from the hall into the bedroom.

He bent to the closet floor, reached for—

A woman yelled: "Who the hell are you?"

12

Plastic bagged shirts grabbed John. His back slammed into the wall. *Balance, get balance,* hands flying up, *gun . . .*

Frank's .45 . . . *was downstairs.*

"What are you doing here?" yelled the woman.

Ebony eyes bloodshot and burning. Midnight hair cut blunt along a long, clean jaw. Skin like café au lait. Her lips were unpainted, wide. She wore a black blazer, denim shirt, jeans.

Empty, her hands were empty. She held her ground by the door, black shoes light and quick on the carpet.

"Who are you?" he yelled.

"Get out of here before I call the police!"

A silly, dangerous bluff.

She knows that, too.

"Frank and I worked together," said John. "Who are you?"

"He's my father."

Believe her.

Once spies walk in the shadows, shadows stay on their lives. Frank and John shared an office, carpooled. Loved movies, books. Respected their lives' protocols. Frank had told John about his wife, how she'd been with the Agency. She was long dead, safe to mention. Once Frank spoke of a child, then retreated from that gem—out of professional caution or from personal pain, John hadn't asked: to push would be arrogant, ignorant. They were friends, colleagues, but first they were spies. In the heartbeat after the woman made her claim, he remembered Frank's nugget of truth. In the next heartbeat, John believed her.

"I'm sorry," he said.

Blinked.

Said: "Do you . . ."

Her face showed the furrows of tears; she knew.

"What are you doing here?" she said.

Give her the best lie: "I came to get him clothes."

"When the lawyer called me, he said . . . that wasn't necessary. Dad's letter of instruction . . . Already taken care of."

"Nobody tells me anything," said John.

She has to trust me.

"Here." He handed her his Senate ID and the power of attorney letter he'd gotten from Glass.

"That's the lawyer who called me." She read the Senate ID. "John Lang."

"Yes."

Her voice cracked. "Are you the one who was with him?"

"Yes." *What else do you know?*

She left the room.

He found her in the hall, staring into the empty pink bedroom. She whispered: "Did he feel any pain?"

"None. Not even a thought."

Her face showed nothing of Frank's image; his strength was in her stance. The soft lines of her features could be linked to the solid-faced woman on Frank's wall only by a stranger or a genetic miracle; this daughter's black almond eyes cradled her mother's studied intelligence.

"My name is Phuong. Phuong Mathews."

In John's grip, her hand was like a sparrow.

"You're with the CIA, right?"

"Yes."

"Like Dad." She snapped on lights as she started down the stairs. "How did you get keys?"

Following her: "With the letter."

"They should have told you everything," she said as they reached the living room. "They never do, though, do they?"

"Not often."

His briefcase waited on the couch, heavy with the pistol.

A black leather carry-on bag sat by the front door, its strap looped down to the bare wood floor like a tired mamba.

"I don't believe I'm here," said Phuong.

A black trench coat with a winged collar lay on the couch. On the coffee table were airline tickets.

"Where did you fly in from?"

"Chicago."

She frowned at the walls, the desk, the video . . .

The shelves of videocassettes: *Don't look. Don't tip her to your treachery. Don't guide her to the dark corners of her father's soul.*

"Something's wrong," she said.

She circled through the living room.

"What?"

"The pictures," she said. "Where are the pictures?"

She ran upstairs.

Her feet clumped in the master bedroom, the pink bedroom, the bathroom. Upstairs closet doors opened, slammed.

On the walls of the dining area, then by the bookshelves and entertainment complex, John found clean rectangles, sharper colors delineated in sun-faded paint. The living room's only painting was a museum reproduction, Edward Hopper's 1939 *New York Movie:* a darkened auditorium. A pensive hay-haired usherette wearing a blue pantsuit leaned against a gold-curtained wall while the shadowed audience watched a blur of black-and-white fiction.

Phuong ran down the stairs. "Where are the pictures?"

"What pictures?" he asked.

"Of me." She waved her arms at the empty walls. "Not there, not in Dad's room, not in my bedroom. Why aren't they here?

"Did you take them?" she asked, stepping back.

"No."

Believe me. She believes me.

Magazines on the coffee table caught her eye. She rummaged through the pile, pulled out a cheaply covered journal.

"This is the only thing with me in it."

Shadows dimmed the room. The light beyond the kitchen's glass door faded to pink, then gray.

Gently, he took the journal from her grasp, said: "I've got an idea."

13

John and Phuong sat in a booth at a Tex-Mex restaurant. Cone lights hung from the ceiling; ferns stretched to the wood beams. Five-thirty was early for the dinner crowd, but the happy-hour herd had arrived, shirt-and-tie computer jockeys and mascaraed realtors. A billowy blonde perched on her usual stool at the bar; she looked a decade younger than she was until the smoke from her cigarette cleared or the hollowness of her laughter echoed above the jukebox. The restaurant smelled of *frijoles* and *fajitas*, cuisine created by Mexican peasants and sold here for prices beyond their dreams.

Phuong drank Scotch, John sipped bourbon. Their picked-at plates of forgotten food had been whisked away.

"This has all changed since I was a kid," said Phuong.

"You grew up around here?" said John.

"I was always grown up. Last years of high school, when Mom got sick, Dad transferred back here—for both of us."

"You were an L.B."

"The official description," she said, "was 'father attached to the embassy staff.' Not 'Langley Brat.' Or 'spook baby.' "

"Did they call you that?"

"I got called a lot of things. Slope. Dink. Orphan."

"Here?"

"Not so much here as London—they weren't more prejudiced there, but in grade school, bullies go for the jugular."

"Was anyplace great?"

"Most places were fine. Rome, Africa. Few times, it was just Mom and me, no dependents where daddies had to go. Paris—"

"I love Paris."

"Me, too. Great to be there as a teenager." She smiled. "Way I acted, out of control, Dad . . ."

She took a deep breath.

"I spent my sophomore year in a Swiss boarding school. Sobering experience, the Swiss. Neutrality equals rigidity, and every family has an Army-assigned machine gun under Dad's bed."

"How old were you when they adopted you?"

"Four—at least, we think so. In Saigon, the center was breaking apart even in 1967. The nuns had faith, not files.

"Dad said that when he and Mom came to the orphanage, I was the kid who held his hand the tightest.

"I pissed him off, I didn't mean to piss him off, he was just . . . Look, I had this thing about him—and Mom, too, though she quit the Agency when they got me, I mean . . . The CIA: hell, they helped run the war that killed my . . . my *real* parents!"

"Everybody was part of—"

"I know that," she said. "But what you know in your head and what you feel in your heart and what whispers to you at night from your closet . . . it all gets jumbled up. Especially when you're young. You can do things. Say things."

She blew her nose on the napkin.

John sipped his drink, gave her a break from his gaze.

"Did he ever talk about me?" she asked.

"He was careful not to," said John. Watching her.

"The spy's highest compliment: guard you like the ultimate secret. Even stateside, he was still an Ops dog.

"What are you?" she asked.

"Congressional liaison," said John.

"Don't feed a cover story to an L.B."

I need her, he thought. *I need her trust.*

"I was Ops," said John.

"Political consul? Military attaché? Chauffeur?"

Give what you want to get back, his mother always said. Training officers urged the proffer of believable lies.

Truth. For her, necessary truth.

"I was a NOC," he told her. "Nonofficial cover. Not attached to the embassy. Station Chiefs knew I was there, but we stayed out of each other's way."

"Where?"

"Did your dad tell you where and what he did?"

"Never directly. And now it's too late."

"Please," she said. "I can't stand polite chatter, I won't take lies, and tonight . . . I have to live with enough of my own realities tonight. Give me some of yours to ease the time."

"My second year of grad school," said John, "Chinese studies, I got an American Political Science Fellowship. They bring you to Washington, three months on a Senator's staff, three months on the House side. I love the process of power, wanted frontline work. Plus I was bored with school, wanted to—"

"Save the world?"

"Something like that."

"That hasn't been chic for decades," she said.

"Now you tell me."

For the first time, he saw her smile.

"They didn't train you at the Farm," she said.

"No," he said. "What do you do in Chicago?"

"Nothing important," she said.

"I doubt that."

She stared at him. Drained her Scotch. John signaled the waiter for another round and she didn't say no.

"In Chicago," she said. "I'm an editor for *Legal Times,* the newspaper that covers lawyers. In San Francisco, I taught school for a year, fought TV for the hearts and minds of the next generation. Lost. In Cincinnati, I worked as a paralegal. In New York, a reader for a publishing house."

"That's a lot of moves in not so many years."

"When I'm ready, I go. Where did they train you?"

"Why should I tell you all that?"

"Because I'm here."

The waiter brought their drinks.

"Don't use being drunk for an excuse," she said, sipping her Scotch. "Trust me about that.

"Did he really . . . Was it really an accident?"

Look her straight in the eyes: "As far as I know, yes."

"Could you have saved him?"

That question: brutal and justified.

"Tried to think of a way a thousand times," said John. "Can't."

She looked away. Said: "I talked to him on Sunday."

"What did he say?"

She whispered: "That he loved me."

She pressed her fist to her forehead, closed her eyes. No tears hit the white tablecloth or diluted her drink.

"That he loved me," she said a minute later, looking straight at John, her voice even, calm.

"How was he?"

"What do you mean?" she asked.

"Was he OK? Happy?"

"You saw him every day," she said. "Don't you know?"

"I knew his work face,'" said John. "He seemed tired."

"He said he was working all the time. Nights. Weekends."

"On what?"

"Are you asking if he broke security? Told me company secrets on an open line? Are you—"

"No."

"—fishing for something, because, hell, there's nothing you'll get. Sure as hell not from me, one thing my dad always was and always will be and always made sure every damn Mathews no matter what the blood was is loyal and . . ."

Her raised voice had attracted stares. She saw them, broke off. Looked at the white tablecloth.

"Sorry," she said. "I'm . . ."

"Doing as best you can."

"Hope so," she whispered. "That was all he ever asked."

They sipped their drinks.

"He called me from a pay phone," she said. "Why?"

"Could be a lot of reasons."

"What happened to the pictures?" she said. "The house looks like it's prepped to stand a shake."

"Where did you learn to talk like that?"

"Parents can't hide all their secrets," she said.

"Why did he take my pictures down? D.C.'s not a foreign posting where Bad Joes can shimmy in to find out where you're vulnerable. Hell, the Bad Joes died with the Berlin Wall!"

"There are always Bad Joes," said John.

"Who were they for my father?"

"I don't know," said John. "Did he ever say?"

"He said he'd see me at Christmas." She shook her head, gave John a second smile: "I guess Dad finally lied to me."

"No he didn't."

"Are you lying to me?"

"I never want to."

"Spoken like a true spy. Hedged better than a shopping mall lawyer. Where did they train you?"

There it is, thought John: the line.

Hell, maybe I'm already over it.

"They had a great idea," he said. "They let the Army try to weed me out. Or make me good.

"The Agency 'guided' my choices. As a reservist, I went Airborne, got in a Special Forces reserve unit, Green Berets. Special ops, unconventional-warfare training. Army intelligence schools in Arizona, Kentucky. A few weeks' Agency orientation at a safe house in . . . New England. I loved the snow there, the birches."

"What's this?" he said, putting the magazinelike journal he'd brought from Frank's house on the table.

"Oh," she said, "that."

The cover read *The New Chicago River Review.*

"It's nothing," she said.

"Don't stroke a trained liar."

"And a trained killer?" She didn't smile.

Neither did John.

He flipped through the pages of black-and-white photographs, drawings, lines of prose and—

"Page 47," she said.

One of seven clustered submissions:

SPRING

Leaf falls to a creek.
Water bears it, swirls over rocks.
A crane turns, walks upstream.

Phuong

"I like it," he said.

"Adequate," she said.

"Why not 'Phuong Mathews'?"

"It's an old poem," she said. "Those days I was still . . . working some things out. Plus, wouldn't you accept a haiku from a
Japanese-sounding name before you'd take one from a hybrid?"

"Who's Vietnamese."

"Who's American. Who looks like all . . ."

"You look like you to me."

She rolled her eyes. "Dad got a kick out of my deception's success."

"If you take out the crane, rewrite the last line using 'I,' you
get the correct syllable count."

"Modern times," she said. "We can break rules."

"But if you change the form—"

"Back then, I liked a crane in my poem better than me. That
mattered more than form."

"Then?"

She shrugged. "Without 'Mathews' next to my name, Dad
could risk this turning up in a shake."

"Don't think like that," said John. "That's my job."

"Where did you do your job? Your real job, not playing
around in the Halls of Congress."

"Did your father ever tell you about me?"

"My dad would never have told me much about you."

"Why?"

"He never wanted me to know men like him."

"Of course he did," said John.

"Is that spoken like a man? Or a spy?"

Say: "Can I read your other poems?"

"No," she said. "Did you work with my dad in the field?"

"Never. I worked solo. Deep cover."

Tell her: the mission objectives won't stay secret much longer anyway, and besides, that war is over.

"Cold War days. My first posting was Pakistan. The Agency was building a road for China, through Pakistan, to Afghanistan. We had a secret deal with the Communist Chinese to help them sell arms to the rebels who were fighting the Soviet communists' puppet government in Afghanistan.

"I was a deep-cover watchdog on everybody and everything. Played the knapsack bum. Smoked grass. Famously. That made me seem like a random lost soul, a Yankee fool, not a spy."

"Did you inhale?"

"Never."

She laughed—strangled it.

"I shouldn't be laughing. Not now."

"Especially now," he said.

"I try to believe that theory, too." She shook her head. "The Agency must have loved you smoking dope."

"The Agency took the same stance police use with their undercover narco guys. Don't confront us with it, we won't see it, we don't sanction it—but keep the intelligence coming. Don't screw up and don't get caught. They're careful during my security polygraphs to focus the questions on current usage."

"So much for glory days."

"Mostly, it was a waste of time."

"Smoking dope?"

"Trolling for product. The dope . . ." He shrugged. "Some laughs, but I have a hard enough time with unfogged reality.

Plus it's bad for the lungs, *ch'i*. The hardest part was not getting roped into anybody's smuggling scam."

"Then what, Mr. Clean?"

"Playing grad student in Hong Kong, taking classes at the university. Calligraphy, Chinese literature, *Pa-kua* and *Hsing-i*."

He explained what they were, resisted the urge to grab her politeness and dive into their depths, their *I Ching* roots.

"Then Bangkok, worked for a real scrap-metal company. Business is the guts of that city. Kept a long eye on Cambodia."

"Vietnam?" she asked.

"Not my primary target.

"Then back to Hong Kong. Import-export job, pretending to be a martial arts bum. Lot of them there. Logical cover."

He drained his bourbon.

"Left Hong King in 1989. Took a sabbatical."

"Why?"

"No," he told her.

She waited. Calmly. Perfectly.

"No," he said. "After that . . . Desert Shield, Desert Storm. With my Green Beret training, I was an Agency liaison for special ops units in Saudi: rock 'n' roll against Iraq. Then I went to work with your father.

"I liked him," said John. "He taught me a lot. Was good to me. A good man."

She looked away.

John said: "He's not dead for me either."

"Look," she said, "thank you for this. I wasn't hungry, but . . . And thanks for helping out with the funeral. Or whatever."

"That's what I should do."

"Duty, huh?"

"This isn't a job."

"What time is it?" she asked.

The new watch John bought on the way to her father's house had both analog hands and digital displays: "Six-seventeen."

"Quarter after five in Chicago," she said. "I'd be at the job, wondering if the L-train would be crowded, what I'd eat for dinner, if I was too tired to write."

"Where are you staying?" he asked.

"At home. Where else?"

"Alone?"

"Of course." She frowned. "The missing pictures . . . Is there some reason . . . Do you think I'm not safe?"

"No." That had to be true. *They*'d already searched the place. No reason to come back. "I just worry about you."

"Don't. Even Dad learned that wasn't necessary."

"Do you have any friends in the area?"

"Do you count?"

"Sure."

She stared at him.

"Then there's one," she said.

"Family friends? People your dad worked with? Trusted?"

"Given my adolescent bullshit, Mom's cancer and Dad's career of secrets, we weren't a social bunch. Whenever people from his work came over, I left. I kept wanting to ask them if they put any of my relatives in the Phoenix program."

The Phoenix program was a CIA-spawned antiguerrilla project that resulted in the execution of 40,994 Vietnamese "enemy civilians" during America's longest war.

"I remember one guy," she said. "Something like Woodman or Woodward or—"

"Woodruff?"

"Maybe. Dad said he'd have had the rank instead of Wood-what's-his-name if Dad had gone straight into the Agency instead of spending extra years as a Marine pilot. I met him and his wife one night when they came over to distract Mom and Dad, play bridge. Mom propped up on the pillows in her bed . . .

"She always wore lilac toilet water, even at the end, so I wouldn't remember her smelling like . . ."

A waiter started toward their booth, saw Phuong's face, walked away.

"She was the best damn woman this world will ever see,"

snapped Phuong. "She gave up her career to raise me, love me, make me feel just like I came out of her womb.

"The best part of me came out of her heart," whispered Phuong. "And Dad's.

"Can we get out of here?" she said.

In the parking lot, John said: "Why don't you stay with the Woodruffs or a neighbor or—"

"Anybody who knew me then doesn't have the best of impressions," she said. "Probably wouldn't even recognize me. Hell, we all look alike, remember?"

"Give the world a little credit."

She blinked. "Sorry. Coming home, old angers are easy to find."

The drive to Frank's house took ten silent minutes.

"Look," he said as they stood on her doorstep. "There may be formalities. People from the Agency who stumble over the bureaucracy, want to talk to you. Police. Whoever. Let me handle them. Call me if they show up or phone you—and don't talk to them or do anything until I'm there to help."

She shrugged: "OK."

"And, ah, if any reporters call . . ."

"I'm a journalist," she said. "Sort of. Remember?"

"No, you're a poet."

"And an L.B.," she said. "Let me tell you a secret."

He held his breath.

"I don't like reporters."

He smiled. She didn't.

"I loved him," she whispered. "All the time, even when I said I didn't."

"He was a smart man. He knew."

She shook her head: "This is so unreal! Here we are. Me. You. Ordinary Wednesday night, feels like maybe . . .

"But now everything's tossed up in the air. Different. Electric and . . . empty. Detached but in your face."

"No balance."

"Yeah." *Yeah.*

"I must look like hell." She dropped her gaze, ran her fingers through her hair.

"No."

A smile she couldn't stop, a flush when she felt its tug.

"You shouldn't drink so much."

"I feel fine."

"John Lang. Huh."

He couldn't give her any paper with his address and phone number on it that might turn up as pocket litter.

"If you need me," he said, "my phone number and address are in the book. It's a short drive from my place to yours."

"The keys," she said.

"What?"

"You have a set of keys to our house. Can I have them?"

John shivered in his suit and sweater. She wore her black coat belted and buttoned, her collar turned up. Streetlights shone in her black eyes.

"Sure," he said, handed her a ringed set of keys.

They said good night. She went inside, locked the door.

Keys he'd duplicated for this house weighed down the shirt pocket above his heart.

14

Funerals are vibrations between yesterday and tomorrow, a breathing space to help the living find their balance amidst the tremors of existence.

Mourners gathered under gray clouds at a D.C. suburban cemetery that cold March Thursday at 10 A.M. Frank was buried beside his wife in one of the few unfilled plots.

We're running out of room for our dead, thought John.

Many of these faces he'd seen at Langley. Some of the mourners were in their 60s; coffins were stacked in their eyes.

The Agency's aristocracy came, including the Director and his bodyguards with radio tubes in their ears. Beside the Director stood Roger Allen and his pretty wife. Other Princes of the Directorates clustered around that royal core. The Centers' Barons jockeyed as close to the crown as possible. Harlan Glass held the arm of a gaunt woman.

His wife? A protruding chin. Nowhere eyes.

Absent was Richard Woodruff. John spotted Kate Woodruff in the crowd, handsome in her maturity.

Head of Security George Korn paced outside the rings of mourners, monitoring guards he commanded.

Twenty paces beyond the crowd waited D.C. Homicide Detective Tyler Greene and his husky white partner.

A dozen staffers from the Senate Intelligence Committee attended. Emma North wore a navy wool coat, a 1920s half-moon black hat and veil. She and John exchanged solemn nods.

Phuong Mathews stood beside the grave, her close-cropped head bare, her black trench coat belted.

The eulogy fell to Miguel Zell, head of Congressional Liaison. Zell read the home-is-the-hunter verse from Robert Louis Stevenson, lied and said he was sure it had always been one of Frank's favorites.

Glass caught John's eye. John's stone-faced shrug was as subtle as Glass's answering nod.

Amen, said Zell, though he'd recited no prayer.

Hands patted John on the back. Voices muttered concern, condolences. The departing crowd swept him toward the parked cars. He edged his way through the stream, turned toward the grave—

White light flashed!

Blind, he was—

Images shimmer back. Sky, trees. A man.

Two men stood in front of him. Detective Tyler Greene and his partner. The white cop held a camera.

"Gotcha," said the white cop.

"What?" said John.

Greene said: "We need it for a photo spread."

"What are you talking about?"

"White male, 30-something, nicely dressed, smart. Uses the name Harold Brown. Walks into our impound lot, monkeys with evidence. Could be obstruction of justice."

"Should be a great picture," said the white cop.

From off to the side, a voice hissed: "Give me the film!"

CIA Security head Korn, his pale eyes narrow and blazing. Two of his men hurried to join him.

"Like hell," said Greene.

"Are you disobeying your Chief?" snapped Korn.

"You aren't my Chief."

"One phone call—"

"Go waste your quarter," said Greene.

The D.C. policemen walked away.

With a nod, Korn sent his two aides in their wake.

"Why are they after you?" Korn asked John.

"Why did you raid my office?" said John. "Where's our files? Our stuff?"

"Your stuff? Did you and Frank have material in an Agency office not pertaining to sanctioned official business?"

"What do you want?"

"Everything you've got to tell me," said Korn. "About your office. What you're doing there."

"My job is to—"

"Maintain cover?"

John blinked.

"You Ops men," said Korn. "Never stop. What were you two running out of there?"

"Us two?"

"Or is it just you?"

"It's just me here talking to you," said John, "and I don't know what you're talking about."

"Games out of your Hill office. When somebody moves a leaf in this town, all the trees rustle. Do you think I'm deaf?"

"Tell me what I'm supposed to hear," said John.

"Either you know and you're a liar, or you're a fool."

"You're groping after phantoms," said John.

"Maybe," said Korn. "But I hear the trees."

As he walked away, Korn told John to have a nice day.

Sunlight bounced off the windshields of departing cars. Toward the end of the row of parked vehicles, John saw a car door open, watched Emma climb in: her black veil, her coat, her trim ankle. The car door slammed.

A sparrow flew toward the nearby shopping mall strip.

John saw Phuong, alone, staring into the hole where her father had disappeared.

He saw the grave.

r

15

The Capitol cop stationed outside the Committee door saw John coming toward his desk, said: "I got stuff for you.

"How was it?" he added.

"Like a funeral," said John.

"Dumb question, huh?" The cop slid open his desk drawer. Inside it, John saw two envelopes. "I hate funerals."

"Yes." John logged in, stared at the envelopes.

"Life," said the cop: "It's a hell of a deal."

"No question." John opened his briefcase for the cop: Frank's gun was locked in the glove compartment of John's car.

"With all we know," said the cop, "you think we'd have figured out women.

"I mean," he said, his fingers tapping the envelopes: "What do they want? If you don't push to meet 'em, they float past you into forever gone. And if you do figure a way to make contact, they shut you down, shoot you right between the eyes."

John glanced at his new watch: 11:32.

"I'm running late," he said.

"It's ghost city in there," said the cop, nodding to the Committee door. "Most of the others still aren't back."

"Then I better get to work. Those are for me?"

The cop gave him the two envelopes.

"The top one Em North sent over with . . . She sent it over. A page brought the other one."

Both envelopes were plain. The envelope from Emma bore

John's name. The other envelope was addressed to "CIA Liaison Officer." The cop buzzed open the door for John.

Who hesitated, looked back at him: "Good luck."

"Is that what it takes?"

The Committee office was silent as John rounded the partition. A receptionist sat at the nearest desk.

"You had a call." She gave him a pink slip marked *CI/LIAS, 9:17, n/message.* "He didn't leave his name."

"Did he ask for me?"

"He asked for whoever was handling Frank's stuff . . . now."

"Did you give him my name?"

"Of course not!"

"Probably one of the guys from our Office of Security. It was a guy, wasn't it?"

"Yes."

"Had he ever called Frank?"

"I don't know. He didn't—"

"Leave his name." John sighed. A carefully sad sigh.

"Is there anything . . ." She trailed off. At first, the staff had mistrusted the two CIA officers in their midst, but she'd discovered Frank and John were human. They asked about her kids.

"To be sure we're not missing anything, can you check the log to see if Frank got any calls from this guy—the guy who didn't leave his name? Just in the last couple weeks."

"I . . . Is this something we should run past Joel?"

Joel was the staff director.

"We can bother Joel if you want, but . . ."

She frowned. The fishbowl had its own phone lines, but often their calls came through the Committee switchboard. The Committee was obsessive about documentation. All phone messages generated a carbon in her spiral message notebook.

The receptionist chewed her lip. Opened her book.

John casually moved so he could read over her shoulder.

Messages flipped past his eyes. Names he knew, offices he recognized: Senators' staff, Agency people.

Eight days earlier, a message for Frank with the "Returned

Your Call" box checked. A message with no identification or return phone number, a message from Martin Sinclair.

Who's Martin Sinclair?

Two more pages of carbons, then she said: "I think—"

"Nope," said John. "No calls. It's probably nothing, but if I
miss the guy again, please give him my home number."

"You're kidding!"

"If he and Frank were working on something for the Committee, I don't want it to fall in the cracks."

"Oh." She told herself not to worry: after all, everyone was on
the same side.

John entered the fishbowl. The fuzzes were switched shut on
his side. He left them closed.

The note in Emma's envelope read: "Need anything else, let
me know Talk to you soon. Take care. Em."

He read her words twice. Smelled the paper: *only ink.*

The one photocopied article she sent came from a January *International Herald Tribune,* Paris edition:

> An American authorities identified as Clifford
> Johnson, President of Imex, Inc., a U.S. company, was
> killed yesterday in an automobile accident near the
> Left Bank.
>
> Police say that Johnson's car was rear-ended by a
> hit-and-run driver. After impact, Johnson's car ex-
> ploded and burned.
>
> Johnson was alone in the car, and there were no
> other reported injuries. The driver of the second unlo-
> cated vehicle is still unknown.
>
> Authorities declined to identify Johnson's model of
> car, but said that a report of the accident would be
> filed with the French automobile safety affairs office to
> ascertain whether other incidents indicated a safety
> flaw in the vehicle.
>
> A statement from the American Embassy said that

Johnson's remains would be flown back to his home in the Baltimore, Maryland, area.

Few weeks later, thought John, someone sends an anonymous letter to a Senator, smearing everybody's favorite boogeyman, the CIA. Frank figures it's a nut case, but the CIA seal makes him buck over to a half dozen Agency shops, to Glass . . .

The second envelope contained a handwritten note on the stationery of United States Senator Ralph Bauman. No internal address, no greeting or salutation:

Get over here right away.

John assumed the scrawled signature was Bauman's. John's watch read two minutes to noon. The Senate would gavel in at 12. Routine morning business would occupy the first hour of floor time.

The overhead lights in the fishbowl burned John's eyes. Often, he and Frank turned off those glaring lights, made their phone calls in the glow filtering through the fuzzes.

John snapped off the lights.

The fishbowl filled with a cool blue fog.

16

"What the hell you been doin'?" snapped Senator Bauman when his secretary ushered John into the Senator's private office.

"Sir?" said John.

Framed photos of Senator Bauman with the famous, the powerful and the popular covered the walls. A portrait of his third wife in her best days presided above the fireplace. Pictures of children, grandchildren and great-grandchildren lined the mantel. Behind Bauman's desk stood flags from his state and the Stars and Stripes of America.

"Where is it?" Bauman bounced out of his chair, circled around his huge desk. Up close, the wispy red-haired, liver-spotted Senator smelled of leather, aftershave lotion and breath mints.

"Where's—"

"Where's my damn list of terrorists? Been since yesterday, 'n' I promised the TV I'd have it and hell, even if I don't get to P-R it out, least I better be able to wave the real McCoy! I ain't going to make Joe McCarthy's phony list mistakes, not this Senator!"

"The, ah, we're clearing it with—"

" 'Salready cleared" Bauman sipped from a blue Senate coffee mug, winced. Popped a breath mint. "You'd be smart to stay on my good side, son."

Would have said "boy," thought John, *but you won't make that mistake anymore either.*

"I aim to be smart, Senator." John let his rural roots carry his words to the short man leaning on the big desk.

"You best," said Bauman, but he nodded. "You have any trouble gettin' what I want got, you call me and you'll see fur fly, yes you will."

"No question, Senator."

"You fetch what I want spit-quick, you bring it to me, we'll all be fine and dandy. We understand each other?"

"Absolutely."

Seven lightbulbs ringed the clock mounted on the wall. One light glowed. A loud bell rang, its message resounding through every Senate office building.

The Senator leaned against the edge of his desk, sipped from his coffee mug.

"Sumpin' else." He unwrapped a breathmint, picked a letter off his desk: "What's this shit?"

The letter he gave John bore the Customs Service logo, the address of its Office of Congressional Liaison:

Dear Senator Bauman:

This is to confirm our response to your oral inquiry made to the Central Intelligence Agency's Legislative liaison, who verbally requested on your behalf any Customs inspection records within the last six months pertaining to a private American company, Imex, Inc. While we have determined that such a query does not violate the Privacy Act, and while we have expended substantial man-hours and agency effort generating the response to the request, please advise us directly as to whether our response should be sent directly to your office or routed as requested through the CIA Congressional liaison assigned to the Senate Intelligence Committee staff.

Don't look up! Pretend you're still reading, that you're slow . . . Don't let Bauman see . . .

No Congressional liaison from one agency would ever "ver-

bally request" any other agency to do something for a Senator.
And in the CIA, only Frank and—

Deception. Smoke screen. Frank covering his own request with a Sena-tor's name, a Senator whose chaotic style could be used to mask someone else's maneuver.

Frank: risking his career, the fragile bond of trust between the
Senate and the CIA.

For something worth a bullet.

Senator Bauman's whine faded back into John's consciousness:
". . . so my administrative assistant—the one I used to have
yeste'day 'fore he messed up—so he walks this in to me few days
ago, asks if I'm doing my own legwork. Neither of us knows
what the hell this is about, but it reads like a Cover-Your-Ass
letter from Customs."

"Yes," said John, "it reads like that."

"The only ass that gets covered by this office is mine."

"Must be . . . a mistake. My coworker—"

"The one who had the car accident?"

"He probably handled this for some other Senator, and Cus-toms screwed it up."

"Figures," said Bauman.

A classic scenario breeds a plausible lie.

"Senator, we'd appreciate it if you let me handle this."

"If there's CYA happening, you best be sure . . ."

"No problems for you, sir." *Take a deep breath.* "But would you
have your A.A. call this man at Customs today, tell him to—"

"Right now, I'm between A.A.'s."

"Senator, 'less I'm mistaking, you got somebody who could
make a call and get things done."

Bauman giggled.

"If'n one o' my girls can't dial, I got strong fingers."

"Bet you do, Senator. Could you give those bureaucrats at
Customs a call to release the data to me? To me only? Don't let
Customs know this isn't your bag, that'll just screw things up
more. I'll straighten it out quietly. And I'll let whatever Com-mittee member asked for this know that you carried his water."

"Son, 'pears you got good instincts," said Bauman. "If you leave the CIA, maybe you should come pick cotton for me."

"Senator," said John, sticking the letter from Customs into his briefcase with the news clip from Emma, "I'm a public servant. I already work for you."

The briefcase weighed down John's arm as he walked through the tunnels connecting the Senate office buildings. Those green walls echoed with laughter and chatter from shirt-and-tie Senate aides, IDs proclaiming them the foot soldiers of America's policies clipped to their clothes or dangling from their necks. So many staffers in their 20s, thought John. So few scars.

Senator Firestone's office door was closed.

Inside, phones rang. In the reception room, a man in a disheveled suit badgered a black woman who stood behind a desk.

A brown-haired woman fresh out of NYU sat at the other desk, frantically answering phone calls.

"Look," the man argued to the black receptionist as John entered, "I know it's not your fault, this is just your job."

The brown-haired NYU graduate gave John a wan smile, punched in another call and murmured the official greeting.

"But I got a job to do, too," argued the man. "And my job is to get the truth to the people, and to do that, I've got to talk to the Senator."

"He's not available," said the receptionist. "I already told—"

"I know what you told me," said the reporter. "Two weeks ago, he and his press secretary were calling *me*, asking *me* to talk to them, print stories about them. Well, now I'm here and—"

"The press secretary is busy right now," said the receptionist. She pointed to a stack of pink message slips: "If you want to leave your name and number, she'll—"

"I don't want to talk to her! I want to talk to him!"

John leaned close, whispered to the brown-haired receptionist: "John Lang, from the Committee. I'm here to see—"

"Just a second, please," she said, punched into a ringing line: "Senator Firestone's office, could you please hold?"

John told her: "I'm from your Committee. Here to see Steve."

The reporter said: "Do you know what a deadline is?"

Brown-haired receptionist told John: "Could you—"

The last two unblinking phone lines rang simultaneously.

The door opened, and a TV news camera crew walked in.

The brown-haired receptionist swore, then whispered to John: "Steve's got the first desk through there."

She angled her head toward a closed side door.

John smiled at her as she answered one of the ringing lines. As he followed her direction, the reporter who'd been arguing with the receptionist saw the entering camera crew.

"Oh no!" yelled the reporter. "Forget it! I'm here first, and if he comes out, I get exclus—"

Then John was out of the reception room, through the side door, its heavy wood sealing off his wake.

And into an office that was more of a passageway between rooms than a suite.

A cluttered desk with a glowing VDT screen and an empty swivel chair. Bordering this work space was a seven-foot plastic partition; beyond that, high windows. Ahead of John was a door leading to Senator Firestone's private office. A Xerox machine filled the wall between the Senator's door and the door to the reception room. The machine cathunked out copies as a red-eyed woman of 30 watched. She stared through John. He glanced at the documents rolling out of the machine: a résumé.

The woman picked up her copies, walked out the side door.

Leaving John alone.

Voices floated over the partition.

FIRST MAN: "—just ride it out!"

SECOND MAN: "I'm getting tired of 'riding them out'!"

He paused: "You could have picked a better metaphor."

FIRST MAN: "The cops aren't pressing charges. Ethics Committee has no reason to—"

WOMAN: "The Ethics Committee? What difference do they make? So what if he hasn't broken any of their cleverly written—"

FIRST MAN: "What do you want? Charlie's got a voting record we're all proud as hell of, and—"

SECOND MAN: "Gonna have to come up with some sort of reasonable blanket response for the press. Damage—"

FIRST MAN: "Why? This is—"

WOMAN: "You think everyone doesn't know this isn't the first time?"

FIRST MAN: "—an unfortunate private matter between . . ."

WOMAN: "They were in a public car wreck! He even made the London papers! How can you pretend this is *private?* You can't keep him locked up in his Capitol office. Camera crews ambush him on his way to vote, stake out his house. And what about her?"

FIRST MAN: "Doris?"

WOMAN: "Yeah, Doris, too, but all we can do for her is bleed and hope she gets a great divorce lawyer."

FIRST MAN: "Hey!"

SECOND MAN: "The girl, what about the girl?"

FIRST MAN: "She won't talk."

WOMAN: "Won't talk? She's a hooker! She'll do anything for anybody for not very much money and you think she won't talk?"

FIRST MAN: "She's got probation violations and outstanding—"

SECOND MAN: "Good lawyer will get enough money from TV up front, so that won't—"

WOMAN: "He's dead meat and he deserves to be dead meat!"

SECOND MAN: "Where'd he meet her anyhow?"

WOMAN: "Where have you been? You drive down the street and—"

FIRST MAN: "You know Charlie. After work Scotches at the Lion. He told me she started talking to him at the bar, they had a couple drinks—"

SECOND MAN: "We gotta worry about DWI charges, too?"

FIRST MAN: "No, she was driving and the police say it was clearly the other guy's fault. He crashed smack into—"

SECOND MAN: "Should have had one of the mail room boys driv-ing him, like we used to do."

He paused, said: "Is Charlie talking about resigning?"

The door to the reception room opened. The brown-haired secretary came in, saw John, smiled. Saw the empty desk, frowned.

FIRST MAN: "I made Charlie promise not to talk at all."

WOMAN: "Charlie's promise?"

She swore: "His poor kids."

The receptionist went behind the partition, said: "Steve, there's a man from the Committee waiting to see you. At your desk."

FIRST MAN: "You let him come . . ."

Whispers. Hushed voices.

The receptionist walked past John, her eyes on the floor.

A bald man younger than John walked around the partition, squinted at him: "I don't know you."

John asked if he was Steve, told him his name.

"I'm from the Intelligence Committee," said John.

"You're not our guy."

"I'm the Agency liaison," said John.

"The hell you say." Steve spun his swivel chair around, sat. He moved a stack of *Congressional Records* off a visitor's chair, mo-tioned for John to sit.

"Been . . . a little crazy around here," said Steve.

John said he understood.

"I'll make it quick," said John. "A couple weeks ago, you sent over an anonymous letter your boss received. About a—"

"Some guy in . . . Paris?"

"Yeah.

"My coworker, the man who died in . . . the car incident—"

"Shit! Was that guy CIA? I remember the *Post* story said he worked for the Committee, but—"

"Reporters," said John quickly: "Any contact you have with them, they might get it wrong."

"They'd love to know—"

"This was just something you learned accidentally." John made his voice cold. "Something you overheard at work."

The bald man glared at him: "Yeah, you're CIA. What do you want?"

"Because of the accident, I have to finish up my colleague's odds and ends. What can you tell me about that letter?"

"That these days, we don't give a shit about it. Even if it's not a crank, which I remember thinking it was, right now . . ."

He shrugged.

"Have you gotten any other mail like that or about that?"

"No. But the guy called."

"What?"

"Yeah. Before . . . Before we got so busy. He wanted to know if we got his letter. I said yeah, said we sent it to the Committee's CIA liaison. Pissed him off. When I asked him for more, he wanted your phone number. Figured what the hell, we had two bills hitting the floor, you guys can deal with it. Gave him the number and he gave me good-bye. And no name.

"So," said the Senate aide. "What gives?"

"We're trying to figure out how crazy he is."

"Don't worry about us. My boss has Capitol cops buffering him from reporters, and they're more persistent than any loon."

"I know." John gave Steve his card, office and home phone numbers to pass along to the nut—if Steve heard from him again. Said, "Good luck."

"Election's in four years," said Steve as he walked John to the reception room. "Think luck lasts that long?"

John said: "Good luck or bad?"

17

Keep Bauman quiet, thought John. *About everything.*

The drive from Capitol Hill to CIA headquarters in the Virginia woods took John 30 minutes—including the stop he made at the scenic overlook along the George Washington Memorial Parkway.

Cars raced by to his left. To his right, through the winter-bare trees, ran the vast gorge for the Potomac River. He locked his briefcase containing Frank's keys, the news-clip from Emma and the Customs Service letter to Bauman in the trunk of his car. John kept the .45 locked in the glove compartment—he couldn't carry it through metal detectors at the Senate. Or at the CIA.

On the Agency reservation, his car could be searched without warning, warrant or admission. John thought the odds of that were slim. But routine security checks of briefcases made it easier to lock everything suspicious that he had in the trunk.

Where no one would look. *Probably.*

Once he was cleared past the Plexiglas-walled gatehouse and inside the electrified fence, instead of parking in his assigned spot in the underground garage, John pulled into a highly visible visitor's space out front of the "old" main building.

Locked his car.

Up the marble steps, into the vast entryway, past the 54 stars on the wall for CIA personnel killed in the line of duty.

You'll get your star, Frank. Stone-cold promise.

The electric turnstiles opened when he inserted his security card. He walked through the maze of halls to the Counter-Terrorism Center, where a guard directed him through yet another maze to yet another set of doors.

The business-suited security guard at the door glanced at John's ID. Then at the phone. Frowned. Buzzed John inside.

Works for Korn, thought John. That can't be helped.

Four months earlier, the vast room behind that locked door had been a secured archive, a windowless cavern inhabited by double-locked fireproof file cabinets.

One wall still held such file cabinets, but now dozens of desks covered the floor, some surrounded by green plastic partitions. Most of the desks were occupied, held computers and phones. The desks were grouped in clusters; near each cluster was a sign: Federal Bureau of Investigation. New York Metropolitan Police. New York State Police. Bureau of Alcohol, Tobacco and Firearms. Naval Investigative Service Terrorist Alert Center. Secret Service. State Department. Drug Enforcement Administration. Customs Service. Marshals Service. Defense Intelligence Agency. CIA.

An electric-blue beacon mounted on a pole slowly rotated its light through the room's fluorescent glare—non-CIA personnel with moderate clearance were in the room. A mute red beacon topped a nearby pole. Stretched between them was a large placard:

CORCORAN CENTER TASK FORCE

A man and a woman playing backgammon directed John to a closed door near the back of the cavern.

"Yo!" said a man's voice behind the door when John knocked. "Come in!"

John closed the small office's door behind him.

The man behind the desk had his tie loose, his suit jacket off. His skin was the color of American chocolate. With two hands, he held wadded paper above his head, flicked his wrists. The paper ball missed the basketball hoop hung from the far wall, bounced to the floor where a dozen more paper balls lay.

"Damn!" said the man behind the desk. "Good thing I'm in the CIA and not the NBA."

John introduced himself.

"Thank you, God," said the man whose name was Kahniley Sangare. He spoke English with a Maryland twang, French like a Parisian and the two main languages of his father's native Ivory Coast like he'd been born there. "A visitor from the outside world!"

"Don't you get many?" asked John.

"These days," said Sangare, "we don't even get many crank letters. At least the main office at the bomb site in New York still gets walk-in wackos to deal with."

John told him about Bauman's list and Allen's promise.

"Yeah, I got memoed on that, but told to wait—in case Bauman forgot. Is he as loony as he seems?"

"He's one politician where what you see is what you get."

"You want to see real power?" Sangare stroked his chin. "Which one of my two dozen stir-crazy and bored, highly trained, multiagency-contributed Task Force warriors should I give your errand to? Who's been sweet to me today?"

He picked up the phone and relayed John's request to a lucky staffer in the main room.

"Sit down. They'll take as long as they can to do this so they could have something they could brag about to their families tonight—if they weren't under oath to keep their mouths shut."

"They're not lazy people—"

"They're wasted people," said Sangare.

"Don't you have anything?"

"We got tons of anything! Did you see that wall of file cabinets? Crammed full, copies of interviews and forensic reports and classified analyses—even one on the weather that week cross-referenced with lunar causation models."

"What?"

"Was it a nut prompted by the full moon," said Sangare. "We

got all that, and what it adds up to here and in New York is fifty of the finest cops and intelligence analysts and spy-counterspy dogs in the world waiting for one teeny-tiny break or—"

He shook his head: "*Or.*

"We've been peeling people back to their own undermanned agencies, low-profile so that nobody gets crucified for abandoning the investigation into what the public thinks is a rare freak terrorist attack on U.S. soil. Hell, last year we had thirty-nine terrorist incidents in this country! And this one case never-ending Task Force."

"Don't you have anything substantive?"

"God, I thought you'd never ask!"

Sangare swung his feet off his desk, beckoned John to a large-screened computer terminal. Sangare turned on the blue screen, called up a multicolored menu, typed a command.

TOP SECRET flashed on the screen.

"You *comprenez* that?"

"Yes," said John.

"Can't be too careful," said Sangare, "you spend your days prowling the leakiest place in the world."

He typed in a code word.

The screen blinked.

Like a television show, a New York street scene appeared in the computer—thick vertical lines obscured the view.

"New York police got this out of a jewelry store's security video camera across the street and down from Corcoran Center. The black vertical lines blocking the view are the bars on the store's security grille. Watch."

Sangare tapped a key.

In slow motion, a man in a black topcoat walked past the store window. The CIA's agent in charge of the Washington branch of the Task Force tapped a key, and the video fast-forwarded until a Datsun rolled past. Long hair hid the driver's face, but even through those wild strands and the smudged glass of the jewelry store and car windows, John registered a line of pink lips.

"Based on the attack on the guards, we think that's a man in a wig," said Sangare. He typed commands into the computer. "But forget about 'her' for a moment. Watch."

The screen changed. The image of the man in the black top-coat reappeared—frozen at the moment when he passed between two bars on the store's window grate.

The screen boxed the man's face in white lines.

The computer filled with that face, barely visible above the coat's collar and beneath blowing long hair.

"He's six-one," said Sangare. "We got perfect digitalization of his nose, left cheekbone, the tip of his left ear and a bit of his mouth and jaw."

He typed a command.

The screen filled with a color "picture" of a man with long brown hair, turned the picture from profile to face-forward to other profile.

"That could be almost anybody," said John.

"Not me or my brother," said Sangare.

"He did it?"

"Not provable in court, but based on what the security guard told us, Mr. Black Coat's timing vis-à-vis the explosion . . . we think so."

"He's the 'witness' the press says you're after."

"Yeah, well, we couldn't stop the leak, but we didn't bother to correct it when it was wrong. Maybe him thinking there's a witness will make him do something stupid. Maybe him not knowing we got this much of him will make him less than cautious.

"If we get our hands on him—or a good picture of him—we got enough to link this guy to the scene, whoever he is. We've run computer comparisons of every vaguely Caucasian terrorist in everybody's files. Come up with zip. But he could be just a hired hand, a freelancer picked up for a onetime deal. We're checking mercenary files, but they're not complete.

"The other one, the 'woman driver,' was definitely involved, but there's not enough there for the computer."

"That's all you got?"

There was a knock on the door. A woman with a gun holstered on her belt entered, gave Sangare a piece of paper with 74 names typed on it. Sangare checked it, rubber-stamped it with the Task Force's logo, initialed it, and passed the list to John.

"No," said Sangare, "we got that, too. Now so do you. And if the Senator leaks it, no big deal, our Agency and CTC kept a few names nobody knows we know off the official list, because if—I mean *when* it gets leaked, the bad guys'll have it, too."

"Thanks," said John. "See you."

"Take me with you?" asked Sangare.

John walked out alone.

Stepped into the hall.

Found two men in suits waiting for him.

"Mr. Lang?" said the taller man. "Director Allen wants to see you."

They made sure he knew the way.

18

CIA Deputy Director for Operations Roger Allen pointed his half-shell glasses across his executive desk.

"Didn't expect to see you again so soon," said Allen.

"No sir," said John.

"And I sure didn't expect to see you out here. At work. Thought you were taking it easy. Perhaps I was misinformed."

"Not by me."

"Why are you poking around that Task Force and the Counter-Terrorism Center?"

John explained that Senator Bauman had ambushed him about the list. Said that he'd come to headquarters to get it, because he knew the problems of an angry Senator outweighed the leave time of a lowly liaison officer.

"And that's what you're doing? Here—and on the Hill?"

"Odds and ends. Mail. Lot of time out of the office."

"Personal time."

"Yes," said John. "Personal time."

"That's wise. Let me see the list."

John handed it to him. "I hadn't had time to report to Mr. Zell or you on this before I was—"

"Before now," interrupted Allen.

"Yes."

Allen slipped on his glasses, scanned the list, noted the transmittal stamps from the Task Force.

"I prefer to keep you relaxing and recovering," said Allen,

"but keeping Bauman's feathers smooth . . . He's put you in the hot seat. You deliver this. But tomorrow, not today. Don't let him get used to us jumping through his hoops."

"No sir." John took the list. "May I ask a question?"

Allen stared over his half-moon glasses: "Certainly."

"Ahmed Naral," said John.

"Yes."

"Senator Handelman and his people are right. The Director even called Naral a terrorist in a speech he made in—"

"Philadelphia," said Allen.

"Somewhere. The point is, Naral isn't on that list."

"No he's not."

"A high-profile terrorist like Naral is not even a suspect in the Corcoran Center bombing?"

"He's not on the list, no."

John's heart was pounding. *Push it:* "Why not?"

"Why put a dead man on a list of suspects to investigate?"

"So Naral *is* dead?"

Allen shrugged. "Apparently so."

"At the hearing you said—"

"I said we didn't know for certain that the man found floating in his own blood was Naral. 'Certainty' means 100 percent—not 95, not 99: *100*. Besides, that hearing was yesterday. Knowledge changes with every tick of the clock. Prompted by the hearing, Ops has now concluded that Naral is 99 percent dead."

"And that's 100 percent true," muttered John.

"Of course."

"But Naral died after . . . And now the list is—"

"Up-to-date. To this minute." Allen leaned back in his chair. "Do you have a problem here, Mr. Lang?"

"Me having a problem isn't the—"

"That's right," said Allen. Evenly. Firmly. "You having a problem isn't the point, and isn't what matters."

"What matters is what happened," said John. "What if Naral was the bomber?"

"Then I'd say him being dead wipes the slate as clean as it can get," answered Allen. "Wouldn't you?"

For a moment, only their breathing filled the room.

"We're lucky," said Allen. "Solving the Corcoran Center bombing isn't per se CIA's task. Co-opting Glass's damn Counter-Terrorism Center and overlapping it on top of the Corcoran Task Force allows us to keep our hands in—but clean. The overlap lets us know everything that's going on. We can maneuver as fast as anyone to get credit for nabbing the bad guys. If the investigation keeps going nowhere, legally it's the FBI's fault, with a ricochet of blame hitting the CTC—thus proving our contention that those damn new Centers aren't worth the budget dollars the Administration and Congress have pried out of Agency allotments and given to them.

"Let the reformers fumble around in a bloody bomb hole while we get on with CIA business."

"What's that," mumbled John, not really asking.

"Right now, it's keeping itself from being blown to smithereens by our ignorant 'friends' on Capitol Hill."

"And being America's first line of defense," said John.

Allen smiled. "I'm glad you understand my testimony. Our concerns. I know we can depend on you."

An Allen aide "accompanied" John to the entrance, watched him go through the turnstiles and step outside to the marble plaza.

The sky churned like a gray sea. Cold wind knifed through John's suit.

He thought: *This is the day I buried Frank.*

19

Alone, sitting at the flat-top desk in his cabin, nine o'clock that night, John heard a knock on his door.

Frank's gun lay in front of him. John's hand closed around the pistol's checkered grip . . .

Don't be paranoid.

He put the gun in the desk drawer.

Probably just the landlord.

The radio played piano jazz.

Mist from the glass of bourbon tingled the air.

On the desk's varnished wood where he practiced calligraphy were the Customs Service letter to Senator Bauman, the news clipping about Cliff Johnson's death, a notebook page bearing the name Martin Sinclair—a stranger who'd merely called Frank at work—the anonymous letter Glass had given John and a yellow legal pad waiting to record his wisdom, operation plans or even random thoughts. He'd stared at the blank yellow page for an hour, trying to sense a pattern worth scrawling on paper, knowing he had too few tangibles to connect and too little time left.

A second knock on the door.

Probably just the landlord.

Outside, a cold rain fell. Wind pushed the cabin.

John slid all his pitiful documents between the sheets of the yellow legal pad, made sure the edges were flush so that a glance showed only unused innocence.

Walked to the door feeling too serious, because after all, this
time of night, way out here, the ambushes by Glass and Green
notwithstanding, this knock had to be just his landlord.

Hand on the doorknob, John hesitated.

Flicked off the overhead light.

Now only the flow from the desk lamp and reading lamp by
the chair and the lamp in his open-doored bedroom lit the room
behind him: why give the night a crisp silhouette?

And just in case . . .

Quietly, slip the dead bolt.

Slowly, turn the knob slowly. Brace, steady . . .

Jerk the door open.

Scared her and she jumped back, one hand to her throat, the
other almost dropping her umbrella.

"Oh!" she said.

"I'm sorry! I didn't know it was you, I . . . should be more
careful. Should have asked who it was."

"That's OK," she said, "I should have called first."

"No, I'm glad you came."

"Oh. Good."

There they stood for a moment, he in the doorway, she on his
front porch. Around them blew the cold night.

"Come in," said John.

She walked past him. A whiff of roses and leather followed
her. He closed the door.

"Can I take your coat?" he asked.

"Thanks."

Step close behind her. There, on the left side of her long grace-
ful neck, her pulse would be beating *there*.

Gingerly, he gripped the dark shoulders of her coat, pulled it
back and down as her arms slid out of the wet sleeves.

"Thanks," she said again.

"Sure."

Maybe she'd changed clothes since the funeral, but her coat
had been closed this morning, so he wasn't sure.

Now she wore a plain dress, a subtle shade of indigo. Low-heeled black shoes. A simple gold loop around one wrist, a watch on the other. No rings, no necklace.

"This is a hard place to find," she said.

"I used to think so."

"Used to?"

"Nothing. Never mind."

"Even with the address, I had to knock on your landlord's door, ask him where to go. I didn't know what to expect. I mean, how your home would look.

"I like it," she added, her eyes lingering on the bookshelves, the black ink calligraphy character painting.

"Thanks."

"I hope I'm not disturbing you."

He shrugged: "I was just . . . Had to do some work."

"I can leave."

"Long as you're here, stay awhile."

She smiled at him, a warm smile.

"Would you . . . like a drink?" he asked.

"Sure."

"Bourbon—or beer, I've got a couple bottles."

"Any wine? Scotch?"

"Sorry. I don't keep much liquor around, don't usually drink much, but . . ."

"Yes," she said. "But. Times like this.

"I'll try what you're having," she said.

As he walked to the kitchen for a clean glass and the bourbon bottle, he steered wide of where she stood.

The music on the progressive radio station changed from piano jazz to a jagged-edged ballad by a female singer.

Wind rattled the windows.

When John turned from the kitchen counter to the living room, she was standing at his desk.

Her fingers trailed over the varnished wood, over the yellow legal pad.

"Working, huh?" she said. Her fingers rested on the yellow pad's blank sheet. "I should be working, too."

Pour the glass of bourbon out of her reach so she has to leave the desk to get it.

She came for the glass.

Their hands didn't touch.

"You know," she said, "last week, I was afraid this year would be just like last. Lucky us, huh?"

"Frank always said luck was what you make it."

"Did he?" She swirled the amber whirlpool in her glass. The indigo dress floated on her: she wore no bra. "We don't know each other all that well."

"Not much at all."

"You don't have to agree."

"I didn't mean—"

The shake of her head silenced him. "Sometimes, the more we talk about things, the more confused they get."

"Sometimes."

"Look, I had all this great speech, but . . . Truth is, I don't want to be alone right now. And of all the faces in this city of death, yours was the only one I wanted to be not alone with."

"Big city," he said. "There's more here than—"

"Don't tell me about this town. Or death. My parents . . . Christ, even a dog we had when I was a kid . . ."

Tears filled her eyes.

"It's OK," he said.

"No it's not." She sniffed: "Sorry. Normally I'm famous for my control. Ask anybody in my office."

"This isn't normally."

"That's the truth."

She raised her glass: "So what will we drink to?"

"Everything."

"Not everything. First, let's drink to Frank Mathews."

They clinked glasses. Drank.

She lowered her glass, half-empty: "Burns."

"You can get used to it."

"I bet I could."

She turned away, walked toward the far wall, trailed her fingers along the back of the couch.

The radio played Muddy Waters, bass thumping, guitar screaming, gravel-voiced Chicago blues.

Rain pelted the windows, pattered on the roof.

"Terrible weather," she said.

"We're OK in here," he told her.

She knocked back the rest of her drink. Fire shook her small frame. She put the glass on a bookcase. Asked: "Do you think I know what I'm doing?"

"You're probably smarter than me."

"I doubt it."

"Call us both right." She stepped toward him.

"Tonight—" She shook her head. Looked up and locked her eyes on his. "Tonight I want, *need* to feel alive. Grab back control. The hell with luck."

She stood so close her breath fanned his shirt. He smelled the bourbon-sweet dampness of her mouth, the warm musk of her flesh. Roses. Leather.

"Tonight," she whispered. "Just tonight."

She raised her face.

His left hand cupped her cheek. Her eyes closed and she rubbed her face along his palm.

Kiss her.

Her lips opened; she was sweet and wet. Her arms circled up around his neck, she pulled herself against him.

Her lips broke away—stayed so close he felt their tingle.

"Tell me the ten thousand reasons why not to do this," she whispered. "But tell me tomorrow."

Then she pulled him down to her kiss.

Fire roared through him.

The hell with everything.

Pull her close.

Dress, soft on her back, her ribs. Roses. Leather. Pounding, head spinning into a vortex.

The crumple of her soft dress. Zipper, down.

Warm, bare, her back so smooth, her ribs frail under his palms. He pulled her dress off the front of her shoulders, down.

Floating down, her dress, down.

Her breasts were bare, sweet small cones high and soft, centered with swollen circles and tipped with rose arrows.

Beneath her panty hose, the curve of a dark half-moon. The scent of her sea.

Around her waist, her stomach smooth, flat, his hands gently slid up.

She pressed his hands over her breasts, cried out, pulled his mouth to hers, then down to her breasts, cried out again as he sucked her right breast in his mouth, his tongue flicking. Kiss her heart, her breast. She moaned, pulled him to kiss her mouth. Her hands popped open the snaps on his shirt, pulled it off.

Her arms tight around his neck. Stand tall and she pulls herself up with him, wraps her legs around his waist.

Low-heeled black shoes fall to the floor.

She weighs nothing as he carries her to the bedroom; she weighs everything.

On the bed, set her on the bed, break their kiss, lay her down. Stand between her knees. Kick off the Chinese slippers, feet bare on the floor as his jeans drop, then his shorts . . .

She rose off the bed. Sat on the edge. Pressed her breasts against his bare loins, pulled his face down to kiss, kisses covering his neck, his chest, her tongue trailing down his stomach, down and she held him in her hands and down. She licked him. Took him in her mouth.

Oh.

Her left hand pressed his spine and held him still and wouldn't let go.

Oh.

Her bare back, smooth ivory, his hands glide up and down, up and down, ribs, fingers brushing round, he can touch, just touch her nipples and they are hardandhecan't

stop

don't

breathe, can't
stop
don't
and he yells as the sun explodes.

Standing straight, eyes opening.
Still there, she was
still there, and he was still there, and he shuddered once again
as she pressed her hand against the small of his back, kept him
sweet inside her.

Pull away. Cup her face and tilted her smile up to his. Her
eyes shine.

Lean over, kiss her.

Ease her down, back flat on the bed. Cover her, chest to chest,
kiss her. Her panty hose scratch as her legs hug his thighs. Kiss
her.

Break off, her lips cling, her eyes open. Her pretty face smiles
up from his bedspread.

Tell her, "My turn."

Kiss her mouth.

His hips press into her, she arches hers in answer. Kiss her
neck. John slid his left arm under her shoulder blades, put his
weight in that arm as he kissed her neck.

There, she said. *Yes.*

As he covered her left breast with his mouth; pressed his lips
around her right nipple covered her other breast with his hand

and she moans and

squeeze.

Oh God, she whispers.

Kiss her stomach, down, between her knees pointed to heaven,
down and his hands caress her breasts

and down, the evening beard on his cheeks scratches the panty
hose covering her thighs.

Hold the waistband of her panty hose. She presses her feet into
the mattress, raises her hips so he can peel the panty hose off
their smooth roundness,

seas, the perfume of sea

and she lowers her hips, points her feet to the ceiling like a ballerina

make her naked.

Panty hose tossed away, flutter, fall.

Kiss her cocked right knee. Kiss her left.

Kneel at the edge of the bed.

Kiss the inside of her thighs.

Grab her waist with both hands, pull her to the edge of the bed, spread her legs wide.

"John!"

Kiss her there.

And he didn't stop. And he wouldn't stop.

The smell of her. The taste.

Like he was drunk, she made him like he was drunk

and he wouldn't couldn't stop

her right fingers in his hair, pressing the back of his head, her hips rock against him.

Eyes open.

Look: her eyes closed, mouth open, panting, her left hand rubbing her breast, her fingers touch her nipple

Oh, she said.

Cried out and bucked up against him and *hold her tight and don't pull away and*

No! she said: Can't

stop

and he wouldn't

and she cried out. Bucked against him her hands pulling his mouth hard against her and

"John!"

Then again he was hard. Fire roars. Slide with her up on the bed, move into her reaching arms, on top of her and

inside her

Oh, they said.

And he couldn't stop he wouldn't stop as they held each other pressing down on her and it went on forever and fire clenched around him and she cried out and still he went faster, still faster, harder and she cried out *Please.*

Then John was gone and he was there and he was everywhere and all the powers in him let go and she was there and she wasn't visionsflashed and her fire grabbed him and he exploded with her as he cried out: *"Phuong!"*

20

"Wrong girl," said Emma.

In his ear, her whisper.

Stomach falls away, napalm roars.

And he knew but said: "What?"

He lifted his face from beside hers, looked at her with as much innocence as he could feign. Felt himself slipping out.

Emma enunciated the words: "Wrong . . . girl."

Still on top of her, *try*: "What did I say?"

"Don't." Emma's thin lips were a hard, straight line. "There isn't a moment about tonight I'll forget. Not a feeling. Not a sensation or a smell. Not a sound."

Her fingernail trailed up his side, across his chest to his neck where his pulse slammed through his carotid artery.

"That's the hell of it," she said: "I always remember everything."

She pressed her fingernail into him, ever so slightly.

"So we both know what you said when you didn't know what you were saying, and it was 'Phuong.' "

"That's, ah . . .

"I shook her hand at the funeral. Guess I should have . . . looked at her with different eyes."

He eased himself off her, careful to keep contact, his arm under her head, his other hand gently on her sweaty stomach. Emma lay heavy and stiff on the mattress.

"I guess I said it."

"Good guess."

"I don't know why."

"Really?"

"Really. I don't know her—only met her yesterday. I . . . Part of what I'm doing is managing what Frank left behind. Even his personal stuff."

"How personally are you taking your work?"

"I was in that car," he said. "What do you think?"

She shrugged, but he felt her tension ease.

The scent of their passion filled the room.

"She must have been on my mind," said John.

"Is that all she's on? Because if this is just head tricks, well, I know about those. But . . ."

"What 'this' are we talking about?" said John. "Me? You? *This* this? Or some other this?

"Words create reality," he said. "Do you want to define everything about tonight right now?"

"Do you?" she whispered.

"This is Thursday night," he told her. "Tuesday morning changed all my definitions. I'm fighting for new ones. My old life got shot to hell. Now comes you."

"I lied when I said just tonight," said Emma. "I've been waiting. I was there before. You know that."

"Maybe I do. Maybe I was waiting, too."

"Ambivalence is such bullshit."

"Ambivalence isn't what you just got from me." He waited. She wouldn't speak. "What are you rock-certain of in your life?"

She didn't reply.

"You didn't come here knowing what would happen," he said. "Even if we think so much alike, I didn't know you were on the way or what . . . What are you rock-certain about right now?"

"Don't lie to me," she said.

"I'll do my best," he promised.

Propped up on one elbow, he watched her. She lay beside him, flat on her back, face to the ceiling.

"How well . . . You and her . . ."

"I met her yesterday when I was at Frank's house, sorting through his life. Her father is dead. He was my friend. I'm point man for the Agency with his family. She's his family."

"What else?"

"We buried Frank this morning. I didn't even talk to her at the funeral."

"Are you going to see her again?"

"Probably."

"She must have made quite an impression on you."

He shrugged. "She must have."

Emma shifted her weight on his arm. Her leg moved closer, touched his.

Wind rattled his bedroom windows.

She turned her face to look at him. Trailed a finger down his cheek. Softly.

"You're not much of a spy, losing control like that. Blurting out secrets."

"I hold up fine under torture."

"That was torture?"

"If it had been, I wouldn't have cracked."

She smiled: "For the record? Is there . . . Do you have anyone else?"

"No."

"I didn't think so," she said. "I mean, I'm no spy, but watching you, hearing you talk with Committee people . . ."

"I thought you weren't a spy."

"I'm not," she said. "And that's the truth.

"For the record," she whispered: "There's no one else I'm . . . I have. Not for a long, long time. A long, safe time."

He kissed her forehead and she nuzzled into the crook of his neck.

"Me either," he said.

"Why not?"

She felt him shrug. "Maybe it's all luck."

"For the record," she whispered.

"Yes?"

"That was . . . phenomenal."

"Absolutely," he said.

They kissed.

"I'm not like that," she said.

"God, I hope you're lying."

They laughed and kissed again.

"Do me a favor?" she asked.

"What?"

"No need to be so cautious. I promise."

"I'll try," he said.

"Try practicing my name."

"Emma," he said. "Emma Emma Emma Emma—"

And she pulled him down to a kiss.

"Em," he said, when she pulled back.

"You know what?" she said.

"What?"

"Where's your bathroom?"

He pointed to the door, she got off the bed and walked to it, smiling. Her brown hair was tousled, her thin lips swollen. Her skin was white, smooth; passion's flush splotched her chest. Her pointed breasts trembled with her step, her belled hips were taut and her thighs were nicely muscled.

The bathroom door closed behind her.

John collapsed backward onto the bed, closed his eyes.

What the hell was happening.

What the hell was he doing.

What was he thinking.

Making a slip like . . . Phuong: *why Phuong?*

Rain pattered on his windows.

The bedspread was wet under his leg.

Behind the closed bathroom door, he heard the toilet flush. Water run, stop. Silence.

For a minute.

For two.

Just as he sat up, the bathroom door opened and Emma came out. Her hair was finger-combed, her face bright and happy.

She belly-flopped onto the bed beside him, kissed him.

"You know what?" he said.

"What?"

"My turn."

She laughed as he climbed off the bed, threw a pillow at him that he caught and tossed back. She hugged it to her breasts, sprawled back on the bed.

"Hurry up," she said.

"Some things take time," he told her.

As soon as he closed the bathroom door, he remembered the documents hidden in the yellow pad

Too late. He stared at his reflection in the mirror.

Don't be silly.

He urinated. Flushed the toilet. Turned on both faucets, washed his hands. Bent over the sink, splashed water on his face.

Heard . . . something.

Outside the bathroom.

Emma yelled *something*.

As the whining toilet tank finally filled, shut off.

"What?" he said, water splashing in the sink.

Over the running water, through the door, he thought he heard a shrill sound and the words: " . . . -et t . . ."

Turn off the faucets.

Silence.

Open the door.

The bed was empty.

Go! Moving, in the bedroom . . .

From the living room came the peal of his ringing telephone.

Through the bedroom door, fast, bare feet sliding on the smooth wood floor . . .

Emma, naked, walking toward the phone, hearing his charge, turning: "I said, do you want me to get it?"

"No!" he yelled as his answering machine beeped and his recorded voice said *"Please leave a message."*

She stopped. Solidly between him and the phone as the machine beeped.

Dancing with Emma, both sidestepping the same direction, his hands grabbing her shoulders, sensing which way she would move before she did and stepping past her . . .

Through the answering machine they heard: "John, this is Phuong Mathews. I . . . No big deal. Just . . . You said to call you if . . . If, huh? If you're free and it's not too late, I'm staying at Dad's and if you want . . . call me."

The machine cut off.

"I guess you didn't want me to get it," said Emma.

She stared at his chagrin.

"I guess this isn't your easiest night," she said.

"Or maybe it is," she added.

"She just called me," said John. "I told her to."

"For work."

"Or for a friend."

"Ah." Emma shrugged. "She sounds good on the phone."

"She'll keep."

"She's the keeper?" said Emma.

"I'll call her tomorrow. Find out what she wants."

Emma shook her head: "Even I'm not that big of a bitch."

They stood naked in his living room.

John said: "I'm trouble."

Emma stared at him, said: "Trouble me."

She pressed against him, pulling him against her warmth, bending him down to her kiss.

Then she stepped back, said: "But not tonight."

"Emma—"

"I'm not a folder, John. I'll fight for what I want. But I can't fight fantasies and I'm too smart to try."

She pressed his hand against her breast: "This is real."

Then she pushed his hand away, angled her head toward the telephone and said: "But you've got work."

"Tonight."

She picked her dress off the floor. "I'll be at the office tomorrow. Don't forget how well we work together."

Her smile was great. Unflinching.

Fifteen minutes later, Emma left him with a kiss.

His new watch said it was 10:47.

The answering machine waited by the phone.

First, put on sweatshirt, sweatpants.

"Hello?" said Phuong when he called. "John?"

"How did you know it was me?"

"Nobody else knows I'm here," she said. "Well, at least nobody who I . . . who would call.

"I'm OK," she added. "Just thought I'd call, let you know."

"What are you doing?" he asked.

"I've got the drapes open. Sitting at the dining room table. Watching the storm outside the glass door."

"It's wild out there."

"Yes. What's that you're listening to?"

The radio played reggae, and he told her so.

"You're a funny kind of spy, John Lang."

"What do you remember about being a kid? Way back."

"In Saigon, it rained so hard you couldn't breathe."

The wind shook John's windows. He sank into his chair.

"Emerald seas in the sky," she said. "Trees outside the orphanage. White dresses. Sleeping with lots of girls in a big room where the ceiling fans never stopped. The nuns' white and black robes flapping in the wind. '*Maintenant mes enfants* . . .' I still have French, studied it in college, easy A's, but . . . but I don't speak any Vietnamese. Not one word."

"You know your name," he said.

"Yes I do. And I remember our—my—first house with Mom and Dad. Had a big mustard wall around it, with razor wire on top, my own room I only had to share with the geckos. I was afraid I'd never learn English and that then these nice people who gave me all the treasures in the world and practically cried whenever I smiled or hugged them, they'd take me back to the nuns. When I was five, I got on an airplane and flew off to never-never land with my mom holding my hand, not ever going to leave me alone like before. I saw snow and laughed so hard I couldn't stop.

"I remember *bup-bup-bup-bup* helicopters and zings and *rat-a-tat-tats* and the nuns shooing us under desks. A big boom tossing cyclos and their pedal drivers through the air like fortune-teller sticks. My dad, like a Buddha, sitting off to the side of the dark living room, eyes on the door, black metal thing in his lap. He wouldn't look at me even when I tugged on his arm and he yelled for Mom to hurry come take me back upstairs.

"Your average childhood," she said. "Growing up American."

"Just like South Dakota." He told her about blizzards from the North Pole, how on a 40-below December night the ice pack cracked under your black rubber overshoes and you could look up and see a million stars frozen forever.

"I love the moon," she said. "I miss him so much."

"Me, too."

"I bet he did like you."

"Even if he didn't talk about me."

"Especially if he didn't talk about you. Where are the pictures, John?"

"I don't know."

"What aren't you telling me?"

"A million things."

"Which ones do I want to hear?"

After a long silence, he told her: "I don't know what to say."

"At least you're honest about that."

"I'll do everything I can to help you."

"Will it be what I want?"

"I don't know." He paused, but she gave him silence. "Don't worry. Everything's OK."

"At the funeral," she said, "there was a woman."

"Oh," said John.

"She has to be seventy. Said she knew my father from the day he came to work. She was a secretary or something—half the time, what you people say you do is cover story. Anyway, she's retired and asked if I'd come see her tomorrow. She only lives over in Baltimore."

"Are you going to go?"

"Unless you can tell me where to find the pictures and whatever else is missing from my father's life."

"The trip will do you good."

"I'll take a late morning train. Stay for dinner."

"I'll call you tomorrow night. See how it went."

She said: "If I get back."

They said good-bye. Hung up.

Exhaustion overwhelmed John. He wanted to close his eyes. He wanted to cry. He wanted to sleep. He wanted to run through the storm and never stop.

Walk the circle.

The living room was shadowed, lit only by the desk lamp and reading lamp, the glow from his bedroom.

He saw the front door.

Realized it was unlocked; had been unlocked since Emma first walked in, unlocked the whole time . . .

Twist the key, shoot the dead bolt home.

Mistake, he thought: *No more mistakes.*

21

Friday morning, the blue sedan materialized in John's driving mirrors minutes after he'd left his house.

Innocent.

Another lemming racing toward the cliff of work.

Then, in front of the Vice President's mansion, the blue sedan ran a light, squealed through the left-hand turn and braked to stay five car lengths behind John's old Ford—desperation too calculated to be mere commuter madness.

Or coincidence.

John's mirrors showed him images of two people in the blue sedan; in that reflected distance, they looked like men.

John cruised down the long slope of Massachusetts Avenue. Past the British Embassy's "V"-flashing statue of Winston Churchill. Past the black-mirrored cube of Brazil's embassy.

The blue sedan stayed with him.

Shadows? Or hunters?

Glide over the Parkway's four lanes. Pass the exit for George-town's narrow streets, acres of grass and trees bordering the black mirror granite wall etched with the 58,183 names of America's Vietnam War dead.

Frank's loaded .45 waited in John's glove compartment.

The blue sedan stayed in his mirrors.

The Parkway split near the Washington Monument. John merged onto the highway from Virginia, six lanes of rolling steel. Horns honked as John edged into the right lane for the tunnel marked U.S. SENATE EXIT.

In the tunnel, John took the choice marked D STREET.

So did the blue sedan.

When he rolled out of the tunnel, the blue sedan was screened in his mirrors by a plumber's van.

Red light. Stop.

A police car rolled past John's windshield. To his left, John saw a dozen police cruisers and unmarked detective cars parked across the street from the six-story police headquarters.

Two uniformed cops led a man with his hands twisted behind him to headquarters' glass-inlaid doors. The man wore a T-shirt against the bitter wind. John saw the glint of handcuffs.

Is Homicide Detective Greene at work?

Who commands the blue sedan?

Green light. *Drive forward, like nothing is wrong.*

Drive straight, go right on H Street. Be predictable.

Are the men in the blue sedan relaxed? Confident?

John drove toward Union Station.

When it OK'd Union Station's government-paid-for renovation, the Senate reserved part of the Station's waffle-layered rear parking lot for its employees. When the Senate Intelligence Committee and the CIA ironed out the agreement for two CIA liaison officers, CIA negotiators wrested one parking permit from the Committee Chairman. In the two square miles of D.C. called Capitol Hill, with its eight major Congressional office buildings, 19,516 employees and 535 Members, parking spaces are a currency of political power.

Frank and John had carpooled to work so neither of them would be stuck paying parking fees or parking tickets.

Union Station's Senate parking was on the first level, officially accessible only through the front driveway. The H Street entrance was for public parking.

Check the mirrors: the blue sedan sped to close the gap.

Do they sense anything?

John drove up the public's H Street entrance ramp.

To his left were yellow public parking ticket dispensers, entrance and exit lanes, a deserted toll collector's booth.

Straight ahead, hanging down from the next concrete level, a sign over a ramp that read WRONG WAY. On the road was a line of giant yellow arrows pointed toward John. The concrete lane beneath the yellow arrows rose to a "hill" that blocked his view.

Lock the steering wheel straight into the arrows.

Punch it.

His tires peeled rubber on concrete as he shot under the WRONG WAY sign, past the red letters reading DO NOT ENTER.

Up, the car surging, G-force pushing him into his seat. Yellow arrows flew at him. Ahead was a band of gray sky between the next concrete level and the crest of the rising ramp, gray sky where a six-ton truck or a mom's orange minivan full of kids or a strolling lost parker could suddenly appear to crash into—

Over!

Gravity battled inertia. Won. John's would-be airborne car crashed back down to the concrete. His stomach quivered weightless, then dropped back to earth.

Horn blares: a salesman's car screeched to a halt as some fool in a Ford going the wrong way almost smacked into him.

Empty ramp down, driving fast against the arrows.

Steal a glance in the mirror: no blue sedan.

Fly down the ramp. Hit the brakes, skid left.

A yellow taxi . . .

. . . swerves out of his way. A curse screamed in Farsi.

The sign for Senate parking: John races the wrong way down the one way toward it, swings left . . .

The tour bus parking zone. Teenagers from Iowa, letter jackets and teased hair, cameras and wide-eyes as they scramble out of the whipsawing Ford's path.

Roadblocks. No Unauthorized Parking.

The parking lot attendant, a patronage college kid earning his

way through American U, hears the squealing car, sticks his head
out of his heated booth.

Empty slots close to the booth: park.

Can't take the gun.

Lock it in the glove compartment, grab the briefcase. Bail out
of the car, lock it, sprint to the escalator.

"Take care of it!" he yelled to the college kid, who was checking John's bumper sticker. "I'm late!"

Run.

Down the escalator. Inside the glass door. Suits with briefcases. Women with giant purses. Janitor pushing a broom.

Down to where trains left for Boston and New York,
Baltimore—would Phuong use the Maryland suburban depot?

The tag team should have reached the escalators by now. John
dodged a woman lawyer with a steaming Styrofoam cup of coffee, her train tickets and *The Wall Street Journal* in one hand and a
briefcase, purse and topcoat in her other.

Don't look back.

Maybe they lost him. Guessed wrong, were hustling out the
Station's center front doors, figuring John was ahead of them,
headed toward the Hart Building.

Explode out of Union Station's west doors, race to the escalator leading down to the Metro subway.

A fat woman in front of the nearest orange fare card machine,
fumbling in a coin purse.

Cut in front of her.

"Jerk! Who the hell do you think . . ."

The machine ate his $5 bill, spit out a magnetized card. He
ran toward the crowd at the turnstile before she finished venting
her indignation.

A hundred commuters hurried around John, half going up escalators to Union Station and work at the Department of Energy
or Congress or the Teamsters building, half rushing down to
catch one of the subways roaring through this gray concrete tunnel.

A crowd shuffled on the red-tiled platform. The air was thick with the smell of their sweat, their damp coats and suits, the leather of their shoes.

No train waited on either track.

John elbowed his way along the platform until a kiosk printed with directions hid him from the escalators. He pressed his spine against the brown kiosk's metal; his legs trembled.

Maybe he'd shaken his shadows. Maybe they hadn't reached the platform yet.

Come on, train.

Don't look around the edge of the kiosk.

Don't show your face.

The air shook. Concrete dust swirled. A roar, a clatter, a burst of light and steel, squealing metal as a subway train barreled into the station, stopped. The train doors opened and a hundred commuters surged out.

Wait.

Dozens of people packed into the crowded cars, angling for seats or a handhold on the shiny poles or overhead grips.

Wait.

Ding-dong—the train's bell, warning the passengers to stand back, doors sliding closed—

John leapt toward the nearest car.

The passengers jammed into the doorway cringe as he—

Slammed into the closing subway doors.

The doors cathunked, gripped his shoulders and trapped him not in and not out of the car . . .

. . . jerked open to let him stumble inside.

The doors slid shut.

Pressed against the bodies of a dozen strangers, John turned to look out the glass panels of the shiny aluminum doors.

On the platform, a face inches from the train, an angry blur as the train roared into the blackness of the tunnel.

The engineer announced the next stop. John realized the train was headed opposite the direction he wanted.

A lucky misdirection—if the face on the platform had been a hunter.

John rode one more stop, got off to catch a train headed back the way he'd come. From his briefcase he took a folded nylon raincoat an unexpected storm once forced him to buy in Hong Kong. The wrinkled trench coat was waterproof and compressible. The tan material didn't breathe, nor did it ward off much cold, but it changed his description.

When his train stopped at Union Station, John stood behind a beefy construction worker. No one's eyes sought John.

He rode the train to Metro Center, certain by the time the escalator carried him back into the morning light that any shadow behind him was his own.

22

Metro Center is in the heart of Washington's redeveloped downtown, not far from Ford's Theater and the White House.

John walked down 12th Street, crossed Pennsylvania Avenue. In front of the Internal Revenue Service, he passed a man lying on a slat-wood bench. Wind rattled newspapers stuffed in the man's clothing. Next to the bench, a shopping cart overflowing with plastic-wrapped treasures was tied to the man's wrist with a crusted shoelace.

A seven-story monolith of a gray stone building filled the entire city block that led John to Constitution Avenue. The edifice was unbroken, a Greek-columned, mythological-friezed mesa kitty-corner from the Washington Monument.

Two men and a woman huddled outside the 13th Street entrance's revolving doors. They stood by the brass plaque reading CUSTOMS SERVICE, smoking an addictive, lethal and legal drug.

After he spun through the revolving doors, John logged in with three revolver-toting guards who were wary of hit teams dispatched by Latin American narcotics cartels. The guards made him clip on a plastic visitor's badge, open his briefcase and go through the metal detector, wait for an escort to the third-floor office where a beefy man with a pale complexion had a phone pressed against his ear. The man motioned for John to sit in front of his desk.

The sign on the man's door read: SPECIAL DIRECTOR AND

LIAISON FOR CONGRESSIONAL AFFAIRS. On his wall hung a diploma from Georgetown Law School.

Night school? thought John.

"I know what your boss wants," the man said into the phone. "But we follow the rules written by you guys on the Hill and the White House. . . . The courts say. . . . OK but . . . but . . . yeah, you can haul our asses up there and whip us for the TV cameras, but all that'll do is bleed my people's morale."

On the bookcase, encased in a plastic stand, was a Customs agent's gold badge.

"Look, not all our 19,000 people are saints or superheroes, but most of 'em give their best, and all of them are bleeding from budget cuts. They keep hearing 'reduction in force.' Hard to work today worrying that you'll get RIF'd tomorrow."

Next to his law degree, this man had taped a crayon drawing of a house: cream-colored paper, a blue band of sky above a black-lined, red-roofed shelter.

"Yeah, I know: the deficit. But cut fat, not throats."

A framed photo on his desk showed a pretty, plump-faced brunette who looked about a decade younger than her husband.

"Which constituent complaint? . . . We checked that out! Benny didn't hurt a thing! If he drooled on her purse in the airport, it was an accident! Hell, it's hot in New Orleans! . . . Last week, the same dog busted a ki-point-five of cocaine. . . . No way is he rabid! . . . Yes, I understand your boss wants him quarantined.

"By the way," the Customs Congressional liaison told the Hill staffer, "in our response, do you want us to include how much answering her complaint will cost the taxpayers?"

After the man hung up, John introduced himself.

"So what's going on?" asked the Customs man.

"Did you get a call from—"

"Oh, I've gotten a lot of calls. Yesterday, Senator Bauman's personal secretary called, said you'd be coming. That was the first time I'd heard from the Senator *directly*."

"Is there some problem?"

"Don't insult me. Your buddy calls a few weeks back, asks us to respond to an oral inquiry he got from Senator Bauman. He gave us some bullshit about why Bauman didn't contact us directly, why all this wasn't in writing, why we were to reply to him instead of the Senator. But we trusted him. After all, don't we work for the same legal government?"

"Now—"

"Now you're here. And your coworker is dead."

"Thanks for your sympathy. We buried him yesterday."

"The newspaper said the cops call it an accident."

"A manslaughter accident."

"He seemed like a nice guy, the times we talked."

"The times? More than one?"

The Customs man's smile slid like a saber from a sheath.

"Didn't you know?" he said. "I talked to Frank Mathews last week. Said he couldn't wait for all the wheels to spin. So he charmed me out of the response we were chopping. So, since your office has already been informed, no need for us to give this to you. We can just send it to the Senator."

"If that's what you want to do," said John. "But that's not what Senator Bauman specifically requested."

"I don't salute anybody just because they're called Senator," said the Customs man. "I do my job, try to give them what they deserve."

"I don't care about what they deserve," said John. "I'm just like you, trying to do my job."

"Does government always roll over for you CIA guys?" The Customs man shook his head. "Even after I got a technical OK from our General Counsel, I asked around about doing this."

"Asked who?" said John. Evenly. Casually.

"Formally, I went up as high as the Director's office."

"And informally?"

"D.C. is a small town."

"Shall we call Senator Bauman and tell him you've been spreading his business all over Washington?"

The Customs man tapped his fingers on the manila file. "Why does he want this so bad?"

"Who knows why a Senator wants what he wants?"

"Is this a first step that's going to turn into a parade marching all over our people?"

"I don't know," said John. He shook his head: "Between you and me, I don't think so. You know Bauman."

The Customs man glared at John. Gave him the file.

"We'll c.c. that to relevant offices," he told John.

"Before you do anything unasked with a United States Senator's request, I suggest you get his permission—in writing."

John stood to leave.

"What is this all about?" asked the Customs man.

"I'm just the errand boy," said John.

The closest privacy was a bench in the deserted American History Museum across the street. The Smithsonian guards paid him no mind. Neither did the few museum visitors.

The Customs Service letter to Senator Bauman—addressed via Frank—read:

> . . . per your request, a search of all Customs Service records of inspection show our inspectors logged only one international shipment from or to Imex, Inc., in the last six months. On 7 December of last year, from the Port of Baltimore, our port authorities reviewed documentation for a shipment of controlled material from Imex, Inc., to the Kuwaiti Military Engineer Corps. The material was aboard a Panamanian-registry freighter named *La Espera*, with a transshipment point of Port Said, Egypt. The cargo's DSP-9 form from the Department of State's Office of Defense Trade Controls and the disembarkment-point American Embassy approval/acknowledgment sign-off for the shipment were reviewed and found appropriate. No physical examination of the cargo was deemed necessary, espe-

cially given our ongoing budget constraints limiting available personnel.

A copy of the Defense Trade Controls' DSP-9 was not attached, but a copy of the two-sentence letter from the American Embassy in Egypt was. That letter said only that the embassy knew of the Imex cargo being transshipped through Egypt to Kuwait—content unspecified—and had no objection. An embassy political consul signed the letter:

Martin Sinclair.

Who'd returned Frank's phone call nine days before.

John used the pay phones on the museum wall. The State Department Locator verified Martin Sinclair's employment, gave John a Washington phone number for him.

"Undersecretary Victor Martinez's office," said the woman who answered that phone.

"Quick question," said John. "I'm c.c.'ing a memo to Martin Sinclair, and I don't have his exact office address."

"No wonder," she said. "He transferred back here so fast, his paperwork is still catching up."

She told him an office number on the second floor of the State Department.

Another quarter linked John to an acquaintance who worked in the State Department. John said he might drop by soon and asked the man to clear him with security. The man was puzzled, but agreed: after all, John was part of the big us.

You're too busy to worry when I don't show up, thought John. Too busy to check with the door guards, find out I entered the building anyway. And the security logs will link my visit to you, not Martin Sinclair.

The State Department is decades more modern than the mountainous block that houses Customs. State has a 1950s feel, a jumble of boxes, flat concrete and steel molding, sealed-glass windows with closed green venetian blinds, low white soundboard ceilings in tiled corridors marked by yellow, gray and blue wall stripes. The doors are blond wood.

The men in the halls were handsome, dignified, visibly busy, most in suits or colored shirts, ties and suspenders. John saw one man hand another a document, heard: "That'll shake up the slots." Both men laughed. In one corridor, John smelled popcorn. He saw a dozen women in the halls, most in serious wool business suits of gold and brown or black, their hair carefully coiffed. All but one of the women wore panty hose that sheathed their legs like thick milk.

Two men in their 50s walked out of Undersecretary for Agricultural Development and Global Drought and Famine Relief Affairs Victor Martinez's office as John entered. One man told the other: "Well, I'm certainly glad of that. I can't imagine your face as you testified."

Inside Martinez's suite of offices, the receptionist pointed toward a closed door, reached for a phone, but John told her not to bother, his old friend Martin was expecting him.

John knocked softly on that office door—more for the receptionist than whoever waited inside. John was already turning the knob when a voice beyond the door told him to *come in.*

"Martin Sinclair?" said John as he entered, shut the door.

"Yes—you the guys with the papers from the landlord?"

Sandy-haired Martin Sinclair had 30 on his horizon. His shirt was white, his tie striped. He wore tortoiseshell glasses.

"No." John flashed credentials: "I'm with the CIA."

Sinclair blinked.

Whispered: *"Leave me alone!"*

The office was a jumble of unpacked boxes. One shelf overflowed with reports, another held only a fading black-and-white photograph of six men crewing a skiff over collegiate waters. A picture of a smiling blonde wife holding a laughing baby girl hung on the wall.

"I'm not here to bring you trouble," said John.

"Tell me another lie."

"You're—"

"We know what I am."

"You were a political consul in the Egyptian embassy."

"There were a half dozen political consuls in Cairo."

John frowned: "Are you one of us?"

CIA intelligence officers often work under State Department cover.

"Not even in hell."

"You signed an approval/acknowledgment letter—"

"I signed a lot of letters, that was my job."

". . . for a company called Imex, back in—"

"What is this? Some kind of test?"

"What?"

"You go to hell. All of you."

"All I want to know is—"

Pain ferried the laugh that escaped from Sinclair.

"What you don't know won't hurt you," he said.

"I'm worried more about you than me."

"Right. You and the last guy."

"Frank Mathews."

"And I told him exactly what I'm telling you: nothing."

"He's dead."

Sinclair shrank into his chair. "That's not my concern."

"It's mine," said John. "Cliff Johnson, the president of that company you processed paper for, he's dead, too."

Sinclair trembled: "Lot of death in this world."

"The smart thing to do is—"

"It's too late for the smart thing, isn't it?"

"No."

"Sure it is. Tell your masters I just want to be left alone. Please. I'm already alone. So I guess it's the hell with you. As long as I stay who I am, and I can't change that, can I?"

"You're not making sense."

Martin Sinclair tossed his glasses on the desk, stood.

"If you're here on business with the Undersecretary, I'll see you in his office. If you're here for anything else, you're wasting your time. Who can afford to waste time?"

Sinclair walked out of his office.

Two minutes later, John left the State Department. He caught a cab in the half-moon driveway out front, mumbled the address for a jazz bar on the edge of Georgetown.

In the dry heat of the cab, the driver wore white muslin, a stocking cap, a wool muffler. He had dark brown skin and thick black hair. Despite the gray sky, he wore black plastic sunglasses.

"The weather we are having this morning was cold," said the driver. "Like now, but more."

"Where are you from?" said John.

"Pakistan, sir."

"Where in Pakistan?"

"Lahore."

The image of Lahore's train station shimmered in John's mind: dust, women yelling at children, soldiers with assault rifles and no smiles.

When the cab stopped and John leaned over the front seat to pay, he noticed the cabbie's foot on the accelerator was bare.

The jazz bar fed him a cheeseburger, a fuel fill-up that didn't dent John's churning mind. Around the corner, he found a pay phone. Dialed the Virginia number he'd memorized.

The phone rang once. Twice. Three times.

The phone clicked.

Silence.

A faint whisper of breath from the man who'd slid open the desk drawer, pressed the receiver against his ear and merely *waited*. Patiently waited.

"Do you know who this is?" John finally said.

"Yes," said Harlan Glass.

"We have to talk."

"Are you all right?"

"Earlier today I had a temperature."

"Are you still warm?"

"No. I took very good precautions."

"I dislike the phone," said Glass.

They agreed to meet at the theater of the dead.

23

They walked the big circle over a floor of smooth white stones. Cold wind whistled through the pillars and billowed over the sunken amphitheater. No one sat in the rows of backless stone benches. No one orated from the quarried cave of a stage. Above them curved gray sky.

"Everything's wrong," John told Glass. "The surface seems legit, logical. Safe. But the center isn't there."

"Figure you're right," said Glass.

"And all the world around me is mad? Or wrong? Or a lie?"

"All the world around *us*." Glass sighed.

Between the pillars John saw bare trees, fields of brown sod, a sea of white stone markers.

Arlington Cemetery's memorial amphitheater sits on a hill above the graves of Presidents and paupers. In a few weeks, spring would lure crowds to these acres of graves across the river from Washington. That March day, except for the dress-uniformed soldier performing his bayoneted-rifle sentry duty with measured steps and clicking heels, John and Harlan Glass walked alone with the dead.

"How frightened is this Martin Sinclair?" said Glass.

"So scared he runs from questions," said John.

"Perhaps that'll change."

"Maybe. He's shaky."

"Until we can find a way to make his terror work for us," said Glass, "don't do anything to make him crack."

"I could—"

"You could set him off so he'd explode in our faces." Glass shook his head. "For now, leave him alone. We'll handle him when it's time. Soon, but not now."

In his tan nylon raincoat, John shuddered. Glass saw his chill: "Say it."

"The Agency nightmare. Frank bumped into something. Whatever it was made him . . . He went under, started a private op."

"To what end?"

"The end he'd lived for. Information. Truth."

"How far did he get?"

"When his routine queries disappeared at Langley, what trust he had of the system evaporated. That included trusting you."

"Frank couldn't even trust me," said John. "We were partners. Basic spy think: your greatest danger and the most logical traitor is the closest person with the most means to effect your betrayal. He sanitized and buffered himself and his op. What I've found indicates that in the least, he dummied queries from Senator Bauman to open official doors."

"Fool! He could have been fired—maybe prosecuted for fraud or forgery, misuse of government office."

"Frank was no fool," said John. "To risk all that, what he was after had to be big. As chaotic as Bauman's staff is, as wacky as the Senator is, Bauman was ripe for co-optation. My guess is Frank'd realized he'd fallen in over his head, was about to risk grabbing for help—starting with me, but . . . too late."

"And all he's left us is Martin Sinclair. A 'controlled' cargo shipped to Kuwait via Egypt. That dead man Cliff Johnson."

Glass frowned. "You can't figure data without context. Plus now Korn has Frank's files."

"I think Korn was tipped before Frank died," said John. "Korn is ex-Secret Service. Frank jerked Customs' chain, and Customs and Secret Service are both part of Treasury. Somebody from Treasury might have whispered in Korn's ear. They wouldn't tell him everything, but they'd hint enough to try to cover their ass. Enough to trigger his suspicions about Frank—and me as his partner, enough to think we were running an op off Capitol Hill."

"Smart," said Glass.

"Nobody's been stupid so far."

The marble was hard and cold under John's shoes.

"Frank never figured the opposition he'd bumped into was so serious," said Glass. "Never figured they would go so far as to kill him to cover them."

From the other side of the amphitheater, at the Tomb of the Unknown Soldier, came the sound of a bugler blowing taps.

"You believe me now," said John. "Believe Frank was hit."

"Our beliefs aren't enough," answered Glass.

They walked in silence.

"Frank must have really had somebody nailed for them to kill him," said John.

"No, but he must have been close. So they killed him. Can you uncover all the trail he left?"

"Can you help me?" asked John. "File checks, computer—"

"No. Even if there weren't a hundred eyes watching my every move, even if we could trust our own Agency . . . there's an operational logic for you to proceed as Frank did. With our key exception of you not going it alone."

"Everywhere I go," said John, "I'm a step behind somebody or somebody's a step behind me."

"Korn's Office of Security?" asked Glass. "Or . . ."

"Or. Or maybe it *is* Korn and maybe he's also no angel."

Glass frowned. Kept walking. "That detective, Greene, has formally requested to interview you about Frank's death."

"I thought—"

"That we shut them down? The General Counsel's Office is stalling, but . . . Police blundering could cause this to explode. Find its way into the press, burn us and let whoever killed Frank cover his tracks, escape. Avoid this . . . Detective Greene."

"Believe me, I'm trying."

"Worse news: Korn has demanded all your files from Person-

nel, from Operations and from the Inspector General's Office.
Raw data as well as finished reports. The Hong Kong investigation."

They took a dozen steps in silence.

John stared at graves: "There's nothing I'm ashamed of in
those files."

"Certainly nothing unknown." Glass added: "In the files."

The wind cut through John's raincoat.

"Will he get them?" asked John.

"Life is a question of timing." Glass smiled. "The only copy of
the Hong Kong file is in Operations. Our old Directorate. Established security procedures prevent its dispersal. Korn got permission to get a copy—but the copy machine in the vault where
the file must remain . . . broke down.

"Today's Friday," said Glass. "You know the problems with
service technicians, working weekends, the orders from the Director and the Office of Management and Budget about over-
time. Korn may not get your file until, say, Tuesday. Late
Tuesday."

"Does he know you've . . ."

"You only know what you can prove." Glass shrugged.

"Are you being very careful?" he asked John.

"Part of a recon patrol's job is to draw fire so the enemy can be
located," answered the spy who'd served as a soldier.

"They'll let you run until they know how far you can go," said
Glass. "If they're smart."

Wind rushed over the sea of gravestones.

"Are you being careful?" asked John.

"Figure as long as you make no mistakes, I'll be safe. As long
as I'm safe, you've got a chance and we can do this."

John leaned against a stone banister between two columns.
Beyond the trees was the river, and beyond that, the city.

A crow cut a black line across the gray-cloud sky.

"Ain't nobody loves you when you're down-and-out." John
smiled wryly. "My mentor even left town."

"Do you know where Woodruff went?" asked Glass.

"No."

"Neither do I."

"But at your level, you should! Does . . . anybody in Operations or Korn . . . you and me—"

"Figure it's just business as usual, not that they know about us," said Glass. "The established Directorates keep the Centers as much in the dark as they dare. Figure that way, they can hold on to their power base in the budget."

"I don't like this," said John. "Doing this. Thinking like this. Talking like this."

"Who said life should be a question of what we like?"

John stared at the natty bulldog man: "How far out of Operations have they cut you?"

"They still have hope for me," said Glass. "Think that I'll come to my senses and return to the fold—as if I've become some sort of heretic for taking over CTC and trying to make it . . .

"Figure I have . . . friends there. Abilities no one could guess."

"Why was—is—Director Allen so . . . *deflective* about Ahmed Naral?"

"Sources and methods," said Glass. "Figure we have to guard them with—"

"But why about Naral? It's not like he's a nobody—or was a nobody. Now Allen says . . . for our purposes . . . Naral is dead."

"So now he's dead," said Glass. "Finally."

"Not like in Beirut in the bad old days," said John.

"Why do you say that?"

"You're a legend."

"Legends are lies."

"Woodruff told me. About you and Jerry Barber."

Glass looked away.

"Beirut was Naral's base. Woodruff was there. So was Allen. Were they—was Allen—working Naral?"

"Figure you know where you're going? Or are you just shooting in the dark?"

"I'm shooting wherever I can."

"That might be a good idea."

The wind blew around them.

"Figure back then, we were all working compartmentalized. Plus what we did and what we reported—you know how it is— different things. I wasn't partnered with them. It was me and . . . Me and Jerry."

"Senator Handelman brought up Naral," said John. "Allen danced around—in the hearing, then on the list Bauman made me—"

"Yes, I know about your visit to the Task Force."

"Can you find out about Naral?"

"Can you find out why Senator Handelman cares?" said Glass, and John looked away. "Not overtly. Figure it's his staff anyway. Not his Committee-assigned guy, but that woman North . . ."

"No," said John.

"Figure we need to know."

"I hate this," said John. "Our work's never easy. There's two sets of rules for Uncle Sam's spies: rules for what we do to targets overseas. And rules that make us the same as everybody else when we're in the States. Rules within those rules. Lines between our two worlds. But walking the lines—in this town, in this thing . . ."

"Borders are negotiations of convenience and power."

"My job—"

"Your job is to find out what we need to know to stay alive and keep the system safe."

"I don't like running intelligence operations in the Halls of the U.S. Senate. As . . . less than perfect as they are up there, they're supposed to be the good guys."

"You figure the people on Capitol Hill are the 'good' guys?"

"What they stand for."

"They stand for themselves," said Glass. "You get in the way of their campaign bus, they'll run you down like a white dog. Look around the Halls of Congress: what do you see? Roadkill."

"Think I'd rather stay fast on my feet than get behind the wheel of that bus."

"Figure both of us have got to do what we've got to do. For the good of everyone. For Frank. For ourselves."

A jetliner roared overhead.

"I'll do all I can," mumbled John.

"What will you do next?" asked Glass.

"One thing . . . one small thing bothers me."

"What?"

John shook his head.

"It's probably nothing," he said. "It's personal."

"Then you better be sure this is the time to pursue it," said Glass.

He stared off at the horizon. Repeated: "Time."

24

On the subway platform at Union Station, John dropped a quarter in a pay phone and counted the unanswered rings from the number he dialed: 19, 20, 21.

No answer.

No one there.

Good.

His watch said 2:33, Friday afternoon.

So much of life is a question of timing.

He doubted his watchers posted a team to surveil Union Station's Metro stop. Such manpower existed only in counterspy fantasies or in China or the USSR at the height of the Cold War.

But they could be on his car. John had parked close enough to the parking lot's attendant booth to make searching his car a high risk. But someone could have strolled past an indifferent college student attendant, ducked down to tie a shoe and slapped a magnetic trace beeper under John's bumper.

No one seemed to pay John any attention as he walked through Union Station. The loudspeaker announced the arrival of a 2:41 train from Boston. No one seemed to be loitering around the parking level for tour buses and Senate staff. A premed student at George Washington University was on duty in the attendant booth; she looked up from her chemistry text as John walked by, brushed her dreadlocks off her ebony forehead and returned to Boyle's law.

His dusty Ford was where he'd left it.

John ran his hand under the Ford's bumpers: found dirt.

Means only nothing *found*.

Car doors still locked. So was the glove compartment, where Frank's .45 awaited a strong hand, a squeezing finger.

No car appeared in John's mirrors when he drove out of Union Station. Drove past the intersection where a bullet shattered Frank's brain three days before. People loitered at the bus stop. A fat woman chattered on the pay phone John used to summon the CIA.

Grip the steering wheel. Drive on.

Run yellow lights, change lanes. Turn, speed five blocks to the east, pull into a driveway, back out, and double back.

Nobody there.

The District of Columbia became the state of Maryland; the only visible change was a street sign flitting past John's window. This is the era of the megapolis. Borders are negotiations of convenience and power. John drove past shopping plazas and gas stations. A fortress surrounded by acres of lawn with the look of a warehouse for the living dead. Franchised burger grease joints, gas stations.

A red light halted him at an intersection kitty-corner from a convenience store with a large parking lot. A herd of sons, husbands, brothers and fathers from Guatemala, El Salvador, Nicaragua and Mexico shuffled over that asphalt, white eyes flashing toward any vehicle that slowed. In the bitter wind, these men wore torn, ill-fitting clothes; some had no coats. At this afternoon hour, pessimism and luck had thinned the herd to these brave few who watched and waited for someone, anyone, to drive up and offer them below-union-scale wages for their muscle and sweat.

Green light. Turn left, drive away.

Only those men filled his mirrors.

Safe to head west, to Rockville Pike, his neighborhood. He drove to a covered municipal parking lot behind a three-story shopping center where in times past his *Pa-kua* and *Hsing-i* group used a mirrored dance studio to practice.

As John parked his car, Korn's question from that first, terrible day whispered in his memory:

"You've run agents in Thailand, Hong Kong. Look at Frank through a handler's prism. Anything unusual about him?"

When John walked out of the parking lot, his nylon coat buttoned against the cold, Frank's pistol was tucked inside his belt. Three blocks away, John found a pay phone by a Thai restaurant. Dialed the number and still got only unanswered rings.

Twenty minutes later, he walked up to Frank's front door, used the key he'd duplicated, and stepped inside.

Phuong wasn't there. She hadn't answered his calls.

The house was tidy. The only trace of her downstairs was a briefcase that she'd left on the desk.

Search her bags, the room she'd slept in, pat down clothes she —

No. Not her. Not that.

She'd told him she'd be in Baltimore, for dinner, maybe longer. She hadn't answered the phone when he'd called.

His watch read 4:10.

Plenty of time. He tossed his briefcase and nylon coat onto the couch, loosened his tie.

The pistol dug into his side.

Put it on the coffee table.

Memorize where everything is.

He stood on a kitchen chair, scanned the titles of the top row of videocassettes. Behind Frank's classic movies, John found the six "adult" cassettes.

He turned on the TV, the main VCR's power, turned the volume low. Stared at the secrets in his hands.

They didn't make sense—or rather, they didn't make sense for Frank, for the man John thought he knew.

". . . anything unusual . . ."

In one hand John held *Deep Throat*, whose star had the name of her cinematic sexual legend adopted as a code name for the second most famous secret in Washington and who, years after her movie was released, tearfully testified to Congress about being raped, beaten, degraded and soul-numbed on the way to fame. In his other hand, John held a movie that had cost its star a lucrative modeling career after the bubble bath company, who paid her to pose naked but strategically covered by their supermarket-shelved product, discovered that she had starred in a strategically explicit cinematic version of a typescript novella passed from furtive hand to furtive hand across the rigid landscape of 1950s America.

At least these two cassettes could claim some sort of twisted cultural value for a collector like Frank, thought John.

Set them on the coffee table.

Next to the gun.

Health Spa: too tragically predictable. On the coffee table. *Love Never Rusts:* too ridiculous a concept to face first.

Which left *Backstreet to Paradise,* with its cover shot of a naked back-to-shoulders, kneeling, curly-haired brunette, and *Exxiles,* on which a thick-lipped, sultry blonde pouted at the camera from her perch on a reversed wooden chair; she wore only a black garter belt, fishnet stockings and strapped high heels.

John loaded *Exxiles* into Frank's main VCR.

Credits listing implausible names. A platinum-dyed blonde wearing red lipstick and a crimson micro-dress kicked the flat tire of her sports car. She sported black high heels, fishnet stockings. A man wearing glasses offered to help her. They went to his apartment. He called a garage. Told her he was a poet. She said she was on the road because we all have to go as far as we can. They kissed. Under her red dress, she wore nothing but her black garter belt and fishnet stockings. He took off his glasses. She did things to him. He did things to her. Terrible music played. The living room. The bedroom. A woman wearing mechanic's overalls arrived . . .

Tight numbness held John; tingling nausea.

He felt removed.

Detached.

Bad enough to break into Frank's. To steal into his secrets, to watch . . .

What he saw. Heartless performances trapped and isolated in the flat, odorless, tasteless two dimensions of a screen.

Pulse beating hard, sure. Eyes burning, seeking, sure. But . . .

Empty. Makes me empty.

John fumbled with the master control wand until he found fast forward. A laugh escaped him as caricatures on the screen flew through gymnastic contortions: this work had not been part of his projections of a career in espionage.

The screen went dark; *Exxiles* was over.

His watch read 4:57.

Plenty of time. Then he could be through with this. Then he could leave. With secrets that left him no wiser, no safer, and certainly not cleaner.

He loaded *Backstreet to Paradise* into the VCR, sank into the couch.

Credits, no names he recognized, few he believed.

Already it's a lie. Not a fantasy, not fiction that reaches out to caress your soul, a lie.

Curly-haired brunette and a weight lifter on a bed. Naked. She had a tattoo on her right buttock, a blue and red butterfly. He had a mustache. They pulled apart. He paid her a compliment. She said gosh thanks. She told him what she wanted to do. Called it paradise. He said he'd never been there. I don't know how, he said. She knelt in front of him on the bed, leaned down on her elbows and raised her buttocks, said—

Frank's front door

Key turning in the lock.

Move get off the couch! Door swinging open—

Phuong walked in.

She saw John, said: "What the—"

John struggled to his feet, fumbled for the stop button on the remote control wand. Pushed the mute button: in the TV, sound died, but the action continued.

"John, why are you . . . How . . ."

She carried a brown sack of groceries; her eyes turned to the flickering TV set.

"Phuong! You're supposed to be—"

Her eyes widened as she saw what played in her father's TV; saw the coffee table covered with lurid cassette boxes.

"You . . . son of a bitch!" She yelled. "Sick, you sick—"

"Don't scream!" said John, remembering the old lady next door. He stepped toward Phuong.

She threw the bag of groceries at him.

He knocked the sack away. Out of it flew glass bottles of Coke, broccoli, meat packages, potatoes, a carton of eggs.

"Wait!" he said. "It's OK!"

She swung her purse by its strap.

John ducked, stepped back as it whirled around again; as she screamed wordlessly at him.

Grab the strap, pull.

But she let go and he swayed back.

She ran to the front door.

Catch her as she grips the doorknob.

"Fire!" she yelled.

Hand on her waist, one on her shoulder: pull.

She flew away from the door, staggered into the couch, fell backward, her black coat whirling around her, her blue-jean legs swinging down to find the earth, her hands slapping the couch, hitting the table.

Phuong grabbed the gun.

"Don't!" cried John.

He dropped to both knees, held his arms wide, *helpless see I'm helpless* as she scrambled to her feet. The black bore of the .45 found him. The gun trembled in her hand. She backed away, circled around the couch toward the desk, toward the telephone.

"You . . . You . . ."

"It's OK!"

"OK? OK? You're nice to me and I think . . . Then you break in here . . . You . . . Bring into *my house,* into *my father's house* . . . And a gun and it's OK? You asshole! You don't know who you're—"

"This isn't about me!"

"Oh, right, this isn't you, you're some cosmic asshole beamed down here by space aliens!"

"I'm just going to stand up." *Slowly, keep talking. Lie:* "My knees can't take—"

"You take one step, I'll blow your knees to hell!"

"I'm going nowhere!"

"No shit, asshole!"

"Listen to me!"

"Oh you're a great talker! But I see what you do!"

She backed toward the phone. Toward the police.

"Don't! Don't call anyone. Not until   "

"You don't tell me what to do! I got this," she shook the gun, "and that makes me in charge!"

The thumb safety—on. *If she knows how to work it, cock the gun, she's got three, maybe four shots before . . .*

"Don't fucking move!"

"I'm not moving!"

"You were moving! I saw you moving!"

"I'm not moving anymore!"

Twelve feet separated them, maybe more.

Time for two shots, maybe three.

"Who do you think you are!" Tears ran down her cheeks. "What do you think . . ."

Her hips brushed the desk. The phone was in her reach.

"I'm here for work. For the CIA. For your father's—"

"My father didn't do shit like this!"

"Just listen, please listen to—"

Her face was numb, blank.

Lost eyes, her mouth open. Staring past John to the TV.

Slowly, turn around, look at the screen.

Muted, silent, in color, a near-Christmas date subtitled on the bottom of the screen: a high fixed camera shot angled down, two men in a strange living room.

Fully clothed men, the back and shoulder of one sitting on a couch, another sitting nervously in an easy chair.

In Frank's house, the gun in Phuong's hand lowered to her

side. Eyes on the screen, John groped on the coffee table for the remote control wand, pushed the mute button off.

"—all new to me," said the man in the chair. He squirmed, his eyes boring into the man who sat on the couch.

"Everybody's got a first time," said the man on the couch. Only his shoulders and the back of his head were visible. He seemed to be wearing a black leather sports jacket. His brown hair was drawn back in a 1990s male chic rubber-banded rat tail.

Turn around, thought John. *Let's see your face.*

The video blinked off in a burst of black-and-white fuzz.

Blinked on: the same two men, same living room.

The man in the easy chair faced toward the camera. Closely styled hair, blue shirt, navy sports jacket, solid frame that had seen about four decades.

But you don't see the camera, thought John as he watched the man's eyes. They didn't flick toward the lens—or dodge it. He talked and moved like an Oscar-level actor. Or an unknowing star: *man in a chair.*

CHAIR MAN: "It's not that I'm not grateful for the business, I mean—"

His costar on the couch interrupted him; sat with his back to the camera.

COUCH MAN: "Glad to do it. We make a great relationship. You deserve—"

CHAIR MAN: "But see, the thing is this . . ."

He leaned across the coffee table. Couch Man leaned forward—

Black-and-white fuzz roared in the screen.

Phuong stood beside John. Her gun-heavy hand brushed his. They watched the fuzz blizzard whirl and swirl.

Blink back to two men in a living room. They leaned back in their seats.

CHAIR MAN: "—so I just like being sure is all."

COUCH MAN: "Everybody likes being sure. But you are, right?"

CHAIR MAN: "Sure. Sure, I guess. I'm sure."

COUCH MAN: "You got nothing to worry about. Already gone this far as smooth as shit, right?"

CHAIR MAN: "Right."

COUCH MAN: "The paperwork—"

CHAIR MAN: "Right."

Beer bottles stood on the coffee table between them. Daylight filled the window on one wall.

COUCH MAN (arms spreading wide—long white hands sticking out of definitely a black leather sports jacket): "I mean, you can't ask for much more in this kind of thing!"

Lean forward! thought John. *Face the camera!*

CHAIR MAN: "I know I have to ask for whatever I—"

COUCH MAN: "That's smart. That's being a good businessman. That's why we went to you."

CHAIR MAN: "I—"

COUCH MAN: "You're a guy who holds his mud. That's why you're where you are."

CHAIR MAN: "And this thing, the whole thing: totally sanctioned."

COUCH MAN: "Sanctioned to the max. After all, that guy we met, right?"

CHAIR MAN: "Right, and—"

Blink off.

Blur of black-and-white fuzz.

Blink on, smear into a tight shot of the ecstatic face of the woman with the butterfly tattoo. The camera pulls back to show her on her hands and knees, hips rocking back and forth against a skinny man John had never seen and she was saying yes un-huh yes.

As the man and woman on the bed moaned, Phuong whispered: "What . . . what's that?"

John smiled, hard and tight: "Call it a preview of coming attractions."

25

"Did you kill him?" said Phuong as they sat at the dining nook table in her father's house. Curtains hid the glass door leading to the backyard.

"I've never killed anybody," said John.

"Did you kill my father?"

"No."

The pistol and videocassette boxes lay on the coffee table. The TV screen was dark.

"Who did?" said Phuong.

"I don't know."

A pool of Coke from broken bottles and shattered eggs congealed on the kitchen tiles close to their chairs.

Tell her: "The best thing you can do is get on a plane—"

"I got on a plane. Came here. Because somebody murdered my father. No 'urban tragedy.' Murder. A wet job. A hit. Your fucking CIA lies to me—"

"They didn't lie to you."

"What?"

"I can't tell you more."

"Can't—bullshit: you won't tell me. Your choice."

"My job."

"My father. My life. The hell with your job."

She leaned back in her chair, narrowed her eyes.

"How much trouble do you think I could make?" she said. "Cops? Newspapers? Congress?"

He sighed: "A lot. Your father wouldn't want that."

"Yeah, well, we can't ask him, can we?"

But her tone was softer. Her eyes dropped.

"I'm not walking away," she whispered.

Believe that. Believe her.

"If you tell anyone anything," said John, "you'll start an avalanche of lies and—"

"I haven't exactly been overwhelmed by honesty."

Outside, streetlights glowed.

"It's that damn tape," said Phuong.

They'd watched the segment of the two men in the living room again.

"I think that's part of it."

"You think? How comforting. Tell me what you know."

"If I do, then you're at risk."

"I saw that videotape. My innocence is already lost."

"That's not enough to sanction your removal for anyone."

"You must not be as smart as my father thought."

"You said he didn't talk about me."

"At Christmas, he said he worked with a good man."

Gotta give her something. Give her just enough.

"Your father . . . Frank accidentally discovered something. He was chasing it on his own."

"Because he didn't trust the Agency."

"Because he didn't know who he could trust."

"Not even you."

John shook his head.

"Yet I'm supposed to trust you."

"What would your father want you to do?"

Phuong walked into the kitchen, looked at the yellow walls.

"He'd want me to run," she said. "Far and fast."

"That's the best idea."

She shook her head. "Nowhere to run to. All this would still be here. How did he get that videotape?"

"I don't know."

"Was it . . . all together like that?"

"I don't think so." John nodded toward the wall of videocassettes, the two VCRs. "I think he had a cassette that was just—"

"Those two guys talking."

"Yes. Then he copied it into that movie."

"Why that movie?"

"The best place to hide a secret is inside another secret."

"The best place to hide a secret," said Phuong, "is inside a truth. What are you hiding?"

"From you? Nothing I don't need to protect in order to keep you safe."

"That's a bullshit answer."

"It's the truth."

"Like I said . . ." Phuong trailed off. "The pictures of me, my father, prepping the house—"

"For a shake," said John. "Your dad knew he'd moved into the target zone. Wanted to be sure you were safe."

Phuong said: "But me, my pictures . . . Just taking them off the walls here, it's not like I don't exist anywhere else."

"There's an answer for that, too."

"You have an answer for everything?"

"Not by a long shot."

Phuong looked away and John cursed his choice of metaphor.

He said: "An inside-the-Agency player might be able to pull your pictures—at least old ones—out of your dad's personnel file. If they knew where you lived, they could always get a fax of your driver's license picture."

"Doesn't even look like me," she said.

"Probably looks close enough," said John. "But never mind how you look: stripping you out of the house creates the impression you weren't important to him. And, if a hunter doesn't have access to Frank's CIA file, a confirmed picture of you might be hard to find."

"Never mind me," she said. "That . . . movie. What about—"

"He copied a video into a 'dirty' movie," said John, "hid that movie with others like it. He bought all of them for cover, figuring whoever tossed this place would find that 'secret' but ignore it because it wasn't a secret they were looking for."

"Where's the original tape?"

"My guess is someone got here before us, found it. Frank probably hid it with the others so they would be satisfied with finding just it."

She looked at the man sitting at the table in the place her father had called home.

"You don't know much more than I do," she said. "But you know who those guys are on the tape, what they're talking about."

Easy: if you lie, and she senses that . . .

"I don't *know*—"

"Bullshit!"

"Listen to me: I don't *know* for certain much more than what you've seen about that tape. *Know.* As in able to prove. Or convince someone else who has less faith without more evidence."

"Try my faith," she said.

"The guy in the chair? I think I know who he is."

"Who?"

"I think he's a dead man named Cliff Johnson."

"Who's the other guy?"

"I *think* he's the guy who set up this surveillance tape. Edited it to remove any shots of his face, got it to your father.

"I remember what he said when we were driving to work," said John. "What he started to explain. How these days reminded him of '72—the year of Watergate. Secret tapings—that living room isn't the White House, but—"

"But it's how my dad might think."

"Yes."

"The tape—"

"A preview," said John, "a tease.

"But not for you," he said. "Go back to Chicago now. Get all the cash you can, fast, buy a ticket, use a phony name, take a trip. No credit cards, tell nobody. Call me when you get back. By then—"

"By then, nobody will care. The dirt will be solid on Dad's grave."

"I won't let him die betrayed," said John.

"Too late." Phuong wandered into the living room. "He didn't talk much about his work. But he loved it. He knew it made a difference, didn't always like the difference it made. But he said that if you aren't willing to fight in the least-bad army, then the worst armies win. Did you know he'd been a Marine pilot?"

"Yes."

"He loved the Corps. *Semper fi,* always faithful. He thought that's what life comes down to: being faithful. Putting yourself on the right line no matter . . ."

Phuong stared at the shelves of classic cassettes. "You know why he liked old movies?"

"No."

"He thought that if he absorbed popular culture, he'd understand America more. He was proud to be an American, but he said he'd lost the feel of being one.

"Plus, in movies there are clear lines and clean battles. The kind he grew up believing in. Not like in this world."

She stared at the curtains closed over the glass door.

"This is where we are," said John.

"Yes," she said. "You said the Agency didn't lie to me. So they don't think my father was killed."

"That's right."

"Then you're not working for them. Then they don't know about this. Who are you?"

"If I tell you more . . . "

"If you don't, you'll have to kill me."

Flat out. No bullshit. No middle road.

Don't lie. Don't hold back.

Because she'll hear your lies. Fly off on her own. Because she deserves . . .
Because.

The bullet. The Agency's response. Cliff Johnson, blown up in Paris. Glass. Frank's missing queries and the phony Senator letter he'd rigged. The unknown cargo to Kuwait and Martin Sin-

clair. The men in the blue sedan. Detective Greene. The layered
steel logic of the crisis.

Everything tumbled out.

Except Emma.

Not important, Emma. Not here. Really. Truly.

"Whoever killed my father is going to die."

"You're not an assassin. Neither am I."

"I can do what I have to do."

"And live with it?"

"On my soul? Sure. I didn't believe in religion, not the nuns',
not Buddha, not karma, not Christ, not any big-time God."

Look at her: "That's a lie."

Her lip trembled: "Maybe. But it's my lie."

"There's more to justice than death."

"I'll take everything I can get. And if you don't help me find
out what happened to my dad—"

"Find out? Just find out?"

"—then the hell with you.

"I grew up in this life," she said. "You had to be taught. Don't
whine to me about danger. I don't give a damn—besides, I'm already on that line, aren't I? Don't argue about training. I know
about compartmentalization, working half-blind, living half-
deaf, following rules nobody else sees."

"There's nothing for you to do," said John.

"I'm the witness," she said. "Making sure that all that gets
buried of my father is his bones."

Change-up, catch her: "Why didn't you go to Baltimore?"

She picked her purse off the floor, dropped a piece of paper
from it on the table.

"That's the old lady's name and number. Call her. She called
me, said she had a cold, asked for a rain check."

The paper lay in front of him.

"I believe you," he said.

She tucked the piece of paper in his shirt pocket. Her fingers
brushed his chest.

"You shouldn't," she said. "Now, why should I trust you?"

"It's the best idea," he said.

"So was America going into Vietnam," she told him. "Look where that got us."

"Here," he said.

"Give me a reason to trust you when my father didn't."

John put the gun in her hands.

"That was another secret of your father's," he said. "You got it, you got his tape. You can cut and run on me any way you want. But you're smarter than that. I give you my trust."

"So I'll give you mine?" she said. "Not good enough."

She cradled the gun in the palm of her hand.

"I had this before and didn't use it. You're playing the odds. And you're willing to die—though you'd go down fighting. That'd be clean for you. Give me something that's not so easy. Something that hurts. Give me a secret."

"I already told you—"

"Not about this. Not about my dad. About you."

"What? Do you want to know who I—"

"You know what to tell me." She stared at him. "I'm a Langley Brat. I know about running agents. Commitment is the key. For some it's fear or love. Ideology, greed. Ambition. Vengeance. Envy. Hope. Anything that races the human heart. For some people, it's the handler knowing them more than anybody ever has. Even saints have dirty secrets. A man like you must have a dozen sins nailed to his heart."

"And I should give one to you?"

"You want my trust, give me something in return. Something that counts. Commit. Or you lose me."

They sat at the dining room table.

John stared at the painting of the movie theater on her father's wall.

She waited, silently. He admired her patience.

She means it. Gamble. Got to.

"I told you I was a NOC," he said. "Deep-cover spy."

"Thailand, Hong Kong," said Phuong.

"China was my target. My cover in Hong Kong was good, but

I should have hung out a sign—CIA agent, here to kick communism. Recruits would have beaten down my door. After being
locked out of China from World War II through the 1970s, in
the 1980s the CIA flooded in. It wasn't just the secret protocols
between the U.S. and China dating back to Nixon, secret deals
to counter the Soviets, to end the war in Vietnam. Or the collapse of Soviet communism. The dragon, the great Chinese
dragon, was stirring in its cave. Change, democracy.

"By 1989, I was running fourteen agents in the Mainland,
with a lot of face time in Hong Kong. Two of my recruits were
in Tewu, their intelligence service: liberals in Tewu tried to save
the democracy movement from getting crushed in Tiananmen
Square by the Army and the hard-liners."

"And failed."

"Eventually. But at the first . . . Even in Hong Kong, the
crowds rallied, hoping that this revolution finally might defeat
history, free China, keep it one strong nation. With good
dreams."

"You did something," said Phuong.

"When Tiananmen Square filled, nobody—not Langley, not
the Chinese secret police or Tewu—nobody knew what would
happen. Revolutions write their own history.

"I wasn't the only case officer with people there," said John.
"CIA had lots of HUMINT—fax machines, for Christsake. Plus
ELINT—electronic intercepts, satellites . . . We knew the odds
were high that there'd be a bloodbath. Half of my people were
safely out of China. We needed more intel. I sent them back in.
Their commitment was hope and trust in me. I used it like a
pro."

"And then tanks rolled over everything," she said.

"My orders were damage control. Disassociate. Don't give the
hard-liners a foreign devil to rally the masses against. Sound ad-
vice, good policy."

"That you ignored," said Phuong.

"I stole $74,000 in black money, operational funds. Conned

an American tourist into letting me take his place on a package tour of China, and went in."

"To get your people out?"

"To give them the only help I could: money.

"We'd set up . . . I got word to a few of them. Guilin is a tourist town for both Chinese and foreigners. Non-Chinese get stuck on monitored tours, no wandering around, only approved hotels. Tour the limestone caves, the embroidery factory . . .

"And go for a cruise-boat ride down the River Li. The river cuts through granite mountains that stick up through mist like the fingers of a thousand giants poking through the earth."

"I've seen paintings like that," said Phuong. "I thought they were Chinese impressionist art."

"They're like photographs," said John.

"The Army forgot to shut down all the tours outside of Beijing, or the orders had gotten lost or whatever. One of my assets made it to Guilin, so did I. He stood on one side of the boat as we glided down the river, I stayed on the other. I taped the money under the boat's bathroom sink. Flew back to Hong Kong. Eventually, two of my people bribed their way out."

"What did the Agency say?"

"If the Chinese would have caught me, I'd have been a disaster for U.S. policy. Even as a NOC, sanitized from Operations, I knew plenty the CIA doesn't want out. The Chinese can sweat a prisoner as good as anyone. Plus the embezzlement, losing professional objectivity, going off on my own, cowboy crazy . . . But two of our people got out because of me, so my 'rebellion' became a 'remarkable success.' I got a medal."

"What didn't you tell the CIA?"

John looked at her: "What do you know?"

"You," she said.

"One of my agents was named Wei. We were lovers. I never told the Agency because . . . I did't want them to exploit it."

"Did you love her?"

John looked at the table, then back into Phuong's eyes.

"She was magnificent. Brave. Smart. We were in something

together that was bigger than both of us, conspiring together, sharing, trusting . . ."

"Did you love her?"

"You tell me what that means."

She said: "What happened to her?"

"One man was caught, broken. Piecing together that I'd recruited him led the Chinese to eight others. They all got the pistol behind their neck. Three we don't know about."

"Wei?"

"Yes. For sure."

"I'm sorry."

"My cover was blown. Antireformists took over Tewu. The Chinese tagged me in Hong Kong, took my picture. In every country where they had an embassy, Tewu gave the host security service a copy. They burned me—globally."

"You never told the CIA about Wei."

"Sufficient truth."

"Sufficient for you."

"And for them. Even with a medal instead of an indictment, it was bad enough that I was burned. The truth would have twisted to show me embezzling money for the woman I was fucking. I would have been an agent who went native, who went cowboy, who lost control, who was a crook, who went bad."

"They'd still think that. Plus the lies you've told to cover yourself."

"Yes," said John. "And if the institution is forced to confront their failure to catch me, they'd need revenge."

He looked at her.

"Is any of that true?" she asked.

"All of it."

"Then you were ready-made for this mess, weren't you?"

He blinked.

"And now I'm part of it," said Phuong. "You got no other choice."

Best deal. Only deal. For now.

Cut it finer, hard: "OK, I'll take you on. As the witness. Otherwise, you don't exist. You know nothing, you say nothing to anyone, now or ever. You do what I want. No questions, no quarrels. Where and how I lead, you follow."

"Long as you're going the right way."

She nodded and he felt himself reply in kind. She said. "You need to do something right now."

Phuong set her father's gun on the table between them. "Teach me how this works."

26

Friday night. Cold. Empty. End of the real-world workweek.

John and Phuong used her father's two VCRs to copy the covert surveillance segment into three of his movies: *The Glass Key, Chinatown, The Big Sleep*.

He gave her *Chinatown*.

"Yours," said John. "Don't lose it."

Backstreet to Paradise and *The Glass Key* went into his briefcase. He mailed *The Big Sleep* to a CIA dead-drop address in San Francisco, sending it book rate and trusting the post office to take at least a week to deliver it. The contact at the accommodation address would forward the package unopened to Langley—at least another two days in transit—where it would end up on the desk of Harlan Glass at the Counter-Terrorism Center.

A double-safe backstop. Just in case.

But not active yet, thought John. Not yet.

They parked Phuong's rental car at a movie theater complex on Rockville Pike between Frank's house and John's cabin. John bought two tickets to the next movie, gave one to Phuong.

"I'll be back as soon as I can," he told her.

She went inside—she had her father's gun, a videocassette. He told her a bar she could meet him in if he didn't make it back before the movie finished.

"What if—"

"Then you're on your own."

He walked down dimly lit alleys and cut through yards to his neighborhood. Saw no watchers parked on the quiet streets.

Lights shone in his landlord's house. A metal sign stuck in the front yard said the property was protected by an armed-response private security company and electronic warning systems. John knew his landlord had stolen the sign, relied on that visible bluff to protect his property.

John hid *The Glass Key* in a bundle of paint tarps on a shelf in his landlord's unlocked garage.

Was certain no one saw him.

Found no one in the dark woods, watching his cabin.

Taped to his cabin door was a cheap shaker of cinnamon and Detective Greene's business card.

Inside the cabin, the message light on his answering machine flashed a three-beat signal.

Two hang-ups.

And Emma.

"Don't tell me you're at work," she said. "It's Friday night, a weekend. Got lots of time. Any suggestions on what we could do with it?"

He could feel her in his home.

So could anyone who heard her call.

John changed to old clothes, packed two suitcases with the minimum he'd need for a week. Donned his black mountaineering coat, turned out the lights, and left.

His shirt was soaked by the time he'd hiked back to the hotel and restaurant strip of Rockville Pike. He set his suitcase and briefcase down in a parking lot outside a deserted ice cream parlor, fed the pay phone.

Have to risk the line's not tapped.

"If this is a solicitation," said Emma when she answered her home phone, "the answer is no."

"It's me," said John.

"Then this better be a solicitation."

"What would the answer be?"

"I'm flexible," she said.

"I'm working," he answered.

Emma paused, said: "With anyone I know?"

In the parking lot shadows, John closed his eyes: "I'm alone."

"Your choice," said Emma. "I went to see you today, at the Committee office. You weren't there."

"I needed . . . some time for myself."

"Oh," she said. "Away from, ah, friends and distractions."

"No—I mean—kind of."

"Ambivalence doesn't become you. Or me. Or us. I don't need it."

John swallowed his heart: "Me either. But I need a favor."

"I think I'm reasonable. Accommodating. For a woman who hasn't gotten a call the next day, which just happens to be the start of a weekend. A weekend with two days. Three nights. The weather report says it's going to be cold . . ."

"Emma   "

"Cold sheets feel so good at first," she said.

"I have to work. All weekend." *Need to keep tabs on Phuong.*

"Oh." Emma's voice carried the night's chill.

"I'm sorry," he said.

"Figures," she said. "This town always wins. Why can't we have real jobs in Cincinnati, nine-to-five?"

"Is that what you want?"

"Do you want me to tell you what I want?" she said.

"I . . ."

"Don't fold."

"Tell me later," he said.

"Promise?"

"Sure," he said, and he meant it, but again he said: "I need a favor."

"I don't do laundry," she said. "Not on the second date."

"Could you . . . do another kind of research for me?"

"You're 'working' all weekend. You guys 'across the river' have the best research facilities in the world. Why are you asking me to—"

"Part of the favor is you don't ask."

"Then you're asking an awful lot," she said.

"I need you to trust me."

"If I didn't, do you think I would have . . . But if this touches our professional . . . John, you better trust *me*."

"If I didn't trust you, I couldn't have called."

"Couldn't?"

"Please, Emma: everything's OK, it's no big deal."

"This isn't the kind of bullshit I expected from you."

Wait. Let her move. Let her settle.

"Shit," she finally said. "What do you want this time?"

"A Dun & Bradstreet report on a business called Imex. Anything else you can—"

Her voice turned cold: "What are you doing, John?"

"It's not—"

"That's the company run by that man killed in Paris. Don't tell me this is 'personal'—that could be bad, too: like helping you with your 'stock portfolio.' Like—"

"Emma, I'm sorry, I—"

"Don't play me. Don't burn me at work, John. Bad enough if you . . . Don't burn me at work. What I do is too—"

"I wouldn't compromise you. Ever."

"Ever?"

"Don't do it if you think I might."

"Might what? Might what, John?"

"I don't want to have to ask. I won't ask you anymore. What I need isn't . . . unethical—"

"That's debatable," she said. "Using Congressional—"

"Just you and me, Emma. Nobody else. No one will ever know."

"You mean I shouldn't tell anyone. Trust you and deceive . . . whoever. Why do you want this, John? What is it really for? For who?"

"It's for me, Emma. Bottom line, it's for me."

She said nothing for a long time.

"You wouldn't ask if it didn't matter, and if it matters—"

"Forget it," he said.

"— if it matters, if you matter, if I trust you . . .

"OK," she whispered. "OK. I'll do it Monday."

"I owe—"

"Don't say that," she said. "If this is a do-for-you so you'll do-for-me, then it's like anything else in this town, and then it's wrong, and then I won't do it."

John closed his eyes, leaned his head against the pay phone. Said, "You're incredibly special."

"Then treat me that way."

She listened to his silence.

Said: "Guess this weekend, I'll have to rent a bunch of romantic movies, hunker down in front of the VCR by myself."

"Sounds nice," he said.

"Come see me. You can choose the movie. Or better yet, make our own movie."

He told her good-bye. Then said: "One more thing."

"Yes?" she whispered.

"Don't call my home, leave a message."

"You know," she said, "if you weren't a spy, I'd say you were a son of a bitch."

She hung up first.

A car drove by the parking lot: a woman's laughter echoed inside the fogged windows.

Do it.

He dialed the number on the piece of paper Phuong gave him; the line rang a dozen times before he hung up.

An old lady. Sick. Probably just not answering.

After they ate a silent restaurant meal, Phuong followed him with her rental car to a quiet street a mile from Frank's house. John parked his own vehicle. When he got his Ford out of the parking lot, there'd been no visible tail, but he didn't want to store his car too close to Phuong in case someone had wired it with an electronic tracer. At her father's house, Phuong offered him Frank's bed; he chose the couch, blankets and a pillow. He heard her lock the door of the pink bedroom.

John put *Backstreet* in the VCR, kept the sound low. He sat on the couch, playing and rewinding and fast-forwarding. He watched the two strangers talk, looking for anything to explain what he was seeing, what it meant, why . . .

. . . *Hard-fast alert, heart pounding:* dark room, TV on.

Exhaustion and the anesthetization of seeing the same scene over and over again had ambushed him with sleep. On the screen, a naked dyed platinum blonde was kissing her way down the chest of a skinny man.

John's watch said 1:02. Frank's house was silent except for low moans in the television. John turned off the machine, closed his eyes.

Didn't know where dreams ended and nightmares began.

Saturday morning it snowed enough to dust the tiny lawn outside the sliding glass back door.

John and Phuong sat at the table. A robin back from the South too soon hopped across the white-crystaled grass. John saw Phuong smile. They divided up the newspapers, drank coffee, read the news, *oh boy*, in silence.

Took turns showering.

Then watched all of the *adult* movies Frank had used for camouflage to be certain he'd hidden nothing else in their secret. They spent five hours at it. Phuong sat in one corner of the couch. John in the other.

After twenty minutes of staring at the screen, silence settled between them.

They found nothing unexpected.

"I've got to get out of here," said Phuong when the last tape was finished. "Are you going to insist on coming with me?"

"No."

She pulled on her coat and gloves. Turned to look at him: "Should I make you come with me?"

"Not if you trust me."

She nodded; said: "Do you want to get out of here, too?"

They took her car.

No one seemed to follow them.

Phuong drove to an arboretum with acres of open grass. A

pagoda overlooked a man-made lake covered with a thin sheet of ice.

"Geese come here in the summer," she said as they leaned on the pagoda railing, looked back over the empty fields, the quiet lake. "Under the ice are thousands of giant goldfish."

It started to snow.

"I loved my father," she said.

"I loved mine, too."

"Does it scare you? The thought of being dead?"

Snowflakes landed on her ebony hair.

"No," said John. "The big change that scares me . . . I grew up in one place. The same white house with a blue shingle roof in an American town where change never came. Before TV made every place alike, that place was special. The land is so stark it's bigger than anything. That's where the ghost of who I was lives. When my mother dies, that'll be rough enough. And when that house goes to somebody outside our family . . . then that ghost of me will be lost."

"And that scares you?"

"Not too smart, huh?"

"I wouldn't know," she said. "I grew up everywhere. Which means nowhere. My ghost has always been floating. Saigon. Switzerland. Here. San Francisco. What scares me is . . ."

"Getting trapped."

"So you say."

In her purse was her videotape; the gun was under her coat.

A seafood restaurant for dinner. John paid with cash, no trail in any computer.

Back at the house, she said she needed another shower.

When he heard the bathroom door close, the water start, he dialed the old lady's number in Baltimore again.

No answer.

Phuong came downstairs. She wore her jeans, a sweater.

"No offense," she said, "but I don't want to see any more of you right now."

Her gesture took in the adult videocassettes stacked on the coffee table. She went back upstairs.

An hour later, she returned. John sat on the couch, pretending to himself he was reading a history of Presidential scandals from Frank's bookshelf. He'd tuned the radio to a classical station. A winter storm warning was in effect.

"I can't stay in my room like it's a cell," she said.

Wet snow covered the lawn. The sidewalk was slick.

"I've got an idea," said John, remembering what he'd read in that day's *Washington Post*.

He turned on the TV.

"No," said Phuong.

"Trust me," he said. "Think of it as overdose therapy."

A black-and-white comedy from before their birth filled the screen.

"I must not understand the Marx Brothers," she said.

"I've never been wild about them either," he said.

"It's slow."

"Ridiculous."

She sat on the couch—in her corner. He sat in his.

A minute went by. Five.

Two images of Groucho Marx faced each other in a doorway, one trying to fool the other into thinking he was staring at a mirror.

John and Phuong laughed.

After the movie, she said thanks, good night.

Locked herself in the bedroom.

At 11:14, John tried the number in Baltimore.

No answer.

Snow fell in the night.

Sunday morning, the old lady next door caught John bringing in *The New York Times* and *Washington Post*. She slammed the door on his polite good morning.

John fried eggs, Phuong made coffee, he burned English muffins, she microwaved bacon.

They sat at the table beside the glass back door, ate and read

seven pounds of newspapers while the sun melted the snow outside and the radio played Mozart.

As she started on *The New York Times,* he took a shower.

Eighteen minutes later, he strolled downstairs.

The radio played Chopin. Newspapers covered the dining
room table.

"Phuong?" said John.

Dirty dishes in the kitchen.

"Where are you?"

The radio announcer said the time was noon.

No one in the living room. The front door was shut. The
chain hung out of its slot.

John ran upstairs: the pink bedroom, empty; the master bedroom, no one.

Look through the blinds in Frank's bedroom. Outside, in the
street, her car was gone.

No answer at the Baltimore number.

He searched her room, her clothes: no bras. Her briefcase was
missing, as was her purse. Gone too were the videotape they'd
copied for her and the gun.

Nine minutes since he'd come downstairs from the shower.

Five more, and he'd dressed in winter gear, long underwear,
jeans, shirt and sweater, his stocking cap and gloves, hiking
boots and black mountaineering coat.

He'd kept his briefcase with his documents and the *Backstreet*
video with him, even when he'd been in the bathroom. Now it
was the only luggage that he took.

Should have kept the gun.

Outside, it was damp and cold, the grass soggy with melted
snow. His prairie boy's senses knew it was spring, not winter,
weather fighting the end of a season.

No one sat in the parked cars lining the street.

No curtains fluttered in any houses.

A boy trudged by with a snow shovel on his shoulder.

Next door, the old lady's blinds were drawn tight.

Newspapers in blue plastic sheaths lay on the front porch of a detached home across the street. The driveway was empty, the melting snow on the sidewalks marred only by the mark of a dog.

From the space between the empty house and the garage, he could see Frank's front door.

Noon became midday. Shadows lengthened. The puddles on the sidewalk froze. His feet ached, his flesh was cold and numb.

At 10 minutes to 4, Phuong drove up, parked.

No car behind her, no one sat in the car with her.

She was focused on the front door, didn't hear him step close behind her.

"Inside," he said.

And she turned, the door opening, his motion propelling them inside the house without touching. He slammed the door closed as she backed into the living room.

"Where did you go?" he yelled.

"Out!"

"Tell me what I don't know!"

"That might take a lifetime." Phuong lifted the purse off her shoulder . . .

He shot his forefinger toward her: "I'm faster!"

She blinked; understood.

"I was going to run," she said.

"Why? Why now? Why not—"

"Because I didn't know if I could trust you."

"So you betrayed me."

"I came back!"

"From where? From who?"

"From the park. From . . . If I don't trust you, I can't trust anybody. And if I can't trust anybody, then . . . then I've already determined how this has to end."

"Pretty clever."

"Pretty basic." She sat on the couch. Didn't unbutton her coat. "I didn't know if you'd be here when I got back."

"What did you think?"

"That if you were still here, you trusted me."

"Or I'm stupid."

His head hurt. He rubbed his eyes, jerked his gloves off his cold fingers and threw the gloves on the coffee table.

"Don't do this to me!" he said.

"I had to."

"Either you're with me, or you're not."

"I'm here."

"Nobody answers that number in Baltimore."

Phuong blinked. "I don't know about that. I gave you her number. If that was a lie, if I was . . . on someone's team, we'd have been prepared for you to call."

"You've got answers for everything, don't you?"

"No more than you."

With his heel, he hooked the leg of the coffee table, pulled it away from the couch where she waited. Sat on it.

"In martial arts," he thought out loud, "an opponent isn't dangerous until he's close enough to touch you. The irony is, you can't counter him until then."

Phuong said: "I'm right here."

27

Monday morning, 8:32.

John sat at his desk in the fishbowl, talking on the phone. The blue glow from the wall of closed fuzzes was cut by the cone of yellow light dropping to his desk from a snake-necked lamp.

"You take the heat for this," said the man's voice in John's ear, "not me. I'm not even supposed to be talking to you."

John said: "I appreciate—"

"There's protocols here. Procedures. You walk outside of them, you walk alone.

"You go outside of them," he added, "you piss people off. Things happen. Things don't happen. You know what I mean?"

"But coming to you directly was the best way," said John.

"For who?" grumbled the man. "I barely get warm after walking from the Metro, then here I am, talking to you. On a Monday morning. I hate Monday mornings."

"It's a simple request."

"No such creature."

"The Committee may hold a hearing," lied John. "We need to double-check our data before we go in, or we could end up making a mistake and more work for everybody."

"My boss will have a cow. Think I'm end-running him."

"Or he'll think you're saving his ass. All this could give him a reason to put you up for a merit award."

"Or transfer me to a coat closet and paper the walls with negative performance evaluations. I should hang up on you."

"Then I'd have to call your boss directly," said John. "Tell him about the Senators' problems. And how you *couldn't* help."

The man sighed: "What the hell, I worry too much about my pension. A little adrenaline is good for the system, right?"

"Cleans the arteries."

"So what do you want from us worker bees at the Office of Defense Trade Controls? Come see us. Central Records has the smallest basement in Crystal City."

"No time for road trips," John told the man whose desk was across the Potomac River. "On December 7 last year, Customs cleared a controlled cargo shipment out of Baltimore, headed for Egypt, aboard a Panamanian ship called *La Espera*."

"Un-huh."

"We've got the Customs records," said John, "but your guys' DSP-dash-9 somehow got lost in the shuffle."

"Why are you asking me about this, too?"

"*Too?*"

"Few weeks ago, I had three clerks jumping through hoops to pull all this together to answer a Senator's query."

"Really," said John. "Well, you know paperwork."

"Never stops, never gets where it's supposed to."

"Now we—the full Senate Committee—need everything you've got on that, everything you sent."

"I'll deadhead a copy of the file over to—"

"Could you do me a favor?" said John.

The man didn't answer.

"We have a time crunch. Send the copy to me, via the Committee, but could you go over it with me now? On the phone."

"I'll owe you one," added John.

"What the hell am I ever going to collect?"

"You never know."

The man sighed: "Let me get the file."

Terrible music assaulted John's ear as he waited on hold.

John was stiff from sleeping on Frank's couch. Tired: he'd skimmed over deep rest, wary of Phuong's footsteps sneaking down the stairs in the night. They never came. That morning, she'd made him coffee. No cinnamon. Scrambled eggs. He'd said nothing about preferring fried. She'd promised to stay in the house. He nodded as if he believed her. Call me anytime, she'd said. The suits he'd packed were wrinkled, but serviceable. No snow remained, but the ground was frozen, the wind cold. He walked the mile to his car, carrying his briefcase with its measly documents, the *Backstreet* video wrapped in a newspaper's blue plastic bag that obscured its cinematic genre. John's car seemed fine. No cars hung in his mirrors as he drove to work.

"Here we go," said the man he'd tracked down by phone. "One Imex DSP-9, et cetera."

John scribbled notes.

"Imex, President Clifford Johnson. Your liasion guy who phoned in the Senator's query—"

"Frank Mathews?" said John.

"Yeah, Mathews. Like we told him, we show this as Johnson's first request for an arms export license. He paid the $250 fee on an Imex check, nobody in the Fed agencies we sent it to objected, so he got a year's license. But he's only asked for one clearance—purchase of and for resale to the Kuwaiti army engineers—not much. Johnson must be breaking into the game."

"What did he ship?"

"Bought from Materials Systems, Inc., over in Baltimore . . . Two thousand pounds of C-4, various detonation—"

"Plastic explosive?"

"Common term, there's—"

"A ton of plastique?"

"Hey, it ain't that much. Material Systems is a research lab for the Pentagon—or used to be, when the Cold War budgets were around. They probably are trying to unload the old days to get into black ink. The Kuwaitis must be using the C-4 in the rebuilding over there since Desert Storm."

Easy . . . Don't rush to—

The man on the phone said: "Johnson's export permit covers this shipment. Like a tease, a onetime special order. Somebody probably did Johnson a favor, cut him in on a quick sale."

"Are there any other names in the file?"

"The sales manager at Material Systems in Baltimore."

John wrote down the man's name and phone number, thanked the bureaucrat for his help. Hung up.

Give this no names. Not yet. Don't guess, know.

Time, thought John.

What about Emma?

Trouble. No matter what, trouble.

The phone: *would Phuong answer if he called?*

Running a mission through government agencies was one thing: John had legitimate influence with fellow public employees. Materials Systems, Inc., was private sector. They could hang up, call the CIA . . .

Had it been quick for Wei? Had they hurt her first? Had they . . . tortured her? Or did they just lead her down to a damp cement basement, make her kneel, press the bore of the pistol—

Gone. Let go.

The sales manager at the Baltimore export firm took John's call after his secretary told him the CIA was on the line.

"You're not our usual contact guy," said the salesman.

"I'm on detached duty," said John. "Helping the Senate."

"Un-huh," said the salesman. "Sure you are."

"Hang up," said John, "get the phone number in Washington for the Senate, then have them transfer you to the Select Committee on Intelligence, ask the Committee if I'm the Agency liaison and get them to transfer you into my office. I don't want there to be any questions about bona fides."

Five minutes later, the salesman rang through to John, said: "You can't be too careful."

"We appreciate that."

"What can I sell you guys today?"

"I'm not buying, I'm auditing."

"Hey, we use your systems. If something's off, it's your fault, not ours."

"Everybody's clean."

"Damn right. Unless the politicians are bothering us guys trying to make an honest dollar."

"Yes." John read him the details of the Imex sale.

"I remember Johnson," said the salesman. "Acted like this was the biggest deal any of us would ever see. Hell, the month before, you people and us—"

"Did he give you the impression this was an Agency deal?"

"He gave me a certified check and all the paperwork the Feds say we need. I shook his hand, asked no questions."

"Was anybody else involved?"

"Nah, just Johnson and his bag carrier in the other car. Johnson was so small-time, he even loaded and drove the truck himself and—"

"Who was the bag carrier?"

"Beats me." The salesman paused. "We got a problem here? Should I get our lawyers on the phone?"

"We got no problems with the law. Why run up your bills?"

"Don't even talk to me about those bloodsuckers!"

"So what can you tell me about the other guy?"

"Let's see . . . Here's the clipboard sheet . . . You know what he wrote under 'Representing' when they signed in at the gate? 'Friend of Cliff's.' "

"Really."

"Since Johnson was the one responsible for signing all the papers, it's him our security boys verified: ID, driver's license, that kind of stuff. The other guy . . .

"Well, well," said the salesman: "What do you know."

"What?"

"One of the guards must have not liked 'Friend of's' attitude. On the back of the sign-in sheet, he wrote 'asshole's lic. plte.' A Virginia tag number. We normally don't do that."

"Give that man a raise."

"Why? He'll work for minimum wage."

The salesman read John the license plate number.

John thanked him, hung up.

If he could trust his own Agency, one phone call would give

him all the official data on that license plate in 15 minutes. If he had time, he could drive across the river to the appropriate Virginia state office, pay a fee, and get the public data himself.

His phone rang. John answered hello.

"Who are you?" said a man's voice.

"Who did you call?"

"Oh, so you're *clever*."

"Who is this?"

"A guy I called this morning told me to call this number and ask for somebody. He said that somebody was handling what I'd called him about. You tell me who I called, maybe you're the guy I should talk to."

"I don't have time for . . ."

And then John stopped. His mind raced, *remembered*.

"Steve," he said.

"Steve is a common name."

"This one works for Senator Firestone."

"You're John Lang."

"Who are you?"

"A concerned citizen who wrote a Senator, ended up talking to a man who ended up dead."

"Frank Mathews."

"He said if I called his office, not to involve you."

"That was a mistake."

"Was it?" said the man's voice. "He was a pro."

"We have to meet. This is mine now. When—"

"Who else is on this?"

"Nobody—I'm who you need."

"I don't need anybody."

"Then you wouldn't have written Firestone. Then you wouldn't have talked to Frank. Then Frank—"

"That amazing, magic stray bullet."

"We don't have—"

"Time," finished the man. "No shit. Your caller ID should have this pay phone locked. See you around, Lang."

The phone buzzed in his ear. Disconnected.

His watch read 9:47.

He could sit there in the blue light, watch the seconds flash by in his watch's analog window, watch the second hand sweep its silent circle.

Wait for whatever happened.

Or he could get close enough to touch.

He picked up the telephone receiver, dialed a number.

28

Like a dream castle, the four-story red brick and white cement high school commanded a hill overlooking the city. The view from those high, arched windows was magnificent: the Capitol dome, the roofs of stately homes, the high-tech glisten of office buildings, trees surrounding the White House, the Washington Monument rising like a beacon into the gray sky where jets soared from National Airport to Hollywood and Paris and Hong Kong.

Rusted iron grilles and bars covered the windows on the first two floors. Metal detectors created a second entrance inside all doors.

Whirling red and blue police lights keyed John which street to turn down across from the high school. He parked, walked past police cruisers and an ambulance to where yellow crime scene tape stretched across the mouth of an alley.

Uniformed cops in blue nylon jackets stopped him when he stepped from the crowd of housewives and teenagers carrying backpacks. A cop bore the news of John's arrival down the alley, came back and beckoned. John ducked under the tape.

The cold alley smelled of garbage. Black plastic trash bags outside back fences had been gnawed open by dogs, rats.

John followed the blue-jacketed, broad shoulders of his escort. Behind them, brakes squealed. A car door slammed.

Twenty, fifteen, ten paces ahead, Detective Tyler Greene and his partner took notes as an evidence technician snapped pictures of a 14-year-old boy sprawled on his back. The boy's coat was zipped; he lay in a black lake that was turning to ice on the alley bricks. His arms were spread wide; one hand stretched toward an overturned backpack and a heap of textbooks (geometry, Latin) and notebooks with pages flipping in the breeze. The other hand wasn't far from a police chalk circle drawn around three shiny brass shell casings. The boys eyes were open. His stocking feet pointed to heaven.

Detective Greene stopped John with a look, went back to jotting notes.

From the mouth of the alley, the sounds of a struggle, orders mumbled and screams: "My baby! Where's my baby?"

Shoes scuffled on asphalt.

"Halt!" yelled a cop.

A black woman John's age and her mother ran down the alley, chased by a policeman who'd lost his hat.

"Billy! Billy!" yelled the mother. "Bill-eeee!"

Greene, his partner and the evidence technician formed a human wall between the charging woman and the boy on the ground. Greene's partner could bench-press 220; he caught the mother by her arms. She went limp the moment they touched, sagged.

"Oh Billy Oh Billy OhBilly!"

"Jesus, sweet Jesus oh my Lord no Jesus," sobbed the grandmother.

But she was strong enough to help Greene and his partner lift her daughter to her feet.

"Not here," said Greene softly. "This isn't your place. Not now. Later. Not now."

"I want to see my son! I want to see my Billy, he's a good kid, he goes to school, he's goin' to be, he has a cold, he has to stay warm, tell the doctors he . . ."

As they gently backed her away, she saw behind them.

"Oh God! Oh God no no God no God!"

Grandmother buried her head in the black cloth of her daughter's coat.

The uniformed cops and the evidence technician led the two women back toward the yellow tape.

"His shoes!" cried the mother. "Where are his shoes? His new sneakers, I bought them for him yesterday! He was so . . . Where are his shoes?"

Greene, his husky white partner and John watched them go.

Slowly, so slowly, Greene turned around. His eyes blazed, filled with John.

And he charged.

Slammed John against a brick wall.

"Ty!" yelled his partner. "Come on! No!"

John's mind spinning, breath coming back, Greene's steaming exhales in his face as John's arm windmilled to—

No: don't.

"Man, come on!" yelled Greene's partner. But he kept his hands to himself.

"There it is!" Greene yelled into John's face. "Here it is! Tell me about *this!* What does your damn *Central Intelligence* know about this? You know so fucking much you fucking white son of a bitch hot shot, saving the world who's going to save him? Fourteen fucking years old and he's dead, Jack! Who gives a shit, huh? You're *Central Intelligence!* Tell me, you tell me, how did he get here! What are you doing about it? Making the world safe for who? For him? For my kids? Which you gonna do, put guns in their hands or bullets in their hearts? Which choice you gonna tell them to make with your damn *Central Intelligence!*"

"Easy, Ty," said his partner. "It's OK. It's not him."

Greene blinked.

Shoved John—but lightly. Pushed himself away.

The black son-father-husband-detective turned, walked toward the yellow tape.

Greene's husky white partner straightened John's suit, said: "You shouldn't have approached a police officer on a crime scene without warning. You could have gotten hurt, arrested."

"Nobody'd want that," said John.

The white cop pointed a warning forefinger to the sky.

Walked away, passing almost close enough to Greene to touch him.

John stayed against the wall.

When Greene came back, smoke drifted in his eyes.

"So," he told John, "you called me."

"You taped a message on my cabin door."

"My Chief got a lot of messages from your people. They all said they aren't talking.

"I say: not yet," said Greene.

"If I can help you, maybe you can help me."

"Why the hell would I want to help you?"

"Because we're on the same side."

Greene shook his head: "You really believe that?"

"Yes."

"Huh."

"Why do you want me?" said John. "What do you know?"

"I know that before you'd have landed that hook punch you pulled, I'd have kneed your nuts up between your ears."

"So what."

"So don't fuck with me."

"Like I said before, you're not my style." John stepped away from the wall. Walked further down the alley. Past the body. He didn't look down. Or back. But he felt Greene walk beside him.

When all they could see were trash bags waiting to be picked up and the yellow tape blocking the far end of the alley, John said: "If you've got something, we'll find out sooner or later. Hell, you'll tell us to trap us. So why not tell me now?"

"The strongest word in 'physical evidence' is physics," said the cop. "You know about trajectories?"

"Enough."

"Took me a lot of grease, but we did a reconstruction that shows the bullet that killed Frank Mathews had to come from the sidewalk or a parked car across the street, not flying from nowhere through the intersection or dropping from the air."

"Physics is religion, not science."

"Grand jury might not agree."

"I didn't see anything," said John.

"Then you better open your eyes." Greene faced him. "And you better tell me what you know."

John weighed the air: "I know . . . Don't let go, but don't push. Not now, not yet."

"Did you just tell me something?"

"No." John looked at the cop. "Setting an ambush to snipe somebody in city traffic is absurd: you have to be certain of the route, the car, have good weather and clear lanes of fire—"

"You told me that bullets weren't your business."

"There's too many variables in your scenario," said John.

"But the odds of 'absurd' drop way down if you've got an inside man."

Greene smiled: "Somebody who can lock in the route, the timing, positioning. Somebody who can put the target in place. Then all the shooters need to worry about is setting up, squeezing the shot, getting away. The inside man even covers their retreat with bullshit."

"You know I didn't do that."

"A cop knows what he can sell to a jury," said Greene.

"They'd never buy all that. And neither do you."

"Might be weak, the idea that you'd put yourself so close to a target you'd set up. Bullets are fickle."

"You probably learned that in the Reserves," added Greene. He shrugged: "Airborne, Ranger, Green Beret: fighting soldier all the way. A routine query to the Pentagon, not the CIA. Course, the bird colonel who called me direct was real curious about why I was asking for information."

"What did you tell him?"

"That I was verifying information received. You never told me you were in the Army."

"You never asked."

Greene said: "So why did you call me?"

"I need you to run a license plate. All the data you can get. And I need it now. Here."

"Say what?"

"We're on the same side."

"Look around again, *amigo,*" said Greene.

"I see you, I see me, I see my dead partner and a lot of going-nowhere questions. I'm looking for the way to somewhere."

"You could start by telling me the truth. That means the whole truth and nothing but the truth."

"No I can't."

"Who's stopping you? It's just you and me in an alley."

"You look around again, *amigo.*"

"If I check it out," said Greene, "I got it, too."

"Random data." John shrugged. "Someday, you might need to use what you get. Maybe someday, but not now, not today."

"Abusing police powers is a violation of law."

"It's just you and me in an alley."

Greene stared at him.

"I want to get out of here," said John. "Don't you?"

"Hey, Detective!" yelled a man from the morgue who'd rolled a stretcher beside the body of a 14-year-old boy who was *goin' to be.* "Can we have him now?"

The homicide detective leaned close to John: "You make a wrong move, I'll feed you your heart."

John stared at him.

"You got a piece of paper in your pocket you want me to look at?" said Greene.

John handed him a note bearing the Virginia license plate number.

"Stay here," said Greene. "I gotta secure and release a crime scene."

Greene walked back to the body. A conference with his partner, the evidence technician. Shell casings scooped into a plastic evidence baggie. An order to the morgue men, who lifted the body into a rubber bag. Pictures snapped of the bricks under where he'd lain. The morgue men wheeled the stretcher bearing the heavy rubber bag out of the alley. Greene spoke to his partner and the technician. They walked to the street. Greene flipped over a page in his notebook, mumbled into his handheld radio.

Two minutes later, John heard the crackle of a reply. Greene filled a page with notes. Flipped to a clean page, jotted another set of notes. Ripped that lime-green page from his spiral notebook, crumpled it into a ball, tossed it on the bricks beside the cooling dark lake.

Walked out of the alley, leaving John alone between two lines of yellow tape.

Car doors slammed in the street. Engines started, pulled away.

At the mouth of the alley, on the other side of a strip of yellow tape, a dozen pairs of eyes watched a white man in a suit who had to be a cop walk to where the boy had lain, pick up a crumpled paper ball of litter.

29

Even with a map, John felt lost.

This neighborhood was seldom seen by tourists. Scarred by railroad tracks, dominated by warehouses and garages, this could have been anywhere in America and was just as ignored there as it was in a Virginia suburb of the nation's capital. Flat-faced rows of brick town houses, peeling-paint houses, fence gates dangling from broken hinges. Cars rusting on blocks in grassless front yards. Backyard clotheslines hung with white sheets.

As John drove, searching for complete numbers on battered buildings, he heard a steady *thump thump thump* of an unseen factory. Or maybe the beating was just his imagination. Maybe it was his anxious heart.

According to the wrinkled sheet of green paper, the license plate he'd given Greene belonged to a brown Datsun Z registered to Phillip David.

Who supposedly lived in these grim streets.

John almost missed the address: a two-story house with splintered gray wood, peeling white paint. A screened-in front porch with holes the size of basketballs in the wire mesh. Broken window on the second floor. The windows were covered. The front yard was a graveyard for last year's weeds. A wire fence imprisoned the house. Mounted next to the closed gate was an aluminum mailbox.

No car in the driveway.

No sign that anyone lived there.

The three-story brick apartment complex across the street was solid and clean. A mother with stringy blond hair sat huddled in a peacoat on a concrete stoop, watching two preschool girls pedal tricycles on the sidewalk. The mother was all of 24, thought John. She followed John's cruising car with her eyes.

At the corner, John turned right, parked.

Phillip David: who'd look for you here?

Lock the briefcase in the trunk: go empty-handed.

Phuong had the gun.

The afternoon was cold; he wished he'd brought his nylon trench coat, even if it wouldn't have helped much.

At the corner, he turned and walked down the street, his eye on the house across the road in the middle of the block.

The cars he passed were well used; bumper stickers for Navy ships, the Marines; parking stickers for nearby Army posts.

From inside the glass door of the apartment complex, an old black man in a hat stood watching John. Down the block, the mother called to the two girls on tricycles.

A For Sale sign listing a local realtor had fallen from the fence surrounding the house. Call the real estate agent later.

The mailbox was empty.

The gate creaked open.

Three wooden steps up to the door of the screened porch. Its hook-and-eye latch was unfastened. The door banged softly in the breeze. Three steps across the creaky porch to the front door.

Knock.

No answer.

Knock again.

"Anybody home?"

During John's Army service, the CIA made sure he cycled through every available intelligence school and training program, including DAME—Defense Against Mechanical Entry, the program that taught agents how to pick locks.

Of course, John was carrying no lockpicks or tension bars or plastic shimmies.

He put his hand on the doorknob, turned . . .

The door opened.

Step away from the entrance: "Anybody here?"

The door swung open, a solid wood plane yawning into a shadowed box.

Watching: the mother on her stoop, the girls pedaling their tricycles, the old man across the street inside the glass door. Minding their own business.

Go in quick, go in smart.

John obeyed his education, took two heartbeats to dart through the entrance and jump to the side, press his back against the inside wall, grab the door and slam it closed.

The house shook.

Dust swirled.

Muted yellow afternoon sunlight filtered through cheap shades and sheets tacked over the windows. The air was thick and heavy and cold. Musty.

The room was completely and totally empty.

A living room. Perhaps a parlor in more elegant days. An open doorway led off to a dining room—also empty.

The kitchen, shades pulled and dark. A refrigerator, unplugged and full of rotting rubber. Cupboards held dust. John tried the sink faucets: air whistled. He flipped the wall switch: nothing. The back door was locked with a twist-open dead bolt.

Every crook in the neighborhood must know this place isn't worth their time.

Upstairs. Two bedrooms. Empty. On one wall was a faded red and green drawing of a stick-figure cowboy and his horse.

Black scum in the toilet bowl.

Downstairs, one jarring step at a time.

Maybe the real estate agent will know something. Maybe the security guard in Baltimore made a mistake. Or maybe had the police dispatcher, or maybe Greene himself. Maybe it was all dead-end bullshit. Like everything else.

He stalked across the bare living room floor.

The heat had been turned off. Even the cockroaches had moved out.

Hand on the front door's knob, John noticed a plastic box screwed into the molding above the door, and as he opened the door to the outer world, the safe outer world, he wondered—

Man shape blocking the doorway light.

Fist hurtling toward John's face.

Rollback/step back/snap left arm up in a rising block to knock the fist away and

John's forearm slammed into/deflected the man's wrist—

fist flicks open:

A grainy black cloud swirled into John's face.

Black pepper. Ordinary, everyday, household black pepper.

Coughing. Wheezing. *Blind.* Blocking blind.

Staggering back into the house, turning.

A kick missed John's groin.

Slammed into his stomach.

Doubled-over, tears flooding, eyes burning, lungs—

Sledgehammer fist hit his right kidney. John crashed to his knees. A fist slammed into the back of his neck and the hard wood floor rushed up to smack him in the face.

Bright *red pain. Roaring.*

Blackness spinning *blackness.*

Door slam, thought he heard a door slam as he fought breath back into his lungs.

A shoe knifed into his side.

Gone, all his strength *gone.*

Blind from the pepper, from pain, from shock.

Hands grab him. Grope his sides, his hips, roll him over on his back. Slap his chest.

Sirens. *Sure, sirens. Neighbors must have called.* Coming closer.

Rolled over, on his face. Blinking, tearing. Wood, he could see the floor's blurred wood.

Wallet pulled out of his pants.

Sirens wail closer.

"Lang!" hissed a man's voice.

Voice on phone.

"John fucking Lang!"

Blink. Vision clear, head swimming, throat retching but see, he could see.

A blur of red light winked outside the drawn window shades.

A hand grabbed his hair, jerked his face off the floor and arched his back and he screamed as red and blue lights beat against the window shades.

Tires squeal on pavement. Sirens cut silent.

Then, before his head was smashed down on the floor, before he looked up and saw the back of a man running into the kitchen, before he tried to push himself up to his hands and knees and collapsed with the effort as the front door burst open, John heard that man's voice hiss:

"If you're real, why aren't you dead?"

30

John Lang stared out the second-story window of the Arlington police station. In the dark parking lot below, arc lights bathed four parked cruisers with a yellow glow.

The throbbing in his head had subsided to a steady roar. His ribs ached, his mouth tasted foul.

John closed his eyes. Opened them.

Still here. Alone, standing behind a captain's desk, staring out the cop's office window to the world.

A police sergeant entered: "You should be sitting down."

"Yeah, and the chair should be in China."

"No can do." The sergeant held the door open. "But color yourself gone from here."

In the squad room, the captain whispered with a man in a rumpled business suit.

Harlan Glass stood by the stairs, smooth hat in hand.

The five cops in the squad room typed reports. Talked on the phone. Looked at no one.

Glass curled his finger and pulled John to him.

"Not a word," said Glass. "Not here."

He settled under his hat, led John down the stairs, past the booking desk where a father pleaded for mercy for his son, out the front door to the winter evening.

When they were on the street, John said: "How bad is it?"

"If your incident leaks to the press, it's a disaster. Questions, everything ripped out of our hands. If Korn finds out, he's got an excuse, hell, the *duty* to go after you. And me."

They walked along the rows of parked cars.

"You deserve better from me," said John.

"Yes I do. So does the Agency. So does Frank."

"Look, I screwed up," said John. "I got jumped, but drawing fire was part of the brief you gave me."

"Containing fire—"

"I'm an agent," said John, "not a magician."

"More bad luck."

Glass swept the street with a practiced gaze. He crossed the lightly trafficked suburban road to a bus stop bench.

"Sit down," he ordered John.

"You're my handler," said John, obeying. "Your call."

"This has never been my call." Glass buttoned his overcoat against the night chill. "Report."

"Frank was trailing a shipment of C-4—one tied to a surveillance video between two men I can't identify for sure. Yet. But they were talking about their enterprise being *sanctioned.*"

"Plastic explosive?" whispered Glass. "As in—"

"As in the Corcoran Center. Two thousand pounds of it in the 'sanctioned' shipment, plus various detonators and gear."

Glass's whisper was flat, clean: "Figure diverting a thousand pounds for Corcoran Center . . . No trouble. Auditing on the other end, in Kuwait, buy one of the foreign workers the Kuwaitis hire to do their heavy lifting, he'll point to a hole somewhere and say 2,000 pounds made it. It's such a small amount of C-4—"

"That it can disappear easy en route from Baltimore to Egypt to—"

"Figure most of it never even left this country." Glass shook his head. "That videotape: do you have it?"

"Stashed."

"Not with you? Not here so I could—"

"Not carried on me, so I could get it ripped," said John.

Glass *humphed.* "Any direct ties to the Agency? To anybody?"

"Probably to a guy named Phillip David. It was his accommodation address, dead drop, where I got jumped—probably by him. Phil David was part of the shipment team, who probably wrote the letter to Senator Firestone—"

"Trying to set up a plea bargain. For the bombing . . ."

"Why?" asked John.

"He got too scared too soon for . . . *whoever* to control."

"Whoever runs the show is slick. And rough."

"Figure he had to kill Frank when he stumbled into the plea bargain Phil David was trying to put together."

"While you're figuring, add in Cliff Johnson. My bet is he didn't 'blow up' in Paris, somebody blew him up."

"Do you have any evidence?" whispered Glass.

"Whatever evidence there was the French have. And I bet whoever did it was big enough to rig a good bomb and cover up any evidence of anything but an accident."

"Why was Johnson killed?"

"After Cocoran Center, my guess is he realized he might be in business with the wrong people. He thought he was doing business with us. With the CIA."

"Was he?" asked Glass.

A city bus roared toward them. Glass waved it on. The bus blurred past them with a *whoosh*.

Again, Glass asked: "Was he? Was it us?"

"Not any 'us' I'm part of," said John. "But Frank's diverted queries . . . that kind of . . . coverage . . ."

Glass pressed his hand against his forehead, tugged the brim of his hat lower. "Ahmed Naral . . ."

Heart pounding. Stay clam. Centered.

"The Centers were thrown together from existing resources," said Glass. "Not just our Agency—which pissed them off enough—but stuff reaped from the Bureau, the Pentagon. Sorting the data chaos everyone 'routinely' gave us, creating new categories, new ways of looking at things . . . The Centers still aren't autonomous enough, still locked in inter- and intra-agency politics. Hell, renaming a file can require a meeting!"

"I don't care," said John.

"You better. *How* something gets done creates the politics of *what* gets done.

"Ahmed Naral . . . I checked everything my Counter-Terrorism Center had on him today. Personally, careful not to leave tracks in computers or file rooms or . . . He's got access designations by code-word levels compartmented beyond what he should have, beyond Carlos or Abu Nidal. And I don't recognize the identifiers—the signatures of people who created his compartments. But it all rests in Ops, and none of it goes below Deputy Director level."

"Allen and Woodruff," said John, "in Beirut—"

"Figure we don't give a damn about Beirut," said Glass. "Figure New York. And here."

"If—"

"Don't!" ordered Glass. "Not until we know more!"

"If we've had Naral as an asset for years, if we helped divert some C-4 for him thinking he'd use it in the Middle East or against Qaddafi or Saddam Hussein—"

"They both hate him now—ex-allies make the most dangerous enemies—"

"—and our old ally Naral decides to jerk us around because—I don't know, ego, more money, more power, less—"

"We don't know any of that."

"No."

"No."

"You can use the Indexes," said John, "manufacture computer runs, track Phil David and—"

"And blaze our trail for everybody, friend and foe—neither of whom *right now* can be sure we're where we are."

The night was quiet. Their eyes watched a man across the street walking his dachshund.

"Where are we?" whispered John.

"Damn!" Glass looked at his watch. "If I don't get to Langley, manufacture countermoves to cover you—"

"Who was the suit you brought to the cop station?"

"He's an assistant U.S. attorney for northern Virginia," said Glass. "Very ambitious. Very cooperative. I've used him before. He'll make sure the captain keeps your mess out of the files and computers."

"So figure how close we are to ending this," said Glass.

"This ends when we nail the people who killed Frank! When we know what he was chasing! Not until—"

"As you said: you are an agent. I am your case officer. You are on *my* string!"

"So pull it," said John. Quietly. His eyes were clear.

Cars whizzed by them, families on their way to the grocery store, exhausted parents motoring home to fragile families.

"You came to me," said John.

"You were already there."

They sat on the bus bench in the cold night, like two school-boys out too late and too far from home. The truth sat beside them on the bench. Quietly.

"We are on the same side," sighed Glass. "We must be."

He checked his watch.

"How did Phillip David know you were at that house?"

"There was a plastic switch box screwed above the door. Microtransmitter, maybe lifted out of our stores or the Pentagon's or the Bureau's or DEA's or—"

"Bought at a shopping mall," said Glass.

"Door opens, switch flips, signal transmits. My guess is he used that house for a mail drop. Maybe he slipped the real estate agent a few bucks. That place wouldn't sell in a good economy. These days . . .

"Anybody who tracked his mail drop and opened the door rang an alarm somewhere nearby. Probably his bunk pad. By now he's long gone, but then he looked out his window, saw me, no backups . . . Still a risky play. Desperate."

"His tactics worked, yours failed."

"So far," said John.

"Can you find him?"

"Or he'll find me. He needs to."

"So you assume." Glass checked his watch, swore.

"Let's bring this in," said John. "Now. Tonight."

"Who would you have us trust?" asked Glass. "After this, after what happened to Frank, who in the Agency can we go to?"

"Go to everybody. Blow all the whistles, ring all the bells. If a few bad guys are inside, the sheer, overpowering number of good guys—"

"Will stumble over their best intentions. And the bureaucracy. Justifiably sealed compartments. The 'believability' factor. And the vital necessity for covering everybody's ass. Figure we have evidence of no wrongdoing—except by Frank, and by extension, you and me. All the powers at Langley, the White House, they'll call it paranoia. Or random, irrelevant mystery. But the hint of scandal will send the Agency into a witch-hunt, and the first to burn will be the messengers who smeared their unsanctioned and unsolved trouble on the Agency's white walls.

"Or am I wrong?" asked Glass. "Do American government bureaucracies inevitably and efficiently serve truth and justice?"

John said nothing.

"What haven't you told me?" said Glass.

"Nothing that's operationally relevant."

"I'll be the judge of that."

"Judge what you want, I'm the one on the line."

"No: the Agency is on the line. I'm on the line. And Frank."

"And me."

"Yes, and you. Figure if Frank was liquidated, you should die, too."

"Not until I'm ready."

Glass said: "Caution, not courage, keeps agents alive."

"Whoever's out there won't whack me until he's certain about what he has to fear from me and whatever Frank left behind."

"Then keep him guessing."

"And draw his fire, draw him out. So you can nail him without burning the Agency—or burning you and your CTC. That's what you want, isn't it?"

"That'll do."

"What about me?" asked John.

"Do your job right, survive . . . I'll keep your head on your shoulders."

"That's sort of my theory, too."

"Sort of?"

John shrugged.

"To me," said Glass, "loyalty is an absolute."

"You said it from the start: you have to trust me."

"You disobeyed my orders and contacted Detective Greene."

"I took the best shot I had. So far, so good."

"So far." Glass thought for a moment. "Korn may force the Operations Directorate or the Inspector General, perhaps the Legal Office, into a position where their hand grabs you—but it will be Korn's force. He may compel your boss Zell to squeeze you. Resist everyone: the moment you say anything, do anything, admit anything . . . we lose control, and this all ends."

"I understand maintaining control. And being squeezed."

"If Korn puts you in a box about tonight, say nothing. Admit nothing, not even that you were here.

"Don't abandon me," said Glass. "Don't abandon Frank."

A car slowed as it neared the bench. Both men tensed. The car's driver was a woman with the look of harried motherhood. She glanced at the bus stop bench, drove on.

"I don't abandon people." John's tone was flat.

"Run deep and hard," said Glass. "Focus on finding Frank's trail, all his tracks. Guard that video and any other data you acquire. Trust no one, confide in on one. Continue normal cover, work liaison, but don't be a sitting duck."

"Instead of a moving target?"

Glass stood: "Do this, John. Find this 'who' and 'what.' Without anyone seeing your hands. Without destroying our Agency and everything we've fought for. Do it now, before it's too late to do anything."

And then the man in the smooth hat walked to his parked car, leaving John alone at the bus stop in the night.

31

His key opened Frank's door.

Phuong peeked around the corner of the kitchen as John shuffled inside her father's house.

"You look awful," she said.

"Who says appearances are deceiving?"

"Sit." Her fingers pressed him toward the couch, helped him slip out of his suit jacket.

"I'm—"

"You're not OK, so save the lie for when you need it."

"Be sure to let me know when that is."

"Figure it out for yourself."

She got a plastic bag of ice from the kitchen, made him tilt his head across the back of the couch and hold the pack against his forehead. The cold burned his skin.

"I didn't know working for Congress was so dangerous," she said.

"It's the moonlighting that kills you."

He loosened his tie.

"Six days," he said. "Do you realize it's only been six days since . . ."

He trailed off. She sat on the coffee table. "Remember our deal. Tell me—everything. And the truth."

Want to. Need to. Tell her everything.

Except about Emma.

That's not in our deal, he told himself. Then he told her everything—except about Emma.

"Did you tell Glass about me?" asked Phuong when he was
done.

"No"

"Why not?"

Head hurts.

"Why not?" she asked again.

John winced, put the ice bag on the coffee table: "He'd have
gone ballistic because I've violated need-to-know—even if I had
no choice. Not knowing this won't hurt him. Or you."

"Don't you trust him?"

"That's not the point."

"Oh?"

"If he knows about you, then I lose some control."

"He's your case officer: he's supposed to be in charge."

"If you surrender all your faith to your handler, you end up
getting shot in China."

For a long time, they said nothing.

"Wei and your other agents knew the risks," Phuong said.
"They were doing their job."

"They weren't in it for a job."

"Neither are you," she said.

"That doesn't change anything."

"That changes everything," she said.

"Dead is dead."

"And here I hoped you weren't a whiner."

"I'm a realist."

"The worst kind of fool."

And he couldn't stop a tight grin.

"I told you not to lie," she said. "to me, not to yourself. I told
you I'd nail you for it."

"Phuong the hammer."

"Damn right," she said.

He smiled and started to shake his head . . . The pain
throbbed and he closed his eyes.

"Just don't hammer my skull," he whispered, breathing slowly, waiting for the ache to subside.

"Only as needed." She put the plastic bag of ice in his hand. "Don't start being a fool."

"I got to stop making deals with you. You're too rough."

"You ain't seen nothing yet," she said.

Her eyes glistened like an icy night.

"This is how agents and ops go bad," said John: "For all the right reasons. Push a line here, violate a technical provision there, tell a white lie or don't report a harmless truth . . . "

"You think you've got a better choice?"

"I think it's too late for that. I'm already on this road. I've done what I thought was best."

"Then you're not to blame."

"Sure I am." He smiled at her. "Sure I am."

"What do you want to change?"

"Being slow to duck."

"Then start believing you're going to get hit."

"Paranoia is Washington's first rule for success."

"For survival." She watched him. "Are you OK?"

"By tomorrow," he said.

"Promises, promises. Are you hungry?"

"Later, I'll eat something later."

"Are you hurt anywhere else?"

"Everywhere else."

She touched the swelling on his forehead.

"I think that's as big as it'll get," she said.

Her fingers brushed the crescent scar on his left temple.

"That's old," he said.

"How old?"

"I was seven. Dog bit me. German shepherd."

"Why?"

"I was in the right place at the right time."

"Must have hurt."

"The fear was worse." John smiled. "After the dog got out of rabies quarantine, my dad borrowed Uncle Alan's Winchester, drove me over to where the dog was penned, shot it dead."

"Then what happened?"

"Then he took me back to school."

"But the owner—"

"Old man Walker knew better than to complain."

"Didn't he have a lawyer?"

"When I grew up, lawyers weren't more powerful than hometown juries."

"What did your father tell you about . . . all that?"

"He didn't waste words explaining the obvious." John shrugged. "You do what you can inside the rules. But you always do what's right. What you got to. And you stand your ground."

After a minute, Phuong said: "Did you ever tell my dad that story?"

"I never told anybody that story."

"Your dad," she said. "Is he . . . "

"He woke up dead one day after he retired. I was in grad school."

The room was quiet. Still.

John sat on the couch.

Across from him, on the coffee table, sat Phuong.

"None of my scars are so dramatic," she said.

"Bullshit. They just don't show on the outside."

"Yeah . . . well . . . " She stood, took the bag of melting ice into the kitchen and put it in the sink.

But couldn't stay safely in the yellow kitchen, let the time pass. She came back to the living room.

"You think you know all about me," she told the man sitting on the couch, "but you don't."

"You're probably right."

Phuong blinked.

"Tell me everything," he said before he thought.

"I don't owe you that."

"I don't want you to owe me anything."

She held up her hands as if to silence the roar of an unseen crowd. "No more!"

"OK."

"Just . . . no more."

"Whatever."

"We have a deal," she said. "And that's that."

"Sure."

She locked her gaze straight on him. Her voice was precise. "How's your head? Does it hurt?"

"Feeling better all the time."

"Good. Good." She brushed invisible crumbs off the dining room table. "You can eat or . . . whatever."

"Whatever."

She said: "Then we'll figure out what to do."

32

Tuesday morning, 9:09.

Echoes of laughter and footsteps drifted down the high-ceilinged, salmon-colored hall outside Senator Ken Handelman's office in the Russell Building.

Two men in shirts and ties chatted with a woman in an expensive but somber skirt as the three of them carried steaming Styrofoam cups toward a numbered office door.

A potbellied Capitol Hill policeman lumbered past that trio of staffers without a glance. Ten steps later, the cop frowned at John Lang's battered face.

John hesitated outside Handelman's open door. A woman's voice drifted to him from inside the reception room:

" . . . so what am I supposed to do? Why me? I haven't done anything to deserve this. I hate his eyes on me all the time! It's like he's always there. Least he hasn't tried the bump-you game, like the guy from Senator Bechtel's office, but come on: what do I have in common with a cop?"

"I don't do anything to encourage him," said the woman as John stepped through the doorway.

The woman sitting at the desk to John's left had cascading honey-blond hair and a year-old cheerleader's B.S. from Arizona State. Her gold dress had nicked Mom's credit card enough so that even she noticed and was styled more for a Hollywood executive than a Senate employee. The dress accented the blonde receptionist's hourglass figure. A gold chain belt looped around her waist. Her skin was flawless, her makeup perfect, from the desert rust of her full lips to her matching fingernail polish to the hint of sunset dusted around her eyes—eyes that weighed John when he entered: his age, his suit, the uncool purple bruise on his forehead, his reaction to her and the serious set of his mouth.

A telephone rang.

"I'll get it, Chrissy," said the woman at the desk to John's right. She had brown hair roommate-cut to shoulder length and eyes of sky offset by dark shadows. This was her fifth year of undergraduate night school before four more years of night law school—if she got in. She answered the phone.

Chrissy smiled at John and said in the voice he'd heard in the hall: "Can I help you?"

"I'm here to see Emma North," he told her.

"I don't think Emma's come in yet," said Chrissy.

The other receptionist shook her head in confirmation.

"Did she leave anything for me? My name is John Lang."

Chrissy swiveled to check a pile of envelopes on a shelf. Her dress strained across her breasts. John remembered a girl in high school who'd never returned his one brave phone call.

"I'm sorry." Chrissy smiled with perfect teeth. "There's nothing here."

"Can I leave a message?"

"Sure."

On the back of a pink phone-message slip, he wrote:

> Emma—I stopped by to see if you had finished that project you said you'd do for me. Please call as soon as you can.
>
>   John

Not . . . enough. He frowned and swore at himself.

"Excuse me?" said Chrissy.

John had scrawled the lines of his note too close together to pen in any revisions, so he was damned to write words obvious as an afterthought below his signature:

How are you?

Not enough, and he knew it: *What else could he say?*

"I'll see that she gets this when she comes in," said Chrissy when John handed her the note.

As he walked out the door, the brown-haired receptionist hung up the phone and resumed her conversation with Chrissy, saying: "I know what you mean, and no matter what, you're right."

Outside the Senate Intelligence Committee door, Jimmy the cop avoided John's eyes as he signed in.

Inside the secure Committee office, the secretary glanced at John, then quickly looked away, pouring her concentration into a letter she was editing on the glowing computer screen.

She doesn't want to embarrass me by asking about the bruise on my forehead, thought John. Phuong's ice packs and aspirin had shrunk the purplish wound to the size of a silver dollar. Almost like a birthmark, thought John, grateful for the secretary's discretion: he didn't want to lie to her again.

Toward the back of the Committee suite, the staff director emerged from his office. He saw John, looked away.

John frowned: *not even a wave.*

The blue screens inside the fishbowl were closed.

He slid his key in the CIA liaison office's lock.

Opened the door.

In the blue-tinged glow sat a lanky gunfighter in a suit and tie, his black wing-tip shoes propped on John's desk.

The door closed behind John.

"Your shoes are scarring the wood," said John.

"Want to turn me in?" said CIA Security director Korn.

"What can I do for you—sir?"

"Less and less as time goes by."

John faced the CIA's head guard dog and reached behind himself, put his palms flat on Frank's desk and rose off the floor, sat on the metal slab. His weight pressed his hands on the desk: *Don't let Korn see you shaking.*

"Did you bring my stuff back?" asked John.

"I know," said Korn.

"Know what?"

The scream of John's telephone: ringing once, twice.

"Aren't you going to answer it?" asked Korn.

"Probably a wrong number." *Heart pounding. Don't let it be Phil David—make him call back later! Later!*

Korn eyed the ringing phone on the desk by his shoes.

"Maybe I should answer it for you," said Korn.

Or Glass, thought John: *If Korn hears Glass's voice—*

"Don't—don't do me any favors," said John. "Don't do my job."

He can beat me to the phone, but I could jump there, yank it unplugged before he could find out who—

The phone stopped ringing.

"Ah," said Korn. "Too late. Maybe they'll call back."

"Still won't be for you," said John.

"Maybe I don't care," said Korn. "I can answer it. It's a government phone. And I am the government."

"Aren't we all," said John. "But that number's not assigned to you."

"Who's got your number, Lang? I know how you got that goose egg on your forehead." Korn smiled: "You think I don't have friends on the Arlington force?"

"Nobody's ever accused you of having friends anywhere."

"I'm your best hope," said Korn.

"For what?"

Korn put his shoes on the floor.

"You either got problems or you are problems," said Korn. "You get to choose. But do it now."

"Do either of us know what you're talking about?"

"I'm talking about your buddy. Phillip David."

John blinked.

"Detective Greene and I reached an understanding."

"The world needs understanding." John felt his shirt sticking to his armpits.

"You can't afford to give a shit about the world." Korn stood. "The door is closing on your ass. Why are you tracking Phillip David? A reunion between Army buddies?"

"I never served in the Army with anyone named Phillip David."

"Never crossed paths with him at jump school, or the JFK special warfare center, or the intel schools?"

"I am not at liberty to discuss any possibly classified elements of my military—"

"Not even with the CIA's head of Security?" Korn shook his head. "You do work for the CIA, don't you?"

"Full-time."

"You kind of forgot that in China."

The phone rang.

Emma—could be—

Rang again.

"Still want to ignore that?" said Korn.

"It's still my job. My business."

The phone rang.

"Your business? Yours and who else's? Your buddy Glass might have half the town webbed, but the other half is still free."

"That bullshit is beneath you. Who's Phillip David and why do you think I care about him?"

Korn frowned: "Maybe you really are the innocent Joe. Then you really got problems."

The phone fell silent.

"Persistent, aren't they?" Korn smiled at the machine linking John to anyone who had his number. "Must be important."

"You say I got problems," said John. "So help me out."

"Are you saying you want to deal?"

"I don't have much luck dealing."

"How 'bout Frank? Was he 'unlucky' too? Or did he smell the smoke of your fire? Pro like him, a whiff is all he'd need."

"Frank was my friend."

"We only hurt the ones we love."

"I'm not dating anybody named Phillip David," said John. "Far as I know, he's your boy."

"Phil was an Activity man. Army spook. You work for them?"

"I never worked for the Intelligence Support Activity."

"Not even when it was called FOG—Foreign Operating Group? Or Tactical Concept Activity? Or its new name now?"

"I served in the Army on classified Agency business."

"Which Agency?"

"Our Agency—at least, the CIA I work for."

Korn shrugged. "Dates of Army duty between you and him don't mesh. But paper trails are made to mislead.

"How about Yellow Fruit?" said Korn. "You know any of those guys they court-martialed in the secret courtrooms they built in Arlington back in '85?"

"Was Phillip David part of Yellow Fruit?"

"His name came up. But he never got nailed. Then.

"Black funds," said Korn. "Big temptation for guys in our business. Millions of secret dollars can blind a guy."

"I've never been charged with financial irregularities."

"No, you weren't charged. No personal misuse or motivation was ever proven. What does your medal say again?"

"You read the citation."

"We didn't pass out 'good dog' stickers in the Secret Service."

"So why did you come to work for us?"

"Us?" Korn jabbed his finger at John. "Check your rank again, Lang: you work for me!"

"And this guy Phil David works for the Activity crowd."

"Maybe," said Korn. "In '82, he was part of the ISA team the Army sheep-dipped into Khartoum to keep Libya from whacking Sudan's President. A coup got that Pres after the Activity withdrew. In '85, Phil David was one of the ISA shooters slipped into Beirut to hit the terrorists who'd grabbed TWA 847, but ISA never got the green light from the White House."

"I never operated in Beirut or Africa," said John.

"So why are you getting beat up in Arlington tracking down an Army spook who did?"

"Questions regarding my work should be referred through proper channels."

"To who? Who's pulling your strings, Mr. Op Man?"

"Nobody named Phillip David."

"Who's pulling his strings?"

"You're the one with the answers," said John.

"Nobody knows about him," said Korn. "When Ollie North and the boys in the White House basement muscled into covert ops, Phil David folded out of sight."

"Privatized? Sheep-dipped?"

"Gone," said Korn. "Just gone."

He leaned into John's face: "Why haven't you told me to shut up?"

"I like a good story."

Then the echo of his own words made John frown: "You're telling me data as much as asking me questions."

"I'm showing you the box you're in."

"No, you're . . .

"You're building the box," whispered John. His voice rose as he said: "If I get put on a lie detector machine, asked the right questions . . . you've told me enough 'facts' so that I can't deny knowledge. You've boxed me in to what you want to find out. Set me up for a frame. Or to be your whore, buying my way clean by doing what you want."

"You lost your virginity on this before me," said Korn.

The phone rang.

"Won't work," said John quickly—*Phuong, could be, why would she call now when—Divert Korn! Don't let him—*

Then John frowned. Felt the sweat bead on his brow. "You know that won't work, too. You're not that . . . dim-witted."

The phone rang again.

"What I am is the last and only guy you can trust," said Korn.

"Give me a break. If I can trust you so much, why did you have guys in a blue sedan trailing me the other day?"

"To see if you'd act guilty," said Korn. "You won an Oscar."

The phone rang a third—clicked off in mid-ring.

"And what so-innocent crap are you doing?" said John.

"I'm trying to find out what's happening to my Agency. That's my job. It's your job—your duty—to help me. If you're really such a Mr. Innocent, you'll do that."

"I've got nothing to say to you." John shrugged. "You've vacuumed everything in here except the dust. If you could nail me on your wall, you would, but you can't—"

"Maybe," interrupted Korn.

"Where are your people? Your backups? A partner to be the official witness? My bet is you're wearing a wire, but this isn't how ex-cops like you work a squeeze. You bring a team you can trust so you can prove what you get and what you did."

Korn reached inside his suit. He handed John a grainy snapshot showing the blurred profile of a lean man wearing sunglasses and no shirt. The smudged background looked tropical.

"In nine hours of full-court press," said Korn, "that's the only photo of your buddy Phillip David my people could find. We got that from an Activity colleague of his who we woke up at four this morning in San Diego."

"If he's Army, intelligence, ISA—"

"All his by-name personnel files and computer references have evaporated. In Virginia, his driver's license negatives have even been 'misplaced.' We were lucky to pick him up in an Index of ISA Beirut team members."

"Who's got the clout or the balls to do that?"

"You tell me."

John stared at the grainy photo: could be almost anybody.

"Don't you recognize who you're tracking?" said Korn.

"Even if I were tracking someone, I wouldn't discuss my work without proper—"

Then it hit John: "You don't trust your own people. And

you're afraid I might be . . . You're afraid you might have me wrong. That's why you're here alone."

"You're the one who's alone," said Korn. "If you cut me out, you cut your throat. Last few weeks, I been hearing rumors that this office of yours was 'active.' Then Frank died, you got beat up. When I found out that Phillip David's files had been purged, I knew I wasn't chasing phantoms. Knew I was right to line up on you. You're an asshole, but you might be mostly innocent. Come clean now, and we can cut a deal."

"Like I said, I'm not good at deals."

Korn stuck the picture back inside his pocket. He walked to the door, looked back.

"Then you better be good at running," he said.

The Security chief turned back and smiled: "If you really are innocent, then you got nothing to worry about, knowing I'm running right behind you."

With a smile, he flipped off the overhead lights and walked out, leaving John alone in the silent blue shadows.

33

John floated in blue light.

Korn had left him alone in his office.

Frank had left him alone on the firing line.

The phone on his desk. Silent.

Glass, a secret phone in his desk. Call him. Tell him what? About Korn? don't tell him about Phuong. About Emma. Tell him . . .

What he needs to know.

This is how it starts. Secrets. Spies. Lies.

Call me again, Phil David. One more time. One more chance.

Phuong. Call her and what? Know that she answers? Guess at her secrets?

The door buzzer blared.

Emma marched past him when he opened the door. By the time he closed it, she stood at his desk.

"We have to get something straight," she said. The ruby line of her lips trembled, unable to hold a smile.

"I'm not sure this is the time or place." Smile. Joke. *Control, don't let her—*

"You're here, so am I, this'll have to do."

She wore a navy-blue linen suit, a simple ivory silk blouse, buttoned at the collar.

"This place," she said, pushing her hand toward the walls of Congress: "This place is too important to play around with."

"I know that."

A black purse hung from a strap over her right shoulder; a folded manila envelope jutted out of its clasp.

"That's wrong," she said.

"Emma, what—"

"You think I can't see something's wrong here?"

"This mess is just because Security is cautious, making sure there's nothing connecting this office with Frank's . . . death."

"And what have they found out?"

"Nothing," said John. "Ask them."

"So I can hear the no-comment company line?" Her eyes narrowed. "You didn't get those bruises shaving."

"Martial arts, at lunch once I told you I practice—"

"You said it wasn't about hitting people. Or getting hit."

"I was working out with another guy. Who was mad at me."

"Oh really? I know how he feels." She shook her head. "You ask me to do high school research when you've got better means than the Library of Congress. I do it, maybe because of high school stuff of my own, because I want to believe you're true."

"It's true. I had questions about—"

"Maybe it's true, but for sure it's wrong. The flow is going the wrong way. *You're* Central Intelligence, not me. You're supposed to tell *us*."

"CIA is who you are," she said. "Isn't it?"

"You know who I am."

"Don't game me. And damn well don't you game me about this place, about my work!"

"This isn't any game."

"Better believe that. You think different, my boss will break your balls, and I'll grease his hammer. If you—"

"Tell him."

She blinked. "What?"

"Tell Senator Handelman what I asked you to do as a friend. But I guess this is Capitol Hill: there must be no such thing as a friendly favor."

"Don't give me that innocent-martyr crap."

"What *crap* do you want?"

The phone rang.

Rang again.

Emma frowned: "You can—aren't you going to answer that?"

John's shirt stuck to his back, his heart raced. "It's gotta be . . . just business."

"Why don't you want—"

The phone rang again.

"You can't even trust me enough to answer it?" she said. "Say, 'Hold on,' or 'I'll call you back,' or—"

The phone rang a third —cut off Silent.

"What 'business' are you doing?" she said.

"Nothing wrong. Nothing illegal. Nothing that concerns you."

"A dead American in Paris? An American whose company has a few piddly U.S. government contracts? You made it my concern when you asked me for help. Plus somebody bruising you? I thought you want me to care about you."

"I do." True. That's true.

"Don't lie to me, John."

"Do you think men and women can ever tell the whole truth to each other?"

"Absolutely." She didn't bat an eyelash. "But this isn't about men and women. This is about me and you."

Got nothing to throw back.

"Don't play me," she said. "Abuse who I am, my work. Already, you've already pulled me too far to . . . to not matter. Don't do it."

"I never want to see you hurt."

"Most people feel that way about dogs. I deserve a lot more than a dog."

"I won't ask you for anything else." *True, make that true.* "I won't put you in a position where—"

"I'm not saying that if you need me I won't—"

"A position where you don't think you should be," continued John. "Your work, whatever. Do what you think is right. You

don't need to, I don't want you to, but if you tell Handelman . . . "

"Tell him what?"

"What you've done," said John.

*But you'd have to lie. You couldn't face him and tell him the whole
truth as you know it. The Senator would shake his head, wonder not
about seemingly unrelated data, but about you and your intuition, your
professionalism, about the mysteries between men and women. You know
that better than me. So you can't tell him. You won't.*

Unless some monster scares you, angers you, pushes you
enough.

Compromised. Boxed. Trapped.

Her eyes reflected that reality even as she fought it.

"Whatever you want to do," he told her. More hollow truth.
"It's your choice."

"Is that all this is?" she whispered.

"What do you mean?"

"What about you? What's your choice?"

Heart pounding.

Look at her.

Look at her.

Don't tell her. Can't tell her. Don't let her know.

Want her. Take her.

Keep her away. Safe. Keep control. Don't let her handle—

"Kiss me," she said. Cold. Wary.

Her breath is quick, jagged as he walks to her. The scent of
coconut shampoo, perfume of roses and leather. Reflected in her
blue eyes, he saw himself draw closer. She tilts her face up.

Bend down to her.

And her lips press his, hard—then soft. Opening. Fire roared
in him. He felt the brush of her linen suit beneath his fingers,
her skirt taut over belled hips. Screams echoed from the death
car seven days gone. The wind of years wanting and waiting.
This was Emma. Just her. Here. Now. Flashing on a vision/no
cinematic lie in the blue light of this room, her naked, bent over,

gripping the edges of his desk, her hips round white worlds, moving into her into her into her as she moans *yes* and knowing

absolutely knowing

that could be true, just that true, feeling that power surge in their kiss,

feeling the limits of that truth and the borders of his lies.

Sensing her feel that, too.

Emma pulled back.

No words.

Keep control! Can't let—

But no words.

Yet she hears. Her mind thinks like his.

"Oh God," she said.

She turned away, stepped away.

"Damn you," she whispered.

"Do you have any good 'why'?" she asked. "About any of it?"

She held up her hand: "No—don't say anything, don't give me any polite lies. This is the way it always is. Should have known. Same old shit. Let me guess. Let me see if I can give it a name. Maybe a face. Maybe mine in the mirror, 'sucker' tattooed on my forehead. Let me not give a damn, doesn't matter, does it? As long as it's just personal."

"What matters is—"

"Don't say another word," she said. "Christ, we're not even breaking up, you never let it get that . . . Just a good time, huh. Just such a good time. A little erotic op."

She gave him a nasty smile: "You'll never ever have a better lover than me."

"I know." And he knew the level where that was true.

"What did you know and when did you know it," she intoned, like a prosecutor. "Damn your lying eyes.

"Damn me," she said. "What a fool."

Just before she opened the door: "You owe me. Get a blood test. Let me know if you've killed me, too."

Murmurs drifted in from the world.

Eyes shining, Emma pulled the manila envelope from her purse.

"All your hard work just for this," she said.

She dropped the envelope on his office floor.

Said, "Wasn't worth it."

The soundproof door swung shut behind her, locked.

Imagine the click of her heels, walking away.

Hope that she walks all the way away. Need her to go that far, she has to go that far, forget it, leave it alone, me alone, her questions, not go to her boss Handelman or . . .

Perfume of leather and roses.

Don't think about ashes in her heart.

Your chance lost.

Can't. Not now. Not important.

Believe that lie. Keep going.

Check your watch: almost noon.

Pick up the envelope.

The wall of translucent fuzzes mirrored John's grotesque image. The blue surface reflected the stain on his lips of Emma's ruby lipstick—a dark smear. Like blood.

The phone rang.

34

The money lay fanned out on Frank's dining room table.

Phuong said: "Twenty-seven thousand, used bills. Plus that bankbook for somebody named Gene Mallette, who has $13,000. Mom used to joke about him, say he was the one who forgot to take out the garbage. Gene Mallette was one of Dad's work names."

"You found this here." John opened an oversized hardback book on the history of movies to a hole scissored in the thick text.

"And started calling you right away. My father never had $27,000 cash in his whole life."

"Not of his own."

"Besides, it's a bush league stash! He's professional and thorough enough to sanitize our house, hide that video in plain sight, jettison my pictures, and then you're telling me he—"

John pressed his hand over her mouth.

Phuong's eyes flared and she jerked back—

Finger to his lips, he let her go.

With a black felt pen, John printed one word in the margin of a book page.

Phuong read his scrawl, stared at him; nodded. She held up one finger. Ran upstairs.

Look out the window: no cars with people in them, no florist's vans.

Phuong bounded down the stairs, a sweater pulled over her

blouse, jeans and sensible winter shoes. She carried a shoulder bag—and from the guest bathroom, John's toothbrush and razor.

As she zipped open her briefcase, he ripped the page he'd defaced out of the book, scooped the money off the table and stuffed it in his suit pockets. In her closet, his suitcase served as a drawer for clean underwear. Hung above it were a few of his shirts, his jeans and mountaineering coat. His black sneakerlike shoes waited on the closet floor beside the suitcase.

Thirty seconds to throw gear in that bag, zip it closed.

Look out the window: no new vehicles, nobody on the sidewalks. No mailman.

Turn around.

Phuong, packing her briefcase with John's razor, a videotape, a framed black-and-white picture of her father, a notebook. She abandoned a volume of poems on the coffee table.

Shoved her father's .45 down the front of her jeans, draped her sweater over it, zipped her briefcase, whirled into her black trench coat. Left the buttons undone, the belt untied.

Nodded to John.

Check the windows: outside, a mangy white Labrador trotted over the dead grass.

Paper in John's hand: the book page.

Excess weight.

Matches next to the kitchen sink. He held the page over the black hole of the garbage disposal. The paper curled as orange flames devoured the word he'd scrawled in the margin: EVACU-ATE.

35

"Drive slow," John told Phuong.

They'd ditched John's car a mile from Frank's apartment, taken Phuong's rental car. For three hours, he'd driven like a pro—doubling back, racing over the Beltway, taking random exits, zipping through city streets again, even parking and running from the car on foot, circling back to watch it from behind rotten-banana-filled trash cans. Finally driving to a forgettable shopping mall café, a quiet table in the rear, fire exit a few steps away and their car visible out the plateglass window. Digesting the computer-generated data Emma had given John: Dun & Bradstreet and other Congressional database-accessible business reports on Cliff Johnson's Imex company.

Phuong never asked John where he got the few pages that showed Imex handled small import-export-transportation contracts overseas for the State Department and Pentagon and private clients.

You wonder, thought John, but you can feel that you shouldn't ask. Or don't want to know. And you're strong enough to trust that.

What they learned from Emma's packet helped not at all.

Now Phuong piloted the car down quiet residential streets.

"Not too slow," ordered John.

"I'm doing fine," argued Phuong.

"We want to look normal. Like we know where we're going."

"We do know where we're going." She glanced in the mirror. "Nobody's followed us."

"Even if they know about you, I don't buy that they'd put a homer bug in your car."

"We don't even know that anybody put one in yours."

"That's right, we don't know."

"Or bugged my Dad's house." She slowed for a little girl running home from school. "We don't know."

Three blocks away, the roof of his landlord's house.

"Why are we going to your cabin?" said Phuong. "You said—"

"Turn left!" he yelled. "There! Up into there!"

Phuong cranked the wheel and the car rolled up the driveway of a large white house. She stopped at the closed garage door.

"This doesn't look like—"

"Down the block." John scrunched low in the front seat, peered out his window. "Just past the corner before my landlord's house."

"That blue van? Probably a plumber."

The front door of this house opened. A gray-haired woman frowned at the strangers parked in her driveway.

"Get out," said John. "Ask her for directions."

"To where?" hissed Phuong as she stepped out to the driveway.

A big smile, a puzzled look—natural. Innocent. A sweet young woman, no one to call the cops about. Phuong asked the old woman if this was the Gene Mallette residence, got a wary denial.

Down the street, a hand flicked a cigarette out the van's driver's window. In the cold air, the van sat still, no exhaust.

The gray-haired woman went back inside her locked house. Phuong got in the car.

"What did you see?" she asked.

"Nothing for sure. Enough."

They drove back the way they'd come, careful not to pass the van.

Phuong said: "Where can we go now?"

36

Four o'clock. Suburban Virginia, a safe neighborhood more popular with the retinue of the previous Presidential court than the minions of the current man. John and Phuong parked her rental car across the street from a three-story plantation-style home.

They could have been newlyweds. Recent appointees or transfers from Kansas. House-hunting for a happy home.

"Don't tell me what I don't know!" said John. "Everywhere I go—"

"*We* go," snapped Phuong.

" . . . somebody's building a box." He shook his head. "No. Not a box. A coffin.

"Operationally, it doesn't matter when they planted the money on your father. We have to assume they know you're in it with me."

"So then it's three coffins," said Phuong.

"Not if we're smart. Not if you do what I tell you."

"I've been doing what you tell me! Look where it's gotten me! You don't know—"

He whispered: *"Don't. Tell. Me. What. I. Don't. Know."*

"Don't tell me what to do," she countered. "If I'm worth a coffin to them, I'm worth more than just following your orders."

He sank into the car seat, his eyes locked on the white antebellum house across the street.

"If anybody else decides there's mystery about your dad's

death, investigates . . . finds his trail that Glass and I have followed . . . then sooner or later, our Security people or the cops,
the FBI, they'd vacuum your house.

"Money is the smoke of sin. If something's deemed wrong
with Frank's death, then the 'good guys' discover that he'd 'hidden' money that was demonstrably not his. No answers, but
more clues. The system might not figure out what Frank did or
what happened to him, but with the secret out-of-pocket investigation he was running, dirty movies and dirty money, he'd sure
come up guilty."

"Who was at your house—if that van was real?"

"My enemies are leaves of trees whose roots I cannot see."

"Don't quote poetry to me now!" snapped Phuong.

"Quote it?" John snorted. "Hell, I wrote it."

"What if this guy's not here?" said Phuong.

"Then we wait. When you called his work, they said . . . "

"All they told me was he wasn't in today." said Phuong.
"What if he won't tell you anything?"

"He'll tell me everything."

She read the expression on his face. They spent a silent
minute. Nothing moved in the windows of the house they
watched.

"How can he afford to live here?" said Phuong.

"My guess is, Martin Sinclair rents from someone who backed
the wrong candidate or believed the wrong economic theory."

John checked his watch: 4:09. In an hour, curious neighbors
would start to return to these quiet streets.

"Come on," he said. "Leave our bags."

They could have been newlyweds. House-hunting.

Strolling up the street. Walking up the sidewalk to the main
door of that big white house. Carefully checking it out.

Or lost, they could have been seeking directions, been lost.

A curved brick path to the black front door. A brass mail slot,
a carved knocker and a doorbell.

Drapes covered the first-floor windows.

The thorny branches of a hedge cradled a blue-plastic-wrapped *New York Times*. A clear-plastic-wrapped *Washington Post* hid in a withered flower bed.

John tried the front door handle—locked.

Rang the bell.

Thick walls and quality insulation muffled sounds inside the house. Standing on the porch, they barely heard the doorbell chime.

Ring it again. Knock once. Knock twice.

"Nobody's home," said Phuong.

"It's cold," she said. "We can wait in the car."

But she followed him around the side of the house. Trees and fences gave the backyard privacy.

Curtains filled the windows in the backyard patio door. Locked—a simple doorknob button. No wires for an alarm.

"Wait," she whispered.

Feel above the doorjamb. Next to the door. Under a stone figure of a wood nymph—a gold key.

Knock on that back door, too—but quietly. Quietly.

No answer.

The gold key slid into the patio door. A turn of the wrist, a gentle push . . .

And they were inside a kitchen full of unpacked boxes.

Whisper in Phuong's ear. She glares, but obeys.

"Anybody home?" yelled Phuong. "Real estate manager!"

Afternoon sunlight filtered through the curtains and drapes.

The smell of cardboard, crumpled newspapers, dust.

"Nobody's here," said Phuong.

They stopped whispering.

"Somebody's dream house," said Phuong, looking around the kitchen with its central island rangetop and oven, its cabinets and counter space, dishwasher, microwave.

A delivery box lay open next to the aluminum sink. Three slices of vegetarian pizza congealed in the afternoon light.

"Doesn't feel like a dream," said John

A message blackboard was glued next to the wall phone. Blank black surface, chalk waiting.

"We're burglars now," she said. "Felons."

"Come on."

Walk slowly in this quiet house.

Phuong said: "If we got in this easy . . . "

She followed John through the hall to the dining room.

Boxes covered a table taped with moving pads.

Wa-whump!

Jump against the wall, whirl and Phuong yells and—

"The furnace." John pointed to a vent in the dining room wall, let warm air blow over his palm. "Furnace kicked on."

"Shit!"

"Least we won't be cold," said John.

The dining room led to a parlor filled with unopened boxes.

"This makes me feel creepy," said Phuong. "Sneaky."

"But it's our move," said John. "These are the chances you pray for."

An afternoon shadow crept across the blond wood floor of the main entryway toward scattered envelopes.

The floor creaked as John hurried to scoop up the mail. He kept his face toward the brass postal slot in the front door, his ears tuned for the sound of a key turning in the front lock.

Behind him Phuong's eyes measured the taped boxes, bare white walls. Solid walls that repelled the sounds of the outside world and sealed inside any sounds of laughter or tears. Or screams.

The architect built this house like a three-story box. He compensated for that budget-enforced boredom by planning the home around skylights. The top two floors encased a room-wide light shaft. Stairs hugged the light shaft's interior walls.

Phuong drifted in John's wake, kept her eyes on him but kept her distance. She backed away from him as he sorted through the pile of other people's mail on the floor by the front door. Her gaze was unfocused, trying not to see *their* crime. She barely knew where she was. Her heel bumped the carpeted bottom step leading up to the sunset flickers in the skylights. She turned.

Purple hands grabbed her face.

Screaming and she stumbled back and . . .

. . . *Purpleblack face* chasing her swinging back and . . . John whirled saw

Phuong, saw

that face, hands, that shape, swinging down from the top of the stairwell . . .

"Oh GodNo oh No!" Phuong pulled the pistol from her jeans, both hands shaking stabbed it at the thing, finger squeezing the trigger, squeezing and it's hard stuck and it won't move won't—

John grabbed her hands, the gun, his other arm circled her shoulders as she stumbled back into him, back, and he held her close, took the gun from her grasp.

"It's OK!" he yelled to her. "It's OK! He's already dead!"

The man's corpse hung upside down above the stairs.

"Shhh," said John. "Don't scream any more. Don't scream."

"He's dead, is he dead, is he—"

"Yes," said John. "Yes."

Blood-bloated, the man's hands and face swung slowly to a stop after Phuong's collision. Hung still. His white shirt was still tucked in his suit pants. One leg jutted out like the awkward forgotten arm of a "K." The other was straight and taut, twisted and hooked out of sight beyond the lip of the second-floor landing.

John flicked the .45's safety off, cocked the hammer. *Rock 'n' roll.* He held the pistol in the two-handed combat grip.

Said, "Stay—"

"Fuck you!" whispered Phuong.

She stepped behind him, where she could see and wasn't alone.

Slowly, edge to the stairs.

That face. Blood-purpled skin. Eyes popped open. Bulging.

Martin Sinclair. Diplomat, U.S. State Department. Mid-30s. Husband. Father. Dead.

No blood on the carpet. No wounds on the white shirt over his chest, his back.

Ease up the stairs, the two of you, backs pressed against the wallpaper, faces and chests tinglingly close to those hands.

Look up: the thick carved wooden slats of the railing that bordered the wide halls of the light shaft.

Martin Sinclair's left foot, wedged between two of those slats above the stairs going down to the first level. Trapped, hanging his body upside down.

A decorative wall lamp angled out from the wall above his body. The bulb was missing.

"We're OK." John locked the hammer on half-cocked, flicked the safety on, tucked the pistol in his waistband. "He's been dead a long time. We're alone. We're OK. We're safe."

"No we're not," whispered Phuong. Her hand trembled in his.

On the second-floor landing, close to where Sinclair's foot was wedged between two banister posts, lay a box of lightbulbs.

The hallway made a corner above the stairs going down to the first floor, the banisters met at a right angle. John saw a dark smear on the wood rail of the banister across the open stairwell from where Sinclair's foot was wedged.

Nausea flowed through John. Then acid.

Damn you! You should have told me when you could! Maybe I could have—

Too late. Too damn late. Not my . . . His fault, it's his fault.

Frank's beast, always a step ahead of me. Laughing.

Watching.

Phuong said: "What . . . What?"

"This is how the cops will write it," said John. "Once upon a time, Martin Sinclair decided to change a lightbulb."

"Where's the old—"

"Doesn't matter, new tenants, maybe a bulb never was there, maybe it's in the trash. 'Maybe' is enough for overworked cops.

"For them, Sinclair is sloppy. Steps over the rail. Reaches. Loses his balance, falls, foot gets wedged in one railing, head smacks the other . . .

"Just another somebody who died," said John.

"But with all—"

"For the local cops, there is no 'all' connected to this."

"How?" she asked. No doubts either.

"Could be one man. Sneaks in. Ambushes Sinclair. One punch, temple shot. Suffocate him to finish it, if he had to. Hits Sinclair's head on the railing lifts him over the other side, lets go—didn't figure on the foot getting wedged, but that wouldn't—"

"Nobody could count on—"

"He didn't count on anything. Except making the kill. Spontaneity. Genius—"

"Genius!"

"You can't train somebody for something like this. Not this smooth. Anybody can kill somebody, but to improvise a scene like this takes talent. Like jazz. Cool and clean and quick."

"Like my father," said Phuong.

"Yes. Like that. However that was."

"Same guy."

"Same guys," corrected John. "Whoever thought this whole thing up uses a pro hitter, a wet boy.

"A brilliant hitter," he added.

"That's what you call it." She turned away from the body.

Phuong started toward an open door to a bedroom.

"Don't bother," said John. "There's nothing here but lies."

"Unless . . . " John ran down the stairs.

Phuong hurried after him, knowing . . .

Have to look at that, she knew she had to . . . look at *that*. Watch it to keep from . . . touching it.

The smell: *Syrup. Sour cabbage and ham.*

His back to the corpse, standing in the front entryway, John cradled an envelope in his hands. The handwritten return address was in Connecticut, "S. Sinclair."

"His mother?" said Phuong.

"Or wife," said John.

"You shouldn't—"

"I bet it arrived after . . . " John tore open the envelope.

"'Dear Martin,'" he read. "'We're fine . . . Miss you, Janey talks about Daddy all the . . . ' Weather . . . Her mother's fine, his mother . . . 'Don't know why you say we should stay up here a while longer. The house sounds wonderful, and it's OK if'—skip that . . .

"Wait: 'I know you'll dodge this if I bring it up on the phone, but I can't bear this anymore. Something's wrong. I know it. Please tell me. I'm scared to death. I don't know which is worse, not knowing or finding out. I love you but I don't even know how to say this: Is there another woman? Someone else who can make you want them? I know I still have some weight after the baby, but you said that doesn't matter. We haven't made love in six months, and it took me a while to realize that but—'"

"Stop!" yelled Phuong. "Leave him alone! Leave them alone!"

"Not our choice," said John.

Phuong turned away from him—saw the dangling corpse—faced the parlor. Took a step, two—but stayed in earshot.

"'I know you've been under stress at work,'" read John, "'ever since Egypt, but it can't be this bad. When I get there, when Janey and I come down to make our family together again . . . .'"

John skimmed the letter. Said, "She wants to go to a marriage counselor. Says they can keep it quiet, out of his personnel file so it won't affect his career."

Night filled the house. A light glowed in the hall where they stood. Lights shone in a room upstairs, from the kitchen.

From the hall above the dangling corpse.

"Get out of here," said Phuong. "I can't stay here anymore."

A dozen other opened envelopes lay on the table in the parlor. John stuck the letter back in its envelope, put it in that pile.

"She'll think he got it, read it," said John.

"Is that what she'll think?"

They walked into the kitchen.

"Don't touch anything else," said John. "The wet boy probably wore gloves."

"Wait!" Phuong grabbed John's arm. "Are you going to just leave him . . . like that? For somebody, his wife maybe, to find?"

John fingered the kitchen curtains, peered outside.

Empty night.

He opened the door told Phuong: "We were never here."

Cold flowed into the house. The furnace kicked on again.

Phuong said, "Give me back the gun."

37

John and Phuong huddled in her rental car, lights out as it idled on a night-filled suburban Virginia street eight miles from Martin Sinclair's dangling body.

The defroster labored to keep the car's windshield clear.

Other cars parked on this street were empty. Inside cozy homes, televisions flickered. The air outside Phuong and John's cracked-open car windows smelled fresh and clean and cold.

"I thought you were never supposed to come here," said Phuong.

"Best-laid plans." John took his eyes off a ranch-style house behind a white picket fence. "You remember—"

"Trust me, I know what to do."

"OK," he said. "OK."

"We're OK," she said.

They laughed.

"Dawn," said John. "Give me until first light, then . . . "

"Then," she said. "If Greene isn't working—"

"Then keep calling until you get him."

"Cinnamon man." She shook her head. But with a wry smile.

Half there as much as he'd ever been anywhere, half lost in nightmares of *what-if*s and bullets and bloated bodies, John whispered: "Everything has one true name."

"What?"

"Wisdom from another time and another place."

"Hell, I can barely deal with here and now," she said.

"But you do, and you're doing fine."

"What if you walk into something like what we found before?"

"Hope that I walk out. You've got the gun. Cash. Woodruff's numbers. Greene's number. The highway and a car rental company that guarantees carefree, happy motoring."

"I'm such a lucky girl."

John's left hand floated up, stretched toward her.

Sitting behind the steering wheel, she didn't flinch.

He pulled off the plastic cap of the car's dome light and unscrewed the bulb.

"Oh," she said.

John opened the car door and the night chilled her face.

Look back, tell her: "Don't let them get you."

Soft as a whisper, shut the car door.

Walk away.

Walk to that house.

Behind him in the night, Phuong's car idled. Headlights dark.

Sit back in your eyes. Relax your gaze. Don't look—see.

Just an ordinary brick house in a comfortable neighborhood. The attached two-stall-garage door was closed. A tan Cadillac sat on the driveway slab. A steel gate locked the Cadillac in the driveway. The picket fence around the lawn was chest-high; steel wires lined the backs of the slats. Black boxes the size of computer screens clung like beehives to the corner eaves of the house; another box hung above the brightly lit front door.

Lift the fence gate latch.

A slight resistance—magnetic circuit broken.

Every blade of dormant grass stood frozen at attention.

Ring the doorbell. No need to announce that a visitor is on the front step, but ring it anyway.

No sound escaped from inside the house.

Eyes he couldn't see crawled over John.

"Figured you might show up here someday," said Harlan Glass when he opened the door. "But figured tonight you'd run to hell."

As John crossed the threshold, he heard Phuong drive away.

Go. Go.

The heavy door closed, locks clicked, and John was inside.

White halls, white rooms, thick carpet. Subdued lighting. The murmur of television.

A mahogany wardrobe was built into the foyer wall. Glance inside that closet: red bulbs glowing on a control panel, TV monitors. On the floor, a pair of overshoes and an umbrella. On the top shelf, the butt of a revolver.

Glass shut the closet door with a secure click.

Soft breathing. The odor of—

A Doberman pinscher crouched in the living room doorway six feet to John's left.

Easy, don't let it smell . . .

Glass spoke a command in a language John couldn't identify.

The Doberman dropped to the floor. Watched his master.

"Move slowly." Glass wore a cardigan sweater over a sports shirt, pressed pants, soft loafers. He looked thinner than in his suits. That night, the canine quality of his features seemed more akin to his guard dog. "Come with me."

Another private language command passed from master to dog. The Doberman trotted behind John's heels.

Down the hall, a dining room and kitchen at the far end. A corridor branched off—probably to bedrooms.

Police sirens wailed in a TV set in the sitting room to their right. Slouched in an easy chair was the sharp-chinned woman John had seen at Frank's funeral. Her feet were bare. She didn't turn her face to see who walked past her life. Her eyes were as empty of the televised drama as her glass was of Scotch.

"Figured tonight, I'd work in my wife's study." Glass walked into a room where a snake-necked lamp dropped light on a table supporting three check ledgers, a pile of letters and envelopes. A raised hand from the master of this house halted John in the study doorway. John felt the dog drop to his haunches behind him. Glass's movements were precise as he slid the cap on a felt-tip pen, closed the ledgers, put letters into files. Respect made John turn his eyes from his case officer's private affairs.

The glow from the snake-necked lamp touched the wall next to John, a gallery of photographs. Rows of pictures. Glass with . . .

John squinted.

. . . Glass with Senators and Congressmen and a movie star who got a special tour of the CIA's sanctified and taboo Counter-Terrorism Center.

The wall looks like . . . some Senator's office.

Washington, thought John: Everybody's secret dream.

A lone family shot caught John's eye: a timeless portrait of mother and daughter. They weren't touching. The girl's smile was frozen, her stance rigid. The mother's eyes looked away from the camera, and her face seemed blurred, a smoother image than the lined countenance of the woman in front of the TV set.

How many years did it take the bottle to win? wondered John. What did that cost this family?

"Not here," said Glass. He snapped off the desk lamp.

John backed into the hall. The dog tensed, but stayed on his haunches. Glass straightened a picture of him shaking hands with a civil rights leader who'd lost a President bid.

Glass led John to the kitchen. Opened an ordinary door to a flight of stairs, switched on the light and tapped a code into a control panel. He walked down the stairs.

Followed by John.

Then the dog.

"Few people ever get down here," said Glass as he tapped an entry code into the lock on the metal door at the bottom of the stairs, pushed it open and switched on more lights. "After you."

The dog followed John inside.

The door clicked shut behind them.

The basement smelled of steel and cement, had no windows. A wall of file cabinets. A computer. A toilet with a curtain for privacy. A coach's blackboard draped with a thick blue cloth.

An antique flat-top desk dominated the room. Three phones

mounted on electronic boxes sat to the left of the desk's executive padded black chair. The desktop glistened like a mirror.

Glass took the high-back black chair. His hand swept John to a metal folding chair facing the desk.

The dog took up a post five feet to John's right.

A command: the dog sat. His front legs stayed stiff, his eyes stayed on John. The Doberman smelled clean. Panted.

The whisper of a drawer being opened behind the desk.

Glass sat with his hands unseen near his lap.

"Figure it's time for you to tell me everything."

John closed his eyes. His strength crumbled against the folding chair's steel.

Words tumbled from him. Money at Frank's. Martin Sinclair dangling dead. Co-opting Emma, not liking it even if both he and Glass knew co-optation was the core of tradecraft. Plastic explosives, Imex's small business profile. He told Glass everything. Phuong.

"No choice with her," said John. "She caught me, she's gutsy and smart and a troublemaker. No choice."

"Figure you're right. No choice. Where is she now?"

"Rolling rendezvous."

"Ahh."

"She trusts me, but . . ."

"Yes. But, is there more?"

"I'm burned-out. Can't think. That's all, that's it."

"Yes," said Glass. "Figure I can trust that *is* it—as you know it. Figure if you were really bent, you would have run to hell, not come to me like this."

The sigh of a drawer being closed.

Glass folded his hands on the desk.

"Do you have the videotapes?" he asked.

"Didn't want to bring them until I knew you were here."

"Until you knew I was alive." Glass shook his head. "I'm much harder to kill than Frank or Martin Sinclair.

"But you," Glass sighed. "Figure you may not even have to be made dead.

"Korn has eyes inside the Select Committee office. This afternoon, when you left work, some of his people dropped by your cabin—officially, to be sure you were OK. You weren't there, they went in. No warrant, but the Counsel can find a dodge if—"

"Why would our legal team care?"

"My sources say that at your house, Korn's goons 'happened' to find $14,000 and a bankbook credited to one of your old work—"

"Shit!"

"Is it your money?" asked Glass.

"Do you have to ask?"

"Yes—but you answered by coming here. And by coming clean.

"There's more," said the CTC chief. "This afternoon, Senator Handelman called the Director and requested a detailed report on the death of an American in Paris named Cliff Johnson. Handelman specifically asked that our Congressional Liaison Office be not involved."

"Emma"

"Betrayed you."

"No." John smiled. "She kept her loyalties."

"Too late to manage that problem," said Glass. "There's nothing about Cliff Johnson's standing-alone death for the Agency to find, but now they're on that trail, too—your trail, Frank's trail. Which has been muddied with money. Who knows what else has been done to construct answers for their questions, but figure you're accounted for in some scenario. And figure this is over."

"No!"

"Collect Frank's daughter and all the meager horseshit you've found. I'll bring the two of you in and—"

"And I'm fucked."

"Your sanction from me will protect—"

"Hell, you're an Agency saint but I have a record of 'appropriating' Agency funds. My dead partner and I are tarred with dirty money. He ran an illegal off-the-books operation—we call it an

investigation, Korn will call it an instigation. Either way, the
Agency will call both Frank and me renegade. Plus the D.C. police think I might have killed him. My guess is that with a few
days of 'reconstructing,' they'll even be able to convince you why
you were wrong to trust me, find some new 'evidence' . . . Hell,
Cliff Johnson and the C-4 shipment, the Corcoran Center bombing—the only key to that is a man hanging upside down in his
house. Guess who found him first, who didn't report it."

"Frank's daughter was with you, she can testify—"

"Sinclair had been dead for hours. Me bringing her back to
find him can look like a move for perfect cover."

"You come in with the girl, we can—

"Do not enough.

"You're right," said John. "It would be over. Even if we can
break the logic of the evidence and convince the Agency that I'm
innocent . . . that the Corcoran Center bombing is part of this
mess . . . In this town, the idea is to manage crises, not solve
them. Solving them means getting down in the mud and blood,
getting dirty and maybe getting caught on a losing side. Admitting and justifying who you are and everything you've done,
right or wrong. Taking your lumps from the public. Managing a
crisis makes more sense. Keep it controlled, keep it quiet. Keep
yourself clean.

"Worse, there's some creep inside the Agency."

"No," said Glass, "figure worse is *if* there is a sanction running through all this, and the creep *is* the Agency."

"Or at least the people running it."

Glass drummed his fingers on his desk.

John said: "If I come in, every move we make, the creep'll see,
he'll cover himself even better. He'll manage us. We won't even
see how. Where can we go that won't need to fall back to the
Agency? The White House—overwhelmed, underinformed.
Congress—even worse. The press? Jackals who can only howl at
the dead meat they're given."

"There's still Phil David," said Glass.

"Right," said John. "Korn's people can't find him—and if

Korn is guilty or innocent, *either way*, you know they're tearing the world up trying. Phil David is linked with Frank, but Frank got killed. He's feeling me out, but if I flip to being one of the inside players—"

"He'll never know until it's too late."

"If I go inside, we'll make it too late—for us," said John. "By now, all Phil David can care about is staying alive. If I were him, I'd be long gone."

"No, if you were him, you'd be close by, trying to figure a way to come in, too.

"Never underestimate the desire some people have to do good," added Glass.

"Give me more time," said John. "My friend was murdered, I've been duped and blocked, set up and framed. Knocked around. Corcoran Center blew up, Cliff Johnson got killed—hell, Ahmed Naral was hung in Beirut! But I'm alive. When you can't find your next move, sink back, wait. That makes the other guy reach for you. Then . . ."

"I know your file, hobbies. This isn't hand-to-hand combat."

"Of course it is."

The Doberman whined.

His bulldog-faced master frowned.

"If I stay out," said John, "we still have some control."

Glass weighed John with his eyes. Shrugged.

"More time would help me set this up better," he admitted.

"You know what I have to do."

"You do nothing without my explicit sanction."

"Sure."

Glass narrowed his eyes. "You'll try to play me. It's your nature. But don't: you can only lose."

The CIA's guru of counterterrorism sighed: "I'll give you tomorrow. But when I say come, you come. Or along with the hounds already on your trail, I'll come for you."

"Understood."

" 'Agreed' was the correct response."

Say nothing.

The dog whined.

John ran his hand over his brow. Glanced at the dog.

"Does he bother you?" asked Glass.

Shrug.

"Ahh," said Glass.

Upstairs, Glass sent the dog in to be with his wife. He frowned toward the room where the television played.

"Sorry," he said. "Sheila . . . She's not feeling well."

"It's OK."

"Figure it is what it is," said Glass.

"I need to call a cab."

"No," said Glass. "Cabs create records, leave trails . . ."

"You could—"

"No. Tonight, I can't leave Sheila alone. And figure I have to start reconfiguring our op again."

He led John into the garage.

Two cars parked side by side. A new Ford with Virginia plates, a dated Toyota with Maryland tags. Much like Frank's car.

"This old one is my daughter's," said Glass. "She's away at college. Use it. These are spare keys, the gas tank is full."

"Close, complete contact," he told John.

Glass flipped a switch. The garage door rumbled up, open.

As John drove into the night, the driveway's white steel pole swung down to keep those inside its span safe.

38

Midnight on a Tuesday in Washington is an empty hour.

John drove the Glass Toyota through the city, from suburban Virginia to suburban Maryland. A perfect spymobile, he thought: functional but forgettable.

Back in the streets he called home. By now, a primary hunting zone for search and locate bird dogs. Or search and destroy wet boys.

They won't know this car, but . . .

He parked in front of a broken bank on the road flowing from Maryland's former cornfields to the heart of chic Georgetown. The bank's padlocked glass doors reflected glowing red and green neon from the movie theater complex across the street.

The movie theater cashier wore the company uniform—white shirt, black vest. She snapped off the lights in the booth as John walked toward her. Behind bulletproof glass, she mouthed, *We're closed.* Grabbed her ticket ledger and cash till, retreated into the theater, out of sight of the man on the sidewalk who was failing to look casual as he stood there, alone for anybody to see.

The parking lot at the 24-hour supermarket eight blocks south of the theater held maybe 20 cars.

Empty, they all looked empty.

John parked in a handicapped slot close to the supermarket's plateglass front windows. The electric doors jumped open when he stepped on the rubber mat. Inside, the store smelled of strawberries, cold tiles and pine ammonia. A mopper worked aisles uncluttered by customers' carts. Overhead speakers crackled with a gutless instrumental version of "Mr. Tambourine Man." Two cashiers gossiped. A security guard fingered the billy club dangling from his belt. John bought a pack of Doublemint gum, strolled outside.

A sedan pulled into the row behind John's car. The driver's door opened. No light came on as a woman stepped to the pavement—

Dyed blond and office weary, divorced left hand and sharp eyes that saw a healthy, scruffy-suited man watching her as he loitered beside a car parked in the handicapped zone. She got back in her car, pushed the lock buttons down and restarted the engine, kept her eyes on the could-be carjacker.

John climbed in the Toyota, backed out of the handicapped slot. Before he shifted from reverse to drive, his eyes met the woman's, saw her censure him for arrogance instead of homicide.

Five blocks north of the movie theater, John pulled into a parking lot shared by a fast-food franchise and a local diner chain. He parked against the brick wall of a discount bookstore, back in the shadows by Dumpsters and empty delivery trucks. Blue graffiti on the brick wall in front of his car read POP MASTER.

The fast-food restaurant was closed, dark.

Cold: John shivered as he hurried around the fast-food restaurant to the locally owned diner.

As he pushed open the diner's door, a man behind the cash register held up his hand: "No *es* open."

John stepped inside the pale yellow food palace.

"I just want a cup of coffee," he said. "Then I'll go."

"We closed. No coffee."

Lay a $10 bill next to the cash register. "No change back."

The cash register man glanced to his side, licked his lips.

Keep eye contact, don't let him bluff you out.

"*Sí,* OK. One cup coffee, no refill, then you go."

The cash register man took the $10 bill with one hand, pointed to booths with the other. The computer cash register didn't beep with a recorded sale.

Turn and—

Sitting at a table in front of dirty plates, their eyes weighing his no-tie shirt, rumpled suit and no-overcoat in winter: two county policemen, brown uniforms and holstered 9mms.

Were there wants and warrants issued? Pictures handed out at roll calls?

A cop suit makes great camouflage for a wet boy.

Walk it slow and easy to the booth. OK to show a little fear: they're cops, they scare everybody. But no extremes, no Mr. Too Nice Guy, no Mr. Too Cool. *Be just a cup of coffee kind of guy.*

The booth squeaked as John slid into it. He faced the front doors the cash register man was locking. Behind John were the back windows and cops with 15-shot nines.

"We'll stick around awhile, Ramon," said one cop.

"Sure OK!" Ramon scurried behind the counter. "You stay long time. I bring you pie. Cherry pie."

Ramon put a large Styrofoam cup of black soup in front of John, dropped a half dozen cream serving cups beside it.

"Drink fast," he said. "Police waiting."

John said: "So I hear."

Even with the cream, the coffee tasted urn-bitter. John forced half the sludge down. Sighed dramatically. Stood, turned. Ramon hovered by the cops and their plates of cherry pie.

Drop a quarter on the table. Let its rattle discourage badge questions. Hurry outside to the car.

Walk the circle.

Don't get noticed.

Don't get caught.

Cold night. *Should have worn mountaineering coat, should have taken the time to change.*

In his mind, he laughed: of all the regrets, *clothing . . .*

Night filled the parking lot, cold night barely cut by a lone light mounted high above the asphalt.

A half dozen empty cars waited in front of the fast-food restaurant. Who did they belong to? Janitors working in the surrounding high-rise office mountains?

No one hid between the Dumpster and the brick wall where the Toyota waited.

Through the car's windows, he saw the backseat was empty.

The subway stop a mile south was next, he thought as he slid the key into the car lock: even if the escalators were chained shut, the trains idle—

Snick-click of a hammer cocked on a pistol.

Freeze. Right hand twisting the key in the Toyota lock, left hand at his side, feet planted, unbalanced—

"I'm alone," he told the night.

The gentle pad of soles on a pavement. Steps stopping, still.

"OK," he said. "It's OK. I'm turning around, Phuong."

She stood between the brick wall and the Dumpster—behind there, she'd hidden behind the Dumpster. An ice breeze cut through John's suit and stirred her ebony hair. The black trench coat cloaked her small form. In the shadows, her eyes shone.

Her two gloved hands kept the gun zeroed on John's heart.

"How did you know it was me?"

"You cocked the pistol. A pro would have been ready."

"Are you alone?"

"Didn't you see?"

"I hid on a fire escape across the street from the theater. No one followed when you drove away. I ran here. Waited. No one pulled in behind you."

"Don't point the gun at me."

"What about the trunk?" The black bore of the pistol stayed on John's chest.

He blinked.

"That car's trunk. And where did you get it?"

John opened the trunk. Pistol held in front of her like on TV, Phuong edged closer, until she could see the spare tire.

"Somebody could see you," said John.

She slid back into the Dumpster's shadow.

"Point the gun away from me," he ordered. "Drop the hammer like I showed you. Put the safety on."

With her café au lait skin, her wide eyes, she was like a fawn.

"Trust nobody," she repeated. "Even you."

But she did as he said.

"Get in the car," he told her.

Turn, give her your back.

John's spine ached, tight, waiting to be . . .

She walked around to the Toyota's passenger door, wrapping the black trench coat closed, the gun nowhere in sight.

"The motel's a few blocks away," she said.

"Wish you'd remembered any neighborhood besides this one," he said as they drove alongside the diner toward the parking lot exit.

"Want to know what I wish?" she murmured.

"Just give me directions to the motel."

Ramon and the two county policemen locked up the diner as the Toyota rolled past. The cops glanced inside that car where two people pretended they didn't care who saw them. A nervous male driver who'd killed time over bogus coffee. A guilty-eyed woman he'd acquired in the parking lot. A midnight rendezvous, headed to a bedroom. The cops had seen it all before.

39

A double-decker motel. L-shaped, with a courtyard protecting customers' cars from crashes and curiosity.

John drove under the motel's arch. The night clerk nodded to Phuong: check in late, leave, come back with a man. The night clerk had seen it all before.

A dark second-story room overlooking the courtyard. Drawn curtains, two chairs, a bed. Cable television on the bureau. White light glared in the bathroom.

Peek through the curtains at the night world. Mist floats above the parked cars. Close the curtains. Snap on the pole lamp.

The heater under the window blew warm shadows across the room. Phuong stood at the foot of the one bed. Hands jammed deep in the pockets of her open black trench coat.

"Not where I expected to end up," she said.

"Your choice," he said.

"Your deal."

"Look, I'm tired, I'm burned-out, I don't need—"

"Oh, sorry I forgot *your* needs. Forgot this was a solo run. Forgot that I'm just a convenience."

"Why are you mad at me"

"You exist."

"If you keep zeroing me with a cocked—"

"I don't want to be found hanging upside down dead from the ceiling in some damn nowhere motel!"

"I didn't put you here!"

"You left me alone! Standing in winter night with this . . ."

A blur: her hand whipped under her coat, out into the open cradling the .45—*How did she draw that fast?*

" . . . this and nothing else—"

"That's the best I had to give you!"

"Not good enough!"

"Then blame your father, not me! It's his damn gun!"

"Don't you dare! Don't you dare yell at my father! It's your fault—"

"It was his damn car! His damn gun!"

Phuong slammed the gun down on the bureau.

"The hell it is!" she snapped. "And it's mine now."

"Then you—"

The phone rang.

Once, a loud peal that made them jump.

Rang twice. Phuong picked the gun off the bureau as John hurried past her, around the bed, picked up the phone.

She heard John say: "Yes. . . . Yes. . . . I know it's late. . . . Sorry, it was the TV, we. . . . No. . . . OK, sure, I understand. Tell them we're sorry, they can go back to sleep."

He hung up the phone.

She slumped back against the bureau. Laid the gun on its wood. Behind her, the mirror showed John standing by the bed table, his head hanging low.

"We have to be quieter," he mumbled, not looking at her. Laughed: "Don't want to get in trouble."

"No," she said. "Not us."

"I didn't mean to yell at you," he said.

"Sure you did. Me, too."

Walk toward her. A few easy steps. Easy.

She stood trapped against the mirrored bureau.

"We just . . . " Smile, it's just a gentle smile, he told himself. "We're pushed over the line, and . . . "

Her face was like a heart. Arched brows. High cheekbones. Black eyes. Strands of her black hair trailed across her forehead.

Café au lait skin, her forehead soft and warm, sweaty as his fingertips brushed—

Shake of her head knocked his hand away.

"So now what?" she snapped. "I get to serve as your trophy? Get to be your China doll?"

"Ni bushi Zhongguoren," whispered John. *"Wo bu yao yi gewawa."*

She blinked.

"The hell with you," he said.

"I don't understand what—"

"You don't understand enough."

He started to turn away . . .

. . . See it coming . . .

And she hit him.

Fist like a small hammer slammed into his chest. He stepped back. She came at him, both fists hammering his chest, her black coat flapping.

Back up another step. *Yield with each blow*—still hurt.

Panting, sweating, swinging harder, she clenched her teeth.

Grab her shoulders, her coat.

He pulled it down, pinned her arms to her side.

She thrashed against the black material, his grip, but she didn't scream or cry out.

Fought her hands free and swung them up to hit him.

Catch her wrists, so thin. With a twist, he pushed her hands down to her sides, threw her fists away. Momentum made her stagger, and he caught her shoulders . . .

She slid between his arms, pushed her face against his shirt, sobbing without tears. Her hands slid around his sides.

Warm, soft, she held him.

Like a sparrow. *Don't crush her. Don't let her go.*

Don't let me go.

Don't let go of me.

Wet on his shirt spread through to his chest.

No tears.

A kiss.

One gentle kiss.

The smell of her hair, dark sun, her cheek soft in his palm, turning, she kisses his hand.

And he bent to her lips.

Sitting on the edge of the bed. Phuong stands, leans to kiss him. Her hands float on his face. Help him off with his suit coat.

Cup her face, her hair brushes the backs of his hands.

Kiss her deep, her lips part.

Her hands on his shoulders as he unbuttons her blouse, shaking. Her breasts, soft, barely there. Brown nipples like pencil erasures. Kiss her *there*.

A soft moan and she says, *"Shhh."*

Pull her down to the bed. Her eyes watch him, wide and scared as he pulls off his shirt. His pants and shoes fall to the floor, socks, shorts. Her eyes never leave his as he unfastens her black slacks, slides them off her, her shoes, socks; her panties.

Small, she was so small.

Her hand circled his neck, pulled him down to her kiss.

Touch her, her thighs, the roundness of her hips, her stomach.

With a feather push, she rolls him over on his back. Straddles him. Guides him. Pushes herself down and her head snaps back as he moves inside her and she is tight, dry, aching for the connection of their flesh not its celebration.

But he wants her, needs her . . .

Against him, hard, moving, her head drops forward as she drapes over him, her breath hot against his cheek, her hands grip his shoulders and her hips slam against him won't let him and . . .

And he's gone, cries out her name.

She lay on his chest, the sheet and bedspread thrown over them, the room dim with yellow shadows.

"I asked for a room with two beds," she said.

"I know."

"It's late. You take what you can get."

"I know," he said again.

He wanted to look and look and look at her. The ceiling filled his eyes.

"I know it's not your fault," she said.

He sighed, closed his eyes.

Think, can't think.

"You have to do what's right," he said. "Otherwise all the lines collapse on top of you."

"This," she ran her hand along his arm, "this bent lines."

He frowned. "Are you sorry?"

Her answer was a soft hug.

"Before   what did you say to me?" she asked.

"*Ni bushi Zhongguoren,*" he repeated. "You are not Chinese. *Wo bu yao yi gewawa.* And I don't want a doll."

He felt her smile.

"Don't tell me what you want," she whispered. "Not now."

He turned his face toward her, nuzzled her hair, its rich aroma. *Remember that always.* Her back stretched away beneath the sheet, long and smooth.

"Tell me everything else," she said.

All he had to tell was of Glass.

"You told him about me," she said.

"Had to. Finally. He's our only link, our only safety. He had to know about you to cover us both."

"Will he? Cover us both?"

"Long as he can stay alive. And he's hard to kill."

"And he gave us tomorrow," she said.

"Doesn't matter much," said John. "He knows that, too."

"What?"

"Coming back out here was a prayer," he said.

"What can we do?" she said.

"Stay alive. Hope that we can get in, convince the Agency that we're not crooked. Or crazy. Convince them to go where we couldn't, do what—"

"So we're done," she said. "You've found the trail Frank left, the evidence. And it's all been . . . changed into nothing. This is it."

"Until tomorrow." He pressed his head into the pillow.

Felt her turn to stone.

"Unless," he said.

"What?" She was warmer. Softer.

"There's got to be a continuum."

"What?"

"A whole is more that the sum of its parts. We've got a lot of parts, but no idea about the whole, the continuum. The underlying force that defines and links all the random everything together. The center."

"For a minute I thought you had something."

"But we must! We've got the Corcoran Center bombing. Private businessman Cliff Johnson's Kuwait deal. Diversion."

"Supposition," she said.

"Phil David writes that anonymous letter to Senator Firestone. Firestone's people buck it to us at the Committee. "

"To Frank."

"Who does a routine check at the Agency. All his queries disappear, but Glass is such a control freak the Counter-Terrorism Center twitches every time Congress or the White House sighs. Glass lets your dad run with the mess. Before Frank gets far . . . "

"*Bam,*" whispered Phuong. Her nipple brushed John's ribs.

"Money gets planted on Frank, on me. Martin Sinclair—"

"Murdered."

"The wet boy. Still busy. Still out there, one or two or however many steps ahead of me—"

"Of us," she corrected.

"On a continuum. If I knew its true name, the beginning . . . "

"Or the end."

"Then maybe we'd have it all, know what—"

"Know who."

"Yes. Who."

He lay on his side so they faced each other.

"I feel like it's right out there," he said. "In front of me. Something simple I haven't done. Something I haven't recognized. Like I can touch it, if I just reach out . . . "

"That's me," she said.

"Sorry."

"Don't be."

Float in the smell of her. Sail away.

"Can I tell you you're beautiful, and can you hear me when I say it?"

"Yes," she whispered.

"You're beautiful, Phuong Mathews."

She smiled.

Kiss her gently.

She kisses back.

"This might be all we get," she said.

"Not if we don't die tomorrow."

"Don't tell me about death now. Or about tomorrow."

She brushed her fingers over the stubble on his cheek. Kissed him. Tender. Slow.

Kissed *him.*

He pressed his hand on her back. She moved against him, her arms circling his neck. Her thigh moved up along his leg, and his hands cupped her breast and this time, *now,* her nipple was swollen and she moaned as they kissed, down her neck, taste her breasts, feel her she now slick, her hips spread to his touch, her fingers dig in his back, she whispers *John* and she's slick

and he covers her with himself as she takes him deep inside her. Her knees come up, her bare feet alongside his hips, rocking back and forth beneath him, panting.

Look at her kiss her, their eyes open, breathing too fast, can't kiss, *can't stop* yes

her knees curl up alongside his chest

thrusting

her eyes open, looking at him, her black hair fanned beside her face on the white sheet mattress

her face bounding on the bed, panting, eyes wide with

can't stop

Phuong moaned and flamed around him and he was gone, too, lost. There. *Here.*

Then later, no words, they switched off the lights.

Darkness cradled their bed.

Heart pounding.

Bolt upright. Awake. Sweating, no breath. Darkness, only darkness. Dream. A

mushrooming ball of exploding fire roaring right at—

In a dream.

Just a—

Phuong, whirling awake beside him.

Metal scrapes on wood. A click.

"John!" she whispers.

Light snaps on—by her hand.

Sitting beside him, naked, the sheet fallen to her lap.

Tousled hair.

Breasts soft as dreams.

The .45 pulled off her bedstand, solid in her grip.

"What is it?" she whispered.

His watch: 5:43 A.M.

No sound of footsteps on the carpeted hall. No street noise filtering through the closed curtain.

Three hours, he'd only slept about three—

John swung out from under the sheet, hurried to the bathroom and flipped on that light. He winced from the white blast.

"Shower," he told Phuong. "Get dressed, fast. Wear a skirt, suit, something professional."

As he turned on the sink's hot water, she got out of bed, walked toward him with the gun in her hand.

Said, "Where are you going?"

40

A cold dawn lit the highway. Shimmers of scarlet glared off windshields and chrome.

Convenience store coffee steamed the windshield of Glass's Toyota. John drove. Phuong's car—registered through the rental company to her—sat in the motel courtyard, place paid for in cash for one more day to the night clerk who'd seen it all before.

"What if we don't get there first?" asked Phuong.

"Then what the hell," was John's only answer.

But he reached across the car seat and squeezed her hand.

The gun filled her coat pocket.

Wednesday morning rush hour snarled John and Phuong on the eight lane Beltway encircling Washington. What could have been a 40 minute drive was an hour-and-a-half steel-river odyssey.

Take the highway north. Cut across the path of the sun.

No frontier waited beyond the official geography of the Capital City. *Out there* meant inescapable infestations of civilization woven into the same web of money and power and myths that trapped Washington. Or New York. Or Hollywood.

But the light beyond the Beltway was different.

Baltimore.

To John, that skyline looked surreal: glistening mountains of glass and steel skyscrapers towering over gritty rivers of commerce and sweat. Blocks of flat-faced row houses, a shrine to

Elvis in one window. A gas station where the old man knew the way, pointed.

Not a national monument in sight.

"We could keep going," said Phuong, her eyes riding the freeway that cut west.

"We are," said John. They knew he didn't mean what she'd said.

American dream streets. Trees. Normal picket fences. Regular houses for regular people

An overturned tricycle on the front lawn of a white wood house. A battered station wagon and a Detroit dinosaur in the driveway. No answer to the doorbell.

To the knock on the back door.

No sign of life beyond the windows whose curtains hung open to the world.

A friendly neighbor told them *right house, try the park.*

Chilly morning air. Calm.

Two blocks away, a park with swings and a slide, monkey bars.

A blonde 2-year-old girl chased a laughing black woman. A 7-year-old boy slumped motionless in a swing. A pale woman in a rusted raincoat and go-to-work makeup begged the boy to smile.

Check your tie, thought John. Hope the shirt isn't too wrinkled, the suit too matted.

Time, this time, let time be on our side.

Put a smile on your face, credentials in your hand.

Walk up to the mother as she sees a warning look register on her son's face. Her bloodshot eyes fill with John and Phuong.

"Mrs. Johnson?" said John. "We're with the CIA. Please, we need to talk to you."

On the park bench.

Mrs. Cliff Johnson, mother, widow.

Sitting on her left, Phuong Mathews, introduced as Agent Tina Chen, an actress John remembered from a movie long gone.

That would have made Frank smile.

On her right sat John Lang—his name had to match his credentials.

The Somalian nanny hovered nearby, her ears straining for every word, her eyes on the little girl who knew how to laugh, the little boy who wouldn't.

"After Cliff died," said his widow, "it all got so hard, so crazy. Lauren will never remember him, but Paul . . . He won't let go of the hole blown in his childhood. He's afraid to lose that because it's all he's got left of his daddy.

"I'm sorry," she said, blinking back. "I'm supposed to be over it now. Getting on with it."

"I know," whispered Phuong.

And Mrs. Johnson believed her.

Belief breeds trust.

"He worked so hard," said the widow. "We'd lived a lot of places. Africa, France, Portugal. Cliff always worked for somebody else, some company. We moved back here, for the kids, and he set up his own export-import company . . .

"But the recession—reces*sions,* they just seem to keep coming. Like bullets. My uncle found me work at his plant—they're hanging on. Coranie helps us almost for free and I find the dimes to pay for everything day-to-day, but you never know."

"No," said John, "you never do."

"Cliff felt so bad. Then things started to pick up. He got that contract, the one he was working on when—"

"What contract?" said John.

"He never told me," she said. "We had the kind of trust where he didn't need to if he shouldn't. I thought it might be for you guys. Or the Army. Somebody in the government."

"Why?"

"Because he said I should be proud of him—I always was proud of him! But that he wasn't just earning money, he was . . . doing good. Though he acted like he didn't understand how.

"He'd been too young for Vietnam. Afterward, there was our

family and anyway, all our wars since then haven't lasted long. But he loved this country, wanted to do something.

"Did he?" she asked.

"His death," she said, "was it—"

"As far as we know," said John, "it's an official accident."

The widow sighed: "Maybe if I could tell Paul his dad died a hero . . . "

"The contract," said John. "Who was it with? For what? Do you have any documents, letters, anything that might—"

"He said he was using his connections in Egypt and Kuwait, mothering a simple shipment. He was due back three days after—

"Documents? The CIA comes to me with questions about my dead husband's business. Comes now, weeks after . . .

"The day we drove to Dulles Airport to . . . escort his coffin to the cemetery . . . our house was burgled. Cliff's office in the basement, our bedroom—everything: trashed. Documents, hell, they were everywhere."

Now nowhere, thought John.

"I'm owed," she said. "Those two kids are owed. Don't tell me you drove all the way out here for routine, for nothing."

"It hurts," said Phuong, "but you have to be patient just—"

"Miss, please don't you dare tell me how to be."

"Did he tell you any names? Leave you any information?"

"He left me with two kids who have no father and a blown-up-life! An insurance policy that barely paid for burying him. Don't you think if he left me anything more, I'd tell you?"

She pressed her fingers to her forehead.

"Don't you think I'd tell you so I could at least pretend that maybe all this pain means something?"

The three of them sat on the bench. The little girl ran in front of the boy, who stood by the swings, a stick clenched in his hand, guarding his mom, uncertain if these strangers were bad guys. His sister tried to make him laugh, but he wouldn't look at her.

"Madam," said the Somalian nanny.

The three people on the bench looked at her.

From her only purse, the nanny fished an ordinary business card, handed it to the widow.

Her dead husband's business card.

"When Mr. Johnson left the last time," said the nanny, "he says take this, and if my wife or children are sick or hurt or you need to get in touch with me, emergency only, not relying on just calling my phone machine in the office . . ." The widow held her husband's business card face-forward where she and the two people sitting beside her on the park bench could read the words that affirmed his name, his existence.

African fingers reached out, turned the card over.

Inked on the back, a Washington, D.C., phone number.

41

Cold morning rain pattered the windshield as John drove back.

"Because we have one shot," he said, checked his watch: 10:32.

Phuong felt the highway rushing under their wheels.

"Go straight to Glass," she said. "Now. Get yourself safe."

"Myself?"

"Drop me off. Let me go."

"We're together." He frowned at her. "You're in this, too."

"That boy's face," she said. "Please, let me go. Let this finish without me."

A truck whizzed by them on the freeway. John turned on the windshield wipers

"I promise," he said, "you'll be safe."

She laughed, cupped her brow in her hand.

"Me, too," he lied. "I'll pull it off."

She saw his eyes burning.

"You like this," she whispered.

"Now we've got a chance," he told her. "A play."

"You've just got a number." She shook her head. "You don't even know what it is."

"That whistle when we called it? Not a fax machine. There were beeps, *then* the whine. It's a telephone paging system, punch in your number, it transmits to a beeper. Foolproof, untraceable."

"Not a good system to give to your Somalian nanny when she thinks she'll wind up talking to a real person."

"What do you expect?" said John. "Cliff Johnson was no genius and a sucker from the start."

"Don't call him that! He had a little girl. And that boy. Don't call him that!"

The green highway sign for Washington's Beltway loomed ahead.

"Not his fault," said John. "He had bad luck."

"How convenient."

The Toyota looped onto the Beltway. Exit signs leading into the city bore street names that made John feel at home.

"You scared her when you told her not to say anything to anyone else, including people from 'our' Agency or the FBI, to go to her lawyer right away and make everything happen through him."

"If she's scared, she'll think twice. She'll run or she'll do it. Either way, we win."

"You can't keep her quiet," said Phuong. "You have no right."

"Maybe, but I need control." John exited the Beltway. "Time. If Glass is right, Handelman asking for an investigation of her husband's death will kick the Agency into gear. Now, when gumshoes show up on her doorstep, she won't talk to them without her lawyer. One thing lawyers are good for is eating up the clock.

"By the time the Agency gets her to open up," he added, "our history will be out of our hands."

"What if it's not 'gumshoes' who show up on her doorstep?"

John drove half a mile before answering: "Nobody has a reason to have her hit."

"She talked to us. We went there, and she talked to us."

He slowed for traffic.

"We didn't have a better choice," he said.

"If you give that number to Glass—"

"Then I give him a job not done," said John. "Then he gets to decide everything."

"Nobody gets to decide anything. One day, you take a road, things just happen."

"You don't believe that bullshit."

"Today, I don't know what I believe."

"You're tired," said John.

The Beltway exit dropped them on Rockville Pike's car dealer, shopping mall and pizza parlors strip. The third electronics store had what John needed. He paid cash.

Driving toward the heart of the city, they passed the cemetery where they'd buried Frank. Neither of them acknowledged it.

The motel day clerk was a woman. John asked a simple technical question, got the yes answer he'd expected. The clerk accepted cash for two more days with a smile.

The maid had already cleaned their room. Packing what they hadn't taken to Baltimore took five minutes.

Rigging the answering machine they bought on the room telephone took less time.

"My guess is Cliff Johnson demanded an emergency number," said John as he unpacked the answering machine. "He was a father, needed his family to be able to reach him. They wouldn't want to give him a link back, but he'd insist—maybe even test it. They didn't want to set up a system just for him, something more to hide, so they had to gamble with somebody's existing number."

He unwound the telephone cord.

"Whose number?" said Phuong.

"It's a switchboard. Yellow page entrepreneur selling answering services to crack dealers, physicians, whoever. An acceptable risk for the op. Before that, also perfect for our somebody's normal, ongoing plans and life. No trace.

"Our guy," added John, "we can't box him if we follow his system. We call him, punch in our phone number, he can take his time calling back. Maybe trace our number, show up while we're watching the phone, waiting for it to ring. Sitting ducks."

"If—"

"If that's what he wants," said John, plugging in the final cord. He smiled: "The hell with what he wants."

John plugged in the answering machine, pushed the button that said RECORD MESSAGE.

"This is John Lang. You want to talk to me. I know what you need. Forget about where this phone is, I'm not there. Four-thirty this afternoon, Wednesday, I'll beep you with another number. You got one minute to call that number back, then I'm gone and you got nowhere else to turn to, no one else to help, nowhere to run. Four-thirty, one minute to call back."

The answering machine beeped, rewound John's message.

"I love this place," said John. "Direct-dial rooms."

He dressed in his jeans, sweater and shirt, black sneakers and mountaineering coat. Phuong kept on her Baltimore clothes.

Look at her. Can't help it: her legs are sleek. Her skin, her eyes.

"Have the bags in your hand," he said, waiting until she did.

Careful. Slow. No mistakes.

Into the motel room phone, John tapped the number scrawled on the back of Cliff Johnson's business card.

One ring.

Two rings.

An answering whine, beeps.

John tapped in the area code and phone number of the motel room, hit the # key. Heard the squeal of electronic transmission, the click of a broken connection, a dial tone.

Hang up.

"Go!" he told Phuong. "Hurry!"

Leaving, he pulled the door shut, locked.

Gray clouds rolled across the sky, reinforcements against the brief interlude of midday sun.

Phuong and John sat in the Toyota, parked at a deserted picnic grounds in Rock Creek. J. Edgar Hoover once silenced liberal activism by a Cabinet member's wife with surveillance photos of her and her chauffeur having oral sex in that parking lot. John kept the Toyota's engine chugging for warmth. Fast-food hamburgers steamed the windshield: 1:17 P.M. They ate because they knew they should, ate in the car because they couldn't loiter in a café.

"I can come with you," said Phuong.

"Then we're one concentrated target," he said. "You're the witness—remember? You have to stay clear. Besides, this is my business, what I do."

"Do it well," she said. "Do it the best."

"Sure."

A Park Police cruiser rolled past the picnic grounds. The cops paid them no mind. A car drove past. A motorcycle. A yellow school bus full of children whose laughter behind the sealed windows looked like a circus chorus of mimes.

In their car radio, an oldie-goldy song cheerfully proclaimed that in the village, the peaceful village, the lion slept.

"What if she's not there when we go back again?" said Phuong.

"We'll keep trying. Or figure something else out."

"What if she's part of it?"

"Doesn't figure. *She* wouldn't be—her husband might, but if he was, then he should have stayed close to any threat. Everybody knows I've been *the* threat since—since they killed Frank."

Baltimore. This morning, could have called that old lady who Phuong tried to have dinner with, could have left her there, further away, safer. Could have—

"I'm scared," said Phuong.

"We'll be OK."

"Do you say that to all your women?"

"You're the only woman I have," he said, "these days."

Thinking of Emma.

Phuong's face showed she remembered Wei.

"It's OK," he said, then before calculated thought, added: "You're the woman I want."

"These days," she whispered.

Looked away, out the window.

"We better go try again," she said.

*   *   *

When they drove up, the woman was carrying sacks of groceries from her car into the house where John had been invited for dinner a dozen times. John pulled their car into the driveway.

"Kate!" John called out as he climbed out of the Toyota.

Make your voice cheery. Friendly. Not desperate.

Fifty had settled beautifully on Kate Woodruff, wife of Dick Woodruff, the number-two man in the CIA's human spies division. She had gray-flecked hair and quick brown eyes.

"Let us help you with those," said John.

"I got them," said Kate. She set the groceries on the floor inside the door. "You're Frank's daughter. From the funeral."

Phuong said yes, introduced herself. Accepted condolences.

"Dick's not available, John," said his wife, who in her youth had spent 10 years working for the CIA.

Knowing that, John still had to try: "Do you know when to expect him, or how to—"

Kate's shrug cut him off.

"You know how it is." She frowned: indiscreet questions didn't become her husband's protégé.

"We need a favor," said John.

"Actually, it's me," said Phuong.

They told Kate about Phuong not wanting to be alone in her dad's house, about needing a place to stay for a few days. Someplace quiet. Private.

"Is everything all right?" said Kate.

Sure, they told her.

"The death of a loved one kicks you off balance," said Kate, her eyes noting John's hand on Phuong's arm. "You have a cabin, don't you, John?"

"The heat's broken there. I hate to leave her stranded, cold, alone."

"You'd be wrong to do that," smiled Kate.

So please, do come in, she said to Phuong. John, too, but he hadn't the time. Plenty of room, said Kate. And John knows the way back here. No bother. No trouble.

"I'll get my bag from the car," Phuong told Kate.

"Of course." Kate smiled at John. "I'll take the groceries inside. Good-bye, John. No doubt I'll see you again soon."

As they walked to the car, John whispered: "You're safer here than at a motel. There, you're a stranger alone, an easy wipe. Here, you're with the wife of an Agency exec. That's a risk that—"

"She's an innocent!" argued Phuong.

"So are you," said John.

"No I'm not."

"Kate's an ex-pro, an Agency wife. She knows the life."

"And you think we can keep everything secret from her?"

They reached the car.

"Keep the gun," he said.

"You promised me you wouldn't need it."

"Not my style," he lied. "You won't need it either, but you having it makes me feel better."

Too quickly for forethought, she said: "You feel OK to me."

He brushed her hand.

"If they're watching, you shouldn't kiss me," she said.

"That's right."

He held her face in his hands, bent to her lips.

Stood back.

"Soon as I can, I'll phone. We're OK. We're almost home."

She watched him get in the car. Drive away.

In the rearview mirror, he saw her standing there.

Alone.

42

Hard rain covered the city that afternoon. Swirling dark skies, angry winds. Slick roads, slow traffic.

At 3:01, John found a pay phone at a gas station. The wind shotgunned icy rain into him as he fed the phone a quarter, dialed his motel room. As soon as he heard his taped message, he tapped in the answering machine's remote retrieval code.

The message tape beeped once, clicked off.

One caller. Who'd listened to John's words, left no message.

Don't be a wrong number. Can't be a wrong number.

Wait. Have to wait.

At 4:10, John walked into the Emerald Glen, a corner bar on an avenue named for a heartland state, an Irish pub sitting under a brown clapboard apartment building. Two Buddhist temples were six blocks away, the Reformed African Baptist Church was around the corner. Except for a drugstore down the block and a jazz bar across the street, this neighborhood had no other legal businesses.

The Emerald Glen had an eight-stool bar, four booths, three tables. Two windows let in what little light the day had left. A pink-faced old man wrapped in a corduroy coat sat at the bar, communing with a shot glass and a beer. The bald black bartender held that day's *Wall Street Journal* in hands like catcher's mitts and read the paper with ex-cop eyes.

A dimly lit hall led to bathrooms. Hanging from the wall between those two doors, John spotted a pay phone.

Inside here was dry warmth, a cloud of whiskey and beer and cigarette ghosts. No blaring TV, no jukebox playing, no radio.

No one looking for anyone.

Eighteen minutes to go.

Take a stool five down from the old man. The odor of wet corduroy coat reached out to John.

The bartender loomed across from him: "What do you want?"

John sighed, "Everything."

One black paw turned palm-up on the bar. Gravel fell into his deep voice: "What'll you get here?"

"Coffee."

"Irish coffee?"

"Black coffee." John smiled to himself. "Don't worry about the cinnamon."

"And I was going to sweat that all night."

The bartender lumbered away.

Sixteen minutes.

In the bar mirror, John saw a burnt, ragged man, wet mountaineering coat and bloody eyes. He smelled of sweat. The man's aching heart kept crashing against his ribs.

Sluggish. Soft. Haven't worked out, practiced in . . .

Walk the circle.

The bartender put a mug of hot coffee in front of John, no cream, no sugar. He shrugged: "Say a buck. That way, I don't have to bring you any change."

"Change, I got change, already got change! Made sure I . . . "

"Just make sure you pay."

The bartender walked to the end of the bar, flipped the *Journal* open to a fresh page. Hanging on the wall to his right was the framed photograph of a gorgeous black opera diva.

John put two $1 bills on the bar, so if he had to run . . .

When it was OK, when it was over, bring Phuong here. Show her.

This bar could be back home in South Dakota.

Thirteen minutes.

Coffee was hot, strong. Caffeine fueled his heart.

Ten minutes. He had to go to the bathroom.

The best cover for heading back toward the phone: truth.

Casual, walk casual.

The old man said, "Another please, Lou."

The bartender sighed, folded the paper to preserve his place.

In the spotless pine-scented bathroom, John flushed the urinal with a resounding whoosh.

Four minutes.

The condom machine on the bathroom wall promised responsibility, reliability and romance.

Two minutes.

With a quarter and Cliff Johnson's business card in his hand, John walked straight to the pay phone on the wall.

The hell with it. Whoever was on the other end of this phone number would be waiting now if he was waiting at all. John picked up the receiver, dropped the quarter in the slot and—

Nothing.

No dial tone. No noise.

Bang the hook up and down. Nothing. Dial zero. Nothing.

John dropped the receiver, let it dangle as he ran to the bar.

"The pay phone's broken!"

"I know," said the bartender, not looking up.

"Another one?" John's digital watch flashed 4:29:57.

"No." The bartender folded the paper, his eyes on the yeller.

"One across the street is broken, too," said the old man. "Nothing's like it was anymore."

To the bartender; "Do you have another phone? Push-button?"

"Not for customers."

"I'll pay whatever, I gotta call my . . . "

"Your doctor, right?"

"Just let me use your phone now before it's too late!"

A hard look, then the bartender reached under the cash register and set a touch-tone on the bar next to John. The bartender barely let go before John grabbed the receiver, began tapping in the phone number.

One digit before he finished, he realized . . .

"The phone number here! For this phone!" John's face pleaded with the bartender: "What's the number here?"

Shaking his head, the bartender dropped a napkin beside the phone. Beneath a color drawing of a Thanksgiving turkey, a gin distributor had stenciled his company logo and the name and phone number of the Emerald Glen.

Punch in the last number from Cliff Johnson's card.

One ring. Two.

The beep. The whine.

Punch in D.C.'s 202 area code and the bar's phone number, hit the # key.

The electronic whine of *message sent.*

John hung up. Five minutes, seven tops. After that, he didn't dare stick around for a callback. Or for somebody to show up. Both hands on the bar, he bent his head, closed his eyes.

Opened them: the bartender had put the phone behind the bar.

"She's going to call me right back!" cried John.

"You got a woman doctor?" said the bartender. Ivory teeth flashed in a charcoal grin. "How enlightened."

John stared at the phone.

The bartender watched him.

The phone rang.

Left-handed, the bartender answered, his eyes never leaving John's face and hands.

"Yeah? . . .

"Hey, baby," said the bartender, his bass voice rich and thick. "How you doin'? . . . Nah, nothin's shakin' here, how 'bout you? So cold and wet out there."

Hang up the phone!

"Nah," drawled the bartender, "you don't need to tell me that. Ain't no big thing. . . . Baby, you do know some ways."

John reached inside his coat.

As his hand disappeared, the bartender's right hand dropped out of sight behind the bar, his eyes on John and the smile of his words intact: "Un-huh, baby . . . "

The $50 bill came from the stash planted at Frank's. John thrust it at the bartender, hissed: "I need the phone now!"

"Well, sugar, we could do that, too . . . " The bartender's eyes flicked to the portrait of President Ulysses Simpson Grant. His right hand floated up to take the $50—

Crumple the money into a ball and toss it beside John's shoes.

"Sure, sugar, you know how I feel. But this old bear don't roll over just for honey and I always told you, special as you are, I hear the buzzin' of a lot o' hives . . . "

No choice.

Before John's hand reached his credentials case in his back pocket, the bartender's right hand dropped out of sight again.

John thrust his CIA credentials at the bartender: *"Get off the damn phone I need it now!"*

"Sugar, there's some static on this line I gotta deal with. I'll call you back . . . When I can. Bye, Babe."

The bartender hung up. Pushed the phone in front of John.

"Should have said please." The bartender scooped something into his right hand from under the bar, walked away to freshen the old man's whiskey.

The phone screamed.

"John Lang public phone!"

Whisper, try not to let the bartender—

"Man," hissed a voice he knew in the phone, "you are truly a lop! Set up a contact time and leave me hanging on a busy sig nal!"

"You're Phil David."

"I know me, but I keep wondering about you! How did you get—"

Dropping into the groove: "Too late for that to matter. What do you know about Martin Sinclair?"

"Never met the dude."

"He's hanging upside down dead in a house in Virginia."

Long pause. A real pause.

"You and I have to connect," said John, "or you and I will end up hanging alongside him. After Frank, after Cliff Johnson, after Martin Sinclair, we're the only ones left."

"What's your Agency sanction?"

"If I had one, I wouldn't be talking to you this way."

"Don't trust that fuckin' place. Any of it. Any of them."

"I don't make that mistake."

"Do and you're dead, babe. They don't dust you, I will."

"You had that chance and passed. That's why I trust you."

"Maybe that was my mistake. What do you got for me?"

"We can buy our ticket out of this shit if we do it together, and if we do it now."

"So you say."

"So you bet," said John. "You bet it with Frank, and now I'm covering his action."

"You come to me," said Phil David. "Solo. Clean. Empty hands."

He told John *how, where.*

When was now.

They hung up.

As John hurried out, the bartender said: "Don't come back."

43

Homeward bound, thought John as he drove through rush hour. The Toyota's wipers swept away sheets of water. A line of taillights danced beyond the windshield. Yellow snake eyes filled his mirrors. A one-eyed headlight swerved on the wet road three cars back, and John eased off the gas. *Easy, go easy. Everybody's homeward bound.*

Me, too, he promised himself.

No one could have followed me. No vehicle pulled away from the curb when I drove away from the bar.

Twenty-one minutes of hard driving to a vertical mall on the District's border. John corkscrewed his way to an empty slot on an upper level of the mall's adjoining parking lot. Lock the car door, walk through to the skyway connecting the lot to the mall.

Lot of cars here for just after work.

OK, it's OK.

Phuong has the gun—don't need it, she's OK, it's OK.

Car horn blares one level down. Brakes squeal. A motorcycle engine guns, backs down, shuts off. A gray sedan wheels around the corner, roars up the ramp toward John, its windows fogged—

A woman driver with a kid in a yellow rain slicker, faces frantic for a place to dump their car.

Forget them: the kid equals innocence.

Through the skywalk to the mall's glass doors. Vendor carts in the mall hallway, a woman selling perfume: *Like to smell some for your lady?* The woman and yellow-slickered boy race past John; she clutches a birthday present tied with pink ribbons.

John stood on a landing overlooking the mall's open center. Steel railings kept the unwary from falling four levels down to the food court, where scores of tables waited—in one corner, green and red helium balloons and yellow crepe paper made a corral for a half dozen mothers and 10 crazed 5-year-olds.

Bumpy the Clown rode the down escalator, sinking through the echoes of squealing children and mind-numbing piped-in jazz.

Walk the circle, thought John, scanning the artificially aromatic stores of discount this and franchised that.

A glass elevator rose from the food court toward the fourth level where he stood. John waited, but the machine slid up one more story to the five-screen movie theater complex.

When he sees you're alone, he'll make contact.

Stay close to the railing. Lets you see other levels.

Walk around the fourth level. Hungry salesmen. A twisted old lady peers into a window of a chain store famous for selling female underwear woven for male fantasies.

Ride down the escalator behind a man in a business suit. The man carried a briefcase, had a mustache, an otherworldly smile.

Not him. Phil David wouldn't own that smile.

Level three: Electronics store. Shoe store. Knife store.

The smiler strolled into a bookstore.

Go the other way.

Past the music store, speakers in the doorway blaring ca-chunking bass lines and macho voice lyrics rapping 'bout—

"Don't stop!"

A man materialized at John's elbow. Green down ski jacket, jeans, hiking boots. Close-cropped dyed-black hair. Phony clear-lensed glasses.

They walked side by side, soft voices and wary eyes.

"So give me your deal," said Phil David.

"Tell me everything," countered John.

"I tell you everything, I'm worth nothing."

"Work with me or you'll wish you were nothing, soldier."

"Soldier? Who you been talking to?"

"Everybody but you, and you're in the middle."

Phil shook his head. "No shit, Sherlock."

A fat woman waddled past, paid them no mind.

"Was the op on the books or off the books?" said John.

"Whose books?" said Phil.

"You answer questions, not ask them. That's how you'll buy your way home."

"Home free?"

"Home with any chance."

"Man, your attitude sucks!"

"Then go die alone," said John.

He stopped in front of a shoe store. Phil David glared at John. Sighed and leaned on the steel railing. Laughter floated up from the birthday party.

"Man," said Phil David, "it's always the foot soldiers who go to the wall."

"Or to New York," said John. *Easy, go easy with him: until you get him to Glass and have got him locked up in a safe house, he can still bolt.*

"Can you get me Congressional immunity? Like Ollie North?"

"I work for the Agency, not the Intelligence Committee or the Senate. Congress would have to vote an investigation—"

"Man, they'd love this one. I could help 'em look like heroes instead of fools."

"Perhaps in exchange for complete testimony, they might—"

"If I name names, I want immunity *and* protection. Some kind of witness sheep-dip. I ain't asking for a reward—"

"For blowing up the Corcoran Center!"

Phil David smiled: "You already got that far, huh? Wanna go all the way?"

Don't hit him! Don't . . . John swallowed, said: "Was it sanctioned by the Agency?"

"Come on, man: give me something!"

"For killing Cliff Johnson?"

"I didn't whack him out!" Phil stabbed his forefinger toward John. "Him dying was why I started blowing the whistle!"

"Who killed him?"

"He hung a 'Shoot Me' sign around his own neck."

They stared at a young couple nuzzling each other: high school kids, not matched guns.

"Cliff started wondering if two and two and two might not add up to a big bang in NYC. Poor simp, he was afraid *we'd* been ripped off, betrayed, tricked. Wanted to tell Big Daddy Whoever."

"Did you kill him?" said John.

Set your balance, don't lean over the rail.

"I only taped him, man. You saw the edited tease I gave your buddy Frank. Figured on using that to keep Cliff in line, if . . ."

"Hell," said Phil David, "never thought he'd be so . . . righteous about a little mistake."

"Did you kill him?"

"I was just a good soldier. I reported back. I thought they'd muzzle him with the flag."

"Was it sanctioned?"

"Who can tell in this business? It's sanctioned by what you can get away with, not by who gave the nod."

Phil leaned away from the rail. John flowed with him. They strolled along the third level.

"When Cliff fried," said Phil, "when I read they had a witness, I figured it was clean-up time and I was a dirty dish. Figured my best chance to stay alive was through Congress . . .

"Shit," he said, "never believe a politician. Read an article in *Time,* figured Senator Firestone would handle it all himself. I knew he was after headlines, but I never dreamed he'd buck my first-pass letter to the C-fuckin'-IA!"

"You covered yourself, didn't sign it."

"Bein' nobody is the safest play. Until you need to collect."

"The C-4 Cliff Johnson bought—"

"We bankrolled him. He even helped us split the load at a rest stop on the way to the Baltimore docks. His magic man in Egypt didn't care, the Kuwaiti end was covered. Should have worked."

Phil David shook his head: "Bad karma, man. Corcoran Center: what a place for a family picnic."

"Nobody was supposed to die," whispered John.

"You want bodies, I can make bodies. But heart attacks and family craziness, nobody can plan them away. Not my fault.

"Hey," he added, "I even had to argue to plan it clean."

"Argue with who?" said John. *Don't push: you let him know what you know, and he'll back away or game you.*

Phil David smiled. "The creep the C.O. paired me with. One weird machine, man. Likes his wet work. Keeps changing his face. Hell, even I couldn't pick him out of a crowd.

"But you should have seen us rock! Great team security—pull together only when necessary, recon, set up, secure . . . But that guy, hell . . . He wanted to make it a horror show, him and his pink lipstick!"

"Who was he?"

"If I knew that, I'd whack him out fast and first, 'cause sure as shit he'll do it to me if he gets the chance and the go code."

"The go code from who?"

"You really want to know, ace? Your guy Frank got dusted because he got too close. The embassy guy in Egypt who was told to shut up, smile and sign off on the arms shipment, you say he's dead—which surprises me, because I was told he'd never be a problem, there was a handle on him already."

"What handle?"

"Compartments, man: his handle wasn't in my compartment."

"What was?"

They rode the escalator down to the second level, John on the lead step, Phil leaning over from behind, whispering in his ear.

No one seemed to notice. No one seemed to care.

"I was Cliff Johnson's handler and one of the in-team. He'd been ID'd and assessed approachable by the Domestic Contact program Casey expanded to use American businessmen as active agents instead of just debriefing them if and when they wandered into Langley.

"Good deal for Cliff, the schmuck. Starting out his business, needing bucks. Probably didn't want to do this kind of work, but hey, times are tough, so he sold himself a red, white and blue lie.

"Hell," said Phil David, "in this business, we all lie all the time, we all lie to ourselves."

John saw their reflection walk through the plateglass window of a closed shop, two images in perfect step.

"No more lies," he said.

"Hey," said Phil: "I copy that."

"What about Ahmed Naral?" said John.

"You crying crocodile tears over him?" Phil David shook his head. "Not my personal work, but figure he was a bonus for America. He's got this apartment in Paris that at the right time, the good guys can link to him and somebody can find a few pounds of C-4 and detonators there. The finder is a hero, Naral takes the fall for a bombing that wasn't supposed to hurt anybody, and it's end of story."

"But why? I don't get why."

"You asking a soldier why?" Phil David shook his head. "Because I got paid."

On the mall's second level. They stood in front of a dress shop with windows full of logos from New York designers.

"It was just a job for you," mumbled John.

"So what's it for you—until you got thrown in the shit?"

John didn't answer.

"So it's not like it's on my head," added Phil. "I'm still a clean deal for the Senators. For testimony. Total immunity."

"Immunity from what 'total'?"

"You think this was a one time op? A stand-alone screwup?"

A teenager in a giant parka and a baseball cap cut their path to lean over the railing, yell: "Yo! Dalmont!"

They walked around him.

"Man," said Phil, "I was recruited five years ago. Sheep-dipped clean of ISA. No more standing in the hot sun with cross hairs on my back for civil service checks. This gig . . . I hung at the beach on retainer for quickies, black baggers—"

"Here? In the States?"

Phil smiled. "The shit I have seen."

"Who?" yelled John. A saleswoman's head-turn toward his insistent voice: "Who?"

Phil steered him back to the escalators, down to the food court, down toward the screams of the birthday party.

"Who?" whispered John as they rode downstairs. "This isn't Agency—I don't give a damn what the 'sanction' is or was. This isn't what we were set up to do. You know it, I know, everybody in hell knows it! So who? Whose op is this?"

"That's what it's all about, Mr. Owl," said Phil. "That's my ticket: I know who."

A mother and child hurried past them, frantic for a bathroom.

"Tell me how," whispered John. "Money, orders, communications, backups, logistics . . . How could you sustain a secret team?"

The elevator opened at the far end of the food court and a quartet of senior citizens tottered out: the early-bird special at the movie theaters had just ended. A dozen moviegoers rode the escalators down to the scent of fast foods and the squeals of the birthday party, to Bumpy the Dancing Clown.

A woman cut between John and Phil David.

His hand steered John close in the growing crowd.

Phil whispered: "Our world is made for this kind of play.

"We piggybacked when we could," said Phil. "In the spy business, you never know whose water you're carrying across the river. Plus we always had money, cash."

An old man frowned as he shuffled past these two men walking arm in arm.

"What was your goal? Where did your product go?"

"This town," said Phil as they circled through the food court tables, chairs and customers. "Where else?"

He coughed.

"If you're lying to me," said John, "you'll need more than immunity."

Phil dropped John's arm, backed away from the accusation. John turned: the ex-Army spy's face glared at him in anger in . . .

Mouth open, eyes wide, Phil staggered three, four steps.

John said: "What—"

Phil swayed forward. His knees buckled. He collapsed.

"Watch it, fool!" yelled a man on a date who Phil jostled.

Then the man turned, saw the green-down-jacketed fool spread-eagle on the floor, eyes wide, mouth gasping like a fish.

The date screamed.

A dozen people turned to look.

Faces, just faces . . .

Phil gurgled. John dropped to his knees.

"What?" He slid his hand under the man's head. "What's—"

The renegade agent's hand twitched across the floor tiles, tried to slide under his right side.

Under there, above Phil's right hip, John felt a pencil-wide hole in the green down jacket. Drops of warm wet.

"Look at his head!" yelled one of the people gathered around the man twitching on the floor and the man kneeling beside him. "He's having a fit!"

Jerking, bouncing, eyes wide, Phil's head twisted toward John.

"Somebody call the cops!" yelled a woman.

Kneeling, people's legs pushing against . . . Look up:

Straight into the lens of a video camera held by a birthday-party mom; the camera's red light glowed.

"He needs a doctor!" yelled John.

"Call 911!" yelled someone else.

Mothers tried to shoo the children back to the party.

The face of the man on the floor paled, his eyes rolled back.

"It's a 'leptic fit!" said a man. "Stick a wallet in his mouth."

Hit, they hit him! Why not both of us? Why—how?

Time froze. Cracked. Ghosts shimmered on the tile of the

mall. A safe-house lecturer who never mentioned his name, demonstrating:

" . . . called the ambassador technique. Ice pick. Hold it flat against your wrist, brush past the target. Swing your arm back hard and fast—it'll look natural. Six inches of steel in and out of his kidney before he knows it. Shock rocks him. Inertia keeps him walking. You'll vanish in the crowd before he drops. The blood fills his kidney, so they'll be giving him CPR but he'll be dead before they even find the hole."

Eyes roll back in Phil's head . . .

The video camera, filming, can't grab it . . .

"Get a doctor," mumbled John as he stood.

"Hey!" said an old man. The video camera followed his pointing finger. "You're with him!"

"There's a pay phone on the second floor!" John pointed up.

And slid between a stunned mother and an old lady as someone he barely saw took his place beside the downed man.

John ran to the up escalator, dodged around people riding its steps, their eyes staring at the confusion below.

On the second floor, he ran up the next escalator, then yet again up to the fourth floor where the skywalk joined the mall.

A man's voice echoed deep in the mall behind John's fleeing back: "Where's that guy going?"

44

Run.

The skywalk—perfume lady loses her smile as he flies by.

Glass doors to the parking lot, slam through them . . .

No bullet hole smashes the glass, rips chest flesh and bone.

No bullets. No backup sniper, no—

Why? Why?

Where's the wet boy?

Glass's car. Engine starts. Squeal out of the striped slot. Down exit ramps, rows of parked cars whirl across the windshield. A dad and his boy jump out of the way. *Got no kids, no son.*

Exit toll barricade points up: free parking after 6.

Rain, dark street—

Truck horn blares, skidding, countersteer—

City streets. Red light. Through it. More horns.

Wet Boy: was he waiting? Had he been on Phil David?

Wipers, hit the wipers. Defrost.

Go where?

Headlights flash in the mirror. Blinding glare from two high riders—a truck, a van. Turns out of the glass, gone. A single yellow headlight slides into that black vacuum.

A deep whoosh through a flooded street corner.

Military Road: four lanes cutting west across the park—

Too wide-open, too easy to be tracked, even in the rain.

The Buddhist neighborhood, temples, *wats,* in Thailand, they call them—

Yellow eye in the rearview mirror. Bouncing there. Floating. One-headlighted car. *Like before.*

No: not a car headlight.

Motorcycle.

Turn left. Still there. Turn right. Still there. Faster.

Coming . . . Coming . . .

Motorcycle.

The sound in the mall parking lot before—

The vision in Frank's mirrors that morning. Clear, crisp air. The street sweeper. Out of its cloud of dust—

Motorcycle. Wind visor and black-helmeted rider. Behind them, all the way to . . .

To the traffic jam on North Capitol Street. Then zooming past them, racing up ahead.

Where it could U-turn back to where Frank and John sat trapped behind a left-hand turner. Set up by foreseeable circumstances for an extemporaneous riff by a gifted, prepared performer. Like jazz.

A riff that could have been aborted right up until the last instant. Frank's Toyota trapped less than four feet away across the concrete divider. A motorcycle—windscreen hiding a silenced 9mm steadied across the driver's left arm as he coasted past the driver's window. A heartbeat of exposure time. A slow-moving, close-in, easy shot. Even if Frank looked, nothing for him to see but the black hole of a tube staring back.

A soft squeeze. A silenced pistol cough buried under morning rush hour traffic. One ejected shell casing carried 23 feet by the inertia of the motorcycle whizzing away as Frank . . .

Still there.

In the night mirror of Glass's car, the motorcycle was still there.

Ram him. Whip around skid around and ram—

Even on rain-slick streets, the bike wold dodge him.

Highway, cut out of town, lose him on the Beltway.

Couldn't beat him there on city streets. Soon as the biker saw the freeway signs, he'd close the gap . . .

How many rounds in his 9mm? Fifteen? Sixteen?

Stop at any red light and he could roll up shooting.

Don't stop—Blow through that stop sign.

Knows, he knows now.

Everybody knows everybody now.

Ditch the car.

Can't outrun a motorcycle on foot, but a motorcycle can't duck into a bar, can't climb a fence.

The yellow light bounced in John's mirror. Six, five car lengths back.

Skidding in the rain. Staying up.

Fly through an intersection and car horn blares and—

Missed, someone cursing as they drove home in the night.

Yellow eye filling the rearview mirror.

Whiz past homes where lovers were snug and safe. Families. Wife, kids, never had. Mom. Heather in sixth grade. Dad. The girl in grad school who loved physics. Wei. Emma. Phuong.

Cut left, south, Georgetown—*No! Too crowded streets, traffic too slow for cars, motorcycles can slide along the curb.*

Windshield wipers whump and—

Up ahead: a bus pulling away from a stop.

Fifty feet past that, a crossroads, a wall of cars held in check by a red light. Wet pavement under the traffic light reflects a flash of yellow.

Gun it!

Fly past the bus. Air brakes squeal as 14 tons of rolling steel swerves, shudder-stops, fills the road behind the Toyota.

Red light changing green, swerve left in front of surging cars *fishtail*

through, the wall of cars honking outrage.

Slide down the side street, countersteer away from cramped rows of parked cars. Turn right.

In the mirror: rain-drenched streets, cramped houses, parked cars . . . No headlights. No traffic.

Cut left, three blocks. Right again.

Mirrors empty. Still.

Lost him.

Maybe. Maybe.

Why is he so good?

Looking for a car, now he'll be looking for this car.

Residential neighborhood between Georgetown and Dupont Circle. Parking here day or night required prayer.

All my prayers are used up.

Roll past an alley. The curb solid with parked cars.

One slot back from the corner: small enough for the Toyota . . .

Fire hydrant, green steel standing sentry against infernos.

Parking there sentences strangers to death or scarring, homelessness because the firemen can't get to the hydrant.

Let them die.

Yellow eye, still not in the mirror. Not yet.

What the hell: odds are, it only means a $50 ticket.

We all lie all the time, we all lie to ourselves.

Whip the Toyota in snug against the curb on the first try.

Empty streets, the streets still are empty. No eyes.

Punch out the dome light—glass cuts.

Shake it off. Out the door. Habit-lock it.

Look back through the closed door. On the front-seat floor: a briefcase bulging with edited videos of a *sanctioned* deal between two men too dead to testify, the pickshit papers collected chasing Frank's ghost.

Leave it there, smash & grab crooks will see it, won't care 'bout what they find but would take it anyway. Trash it.

Carry it, slows you down, fills your hands. Means when Wet Boy sees you, he'll think if he gets you, he gets it all.

Unlock the passenger door, close it. Lock button sticks up on that side only, but hell, let the smash & grabbers have the radio. Unlock the trunk. Toss the briefcase in there, safer.

If the city tows the car—Greene's number in the briefcase.

Slam the trunk shut. Locked.

Rain beats down. Wet hair, face, dome glass cut wet hand.

Wet Boy.

Softly glowing windows. Black mirror streets.

Run.

No—*walk.* In the shadows, blend into the shadows.

Blend into the night. Into the rain.

Past houses, no one looks out. Car drives by, a Wednesday night double date, scanning for a parking spot half a mile from the hustle of Georgetown. *Why are they looking all the way over here?*

Duck behind a parked van until they've driven by.

Gone: *Their prayers must have been bogus.*

Quickly finding cover every time a car rolls by. Two blocks, three. Down a block to the right.

The edge of the quiet streets.

Four blocks ahead,

shining through the city night's million falling tears, the glow of a bridge over Rock Creek Parkway, a bridge with sidewalks and high-intensity streetlights, a bridge leading to Dupont Circle, D.C.'s Bohemian zone—theaters, banks, bookstores, and gay bars. So many shelters. Pay phones.

Just across that well-lit bridge.

The subway was there, too. Underground. Dark. Safe. Fast. A high-speed ride far from this killing zone where a motorcycle must be roaming the streets. A subway to a phone. Call Glass. Call Phuong, she had a car.

A woman with an umbrella hurried toward the bridge.

Footsteps click in the shadows—*whirl:* nobody there.

Imagination breeds monsters.

Catch the woman.

Don't look back.

Catch her, she's tall, umbrella held high. Above the pelting rain on her umbrella, she hers running footsteps, turns—

Duck under the umbrella, walk beside her.

"Don't let me melt."

Grip and trap her hand that holds the umbrella, pull it lower over the two of you.

She says: "My baby needs me! You can have—"

"Just walk me to the end of the bridge. Keep me dry."

Hold her shaking hand steady, keep the umbrella low, a black dome hiding their faces from vehicles whooshing across the bridge. Look like just another anxious couple walking toward morning.

Can't see beyond the edge. Rain drums on umbrella fabric.

The woman cries, her hand shakes. She tries to walk slower, then faster. Her arm strains like she wants to break away, flee.

Squeeze her hand around the umbrella handle.

The end of the bridge. The woman whimpers.

Let her go. *Run.*

Dodge around a man holding a newspaper over his head. Jump a leash connecting a soggy poodle to a fat man in a duffer's hat.

Run. Don't look back. *How could anyone be there?*

The traffic circle, a round park where a white fountain overflows with rain. Across the street, the tunnel mouth with two giant escalators leading down to the subway. A matted-haired man in a torn Army coat stands there, staring into nowhere. Beneath a building's walkway, two boys and a girl argue about a cigarette. The girl's hair is dyed taillight red. They all wear black leather motorcycle jackets.

The escalator, almost half a football field of moving stairs sinking into the earth. Ride down into that dark tunnel.

Breath, catch your breath.

A dollar bill buys a fare card from the vending machine. The turnstile eats the fare card, spits it out and clicks open. Another escalator down, 15, 20 feet.

The subway platform. Red tiles on the platform facing the tracks. Brown kiosks with train information. Gray concrete benches where only an old woman with thick glasses sits—homeward bound.

Empty tracks in the misty yellow light. No trains.

Stand in the middle of the platform.

Wait.

The old lady's thick glasses stare at the same track.

Wait.

Hollow laughter echoing down the tunnel tube from the world above. Clumping feet. A howl of delight—a girl's voice.

Come on, train.

Bouncing down the short escalator to the platform, the girl with fire hair laughs with a 20-something greased buzz-cut guy in a dirt-smeared green raincoat. The taller of two boys in biker jackets says, *for like even five bucks, man, I'd do anything,* and his black-jacketed bro bringing up the rear mutters, *shit.*

Come on, train.

The so-cool quartet shuffles 15, 20 paces away.

Warning lights flash next to the edge of the platform

The air rumbles.

Way down to the left, the far end of the platform:

A big man wrapped in a trench coat steps out from behind a kiosk. His gloved hands are empty. He doesn't look John's way or watch the train rush out of the tunnel, screech to a halt.

Subway train brakes hiss. Bells ding.

Straight ahead, a train door slides open. The car is clean, well lit. Plenty of seats. Few passengers. No one gets off.

The old lady shuffles onto the car, a whiff of baby powder and wet rubber in her wake.

Off to the left, the man with gloved hands still stands on the platform—grandly checks his watch.

"Cool, man," says the tall, black-jacketed guy behind John. "Thanks."

The sound of a kiss.

Laughter.

The closing-door warning bell dings.

Two cars down the platform, gloved man strides onto the train.

Quick, step toward the closest car.

Three biker jackets, already in, jostling, laughing, only 3, scarlet-haired girl's eyes look this way go wide—

Whirl right, blind, corkscrew right arm up—

Slamming into a green-coated arm. Glistening steel stabs past John's eye, through where the base of his skull had been as—

Warning bells ding and the subway doors shut, the rubber edges grab the shaft of an ice pick.

The train roars away, carries the jutting ice pick into its dark tunnel.

Whirl, step, palm strike against Green Coat's ribs, whose own left hand throws him off balance as it follows through on the push into the train of the body that suddenly wasn't there to stab.

Green Coat stumbles back.

Wet Boy, right hand diving under his flapping green coat . . .

Brisk, quick, stay soft . . .

Stuttered three-step *Hsing-i* charge slams John into Wet Boy's space. John's right hand drills up. The killer jerks his head to dodge the blow as John's left hand drills down—

Catches Wet Boy's gun wrist, turns the 9mm away from John's pivoting body. John's right arm snakes under the killer's gun hand, folds over as his shoulder slams into the man's chest.

Wet Boy slugs the back of John's head.

Fire, pain, try to snap his wrist—

The pistol clatters to the tiles.

Another punch rocks John's head.

Whirl out. Slam a palm heel into Wet Boy's chest.

Knocked him back.

Wrong: not force against force, *ch'i,* use—

Wet Boy charges, front snap-kicks, one, two—

But John isn't there, circles, palm facing the center, other hand low: soft and flowing *Pa-kua.*

Against Wet Boy's external style, karate or Tae Kwon Do or a Chinese Shaolin system: hard, fast, brutal.

And he's younger, all-purpose prepared white shirt and tie under the green trench coat, motorcycle leathers shed with the bike, quick as a cobra, he's—

Wet Boy threw a brick-breaking punch at the man who

skated strange circles around him instead of bobbing up and down like the guys in the dojo.

Not strength against strength, don't be hard and tense like him, relax, don't attack like him, don't be like him.

Wet Boy's center punch missed. Hard and fast, follow up with snap-kick and the damn guy whirls, changes directions, his arms deflecting the kick. There, his head will be there, follow up with a roundhouse kick there—

Miss, where the hell is—

Whirl around, balance, get—

Drop down, sweep kick—

The green coat whirled like a matador's cape with the man spinning on the ground.

Connect, the killer's extended sweeping foot connected . . .

To John's weightless foot that floated with the force of the sweep. But John's balance stayed centered, and he stayed upright as Wet Boy's sweep spun the gun off tiles, lost it on the tracks.

Wet Boy's guard locked solid as John charged, both hands knifing in, both hands blocked—

John stamp-kicked Wet Boy's right hip joint.

Caught, John caught a punching arm, felt Wet Boy's retreating *ch'i* and stepped in with a palm strike that added force to force and sent the killer crashing back into a kiosk.

Smash his face. The ribs above his heart. Knee his groin.

Frank, he killed Frank . . .

Knee his face, his head slams against the metal kiosk, and the subway attendant standing on the upper platform shouts.

Martin Sinclair hanging upside down. Paris car bomb. Ice pick.

Cocked knife-edged hand aimed for the lethal windpipe strike.

Don't be like him.

John's backhand slap knocks Wet Boy to the tiles. Out of his shirt pocket falls a plastic baggie—inside it:

A press-on mustache.

Clear fake glasses.

A tube of lipstick.

"The cops are coming!" yelled the subway attendant, then he scurried into his locked and bulletproof booth.

A man running down the short escalator wore a leather flight jacket and blue jeans.

Could be an undercover cop. A citizen with superhero dreams. Reinforcements, backup, could be—

The Wet Boy on the tile moans, curls his legs to stand . . .

Hired hands, just a set of hired bloody hands.

Don't get caught, not now, not yet.

Gotta kill him. Or gotta go. Can't hold him, no way—

The flight-jacketed man reached the subway platform.

Warning lights flash for an arriving train.

Can't beat two men. Getting caught equals getting killed.

Run.

The far escalators, the Q Street exit.

Thigh hurts: Wet Boy's kicks. *Limping, don't limp.*

Up to the turnstiles. Scramble over them. To the main escalators: longer, steeper than the ones ' went down.

Slotted steel steps, run up. Out of breath. Leg burns.

The tunnel slants up to the gray light of falling sky.

Up, halfway up—

Hands slam John down to the steel steps.

Push off, twist, drive back with elbow, get on ' back—

On the escalator carrying them up, John sprawled on his back, on top of him, face-to-face . . .

Wet Boy, white shirt splattered with his own blood, tie dangling, green coat flapping—

He loops an olive-drab, yellow-striped fuse cord around John's head, crosses his fists and jerks the garrote tight.

Breathe, can't—

Kick—legs pinned—

Black. Spinning.

John drove his thumb into Wet Boy's eye.

Screams. Garrote loose. John pulled the killer's hands off the cord. Wet Boy grabbed his wrists. The killer pushed his weight into John, tried to slam his forehead into John's face. John kept his chin down, his throat covered from ripping teeth.

Steel stairs carried them up.

Rain beat on them.

The top of the escalators, four heartbeats away.

The chic tie Wet Boy wore just in case he'd need such camouflage dangled free. Dangled down. Dangled past John's face.

The escalator ate Wet Boy's tie.

Steel stairs rolled home, the force of a thousand horses cycling them back down the tunnel.

The escalator swallowed Wet Boy's neck-circling tie inside its machines, sucked his face against the crack at the top of the relentlessly rising stairs.

A scream. Bone snap. Gurgle.

John scrambled from under the kicking body.

Wet Boy flopped as the escalator fought for his meat.

John stepped on the writhing corpse, ran into the night.

45

Back, run back.

Down the street, across the bridge.

Backup, Wet Boy had no backup.

Never killed anyone before, never—

Run. Or die.

A car splashed a puddle over John.

Run, streets of houses, the neighborhood where—

Glass's Toyota, parked by that hydrant.

Stumbling, slipping on Georgetown's wet brick sidewalks.

The car, driver's side, fumbling for keys, standing in the street
where a truck could roar down, smear you against—

Through the window, John saw the passenger door's lock button.

Pushed down. Locked. Secured.

Not standing up for the smash & grabbers to steal the radio.

Been in here. Somebody—

Wet Boy'd found the car. Opened it—quick recon, no time to
pry the trunk. Driver's door locked now, and when Wet Boy got
out, habit, he forgot and pushed the passenger lock down,
slammed the door, ran off to play his subway hunch. Or he could
have been close, close enough to see—

Could have planted a tracer bug inside Glass's car.

Wet Boy's reinforcements coming. Primed to the tracer.

Leave the car. Get out of here.

Down the street, turn the corner: halfway up the block, wedged between two cars.

Motorcycle. Windscreen. Locked plastic compartments. Room for helmet. Foul-weather gear. Maybe a portable phone, weapons.

A door opened on a house across the street, sent a yellow shaft of light through the rain to the motorcycle and John. The host couple started a long farewell to dinner-party guests.

They'd call the cops on a motorcycle thief, a vandal.

Leave it. Run.

Killed him, no choice, Corcoran Center and he ice-picked Phil David, bombed Cliff Johnson, Martin Sinclair, shot Frank, tried to . . . Killed him.

What was his name?

Wet Boy.

Rain soaked John as he ran through the night.

Bright streetlights, windows of closed clothing stores, a tourist hurrying in the rain. Georgetown cafés and trendy shops, gold-chain stores catering to drug dealers with pockets of cash.

The French café on the corner.

"May we, ah, help you?" said the maître d' when John stumbled inside.

Cigarette smoke and espresso. Golden light. A bar. A married couple ate dinner at a table; with practiced skill, they avoided each other's eyes. The scrape of their dinner forks filled the silence between them. At a table by the door, three men laughed. In a booth sat a man with a bow tie and tear scars on his cheeks.

"In the back." John nodded to a table.

"Certainly . . . sir."

As the maître d' led John to his spot, the three men protested to their blonde waitress that they'd ordered white, not red. She wore a white apron over a white blouse, black pants. As she whirled back to the bar, not a drop spilled from the three glasses of red wine balanced on her tray.

The maître d' pulled a square table out from the wall and swept John into the back chair with a glance.

"What may I bring you?" The maître d' pushed the table in front of John. Snug.

"*What?*"

"Do you want a drink or are you ready to order right now?"

Rain trickled out of John's matted hair, down his sweat-caked cheeks. In this soft café, his black mountaineering coat smelled of the outdoor life. City rain had stained his blue jeans black.

"I . . . Wine, you can bring me, glass of wine."

The maître d' plucked one of the red wines off the waitress's tray, swept invisible crumbs off the white tablecloth and placed the wineglass in front of John with a quiet little clunk.

"And will there be anything else?"

Drop a $50 from the stash at Frank's next to the salt and pepper shakers: "Maybe later."

Shake, don't let your hands shake, he's walking away don't—

John clasped his hands together under the white-clothed table. His shoulders trembled. The chalice of red wine pulled his eyes.

Breathe, OK, breathe. Think, need to . . .

Never killed anyone before.

Never died before.

John held the wineglass on the white tablecloth, pushed the table back and slid out. He spilled not a drop of red wine.

From the front door, the maître d' watched John limp back toward the bathrooms and pay phone. The $50 stayed on the table.

Turn your back to the café, to the entrance, thought John. He fed the pay phone a quarter and tapped in the number.

"Hello?" answered a little girl.

"Is this . . . " said John, then added the number he wanted.

"Yes. Mommy's sleeping in the chair, but my father—"

That man's voice in the background said: *"Irena!"*

"Father-I'm-sorry-but . . . The phone rang and Mommy is, she's just, in her chair, 'n' the phone was ringing and I *had* to get it so everything would be—"

Muffled motion in the receiver pressed against John's ear.

The toilet flushed in the café's ladies' room.

"Go back to bed, Irena," said the voice holding the phone.

"Yes, Father!" A faint, fleeing voice.

Then her father asked the caller: "Who is this?"

"Me!" said John: "We're all gone to hell!"

Harlan Glass said: "Calm down! Are you where you can talk?"

The door to the ladies' room opened. The woman bartender came out, smiled at John on her way back to work.

"No," he said. Whispered: "Yes."

"What—"

"We've gotta go in now! It's too late. Phil David, found—"

"Where? How? What did—"

"He's dead. Wet Boy—"

"Wet Boy, who's—"

"The erasure man," said John. "Killed Phil David before—"

"What did Phil say?"

John fired staccato whispers about an American op gone bad, renegade teams, car bombs.

"Did he say who?" whispered Glass, safe in his Virginia home.

"He died holding on to that chip."

"And—"

"I killed Wet Boy. Twenty minutes ago. Dupont Circle."

"Are you sure?"

"That he's dead? Or where I am? *I'm over the fucking edge!*"

Turn around, slowly look back into the restaurant where those last screamed words echoed.

Faces, turning away from the ragged man in the rough black coat and back to their own business.

Curious faces. Powdered with realized urban paranoia.

In the phone, Glass said: "Where are you?"

Turning his back to the café crowd, John told him. "Ran here. Ditched your old car, trunk's got all the pickshit."

John told him where.

"What about Frank's daughter?" asked Glass.

"I left her at Dick Woodruff's house."

"What did you tell Woodruff?"

That question roared around John like a hurricane.

"He's supposed to be out of town! I didn't see him, I left Phuong with Kate, and—"

"Told the Woodruffs nothing?"

"Woodruff isn't supposed to be here! I—no, nothing."

"Listen to me," said Glass. "Figure, as long as you're alive, the girl will be, too, no matter who she's with. Stay focused. Stay where you are."

"If I catch a cab to the Agency—"

"You'll drive into the bull's-eye. I'll come get you. We'll slide safe together."

"I'm not waiting for—"

"Figure fifty minutes. Don't call anybody. Don't go anywhere. You'll fly apart if I make you sit longer and that's not enough time to figure this right but *damn you:* give me fifty minutes. It's a hard drive from my house in the rain."

"Fifty minutes." John noted the time on his watch. "From now."

"That girl: Phuong . . ."

"What about her?"

"Figure you can trust her?"

"Forty-nine minutes," said John. He hung up.

Held the wineglass as he slid between the table and the wall, settled in his chair. Not a drop spilled.

Eyes in the café floated over the madman sitting at the white-clothed table in front of untasted red wine.

Early in the night, hours until midnight. Eight days since Wet Boy shot Frank. Forty-seven minutes to go.

Two months until my birthday.

Bumpy the Clown, dancing in the corral of balloons.

The wine tasted full and rich. Strong.

Put the glass back down. Don't spill even one drop.

Pick it up and drink it all, fire hits blood.

Maître d' plucked the second glass from the tray on the bar, whisked away the empty, and without a spill, put another red wine in front of John on the virgin tablecloth.

And then there was one.

Remember.

Emma when she'd come to his cabin, logic beyond fantasy, true to who she was. Trains, when he was a boy, loved to watch freight trains roar through his hometown, and sleek passenger machines carrying people away to the real world. Phuong, skin like pale chocolate, her eyes knew. Ten years old, festival on the Sioux reservation, hot sun and moccasined dancers in white buckskins and eagle fathers, Indians fascinated Wei, they danced shaking tomahawks and medicine bags, drums beating—

Wineglass, second wineglass, empty except for the swirl in the bottom, the taste in his mouth.

Twenty-seven minutes left.

The married couple rose. Husband ripped his copy off the credit card slip. They mumbled *good, just fine,* to each other. Buttoned their coats. Wife had an umbrella for the rain.

John dipped his forefinger in the red moon at the bottom of the wineglass, undergraduate dining room time rubbed the finger around the rim until a whine vibrated the café air. Eyes flicked his way. His finger circled the rim. *Walk the circle.*

Sioux drums beating.

Bumpy the Clown whirling in a corral of crimson balloons.

Children laughing.

Trains.

The maître d' snatched the wineglass from under John's finger, slid the last full one in its place, disappeared.

Nineteen minutes.

Children laughing.

John's finger wobbled the full wineglass—tipped and he caught it, but two drops,

two red drops

fell to the white tablecloth, their stain soaking into rusted circle smears.

Children—

John shoved the table away. The full wineglass tumbled over, red stain mushrooming across the white tablecloth as the glass rolled and he stumbled to the pay phone, dropped in a quarter, his trembling hand punching in the number he prayed he remembered.

Wineglass shattering on the café floor.

In the phone, one ring.

Answer! Come on, answer!

Two rings.

Too late! too late!

Three—

"Hello?" said Kate Woodruff.

"Listen to me!" said John. "What—"

"John! Look, whatever you and my houseguest are up—"

"No time! Just listen! *Tell me!*"

"What?"

"How many children does Harlan Glass have?"

"Glass? That snake! Married the lost heiress, lucky her being rich *and* a drunk, then to prove he had some sexual orienta—"

"Kids, how man—"

"One."

"How *old?*"

"Can't be more than ten. If she makes it to high school—"

"Phuong, let me talk to Phuong! Grab your coat!"

"John!" said Phuong seconds later: "What—"

"It's Glass!" he told her. "Harlan Glass, all along! The car, he had to give me a reason he had it so I would take it, but . . . He's the lie at the center of everything! Don't know why, if he's in it alone, but he knows where you are. *Run!* Take Kate, tell her everything, tell her ' get both of you inside!"

"But—"

"Go! Take the gun!" He hung up.

Understanding now that the train he was on was also the train chasing him down the track. Roaring closer. Closer.

Fifteen minutes.

Close your eyes. Breathe. Think.

Fresh air flows around him.

Call the Panic Line—no, it's inside the Agency. Don't know where Glass's tentacles—

Korn—maybe he's straight, but he'd have no teams who could respond in—

Homicide Detective Greene. City man. *Street man.*

His card—in wallet. Get another quarter from—

A hand dropped on John's shoulder.

Whirl—

"I'm early," said Harlan Glass.

46

Raindrops fell from the brim of the fedora Glass wore when he wanted to leave a memory of someone else. The umbrella from his security closet was closed, its steel tip kissed the floor.

The phone filled his eyes: "What are you doing?"

Beyond him, John saw the café's closed door.

"Guess I don't need that quarter," answered John.

"Guess not." Glass smiled. "You look like you've seen a ghost."

"It's been a hell of a week."

The man John had called swept his gloved left hand toward the table at the back of the café: "You were sitting there."

The table jutted out from the wall. On its white tablecloth, a $50 bill lay beside a drying crimson lake.

"Perfect place," said Glass. "Let's sit. Calm down. You can tell me everything."

Don't give him control! Don't step into his setup!

"Been here too long. People are starting to notice."

Logical. Professional. *Hold ground. Wait him out.*

"All right," said Glass, "but figure it's wet out there."

He swept his gloved hand toward the door.

John nodded for him to lead. Waited.

A bulldog smile, then Glass walked toward the front door.

The customer with the bow tie didn't care. The three men laughing at the table were glad to see John go. The blonde waitress read a magazine at the bar. The bartender polished glasses.

The maître d' was already spending $50 copped from recycled wine.

Glass wrapped his gloved grip around the door handle . . .

Pulled it open, and stepped aside for John.

Parked cars lined both sides of the street. All their windows looked rolled up.

Step into the rain.

As Glass closed the door behind them, the maître d' said: "Have a nice night."

The storm beat down on two men on the sidewalk.

"Aren't you going to use your umbrella?" said John.

Glass swung the wrapped umbrella up like a sword.

"Almost forgot I had it." He unsnapped the umbrella's canopy. Opened its cloth shield. "Where to?"

"Figure we'll walk awhile," said John.

"Ah. Figure that."

He raised the umbrella. Nodded for John to share its shelter.

Need to be close enough to touch to have any chance.

Shoulder-to-shoulder, two spies strolled uphill in the rain.

"How did you get here?" said John.

"Don't worry," said Glass. "No one followed me. Drove in, parked at a downtown lot. Caught a cab at a hotel, got out down from the café. Told the driver I was from Missouri.

"Never liked Missouri," he said.

"No tracks," said John.

"We're both professionals."

A bus whooshed by.

"Have you activated backup systems?" said Glass. "Fallbacks? Double safes? Time triggers?"

On the sidewalk, their footprints etched lines in water.

"Guess we'll see how good I was."

"Figure you couldn't have done much. Not enough time, resources. Reason. You had me. No one else to trust. No one who trusted you. Woodruff sent to Argentina. Leaves you with Korn and your credibility problem from China, all the data flowing against you. Confusion. Figure even now, no one'd believe just you.

"That Phuong," said Glass. "Does she know everything?"

No good answer. "So far."

"Do you trust her?"

Across the street, a pink neon sign glowing in a curtained window advertised a tarot card reader.

"Yes."

"Does she trust you? Will she come in—for you?"

"She's not working for anybody."

"She could have been."

"Yes, that would have been smart."

"Sometimes you can't recruit all the key people," said Glass.

A car honked: both men flinched.

Not expecting that either, thought John. Not expecting—
Anybody else.

"Where did Wet Boy come from?" said John. A question on the edge of innocence.

"You can buy bad boys," said Glass, a speculative answer this side of guilt. "If you know where to look."

"Guess everything's for sale."

"For sale. For grabs."

They stopped at an intersection. Traffic light changed from red to green above a city crossroads.

Ahead, Wisconsin Avenue, well-lit blocks of bars and all-night drugstores, a steady flow of headlight eyes.

To the left, cobblestone streets running toward dorms at Georgetown University. Students darting to and from libraries, basement apartment erotic discoveries.

To their right, narrow residential streets leading back the way John had come. Dark roads of million-dollar matchbox homes.

John sensed Glass's next step: forward motion more confident with each footfall.

Figure going straight on this well-lit way was smart, logical for a man afraid for his life. Glass would figure that, too.

A vision of terrible beauty seared John's eyes.

Then left him in the rain.

John nudged Glass to the right, down that dark street. Away from the safety of logic.

A bulldog frown: Glass didn't know why he'd been turned that way, but John felt him adapt, embrace the shadows. Grow.

"Bombing Corcoran Center must have somehow been a brilliant idea," said John as the well-lit main street receded behind them. "Was it yours or Allen's?"

The umbrella above John's head swayed.

Take a step. Another. Two beings in stride.

Glass said: "Figure what's important now is your price."

A *lie,* thought John. *Time buyer. Feint. Figure in your eyes, I'm already a corpse looking for a place to fall.*

Feint back: "Allen is the C.O., Allen needs to talk to me."

"Allen?" The being with a bulldog face stepped in a puddle and made no splash. "Roger Allen, the man who's staked his crown on an empire whose time has passed?"

Glass slid his empty gloved hand into his coat pocket.

John said: "So it's just you I need to bargain with."

A police car cruised toward them in the night rain.

"Just me." Glass smiled.

The police car rolled past. John did nothing. Glass sighed.

Each step led John further away form the bright lights. Words rolled out of Glass, beacons he lit to draw John further into the lonely darkness.

"You're smart to look for the angle on this," said Glass.

Truth, lies, the mix doesn't matter now: just words.

John said: "The angle is you. Your team."

"Figure I've been careful with my recruitments. I need a smart, ambitious man like you. Guy with big dreams. Guy who'd go all the way for them—like you did in Hong Kong. Rebel."

Parked cars, thought John. Too many streetlights. Not close enough to there yet.

Tired. Leg aches. Head burns. Heart . . .

Keep Glass talking. Walking.

"Rebels aren't your style."

"But you are—aren't you?" Glass chuckled. "Could have used you the last few years. Careful work, quiet work. Small ops here, there. Building. A handful of pros in the know, strings on a few unwitting assets, few Senators, Congressmen, wife's money dumped in their campaigns. Access bought for when the time is right to suggest nods toward ideas that sound good anyway.

"Others . . . Senator Firestone gets a damn letter, bucks the letter into the system. So a whore facing jail gets new friends and learns that if she opens her mouth wrong, *Wet Boy* rams the blade all the way into forever. She visits a bar, strokes a vain man's thigh, gives him a ride . . . Whoops! A car driven by a citizen nobody suspects crashes into them. Cops get called. Reporters swarm like flies and suddenly sex-scandal Firestone can't give a damn about a whistle blower letter."

An old couple with a sheepdog on a leash turned the corner and slogged toward them. *Witnesses. Screamers. Interference.*

"How—"

"Why not?" said Glass. "If you're born with the eyes to see, why not? Wasting good vision may be the only sin. And if you're born hungry . . . Power is the only meal in D.C.

"J. Edgar Hoover," added Glass: "He had the brains, but not the balls. He could have done it in his time."

The old couple led their sheepdog across the street.

"Corcoran Center," said John: "If the op would have worked—"

"Figure it has," said Glass. "Or it still will. Would have been cleaner and easier except for those damn civilians . . .

"Least this time," said Glass, "when my op went bad and I had a Company man about to burn me, I didn't have to carry his corpse through a war zone's rubble."

"Beirut," whispered John. "Even years ago, you were . . . Jerry Barber—they gave you a medal for that!"

"You once got a medal, too," said Glass. "Worked out better for both of us than we could have planned."

"Everything you've done," said John as they walked deeper into the night, "bombing Corcoran Cent—"

"Riding history," said Glass. "Or creating it: A high-profile terrorist incident. The old CIA—driven by Ops and Allen and Woodruff and inertia, the FBI, Pentagon—nobody can solve it. Then, when everyone's given up hope—"

"Harlan Glass's Counter-Terrorism Center pulls a rabbit out of the hat," said John. "Harlan Glass—hero, genius."

"The man who nailed Ahmed Naral—who when he was dead could protest nothing—as if anybody would have believed him."

"Was Naral an Agency spy?" said John.

"Allen has owned Naral since Beirut—something about the great Palestinian warrior's long-lost love being Jewish. I took out Naral to deprive Allen of his best asset and give me a victory over a villain, all in one!

"Served a bonus when I got your skin," said Glass. "They slingshotted Woodruff to Beirut to nose around Naral's death, cover up the truth that he was their boy. That left you alone, with your rabbi out-of-pocket. Now I can add to that bonus your—Frank's—secret investigations as evidence of Allen covering up the 'horrible truth' that establishment CIA's trusted asset Naral had turned into a Frankenstein monster who bombed Corcoran Center. Don't know whether to make Frank the martyred hero who was uncovering Allen 'backing' a rogue terrorist, or whether to frame Frank as part of Allen's cover-up. There are so many possibilities when all reality is shadows and secrets and lies."

"Then there's me," said John.

"Yes—how will we figure you?"

"What do you get out of this?" said John: the elderly couple's sheepdog sniffed a fire hydrant while they huddled in the rain.

"Counterterrorism, it's the wave of the future. If its necessity is proven and there's a new, untainted team waiting to take over, the budget's big dollars—"

"This was all about the budget?"

"Dollars equals power, power equals everything," said Glass. "Yesterday is dead history, the old power bases are crumbling. Resources are scarce. Acting fast, acting smart . . . In the Depression, Hoover realized that fighting Reds and bank robbers created a safer throne than attacking the Mob or drugs."

Across the street, the old couple hurried their sheepdog home.

Further, make him take you further out . . .

"Martin Sinclair followed your CIA orders!"

"He made the mistake of filing a medical insurance claim for a blood test that came back HIV positive. His real self got out one night in Cairo. If he told the State Department he had AIDS, that would have admitted he lied on security forms, admitted he'd discovered he was gay. Enough of an excuse for them to kick him out and pull all his insurance. His daughter and wife would lose everything. Including their myths. First he did his job, then when he doubted, he kept his mouth shut because it was his family's only hope. But you said he was cracking."

"See?" said Glass. "You've already drawn blood for me, time to draw benefits."

"I'm not an assassin!"

Dark street. Jagged brick sidewalk. Alleys.

"You killed Wet Boy," said Glass.

"That—"

"Evil is a winner's definition. Politics is any human interaction involving power. Like a million eager kiss-asses and would-bes, you chose this town, and that's politics. Have the brains and balls to seize your life."

"Like you?"

"Like who *you* want to be."

"Frank—"

"You've saved me from him," said Glass. "Now I know how far he'd gotten, now I can counter whatever crawls out from rocks he turned over. Frank was smart, tough. Discovered his system was bent so he played his own game. Got ahead of my curve. I couldn't let him link up with Phil, that fucking worm. Frank was supposed to be neutralized cleanly, but . . . *Wet Boy* could never resist a clever dance. Frank was good. But first, he'd trusted the system."

"And you," said Glass, "figure you trusted yourself."

"This city," whispered John, "this city won't let you—"

"This city is dying for me," said Glass.

John slammed his palm heel into Glass's ear.

Glass staggered, crashed the umbrella down on John.

Who missed grabbing the other man's arm, Glass whirling—

a blur of revolver

rising across Glass's stomach as he spins and John slams his body into the older man.

The older man who hadn't already been battered that night. Chased by a train. Betrayed. A wiry, trained middle-aged bulldog whose thigh muscle wasn't bruised and torn.

Grab down, gun—

Got it! Twist it! Move—

The revolver roared.

Fireball slams along John's ribs but he held onto the bucking wrist, the gloved hand—

Window shatters.

A Burglar alarm rings.

Slick bricks, shuffling, balance, pushing, scrambling for—

John twisted the gun hand until the revolver pointed up into the rain between the two men's straining faces.

Glass kneed him—missed the groin, hit the stomach and the shock novaed through John's wounded ribs.

Scream, don't scream again, breathe—

The gun, Glass's finger on the trigger, snub-nosed barrel bobbing back and forth between them.

John pushed the release button for the revolver's cylinder. The gun's cylinder swung out. Six brass cartridges fell to the sidewalk like golden shafts of rain.

Glass raked the unloaded revolver across John's eyes.

Blind, screaming, John shot a palm-heel strike straight out—

Move! Jump sideways, blink:

Glass, folding the umbrella's canopy down, twisting the handle, the steel tip—

Dodge—umbrella thrust at John's guarding hand.

Doesn't care if he hits a vital organ.

Poison. Old KGB stock. Maybe a new neuroagent.

Wet steel blade knifed like a snake past John's eyes.

John threw an empty metal garbage can at Glass. Knocked him back, aluminum clattered.

Run!

Limping, he sees me limping—

Alley, down there, right way—

Rain. Wail of the burglar alarm—police siren answers. Glass's feet pounding closer. Glistening black plastic trash bags.

White board fence, 20 feet, 15. Taller than John, a curved archway gate—closed. *Like in basic. Special Forces school, run faster, harder, good leg, use good leg to*

push off

jump, grab the top of the fence, its rim crashing into bullet-scraped ribs and *SCREAM* flop over it, kicking high . . .

Slam down on the other side, legs driving down into shoes, into the patio sidewalk—

Black Rottweiler charging, roaring, white teeth—

Scramble back slide up the hard wooden gate, fumble, the metal bar lock, jerk it, the latch—

The fence gate flew open and swung John back into the alley inches ahead of the charging dog. Inertia smacked the 130-pound animal into Glass's chest. The collision knocked the man back. He staggered as the dog crouched and snarled.

John leapt back into the fenced yard, swung the gate closed behind him and shot the lock bar home.

Unseen growl, roar.

Limp across the patio as lights go on in the house's rear den. Climb the pile of slippery firewood.

A dog howls.

Drop over the fence into the next yard. Hobble to the low ornamental gate leading to a passageway between row houses.

Leading to the street a solid block of homes away from Glass.

Run, drag the leg, leg don't drag—run.

Slipping, stumbling, crash into parked car, keep running.

Get there. Get there first.

One block. Two.

Suit-and-tie topcoat guy on the street glares at another home-
less crazy runner in the night rain.

Hell of a thing for the nation's capital.

A jagged brick tripped John. He sprawled headfirst.

Flat in the street. Like roadkill.

Crawl.

Across to the accidental park. Border of the Parkway.

Mud. Wet dead grass. Sticks. Trees, through the blood running down, rain, chest on fire, see trees, leafless silhouettes waving in the night.

Gravel ditch. Flop into it, look back at the block of Georgetown homes, the row of parked cars.

At Glass's nonexistent college-aged daughter's Toyota.

Heartbeat, breath slowing—*Don't breathe fast, pant, don't send
up a visible steam cloud of exhales.*

Listen.

Hurrying feet. Not running feet that would attract a cop or a
homeowner with a phone and witness eyes.

Across the street, just a man in a fedora carrying an unopened
umbrella in the rain, looking, seeking—

For his car, obviously for his car.

Leg stiffening—*Don't move it! No sound!*

The car that could maybe be linked to Glass. The trunk that
John had told Glass held the only tangible evidence.

Phuong, alive, please alive . . .

Still alive. Glass'd fix that, too. Have to.

Glass had to get to a center. Probably headquarters, where he
could twist John's attempts to come in. Where he had secure
phones to other contract hands. Where he could build a castle of
lies and insanity in which John Lang ruled. Embezzler John
Lang. Once or twice or three times a murder suspect John Lang.
Dirty money. Dead dirty partner. Phuong—unwitting accom-
plice, dead victim . . .

Glass unlocked the Toyota's driver's door.

Spinning a thousand new webs.

One will trap me. You'll skim across that web so fast . . .

Wipe away the bloody rain.

The Toyota pulled away from the curb. Glass cranked the steering wheel, turned the car around 180 degrees—

Headlights swinging through the falling rain—

Duck!

Glass drove the Toyota away. Turned right on P Street where it bordered the accidental park. John raised his head out of the ditch, watched the car drive over the bridge he'd run across twice that night. Glass's turn signal blinked on, no traffic violation to generate a record. Stop at the stop sign. The Toyota turned right, drove down the entrance ramp to Rock Creek Parkway.

Going, the Toyota that Glass had set John up to take. The car that had a tracer bug planted in it long before John gratefully accepted its use.

Stand up, look, better chance to see . . .

Going, the car that Wet Boy hadn't needed to see to follow. The car he'd closed in on as soon as John parked and fled, ran without seeing who'd coasted a motorcycle to a stop around the corner. Wet Boy knew that John was there, saw him sneaking toward the bridge, toward the subway where maybe he'd escape.

Stagger to the trees along the Parkway . . .

Going, the car John would logically have reclaimed—if he'd escaped at the subway.

Headlights, just headlights now, snaking along the deserted Parkway, accelerating . . .

Going, the car whose passenger door had been unthinkingly, habitually locked by Wet Boy after he'd been inside it. Nothing there for him to bag. Wet Boy who'd killed Cliff Johnson wouldn't have chosen to burden himself with anything John had left in the car—why bother? Especially when he had a chance for a creative dance. If he hurried. If he was quick. If he didn't waste time going inside the car. Or if he used only a minute, two. But not to plant a tracer bug in a car where one already functioned.

Rain pounded the nylon shoulders of John's mountaineering coat. Trains. Sioux drums.

Going, the car, around an unseen bend. Creative and professional backstopping so-cool, wanna-be-sure, trained and practiced Wet Boy, dancing-fighting, ground mud-smeared green coat, subway, escalator, his makeshift garrote an olive-green and yellow-striped fuse cord *remember* Special Forces training and Paris, we'll always have Paris—

Bright orange flash beyond the trees, on the Parkway.

A push of hot wind, the stench of volcanic gasoline and burning metal, and the roar,

that roar

engulfed John,

then was gone.

47

Funerals are vibrations between yesterday and tomorrow, a breathing space to help the living find their balance amidst the tremors of existence.

That Saturday morning, spring filled the air at Arlington Cemetery.

Sunlight glistened on the sealed coffin.

Six pallbearers unbuttoned their topcoats: Roger Allen, who was responsible for the Agency's spy dogs; Richard Woodruff, his second-in-command; Miguel Zell, the Agency's pilot through political waters; the Agency's chief in-house lawyer; Kahniley Sangare, the CIA executive in charge of the officially eternal Corcoran Center Task Force as it entered "Reinstitution-alization Phase One" and folded back into existing agencies and locked file drawers; and George Korn, commander of the guard for the CIA's walls.

Plus one to count cadence, thought John Lang as he watched.

Because you can never trust the weather, the escorting sol-diers wore winter dress uniforms. The widow wrapped herself in a heavy wool coat and blank stares. Her daughter smiled bravely.

With one hand, the child held on to Mommy. The doctor had given Mommy lots of medicine. He didn't know about the medi-cine flask Mommy had in her purse. With her other hand, the little girl held on to the woman named Mary, who came to the house late that awful Wednesday night with men from Father's work. The child had to quiet the Doberman, open the front door. Mommy had been . . . asleep, Mary explained after the girl let them in. Men sawed into Father's basement. They shot Father's dog with real bullets. They called a doctor, who woke up Mommy. The child remembered how Mary sat with her in her white-walled bedroom where everything was *yes sir* in its place. Mary held her hand, and told her she had to be a very brave little girl. They talked about dreams.

At the widow's request, no eulogy or sermon was delivered. With her shaky signature, lawyers from her husband's work took control of probate, audited all the family finances and possessions. The morning after her husband died, a moving van hauled metal file cabinets away from the house.

A drill sergeant barked. The honor guard snapped to attention. The pallbearers set the coffin on straps across the open grave.

Friday, the day before, Maryland authorities just across the invisible Distict of Columbia border shipped an urn with the ashes of heart attack victim Phillip David to his aunt in Cleveland.

That same Friday morning, an unknown male was buried in a pauper's grave in Washington's municipal cemetery. Besides two gravediggers, the only witnesses to the cold interment were John Lang and police detective Tyler Greene, who'd investigated the John Doe's tragic death by misadventure. That Friday, Greene was promoted to detective sergeant and offered a transfer from Homicide to the city police's Intelligence and Organized Crime unit.

Police in the suburb where Kate and Richard Woodruff lived genuinely had no answers for their neighbor who'd called 911 just before dawn on Thursday, claiming that he'd seen four carloads of men converge on the Woodruff house, race inside, then emerge minutes later leading two men in handcuffs to the cars that then raced away. One of the captives, said the neighbor, was as roly-poly as a Buddha. When the responding cruiser arrived at the Woodruff house, no one was home. A follow-up visit to the couple, who had been out of town, revealed nothing unusual. The neighbor considered calling *The Washington Post*, but then realized he'd be written off as a crazy by the reporter, or maybe worse yet, a story *would be* published and the ensuing rumors of crime in his neighborhood would cause his property values to crash.

The pallbearers stepped back from Harlan Glass's grave.

The funeral director pressed a foot pedal.

The coffin sank into the earth as a bugler played taps.

That morning's *Washington Post* ran an obituary for Martin Sinclair, a promising State Department officer who'd died in a household accident and was discovered by a pizza delivery man. In the mail piled on a table in the house he'd rented, his widow found an envelope containing a life insurance policy with an accidental-death provision for $250,000, a supplement to their already overinsured financial plan that he'd never mentioned. She never noticed the envelope was not postmarked, never questioned the speed with which the insurance company she'd never heard of processed her claim. She followed the funeral director's advice—he'd been chosen by the ambulance that processed her husband's body—and Martin Sinclair was cremated.

As Harlan Glass's coffin sank into the ground that Saturday morning, Senators on the Select Intelligence Committee and their counterparts on the House side rode trains and planes and cars back to their home states for a long-planned recess.

They needed their break, the rest. The distance.

Friday morning, they'd received a Members Only briefing from CIA Deputy Director for Operations Roger Allen, CIA Congressional liaison chief Miguel Zell, and John Lang—whose bandaged face drew nervous looks.

Allen had argued for holding the briefing on Congress's turf instead of the White House: keeping the members on the Hill made them feel more in control, and keeping them out of the

White House made the briefing—which was never announced—easier to conceal.

Having Allen give the briefing—and dodging protocol by having the Director in Paris, where he'd rushed to *diplomatically manage* the crisis—insulated the Administration from immediate political explosions, should control be lost.

Allen began by telling the Committee he would answer questions about his statement as they demanded—but at their own risk.

The Senate Chairman—whom Allen had favored with a cursory before-the-hearing private meeting—led the Congressional team.

Allen told them the following truth:

The Corcoran Center bombing was a private criminal group's rogue intelligence operation that had accidentally gone bad when five innocent people died. The operation had also neutralized—here Allen paused, repeated himself—neutralized well-known terrorist Ahmed Naral, who was believed to have been linked to the 1983 car bombing of the Marine barracks in Beirut that killed 241 U.S. Marines.

As a consequence of this rogue operation—which the CIA had uncovered and neutralized—besides the five innocent civilians killed in the Corcoran bombing, five other American citizens had died in deaths unlinkable to the Agency and unharmful to long-term U.S. security interests. All five of those deaths, said Allen (not naming Cliff Johnson, Martin Sinclair, Phil David, Frank or Wet Boy), were of people who were either involved in the rogue operation, to one degree of guilt or another, or who were Agency officers who gave their lives in necessarily secret devotion to the highest duty.

The only completely innocent victims, interjected liaison chief Zell, were the architect and her family, who chose to wander into the field of fire, and the elderly security guard, who the coroner believed to have had a previously existing heart condition. None of the innocent dead left direct heirs, so restitution or revenge for them was neither possible nor necessary.

Allen paused to let the shock wave roll through the members, then interrupted their building murmurs.

Unfortunately, said Allen, several Members of Congress—several members of this group—had been innocently put in political jeopardy by the rogue operation.

The architect of the operation, announced Allen, was former head of the Counter-Terrorism Center Harlan Glass, who—

As the Committee roared, Allen increased his volume:

—*who* may or may not have lapsed in stability prior to these events. All pertinent criminal rogue activities were rooted in Glass's semiautonomous CTC, not the established mainline CIA.

However, added Allen, CIA investigations had also alarmingly revealed large sums of money from Glass to the campaigns of many unwitting Members of Congress. Some contributions were of questionable legality.

Before Glass could be arrested, said Allen, he had perished in what had been ruled a one-car accident by federal Park Police.

The renegade operation, Allen said, was neutralized. Its postmortem was being undertaken by a team headed by Security chief George Korn and Congressional liaison officer John Lang, whose job it was to keep the Committees fully apprised, as deemed necessary.

Congressional liaison chief Zell pointed out that the sizable political contributions Members of both political parties had received from the clearly guilty terrorist bomber Glass were part of the secret investigation, but, as with all other aspects of the probe, no public disclosure of such connections was planned.

Appropriate reparations were being made, Zell quietly added.

On cue, the Senate Chairman asked about the White House response.

The President, said Allen, had expressed his desire to cooperate fully with Congress. If the Committees so chose, he would launch a public investigation into all aspects—all aspects, re-

peated Allen—of the affair. The Attorney General had already
moved to investigate indictments of those involved.

However, said Zell, most of the guilty parties were dead.

Except, he added, of course, various Members of Congress who
had received campaign funds laundered by Glass.

The damage that has been done cannot be undone, said Allen.
But it can be made worse.

For example, he said, to sully Congress and the CIA with false
blame for a non-CIA rogue operation that killed only five completely innocent people and caused minor property damage,
would serve no strategic national good and would further under-
mine the credibility of Congress and Washington just as "we"
were trying to solve dozens of other politically sensitive crises
while moving legitimately into the future.

The press, he said, would be unable to make the necessary dis-
tinctions of blame clear, and scattershot anger from an ill-in-
formed public would damage vital American institutions like
the innocent CIA and Congress, and would also wound various
public officials linked to Glass.

"As it stands," said Allen, "the slate's clean. Nobody—not justice, not America, not the public, not you in Congress or us in
the CIA—nobody is better off if we throw gas on the ashes."

Indeed, he added, public investigation of the for-all-practical-
purposes-closed affair would directly expose a heroic CIA intelligence officer and an innocent American citizen, with consequences
that no one could predict or control.

I built the coffin, thought John as he watched Allen roll that
unsubstantiated implication of unspecified harm to the Congressmen, *now I'm a nail to keeping the lid on. Phuong, too, "Protecting" us lets the Committee justify protecting themselves.*

Perhaps, suggested Miguel Zell, the best compromise in the
interests of the country would be for the two oversight Committees to mandate the CIA to report fully all pertinent aspects of
its ongoing classified investigation at an appropriate time to the
Committees in closed session.

Senator Bauman made a motion to that effect.

The night before, in the locked study of his home with John, the CIA's lawyer and a clearly trigger-eager Security chief Korn, Bauman drank four tumblers of Scotch as the men from the CIA gave one of the Senate's senior Members a heads-up. Should a public probe be launched, Bauman learned that he *by name* could be identified as getting money from a terrorist bomber.

As required under the rules, the Committees voted. The motion that, in effect, authorized and sanctified a forever-secret internal CIA investigation passed.

In an unusual move, the Senate Chairman showed his position by loudly casting the first vote: a YES for his fellow senior Senator's motion.

Senator Obst smelled rotten fish and voted NO.

Out of reform and image-minded reflex, Senator Firestone voted NO. The morning before, two of his former women staffers issued a press statement claiming that he'd fondled them. Even though he'd broken no laws during the car accident when a woman he met in a bar was driving, he and his A.A. decided that Firestone would announce he was seeking treatment at a celebrity alcoholic recovery center. Four years later, he lost his re-election.

Senator Handelman wanted to vote YES and support his President, voted NO and supported his troubled conscience.

After the Committee briefing, John led Handelman to a corner, whispered that Emma's vigilance helped uncover the wrongdoing.

Handelman frowned. "What can I tell her?"

"Nothing," said John.

Handelman knew that was true.

But he didn't yell at Emma for two weeks and gave her a larger raise than she'd expected. He never told her or his A.A. why. His Committee had voted secrecy, and Handelman was an honorable man.

As the closed-door Committee hearing was about to adjourn,

Zell informed the members that *luckily,* since this was a staff-free Committee meeting, any leaks would obviously have to come from a member breaking high-security laws and betraying his fellow members, and *luckily,* that would never happen and require another historically bitter round of finger-pointing, ethics investigating and public blame-taking.

Amen, said the Senate Chairman, then he banged his gavel.

When CIA doctors treated John for the bullet crease on his ribs and gashes on his face, he had them draw a test tube of his blood, send it to a reputable outside lab. The results came back negative for HIV. John spent a night agonizing over a letter, finally mailed the lab report to Emma in an envelope by itself.

Figure she never wanted to hear of him or from him again.

Figure he could never tell her what her heart needed to hear.

Rifles cracked at Arlington Cemetery that spring Saturday morning as Glass's coffin hit the bottom of its grave.

One volley. Two. Three.

Sparrows kept their perch in the budding trees. They'd heard so many guns here, they'd lost their fear.

John flinched with each report, looked away from the grave—

Something in the trees moved.

The sparrows took wing.

A shape in the sunlight—

Oh.

What to do about two lowly clerks in the CIA's mail room flicked through John's mind. They had thought they were helping CIA legend Glass foil Israeli penetration and manipulation of American government. They diverted all mail from the White House or Capitol Hill to a blank-doored office where flaps & seals men loyal to counterterrorism guru Glass had two hours to open envelopes and report to their chief. That Saturday morning, the not-stupid flaps & seals men were locked up with Korn's quiz whizzes and hard boys at a safe house on the eastern shore. The two mail clerks were under nervous voluntary house confinement.

They're as guilty as . . . me, thought John.

Cut them slack. Give them their jobs, save their pensions.

Be sure they know their savior's name.

The honor guard snapped to attention.

The squad commander slow-marched the folded flag that had covered the coffin to the widow. She stared straight ahead, clutching her purse to her chest.

Stymied, the square-jawed squad commander hesitated . . .

The daughter let go of her mother, then dropped the hand sent by the government, took the flag and the salute that followed.

The honor guard marched back to the bus.

Mary walked the Glass survivors to their limo.

Korn swept his pale eyes over the departing CIA executives, checked to be sure his security team looked sharp. The nod he sent John was crisp, and John swore he saw Korn wink.

As the other attenders walked to the parking lot through the gardens of stone, Dick Woodruff came over to John.

"No sense hanging around here," said Woodruff. He'd been named interim CIA coordinator for the Counter-Terrorism Center. "We've got meetings scheduled for tomorrow. By tomorrow night, I think Kate may have forgiven you enough to have you over for a quiet Sunday dinner.

"Don't mention the house, though," cautioned Woodruff. "We're going out now to buy a new rug."

"I think I'll give her more time." John looked at the open grave. "Who'd have figured this is how it would end?"

"You made the right choice," said Woodruff.

"Agreeing to be part of a lie is right?"

"Not a lie—a secret."

"What's the difference?"

"Those who need to know the truth—do."

"Do they?"

"To the best of our efforts and their wants, yes."

"What has that cost us?"

"Did you think you could smite evil without evil smiting you?" said Woodruff. "No matter how soiled this may feel to you, what cleaner, less harmful good could you have done?"

John dropped his eyes.

"Turns out, Glass was brilliant," said Woodruff.

"What?"

"A terrorist incident like Corcoran Center—no matter who perpetrated it—no question remains that a strong international antiterrorist analytical and investigative force is necessary.

"Of course," Woodruff smiled, "centralized control has proven to be equally necessary. And 'Central' is our first name."

Car engines started up in the distance.

"Don't stay out here too long," said Woodruff. He left.

When only John and the gravediggers remained, the watcher walked out of the trees. Stood beside John. The gravediggers said the hell with it, shoveled dirt down onto the coffin.

"I thought you didn't want to come," said John.

Phuong said: "I want to rip open that box and drive a stake through his heart."

"There's only ashes in there."

"But you're sure it was him?"

"Oh yeah," said John. "It's him."

She wore the black trench coat from her father's funeral nine days before, the same blue jeans she'd had on when John left her at the safe house to see Glass buried. Her head came to John's shoulder. Her hair smelled fresh from her shower. The sun warmed his back. He loosened the tie on his new shirt.

"Look away," he whispered.

Every direction they turned were white tablets of stone.

He led her toward the theater of the dead.

"I signed the papers," she said. "Even the nondisclosure form—to protect you. Gave them to one of our baby-sitters."

"The Agency would have helped you find a lawyer to—"

"I hate lawyers," she said.

"You'll get a quarter of a million dollars."

"Hell of an insurance company," she said.

"You won't have to work for that newspaper in Chicago," he said. "Writing about lawyers. You can be a poet—"

"Money doesn't make you a poet—"

"Keeps you from starving."

"—or buy you a father," she finished.

They walked into the open-sky stone auditorium. Alone.

"What did you get out of this?" she asked.

Think about it.

"More than what I went into it for."

She looked at him.

"Was it worth it?"

He looked away. "They gave me another medal."

"Congratulations," she said. "I guess."

On Monday, two days away, John and the CIA's chief lawyer met with Cliff Johnson's widow and Somalian nanny in the Baltimore office of the widow's lawyer.

Explaining nothing, the CIA lawyer offered the widow $250,000 tax-free, if she signed papers agreeing to hold all parties known and unknown blameless for her husband's activities, including his demise. She had to sign a nondisclosure agreement. Her signature also made her children beneficiaries of a $50,000 trust fund geared toward their education, to be invested and administered by trustees she'd never heard of. Under a similar contract, the Somalian nanny would receive a $25,000 "finder's fee" and be placed on a protected fast track for U.S. citizenship.

The Baltimore lawyer spread his hands: "We bargain, you get nothing."

The two women signed where they were told.

When the paperwork was finished, John waited in the lawyer's mahogany-walled conference room. The air smelled of fine leather.

A soft knock on the door.

He said, *come in.*

The only living Mr. Johnson entered. The door closed behind

him. He stared at the man from the park with wide eyes that were missing yet another day of second grade.

The man from the park made him raise his hand like in Cub Scouts. The boy swore a blood oath to never tell anyone. The man held out a red velvet box. A name label had been ripped off the velvet that morning, but the boy never knew that.

The man opened the box.

The medal inside had a 'Merican flag ribbon. The round metal showed an eagle and a shield and olive branches cupped by a half-moon of letters reading CENTRAL INTELLIGENCE AGENCY. Etched in bronze by the eagle's beak were the words FOR MERIT.

The boy's trembling hands took the box. The man turned the medal over.

That morning, a Baltimore jeweler had earned $200 of the cash planted in John's cabin by engraving the back of that medal: CLIFF JOHNSON.

Your father won this, said John, he'd want you to have it.

All his life, John would remember the boy's arms wrapped around him, the 7-year-old's shaking body, his burning tears.

The night before Glass's funeral, Dick Woodruff presented Phuong with an identical medal for her father. In keeping with CIA security procedures, its back was smooth, blank.

One midnight three weeks later, John watched as workers discreetly mounted a new memorial star on the lobby wall of CIA headquarters.

The morning they buried Glass, as John and Phuong walked the circle of stones in the theater of the dead, she said: "My bags are in my car."

Darkness the night before. In the safe house.

Made love, afterward, her hands pressing his back, her thighs locked, pulling his weight down on top of her, not letting him move but they couldn't help it, stop it: he slid out. Her whisper said that wasn't a tear trickling between their cheeks.

Sunlight reflected off the white stones.

"Don't go," he told her. "Please."

Like a hollowing wind, all around.

Calm, so strange, calm. Walking the circle.

Knowing that later he'd scream.

"You just want to marry a rich girl," she said.

Not even blinking at the word *marry:* "I only care about you."

She slid her hand around his: "Why me?"

Burn away her no with your eyes.

"Can't . . . I don't . . . Say maybe because anybody who writes, poet, have to be an optimist to be a writer. You have to believe. I need . . . You're frustrating as hell and tough, so tough . . . We don't think alike but . . . This life, you know it, and it shapes me, is me. I don't need to explain it, you've lived it, know it, know me.

"Don't ask why, I don't know why: I just know yes."

Her fingers brushed his face.

"This life is you," she said.

"I'm more than—"

"South Dakota boy, Saigon girl." Her cheeks were wet. "Even if I can touch your soul . . .

"This life. Your world, your town: I've spent forever trapped in it. Orphanage to my family, living those rules. Maybe I'll never get out, but if I marry it, I'll be damned."

"Or happy."

"If I risked it, you're the only chance I'd trust."

She stood on her tiptoes, brushed her lips over his.

Leaned back and said: "Gotta go."

"You never even saw my cabin."

"I know where you live."

Then she walked away.

Remember always her black hair floating in the spring breeze, her black coat fanned out behind her as she disappears down the white stone steps; the taste of her skin.

Walk the circle.

But that morning, he couldn't.

Skirt around the whispering tourists with their flashbulbs popping; the lone soldier, bayoneted rifle on his shoulder as he stepped out the watch at the tomb of his unknown comrade.

The air smelled green, alive. Hurry past the gravestones standing guard.

Go through the trees.

Should be at work. Work.

There, the river,

wide and rolling, unstoppable gray.

On the other side, like in a dream,

that marble city,

its sky. Clouds.